ELEMENTS

An American Adventure In One Year

A Novel
By Solomon Deep

Perpetual Imagination
Boston · Northampton · New York

881 Main St #10
Fitchburg, MA 01420

info@perpetualimagination.com

Manufactured in The United States of America.

2 3 4 5 6 7 8 9 10 1

Second Edition

ISBN-10: 0615728707
ISBN-13: 978-0615728704

Library of Congress Control Number: 2012953952

To discuss literature fundamentally, and to have that discussion be opened in an introduction by the author is considered blasphemy in certain circles. It was very common to see author's notes and author's introductions around the time of the Romantics and the Victorians, but it seems that in modern times we have traditionally deferred to the scholars or to other contemporary artists in their interpretation of the work and what makes it important. In turn, they tend to either gush on the merits of the work, or attempt to prove that the work is even worthy of our appreciation years after it has disappeared from the bestseller lists and bookshelves of the proletariat.

I understand both sides of the argument – from Roland Barthes discussing the death of the author in our postmodern reader response approach to literature, to the very opposite in our consumption of all but written media as motion pictures come with extensive commentary by actors discussing their craft to directors exploring the minute deliberate and accidental choices in the finished product that made it to theaters. There is no doubt in my opinion that the discussions on the manifestations that arose during the creation of a work are splendidly intuitive and exhilarating for even the average reader. Yet for an author to write his own introduction seems blasphemy – as if I am the person in charge of filling one of those roles of introducing you to why the book you have just opened or pulled up on your ereader is worthy of your time ten years after its debut. The majority of the time, this introduction should also completely give the entirety of the plot away prior to even beginning the book, as if it is your own ignorance that should lead to the spoiling of the plot since everyone already knows what it is about, don't they?

This is why I decided to write this introduction.

Close to a decade has passed since the original release of this novel, and what is interesting is how the evolution of the meaning of the work itself has progressed in this short span of time. I would like to break some of the cardinal rules of authorship in this new edition by explaining some of the more misread elements of this text and write precisely what the point is, especially considering the fact that we are living in our own bleak alternate version of the bleak future that Alan Levy found himself in.

To begin, there was a clear point in my mind that I could precisely turn to that led to the creation of this work. While today it is cliche, the book was inspired by the sprawling confusion that arose in our next generation of the young during the years immediately following 9/11. Young men and women that I was speaking to had no concept of the future and what it held in store for them. I noticed a tremendous amount of guilt, of fear, and of confusion in physical, educational, and spiritual matters. This led to my own interpretation of what was happening to these young men and women. The idea that in the face of uncertainty, they became uncertain. In the face of reality television, they became the center of their universe. In the face of an economy that stagnated and then fell sharply, they began to redefine what a successful life meant to them. The very nature of fear - that one had no control over one's own destiny - has led to the marketing and publicizing of oneself so that there was some semblance of everyone knowing that one existed on this planet.

Out of the dust of all of these events and my interaction with young Americans did the character of Alan Levy rise, and the themes of this book began to become clear.

While no character in this book is at all meant to be perceived as a three-dimensional, living, breathing entity, Alan was a conglomerate of many stories and attitudes of the youth I met in the early 2000s. There was a fear of war, fear of being watched, fear of being ignored, fear of poverty, fear of work, fear of being forgotten, and an ultimate fear of everything. I wanted to write a narrative that was able to embrace this, and embrace the ignorance that went along with it. I wanted our narrator to sound like he was just as ignorant and afraid. He would be almost one in the same with Alan, but ignorant to his desires, and even to the text itself. Original drafts of the novel were rife with poor grammar, misspellings, and mostly used the passive voice. I tried to do the same with Alan.

When I was marketing the book, it was difficult to convince agents and publishers that these choices were deliberate, and were meant to make the audience unsure of the stability of our narrator entirely. As if Alan or our narrator would go off the deep end at any moment, forget how fragile we are, and make a series of bad choices that would bring an untimely end to the book. There were many times that I considered removing the first section entirely, because it was slow to pick up, and embarrassingly whiny and formulaic. I also thought of making the book a great deal longer than it is, and put the audience in the same stagnation as our characters. To feel bored, or desperate for something to happen. Desperate for an ending, at least.

The one thing that was hard to sell was the fact that the language and writing matures as the book progresses. The errors and passive voice decrease. The maturity of the diction and syntax grows with Alan. My favorite parts of the book are two-thirds of the way though to the ending, but that is not what sells books.

Alan is meant to be ignorant and selfish, childish and bratty. The book is about his development. While the motifs do exist, it is important to remember that as an audience member the frustration that Alan produces for us in the avenues of Americanism, American Sexuality, American Race, American Culture, American Religion, and American Consumption are all criticized by him – and ultimately the criticism should fall on Alan's shoulders. The book is about all of these things, but they are meant to showcase Alan, not teach the audience to adapt to the same opinions. His opinions of these motifs and even other characters in the book are immature and misguided. They reflect a lack of education and understanding of the world around him. But most interestingly, they become moot in the final quarter of the book. It is not a book about Americanism, American Sexuality, American Religion, and American Consumption, but rather, a book about love and learning to focus on love.

What else is interesting is some of the amazing developments that have happened in America since I wrote it. I had always intended on the book to be an alternate future, in the hopes that when the book was finally published, there were many differences between what happens in the fiction and what really happened in our real lives. There are only a few dates and historical facts that I can be certain is mentioned in the book. One is the year 2015, spoken of in the past tense. The book mentions the illegality of gay marriage (as of the time I am writing this essay, five states allow gay marriage without restriction, and many more have civil union laws and pending legislation), that there are restaurants and businesses that have gone under, and many other things that none of us knew would be happening in the future when I originally wrote it. There is a mention of the Iraq war in the past tense. Fantastically, the idea of entire businesses having been started using the self-promotion I mentioned earlier in this introduction as the entirety of their business model, such as Twitter and Facebook, is simply staggering – but since these services had not been around when I first wrote the book in the way we know them and the dominance they have on our relationships and society today, there is not one mention of them. I tried to be as unspecific as I could with technology – it was no mistake that he wrote in his journal in longhand, and typewriters make an appearance.

I had never considered updating or revising the text in any way that would have affected these elements. In *this* alternate future, this is the way things are. It captures the atmosphere of the period I was trying to cover so well that it would be impossible to ignore the importance of it. If anything else, it reminds us how desperate times were, and how unfortunate the civil rights, war, and other situations were. But to revise it to make it more appropriate and applicable to the time that we live in is not a good prospect. Bizarrely, *Elements* is a document not only about the fear, oppression, and life in the world that Alan lives in, but it is a direct reflection of the world that myself and the young people that I interviewed lived in in the time that I wrote it in 2004. It is a document about the feelings of helplessness and insecurity. Unfortunately, it is also a document that reminded me that there are some horrific and dangerous political and social choices that were made in the past ten years that I could never have fabricated in my wildest imagination.

Something that many fans of the text do not realize is that there were several working titles to the book. To begin, the book is known as *Elements*, but the first printing of it also had the full sub-title, *Elements: An American Adventure in One Year*. The first working title for the book was *Elements of Life: An American Adventure in One Year*. The title seemed too long, cumbersome, and seemed cliche before the book was even finished. In the context of where the words "elements of life" appear in the book itself, I always thought it was beautiful, but book jackets aren't for context. The next title, *Elements of Ignorance* seemed as though it was misleading. It served several purposes, such as inviting the audience to wonder who the title was referring to and making a suggestion about the entire cast, perhaps. But it didn't fit, it didn't occur in the book anywhere, and it was ultimately scrapped. *Elements*, therefore became the catch-all sibling of these two ideas, and was simple enough to exist on its own without any peers in a sea of one-word titles.

Another interesting thing about the book that I will entirely admit to was that there was music that seemed as though it absolutely had to be included in the text, but was eventually scrapped because it was difficult meshing the vintage qualities of the songs with the context of their appearance in a book that is supposed to take place in the future. I am eternally grateful to the musicians whose work shaped my hours and hours of writing and editing and meeting the characters in my work, and I highly suggest you find their work. I also was unsure about the murky licensing waters of asking a musician to share the rights and including lyrics in a book. I figured that it was just easier to remove any reference to them, and leave it at that. Regardless, the artists work that somewhat colored my prose in certain scenes and whose words at one time were imprinted in the text include Elliott Smith, Ben Folds, Aaron Perrino's The Sheila Divine, Hugo Ferreira's Tantric, and

Frank Black's The Pixies. These artists all have some intimate connection to Boston, and I thank them for everything they have done for Alan, myself, and my work. The original drafts to the book not only contained the lyrics, but were also included in a page long acknowledgment section in another language at the end of the book that is no longer present.

Finally, another small element of the text that had changed from the first printing was the use of actual phone numbers. These numbers could be called, and you could reach myself and people that I know who agreed to this experiment. As far as I know, no one has told me that they ever received a call. Interestingly, all of the numbers from the original edition have been changed – but only for the reason that phone plans have been switched, land lines canceled, and a variety of other unrelated reasons.

I hope that this edition of the book finds you well – the past decade has personally been a whirlwind of progress, work, development, realization, and awakening. If you have never read it before, I hope that it gives you perspective and an intelligent broadening of understanding in this complicated world that we live in. If you take nothing else from it, I hope that it is entertaining, and that you are allowed to share the gift of literature and appreciation with someone you know by recommending it. Until then, enjoy the ten year anniversary of my first novel, *Elements*.

AUGUST 2012

For Lauren.

I love you. Always.

ELEMENTS

An American Adventure In One Year

A Novel
By Solomon Deep

Part I

Spring Song

In what arena of discontent,
We live our daily lives.
We have the resources to disappear
And away from whence we drive.

But do not wander fro, my friend
A land rampant with regret,
For in the end, you'll be surprised
When you ask for what you get.

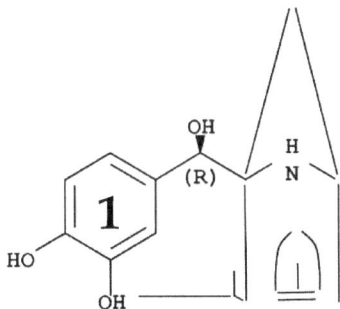

The final decision came while Alan Levy argued with his girlfriend in the modest two level home her parents still allowed her to live in and a gigantic blast in the backyard shook the home, Alan and Jane, and even the brittle bones of the family's aging feline. Of course the argument that was in progress screeched to a halt, and why wouldn't it? A mere discussion on the intricacies of a move eighty kilometers east to Boston that turned heated upon five minutes was always sure to end with a destructive blast; but never like this.

Alan continued looking at Jane Rarus after the explosion, and she stopped speaking only to look back at him with her token frightened expression. The slender, blond looked straight ahead and blinked her eyes. As she blinked, she would also simultaneously nod her head and sniffle heavily through her nose every time her eyes closed. Alan always thought that her passive fright made her look like a doll that a friend of his little sister had, Little Miss Typhoid, or something; a sick baby you had to take care of but always managed to look as though it were possessed. Usually this look came to Jane when she was driving and someone pulled in front of her three blocks away. Today, Alan actually thought that it was finally an appropriate response considering the circumstances. What she would probably do next, he thought, is ask what the noise was, as if he knew.

"What was that?" Jane asked.

Brilliant. Alan continued to look at her, and staring at her was the face of a man who didn't really care anymore, a man who had to listen to her ramblings on "who would her friends be?" when they got married and moved to the city. They would all be here, and she would never get to see them. Poor Jane. Poor, poor Jane. Truth is, that is exactly one more reason that Alan was ready to leave. One more reason atop many.

The two moved from the small wood paneled living room that was situated in the front of the house, through the small kitchen, and into the very tiny connected atrium which had two doors, one leading to the driveway and the other which looked onto their backyard. Each footstep creaked - the only utterance the home expelled until today, each plank and board screaming for deliverance into a new era. Usually the backyard was mainly empty except for a small drying carousel, a picnic table, and a small shed. Today there was a giant plume of smoke billowing into the sky, so thick and black that it blanketed the air and the the bottom of the steps in front of the door, blocking the ten or so meters to the other end of the yard. Heat radiated onto Alan's face through the storm door, and the noxious smell of burning plastic and fuel choked every breath.

"What happened? Did something explode?" she inquired.

"How should I know? Call the fire department..."

"Where's the cat?" she asked quickly. "Do you know where the cat is?"

"Give me the phone."

"I got it."

In his 22 years, Alan had never seen someone's backyard explode. But in this case, it was a great excuse to get out of an argument, and will probably go down in history as the best ever. As he stood looking out of the window, he thought about how he would break it to Jane, his friends here, and everyone else that it was time to go. Another blast rattled the aluminum door, its thin window, and a magnesium flash electrified the smoke with an orange fireball bubbling toward the sky.

"I called and they said that they already knew about it. I guess they thought it was the house or something because the people across the street called. I told them that it was just the backyard."

"Are they still on the phone?" Alan asked. Jane looked back at Alan blankly.

Jane lived her whole life here, along with her parents, their parents, their parents, and their parents before that. The once bustling town known as Chapmansville now just stood as a wasteland of cement and people always looking for jobs. For generations before this one, residents were always gainfully employed by the paper mills and the plastics factories that spotted the landscape. Now, all the businesses that originally made the community and its residents wealthy and happy stood desolate and rotting, making a concrete elephant graveyard of the landscape where all the industry went to die and decompose.

Life still went on, however. The only thing keeping the city alive was Chapman State University that sat in the middle of town. It was named after the city, which was named after the man who planted the now giant apple trees that dotted the college's gorgeous ivy covered brick structures, the boozy scent of their decomposition heralding fall, books, and the eventual rebirth of the campus. Here stood the best college to attend in the country if you wanted to become a teacher or get a well rounded degree on little money. It seemed anyone in the area who held a decent job was a graduate, and if you weren't, you easily subsisted on welfare or proceeds from selling drugs.

It is because of the great college and its value that Alan traveled to from Boston to Chapmansville: to attend college and get his degree in English. He wanted to become a writer, but figured that a career as an English teacher could help him earn money until he was able to live on his writing. Of course he knew that a lot of writers weren't able to live on their own with just their writing, but he looked forward to the day that maybe he would be lucky enough to do it. He was already publishing short stories and writing for the local paper, but he wanted more.

Alan could already hear the sirens squealing from the distance. He looked at his watch and then looked back up at Jane who was staring mesmerized into the backyard. He wasn't sure that he wanted to be here when the emergency personnel arrived. Jane's fragile nerves would certainly overcome her when they came, and he didn't want to be there for it. Besides, he had an appointment in a half hour at the college and it would certainly be more important to him than seeing what results from this bizarre fire in his girlfriend's backyard. It wasn't spreading. Everything would be okay.

"I think I am going to hit the road, I have to head over to the college," Alan said. Jane looked over at him again with a blank stare.

"You're going to leave me like this?" she responded, and began to laugh with an annoying contempt. She did this often, and Alan hated it more than anything.

"The firemen are right up the street; you don't need me to be here. Besides, I have an appointment in a few minutes."

Shaking her head, she responded, "You know what, whatever." She paused. Still shaking her head, she continued, "I don't know about this…about us."

This was a constant; bold statements about their relationship that sounded to him like lines from a trashy teen romance novel dotted almost every interaction. What would happen if he responded cheerfully to these statements, "You know what? You're right! Bye, kiddo!" and then never talked to her again?

Alan turned around, opened the screen door, and made his way down the three steps to the small driveway. He dealt with Jane the best way that he learned to deal with Jane; he just walked away. He didn't notice that behind him, she ran to the door to watch him, or turning toward the front of the house to get into his car, several ambulances, fire trucks, and police cars sped up toward him, and the personnel jumped out and ran through the driveway toward the backyard in slow motion.

• • •

"What have you been up to lately?" Dr. Furman asked. Alan continued to look at the ceiling. "How are classes? Are you still working at the diner?"

Alan lay on the leather couch in the very small office, his feet comfortably raised on the portion where one's head normally rested. It looked exactly as you would suppose a psychologist's office at a state college would look. It was narrow and the walls were white. The office door could hardly open without hitting the doctor's desk, a sixties-era number with a matching chair that was solid metal and easily weighed several hundred pounds as a set. The couch practically stretched the entire width of the room, as if the room were built around it... There was simply no other explanation as to how it got into the room. Furman sat in one of the two leather chairs that faced the couch, and a tall floor plant towered behind him. Other than the plant, a small window by the desk, and the doctor's certificate on the wall, the room stood bare.

"Dull. It's all dull. I told you before that I was sick of it all."

"Well, refresh my memory."

"Classes are dumb because I don't think that I am learning anything. I am not even taking any English courses this semester, they're all electives and they don't interest me or anything that I will be doing in the future."

"What do you mean?"

Alan began to think about a diagram in his secondary special needs textbook that outlined how to insert a catheter into a student. The drawing, so as not to be vulgar, looked like a person was feeding red licorice to a snake. All of the side notes constantly referred to the child as the 'student'. Furman just continued to look at him, not quite sure where he was going with it. Alan continued, "Well, even if I decide to become an English teacher, and I have an inclusive classroom with a student who just happens to have special needs and also happens to be incontinent, will I really be the guy who has to change his catheter?"

"Well, no. Why do you suppose that they are making you take this class?"

"They say the state, licensing, you know? Honestly, I have no idea where they are going with this... I don't even think they are all on the same page. Majoring in English is fine, if I was taking English classes. But this. Education. I feel like I am majoring in Unicorns or Dungeons and Dragons. Applicable, but..."

Alan was disappointed in the ever-changing requirements for teacher licensing in Massachusetts. There was a standardized test that all potential teachers had to take, and as far as he could tell, all it did was give a company an outrageous amount of money to administer a test that was just created to make parents across the state feel better about the teachers in their schools; but it just showed that all those who pass and become a teacher that they are licensed to be a certified test taker. While he loved literature and wanted to become a man-of-letters due to his experiences so far in college, Alan was just in it so that when he graduated he could eat until he could live off of his writing on his own. Alan made that point very clear to everyone he knew, and some of his professors who were passionate about teaching in the public realm resented his statements on the matter.

"I agree. But the payoff will be great when you get into the classroom and get a job without needing anything more than your degree and license, right?" Alan turned his head to the doctor and glared at him. "That is of course, you won't even need to if you become a famous writer first?" Alan looked back up at the ceiling.

"Right," Alan sighed.

"How is the diner?"

Alan worked at an all-night diner called "Dan's." It was situated across town and was sandwiched between a cheap motel and the interstate that reminded him that he could be in Boston in only an hour. It was an inexpensive chain that still managed to charge way too much for what they served. Alan began working there a few months earlier during the winter when he first moved to Chapmansville. That was before he knew every horrific aspect of its local reputation, the fact that they were one of the top companies to be sued in civil court, and this was Alan's favorite, one of the last companies in America to rid itself of segregation.

"It's fine. I am not making that much, and certainly not enough to make up for the sales I have at the end of the night, but..."

"But what?"

"Well, I like the people I work with, you know? I like the fact that I can be goofy with the customers and play with them and not get in trouble with my boss. I am my own job security, in a way... I simply don't give a shit. Moreover, I am not sure how, but I think I get better tips because of it."

"But not enough?"

"I probably walk out with ten percent of my sales, and that is if you take into consideration that there are people I have to deal with that don't tip over eight percent and then the people that tip thirty. Sometimes it averages out to fifteen; even though I know I am worth more."

The doctor scribbled something on his notepad.

"Tell me, how are you and Jane doing?"

Alan contemplated what he wanted to tell him. So far, Furman's suggestions on their relationship were helpful, but Alan didn't want suggestions, he wanted results. No matter how many things that Furman suggested to him that were actually implemented, Jane would still be impatient, selfish, and anxious, and Alan couldn't do anything about it.

"We're the same. It's all one big conflict of interest... We don't want the same things." Dr. Furman continued to stare back, waiting for more of a response. "We were arguing today, as a matter of fact, until her backyard blew up and interrupted us. Our relationship, conversations, and arguments don't seem to go anywhere. Nothing with her does."

"How is her...what was it, anorexia or bulimia? How is that going?" Furman asked. He loved bringing up the fact that Alan spent a great deal of time nursing her out of her eating disorder. It was getting better, but it was sure to come back at some point.

"I don't care anymore…Frankly, I am starting to think that I am ready to go home and get out of here."

"How much school do you have left?" Furman asked.

"Well, I have at least a year and a half left, but honestly I can just transfer my credits somewhere else. I don't really think I am learning too much here, and I hate it."

"You grew up in a big city, you were in the middle of it all, and now you aren't. Are you bored? Do you miss your friends? Is something keeping you here?"

"You got it. But it is even more than that. This is like… Like the worst time warp I think I have ever seen. It's bizarre. There are no decent paying jobs around here, cement covers everything, people are living from paycheck to paycheck, and everyone is in constant debt and despair. I made way more at home, in some really awful jobs."

"Welcome to the Midwest."

Alan wasn't entirely sure what he meant. They were in New England. Was it an entirely different country than the rest of the U.S.? Did he mean here? Was it Midwest Massachusetts? "I don't -" Alan was about to explain, but Furman interjected.

"A great author, his name escapes me at the moment, but a great author once wrote something that I thought was pretty impressed with. He said that beyond eighty kilometers outside of every major city in the U.S., it automatically transforms into the Midwest. I think what he said is very true. I think about it every time that I come to work and drive through downtown…. What is key is how *you* perceive life, how *you* go about things. You have to remember that you aren't ghetto or even Midwestern, just because you live in a place that resembles the idea itself."

Alan thought about this and was reminded about why he came to therapy to begin with. Furman was right; the city only affected Alan as much as he allowed it to.

Was life automatically "Midwestern" when you got outside of eighty kilometers of any major city? What is "Midwestern" anyway? Is it the pursuit of greatness, but the settling over only the attainable? Is it life below a certain degree of something? Money? Intelligence? Education? Is it just the fact that a certain group of people enjoy eating grits and butter, and they just happen to live congested in the same place? Why did they eat this at Dan's? It certainly wasn't Alan's first breakfast choice, for nutrition and for flavor. Alan thought that he would like to pursue this concept at some point in his writing.

Furthermore, why did it take almost an hour for the therapy to start doing something for him? They should offer two-for-one sessions where you get two hours of therapy, the second hour being the hour of power where you learn all of life's secrets and can truly get down to business.

"Well, Alan, it looks again like our time is up."

"Just when we're getting going."

Furman paused and looked back at Alan, his forehead wrinkled up. "Did you say something about Jane's backyard exploding?"

"We were in the middle of an argument about a half hour before I got here, and there was just a loud boom, the house shook, and the backyard was on fire."

"What was it?"

"Oh, I have no idea. Most people around here have septic systems, right? That was my guess, but I don't really know. I didn't know those exploded."

"Was anyone hurt?"

"No, and just as I was leaving to come here, all of the emergency personnel were pulling up. Even before the explosion, I just thought, 'Christ, I need to get outta here…'"

"Wow. Well hang in there and let me know what's happening. I'll be seeing you next week?"

"Yeah," Alan said, as he fingered his key ring in his pocket.

Alan started out of the office, weaving around the furniture, and opened the door to go out. He turned around as he closed the door. Dr. Furman was still writing. The door closed, and Alan turned around and started walking to the elevator that was up the hallway.

Alan wondered what Furman had about him to write about. Was he depressed? He thought that it was a great possibility because it runs so rampant in his family. It was also a great possibility that he was schizophrenic, an alcoholic, and senile, and it would be interesting to find out if that is the way the rest of the world sees him and he just didn't know it. Was he speaking his inner thoughts out loud at that exact moment without realizing it? No. But he did remember from psychology that he is at the age where this begins to happen and he thought that it probably has something to do with what Furman was writing on that paper. He thought that there was also the possibility that he was just paranoid. A paranoid schizophrenic. With a brain tumor.

The elevator opened, and Alan stepped in. He looked at the numbers as they lit up and brought him down the various floors of the college library…the countdown.

• • •

Charles Hobbeston stared with is arms outstretched towards Alan. He was beginning his descent, Alan thought, his descent into the meaningful part of the program where, books and money aside, he delivers the true message. Peering through the television screen from some studio in Las Vegas, he works his magic; his religion. He moves his hands down, stares at the audience, and begins.

For as long as Alan could remember, television evangelists had always captivated him. Many were just looking for money, while others had other perogatives such as feeding the homeless (looking for money), teaching others about the wonders of Christ (looking for money), or delivering people from war torn countries (looking for money). He liked to watch as someone could make thousands of people believe in and find personal worth in them. The worth that they sought was an empty hole in their own lives, and the preachers tried to fill their own personal hole with the money that people would send to them. It was fascinating.

The Reverend Charles Hobbeston was Alan's favorite. With his perfect blonde hair that resembled a flowing holy mane and a perfectly pressed gray suit, he would address the nation of believers and non-believers as if he hosted a news program of worth. The show, The Sacrosanctity Society, consisted of four parts: a short news program which talked about scary music or violent video games and let you know that they were brainwashing today's youth, a second part which had a testimonial of how by a viewer giving the show money they were in turn blessed with income, a prayer service where Hobbeston, his wife, and his reporters would all hold hands or put a hand in the air and pray, and finally the 'sermon' of sorts which would deliver a message to the world.

When Alan had gotten back to his studio apartment, they just finished introducing a new segment during the prayer service that was complete with theme music and animations flying across the screen. It was "Operation Supreme Affliction," and was based on yet another senatorial decision to allow gay marriage somewhere else in the U.S. The point of the segment was to pray for the "sick, old, and tired" senators to come down with a sickness of some sort that would subject them to step down from their position.

Currently, the sermon had begun, and Alan was as he always was in this part of the show - intent to listen to the powerful words of the greediest of evangelists. When the reverend had begun, there was no speaking, and the television show was replaced with a sweeping blue screen with the words "NEWS SIX, Special Report." Alan watched intrigued as he had never seen a midday show interrupted by a special report. The local newscaster appeared on the screen and began her monologue on the news that was unfolding.

"Christine Barre here with a special report from the NEWS SIX Action Team. It appears that a small commuter plane has violently crashed into a residential neighborhood less than an hour ago. Let's go live to Alice Christie in Chapmansville. Alice?"

The screen cut to an attractive young woman standing in front of Jane's family's home. She was surrounded by a throng of emergency personnel and flashing lights. There was also a great deal of very sharply dressed men in suits walking around with clipboards making notes and talking with each other.

"Hi Christine. A frightening blast shook this quiet neighborhood about an hour ago when a small commuter plane on its way back to Chapmansville Municipal Airport from a flight to Worcester ran in to an unknown failure, and was forced to crash into the backyard of this small suburban home."

The camera immediately cut to a montage of people running and hurrying around the small white house that Jane grew up in. Alan suddenly felt awful for leaving Jane like that, but he reminded himself that she was being irrational and he definitely needed his therapy that day. There were a few short quotes aired by some of their neighbors who were home at the time, and footage of the firefighters trying to douse the smoldering ash without disturbing the scene of the accident. Surprisingly, there was no footage of Jane in her frail state. She would have been the camera crew's prime target for a totally traumatized witness. Regardless, the camera cut back to the reporter.

"Aside from the pilot of the plane and his flight instructor, there were no fatalities or injuries in the accident. The flight tower has no information on the flight, as they lost contact with the plane a whole fifteen minutes before the accident. More information as it is available to us, Christine, back to you in the studio."

"Is there really no information leading to some kind of explanation of the accident?" Christine in the studio asked. The screen was now split in two, the field reporter on the right and the studio anchor on the left.

"Well, Christine, the FAA is already at the scene and are performing some initial tests. It is obvious that they will be looking for the cockpit data recorder – this small plane used mainly for instruction had one for insurance purposes which is unusual for aircraft of this size and type – and the flight plan if it still exists to note anything unusual in the coming days and try to solve this mystery as to what problems they had in the plane. The question this evening remains, why did they chose to land it here in such a dense neighborhood when the airport is only about a half kilometer away from the scene of the accident. An important side note: the plane had just passed its inspection only a week ago, so it will be interesting to find out what the cause of this devastating accident was."

"Thank you very much Alice. That was Alice Christie reporting live from Chapmansville. We will certainly bring you more developments as they occur. Now, back to 'Our View', already in progress."

Alan stared at the television and was fixated in what he saw. Only there, only then would that happen. He didn't realize it, but he was rolling his telephone in his hands. He contemplated calling Jane and then decided not to as she would probably be too distraught to speak, swooning over the disaster and emergency personnel in her house.

Alan stood up in half of his tacky work uniform, grabbed his work shirt, put the phone down, opened the door to the hallway, and left. As he walked down the hall to the exit, he thought about the accident as it happened earlier. They were arguing, there was a bang, and two people were dead. Just like that. They could have crashed into the house and killed all of them, but they didn't. How bold, and yet how sad; it was despair that soaked every borough of this sad community, and he knew this. As Alan left the tenement building and entered his car, he realized that when he was zoning out for the news report and the evangelist, he was wasting time.   Alan was already twenty minutes late for work.

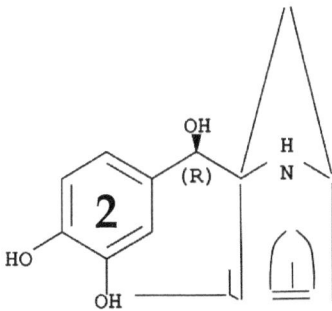

Dan's stood at one end of a barren wasteland of pavement that stretched to the gigantic Home Warehouse that was about a kilometer up the road away from the interstate. In between the two, the sprawling space featured various fast food restaurants across the street from one another, six strip malls, a movie theater, and a full size mall. The mall was the equivalent of an oasis in the desert of cement, a place where you could cool off in the air conditioning, get a soda, and walk around the stores. There was a video game store, two fat-lady stores, a dollar store, a couple of fast food places, and a surfer store, which Alan always wondered about because there was nowhere to surf aside from the lakes that dotted the area. If you did want to surf, you could have driven two and a half hours to the coast, where there were no waves.

Dan's was open twenty-four hours a day, seven days a week. The only time it closed was for Christmas and less than every four Thanksgivings or so. Being an establishment such as this, one could imagine the fine and upstanding clientele that Dan's catered to. It was only the previous Thursday, only three days before, that the restaurant beat its own record for "longest time that went by without a fight on a Thursday overnight." This time around, it had been exactly seven weeks since the last fight-free Thursday, and the staff celebrated.

Alan drove his small blue hatchback into the driveway, and parked alongside the building. Alan had not always had a car, and bought this one right before he moved so that he had some wheels to get around on. It was his second car, and it was a steal when he bought it used with a hundred and fifteen thousand kilometers on it for only three thousand bucks. He bought it after finding out that there was no local public transportation in Chapmansville.

As he walked to the door of the restaurant, he surveyed the area. One thing that he always wondered about the town was why there wasn't a spot of grass or trees in these congested shopping areas. He wondered many times how these retail deserts were created? Who was the guy in charge that just said, "Okay, here's the plan. We're going to bulldoze all of the trees down so we can build our shitty stores. Then, we'll cover everything in pavement, build the stores, and then, get ready for this, we will *not* make any new gardens to plant trees or grass in to make it look nice! What do you think?"

Of course the town's planning board and zoning board looked back at the man open-mouthed, blinked their eyes for a moment, and stood up cheering! They just had to hold themselves back from jumping on the chairs and the tables, bringing themselves down to the level of apes. The human condition stood in its most raw and uncanny form.

"Revolutionary!" one board member shouted.

"I wish I came up with the idea of covering the earth with sweltering tar!" said another. To this day that brilliant man lives as a legend in the hearts and minds of all Chapmansvillians, young and old. He is known as the man who risked everything and had the guts of taking on the system and making his dreams come true.

While that is not exactly how it happened, Alan thought, it made the most sense because there was no way any moron could accomplish the feat of tearing an entire square kilometer of forest down and sprouting up icons of corporate America in its place. Alan could never imagine such a place because even in the city, a place that is constantly bombarded for being so deadbeat and covered in pavement and congestion, there always were parks and trees and bushes about every three meters in the sidewalk.

Alan opened the door to the diner and entered. It was a rather hot day out, and he would expect that a refreshing gush of cool air conditioning would whoosh over his ears as he entered the building, however it didn't because they can't afford to pay the electricity bills when it was running. The restaurant was somewhat cooler than it was outdoors in several spots, namely the ones away from where the wait staff had to stand on account of the hot grills. Many customers have even been lost on account of the lack of air-conditioning in the restaurant, choosing to battle the heat out and driving to another restaurant...an air-conditioned restaurant.

The restaurant was big as far as breakfast diners were concerned. The dining room itself was horseshoe shaped, the bulk of the dining room's size being in the front. When you walked in, the bathrooms were straight ahead, along with a counter to sit at that wrapped around and led to some booths. When you turned to the right, you could see the kitchen's service window to the left, a counter with seats in front of that, and the dining room lay about 15 meters straight ahead with booths lining the walls, and free standing tables in the middle. Lights hung from the ceilings on cords with big plastic faux frosted glass lampshades that reminded Alan of cymbals. The windows were large, and had steel blinds that made it look from the outside as though everyone inside was in some kind of bizarre futuristic prison with bars that went side-to-side rather than up and down.

"Alan. The Man. The Myth. The Legend." Edward Donohue, the store's manager, always greeted Alan this way. He was trying to be a man comfortable enough with himself to greet another man in this fashion, much like Alan did. Alan hated it.

"Hey Edward. How are the ladies treating you today?" Alan responded.

"Which one?" He responded. Edward was married and never seemed to have any kind of good experiences with his wife, and made up for his tattered relationship by hiring attractive young women who worked at Dan's for a month or two and then left. About one in five sued him for sexual harassment, and all of them could not afford the lawyers and court fees necessary to finish what they started. Such was the case for a lot of things that people did out here...no one finished anything.

Edward was about forty, and he wore his hair slicked back into a black gelled helmet. He would always wear a dark wool suit to work that was at least five years out of style, and tanned so regularly that it made his skin and appearance almost leathery and beaten. Traditionally he was always at work when Alan arrived, and would leave an hour or two later. Alan never liked it when Edward was around because he had a tendency of taking his poor attitudes out on everyone from staff to customers, and the fact that he was intimidated by Alan didn't help much either. Today, it seemed as though he was in a good mood.

Alan punched in on the one computer that still worked (the restaurant couldn't afford to fix the other two) and went to change into his uniform in the back room. The uniform, half of which he was already wearing, consisted of black pants, black shoes, and a tacky yellow bowling shirt emblazoned with "Dan's" in an explosion of color on the back. In the catalog that the company ordered the shirts from, they called them "camp shirts," and Alan always wondered aloud 'why wouldn't they?'

"Alan, listen, I am going to need you to go and take care of wiping down your seats and blinds before you start taking any tables, alright?" Edward requested. Usually, while Edward was always around for a good hour or two before the night shift manager arrived, there usually weren't any tables that came in and the restaurant lay dormant until four thirty or five o'clock. Edward didn't use this time to make people come in late to save the company money, but rather, used the wait staff with their two-and-a-half-dollar-an-hour pay scale to janitor the restaurant until business picked up. Yeah, he was still saving the restaurant money, but he was wasting the wait staff's time at the same rate, and the restaurant's money wasn't his anyway.

"Yes, Edward." Alan responded. He was a yes man.

Whenever Alan was toiling at something that he didn't really care for, he enjoyed playing certain games with himself. For one, he liked to look at people in general and try to figure out their story, or fabricate one that transpired into something strange that could only happen in real life. Working at a restaurant made this activity all the more easy. There were all sorts of people that came in; tall people, skinny people, fat people, people with disabilities, and don't forget the low class white trash stock character. Along the same lines, he also liked to work out stories that he was planning on writing at some point.

Spraying industrial cleaner onto a rag and wiping dust and fly droppings from the plastic and steel, he cycled through everything that was on his mind: school, Jane, work, and the constant yearning for home. What if he ended it like he had been wanting to? What would it be like if he just packed up and left Chapmansville and everything here and headed back home? Setting: a barren wasteland of cement, steel, and glass. Little ketchup packets served with your microwaved egg sandwich breakfast lay in front of a couple that aren't much of a couple. The sanitized life resembles a game show with couples competing for big cash prizes, but is really only a dry representation of a life no one in the town can attain… He could win.

"Alan, you ready for a table?" a waitress had asked. Alan was staring out the window across the vast emptiness of parking lot between Dan's and the mall, transfixed by the haphazard crossed telephone wires. It was getting darker out. Alan collected his thoughts and looked up at Rosie holding two menus and standing with familiar faces. "They requested you."

"Oh, sure! Send them over!" Alan walked over to the cleaning cart and put the spray bottle and towel down. Alan had to serve tables in the back of the restaurant today, and on a Sunday night, that traditionally meant that he wouldn't make more than thirty bucks if he was lucky.

The couple that approached one of his tables was Diane and Johann, a recently married couple who treated him and Jane to dinner one evening. They had been two of the friendliest people that he had met out here, a couple who beat all odds to be together and had a relationship that existed as love in its most pure sense. They had met on the Internet over a vast ocean, exchanging only words between each other without actually meeting or even seeing each other's faces.

Diane's husband had just died, and she was having a difficult and desperate time finding her way out of her home. She reminded Alan of his own mother. Through her own desire to do something for herself, she connected her computer to the Internet and joined a widow support group in Belgium. One of the counselors for the site was a social worker that had also lost a partner and professionally worked with the developmentally disabled.

When Diane and Johann first met, they immediately hit it off, and communicated regularly for a period of a year, and when they met for the first time in Boston when he flew in, it was love at first sight. She was a 37-year-old short and stout soccer mom who wore glasses and short red scraggly hair, and he a 45-year-old tall, skinny man with long black hair who didn't go anywhere without his black leather vest, black leather cowboy boots, and various pewter necklaces around his neck. They held each other for a moment, looked each other over, and made their way to her car. When it started, the music of a popular loud metal rock band from Germany filled the air, and they knew from that moment on that they were perfect for each other when they both began to sing the lyrics.

Every night that they came into Dan's was magical. To most, it was a crappy truck stop diner that they hit up because they could only afford a crappy truck stop diner, but Diane and Johann savored their buffalo chicken fingers and hot turkey sandwich as if it were the greatest meals ever served to them. They would chew, dream into each other's eyes like teenagers, and hold hands. They spoke little, and what was said was usually spoken so softly that only they could hear it. There were only a couple of times that he had seen the two in bad spirits, and that was when his temporary citizenship visa was up, and he had to return to Belgium.

Tonight, the couple was engaged as their usual bubbly and excited selves. They sat looking up expectantly and smiled at Alan. He was happy to see them not just because of who it was, but because they were his first table.

"How are we doing tonight kids?" Alan asked.

"We're fine, just fine," Johann responded softly and ethnic. They were smiling up at Alan from their seats. The couple radiated warmth that was unparalleled to anything that Alan had ever experienced when they were around. It was wonderful.

"Did we do anything exciting today? Did you guys go to the movies or anything?"

"Actually," Diane began, "I just got out of work, and we were going to go to the mall after this. We were going to check out the sale they were having at The Body Store and see if there were any wonderfully perfumed massage oils or fun bath things we could get to play with."

"That sounds fun..." Alan crouched down beside the table to level himself with his guests. He put one hand on the floor to steady himself.

"How have you been?" Diane continued.

"I have been okay, thanks. You know, trying to keep my feet on the ground between school, work, Jane; the usual." While he should have been less candid with these people who really just amounted to strangers, or perhaps mere acquaintances, he was strangely comfortable.

Alan thought about going into detail about the plane crash and everything else, but he didn't really want to dampen their spirits. Alan didn't really feel like working tonight, so he would just take their order, and disappear. This worked so well with Diane and Johann because they didn't demand a great deal of attention aside from a little small talk, food, and a smile. As friendly acquaintances, he could talk with them for an hour, and as customers he could just serve them without much else. Tonight, he just wanted to do that; serve them their food and let them daydream while he went out of the back door of the restaurant, sat on an empty plastic milk crate, and thought up some stories or wrote a little.

"Do you folks just want your usual?"

"You got it," Johann started. "And two cappuccinos afterward, please."

"I know, I know," he responded. What normally passed for a rude retort by a server was always ironically met with humor.

Alan turned around and made his way to the point of sale computer where all of the wait staff put in their orders. He punched in a buffalo chicken strips and a hot turkey sandwich, omitting the cappuccinos that he never charged them for. He figured the company was already making a lot of money off of their overpriced items and it wouldn't make a difference if they lost the penny or so that it cost them to make the drink, let alone the two-dollar profit they would make if he did charge them. Fucking capitalism. He hit the 'send order' button.

He walked through the swinging door that was immediately to his left, passed the kitchen and the dish room, and walked down a short hall to the back door. Without looking where he was going, he inadvertently walked right into the cook on duty, Ted. He was a large man at five ten who would quite literally douse everything he ate mayonnaise and fit the mold as your 'Average Unhealthy Joe' in every public health campaign that ever existed. At twenty-two he was a prime candidate for a happy-birthday angioplasty when he turned thirty, and his average Central-Massachusetts ignorance to the world was exhibited to Alan in his first week of work. After a plate had come up in the service window with too few fries on it, he asked the cook, "why are you jewing the customers?" Ultimately he was only a product of the area, as he had apologized to Alan after realizing his folly, and he continued on to correcting another employee after he had said it once. Deep down he was a good man, and his ignorance was not self-inflicted.

"Whoa there. Where are you off to?" Ted asked.

"I'm going outside..."

"Doing your reading or whatever?"

"Yeah."

"Did you put some food in?" Ted was breathing heavily from whatever light work he was doing a minute earlier, and Alan always thought that the wheezy intake of air would just halt one day and he would have to enforce some CPR or boy scout first aid that he hadn't ever had to use.

Ted had always commented on Alan's academics. He had never finished high school and he always thought it was great that Alan was as ambitious as he was, living a life that he never would. As Alan looked at Ted, big, sweaty, and soiled with work, he looked at his clear blue eyes; two apparitions of blue puddles sloshed with goodness and purity. They looked at Alan as a child's eyes would, with virginous ignorance.

"Yeah, I put an order of buffalo strips and a hot turkey... Could you shout out and let me know when it's done?" Alan said.

"Cool. I'll let you know."

Alan made his way to the back door, a once white, but now filthy barrier between the humid dish room and the clean nighttime air. He pushed the cold metal bar to open it, and as he did, the box to the left of the door began to scream in an inconsistent and desperate manner. The door was armed with an old alarm that didn't know when to go off, so Edward had left the disarming key in it so that the employees could shut it off whenever they wanted to go outside for a smoke, or in Alan's case, a short break from his halogen nightmare.

Alan looked at the back parking lot at what the environment had to offer him tonight. He thought about his views on the area as he surveyed the parking lot, which was a rectangular and flat land of tar cut off ahead by a line of cement that raised the terrain a couple of meters, and then changed back into splaying blacktop for the parking lot for the strip mall behind Dan's. It was a strip mall with only an office for an auto club and a skateboard shop, the rest of its four shops standing as empty and desolate as the city itself. Flies and moths darted around the gigantic halogen lamps that dotted the sky around the empty parking lots. They created spotlights on the ground for tonight's staging of Chapmansville: The Musical, starring no one at all.

He reached over to the stacks of plastic milk crates lining the walls and took down four from the top. The rest of the pile accidentally crashed down onto the ground and danced around his feet into the parking lot. He took the two in each of his hands indifferently and placed them firmly on the pavement in a stack of three and a stack of one in front of that, making himself a king of the parking lot sitting on the throne of industry behind Dan's on a quiet night in suburbia.

Alan removed a small black leather-bound notebook out of his apron, along with a pen. He removed the leather strap from its brass clasp and fanned the book open to a fresh page. The book contained his secrets to his life: thoughts of things happening in the world, musings on what he read, observations on people in his world, and random data like phone numbers and television show times where the book came in handy as the only available paper. He put the pen to paper and began to write, a reflection of what he experienced in his day.

"Spoke with Dr. Furman today again. Discussed current and extended disgust with the area, and how to keep myself fitfully sane in this horrid place. He said that it was probably the fact that I am not used to the 'midwestern' attitudes being a city mouse and all. Thought exploring this concept would be a fantastic story idea, in fact, writing about someone who leaves everything that is upsetting himself…"

He paused for a moment reflecting on the day; the argument at Jane's house about moving back to the city, the plane crash, and everything else surrounding it. He looked back at the paper and began to write again.

"…A story of someone who is fed up of the ignorance and naiveté that surrounds him and decides to end it all… But not by exploding or killing or flipping out, but just by leaving. Should do his best to make the greatest out of his situation, and even have an almost cynical optimism."

Alan looked at what he wrote and was very pleased with the result, and he wanted to write a complete story soon. His last great piece here in this town, and he would pour his heart into it. It would be a story of love and loss when there is only one to be loved and cared for, and that one has no idea how to return it as they are so personally centered in their own world that nothing else matters. Magnificent.

His focus was shifted from his book down onto the ground between his legs. There was a small ant crawling across the pavement. He hadn't noticed any bugs ever doing this at night, but it was likely that it was because they would be killed by the smoldering sun on their backs, heating the ground to sizzling temperatures. The nighttime was a much more reasonable time to move, and at a closer examination, the ant was carrying a leaf and there were others doing the same. Such trifles are nature's way, the survival of such small creatures in the immeasurable desert of the parking lot. They had to survive, and to do this they brilliantly adapted their pilgrimage to six o'clock at night.

"What the fuck?" Ted's voice erupted from the back door of the restaurant. He was surveying all of the crates on the ground.

"Oh, hey…they fell…" Alan responded.

"Oh. Well, your food is in the window."

"Thanks, brother."

Alan felt the weight of his heart on his feet as he stood up. He began to walk towards the door and felt his stomach turn inside of him. He was hungry. It was a feeling that he was used to out here, not because he wouldn't be able to afford food on this particular night, but it is also very similar to the emotional feeling of despair and heartbreak. He opened the huge steel door, and wrote one more word in his little journal, "Hungry." He placed the precious little book in his apron and moved through the back of the restaurant, determined.

Normally when Alan was ready to write, he put all else aside and sat down to just pound something out until he was finished. The words would just purge forth through his fingers onto the page as if they were a river flowing from the mouth of a majestic waterfall. There have been times that he was known to just stay up at all hours of the night just to complete a manuscript for only himself. Brushing aside personal commitments, schoolwork, sleep, and other important aspects of his life, he would enter a zone of productivity and creation that was rivaled only by god himself. He was a god in these moments. God had created Alan in his own image, and so, Alan creates.

Alan reached the service window and retrieved the sandwich and the buffalo strips. The restaurant still stood empty for the most part, and as Alan turned with the plates in his hands to present them to his customers, he was surprised to see that the couple at his table was missing. Looking out of the window towards the front of the building, he saw that the couple was talking wildly and waving their arms. They were fighting.

Taking this in, he wasn't sure at what juncture it was that he had begun to think that they were such a perfect couple. Whatever the circumstance is surrounding their little argument, it is certain that any healthy relationship must have its small spats and fights, but to what degree is it healthy? Certainly the way he and Jane fought was not healthy in the least; he felt like dirt afterward. Alan had totally trusted them; he had trusted them to have the relationship that he never could with someone else; one with such a passion and flame that would certainly make anyone else think about himself and his partner what he was always thinking about Diane and Johann.

While he pondered this, the couple entered the restaurant again. They seemed as though they were back to their old selves, and Alan hadn't bothered bringing the food back to the window to stay warm. He placed the platters in front of the couple after they reseated themselves.

"How are we looking guys?" Alan asked.

"Well, we're missing something." Johann asked softly. Alan wasn't sure what he meant for a moment, but thought about it and immediately grabbed the plates off of the table again.

"Ooh. Sorry." He cleared his throat and continued, "okay, kids, are we ready to rock and roll!?" The couple stared back up at him with smiles, happy with their return to the warmth and fun that brought them there to begin with.

"Sure," Johann said as he nodded in approval. Alan returned the plates, turned, and walked away.

Alan shuffled over to the counter toward the front of the diner where the coffee machine sat and poured himself a cup with cream. It was cozy and refreshing. He sipped as he walked back towards the back door and outside. The milk crates were a mess, and unfortunately he wasn't about to pick them up. He wasn't feeling lazy on this night, however, he didn't feel it was necessary. They were on the ground, they were everywhere, they weren't in anyone's way, and that was okay.

Looking up he saw a man and his dog crossing the parking lot. The man walked scraggly and hunched under layers and layers of clothing. He pushed a shopping cart filled with bags, and the dog strolled unevenly alongside him. The poor man. How did there exist any degree of poverty out here? Where was a man like this supposed to go? How did he get to where he was?

Alan began to characterize this man, something that he often did. He considered it his most valuable personal creative asset, but also his biggest character flaw. Judgment. Going easy on him, Alan pictured a man who had graduated from high school with high honors, and the subsequent bachelor's degree he received from Columbia in business. The man worked his way up the corporate ladder, and worked at a successful day trading firm in the World Trade Center in New York City. On September tenth, 2001, he was supposed to take a small jetliner to a consultation meeting with a small plastics company in Chapmansville, Massachusetts on how to fully maximize the appropriate spending of the company.

His plane was delayed, and the next available flight was leaving the next day at seven o'clock in the morning so he could arrive in Chapmansville by the beginning of the factory's opening. After working in the tower overnight, his plane departed for Massachusetts. When he arrived, he found out about the awful tragedy that happened that day, and watched it unfold on the small television mounted on the wall of the airport. He had nowhere to go from there, and after the airport told him that there was no way he could possibly stay there any longer after a week, he became a suburban nomad.

Alan just knew others didn't see the man crossing the parking lot in this way. Some would have passed him by as a crazy drunk, a homeless drug user who had run out of money, a filthy man with his ragtag mutt, but not Alan. He had read once about the Buddhist way of seeing every person as the Buddha himself, and he was usually embodying the least fortunate of us that he is. Alan adopted this vision as his own. God could be anyone, and thus, we should be as empathetic as possible.

But why is no one this way in reality? This effortless way the people of central Massachusetts embrace the concept of 'midwestern' was unfortunate, and it further added to the confusion that Alan had about the rest of his country. Why was everyone so apathetic, distant and egocentric? What made this country so religion based, yet what made it the least religious? Was in fact everyone eighty kilometers outside of every major city as 'midwestern' as they were here? Was everyone hungry for something they didn't have, or was it something else?

During his whole internal dissertation, he was staring at the ground and his leg was bouncing compulsively on the ball of his foot. Ted had quietly returned without Alan noticing until the light cast off by the small bulb attached to the wall in a steel cage began to fade.

"Alan, it's pretty dead tonight. Do you want to hit the road after this table is through?"

"I would be happy to."

"Great. Clean up these crates, start your side work, and hit the road...How have you been, man? You alright?"

"Yeah, I am okay. Jane and I have been fighting, and I really miss home."

"What's new, huh? You are always saying that. You should do something about that."

"I am seriously thinking about it."

The two exchanged glances for a moment, and then Ted turned back toward the kitchen without saying a word. His social skills weren't all that fantastic, Alan thought. Alan left the milk crates where they were, and turned to go back inside the building. The steel door slammed in the night, adding two more fallen stacks of crates, leaving a small mountain of black plastic cages.

Alan returned into the dining room of the restaurant, and began his side work. Diane and Johann had finished their dinners and they were talking over their cups of cappuccino. Alan went over to their table to drop off their check, and Diane was crying. Johann looked up from his cappuccino and had an awfully sullen face on.

"Sorry that we were fighting there, Alan. It's just that I don't agree with her baby sitter choice all the time, especially with her daughter's issues. She demands a great deal of attention all of the time, and I am always looking out for her."

"That isn't what she is upset about, is it?" Alan replied.

"Well, no. I am leaving for Belgium again on Wednesday, and we were also discussing whether or not the kids would be going to drop me off." The conversation was awkward, because Diane remained at the table crying.

"Oh, that's too bad." Alan's stomach sank thinking about how Diane's children must feel when she dives so hard into her depression. She sat at the table sobbing hopelessly. It was a depressing sight, and it was uncanny to think what she did with her time outside of when Johann was visiting. Her seventeen year old son told her during one visit that she just slept in her room all day for weeks at a time. How terrible, he thought. Alan was reminded of his own mother.

"I am coming back, of course. We can't keep doing this. I need to come back and stay at some point. It is also getting unbelievably expensive, as you could imagine."

"Of course."

"Are you working any time before he has to leave?" Diane asked between her sniffles.

"Honestly, no." Alan replied.

Of course, Alan was working after class the next day at four in the evening, and then again on Wednesday afternoon after class, but he didn't have the heart to tell them this so as not to complicate their situation. He knew they would absolutely have to come in to the diner before he left. But why the waiter?

Johann stood up and shook Alan's hand. Unexpectedly he wrapped his arms around him, the squeaking and the smell of his leather vest made him dizzy. He thanked Alan with a warm heart, and then sat back down. They gave him their goodbyes, and Alan turned around to leave. Alan did the rest of his evening's work, the entire time longing for escape and to just disappear from where he was at that exact moment. It was a nightmare. A phantasmagoria of white trash, humidity, laziness, people and faces that were unkempt and rotting. A garish apparition of the midwestern dream deferred.

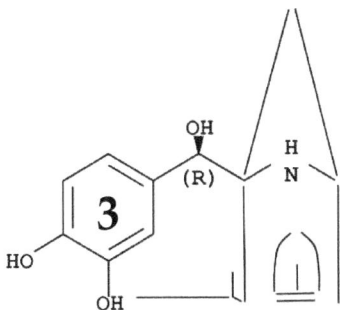

The screen of his computer was blank. A clean canvas ready to be painted with his imagination; with a story that would have a fantastic staying power and would reach out to millions of people ready to withdraw from their dull and horrid suburban lives. His black leather notebook sat next to his hand on the desk, open to the latest entry. There was only one thing that was delaying his work.

"I feel like I just ate a hockey puck," the familiar voice on the other end of the line said. Alan had been listening to Jane talk about the dinner her friends took her out to for the last half hour. It was the same thing, over and over again. How many pieces of popcorn she had eaten. She had twenty four. How many French fires she ate. Five. She said she ate her cheese burger, but chances are that only meant that she had 'eaten' it. More than likely, there were three real bites, four fake ones, no bites of the bun, and she used the rest of the duration of dinner to cut the burger into tiny pieces and spread them around on the plate to somehow make it look as though she ate more. Alan was a professional at reading her eating disorder.

"Yeah." He responded. That was the forty-sixth time he said 'yeah', and it was not the first time that he thought a twenty-four year old woman needed something else to do with the last thirty minutes of her life. Alan wasn't insensitive, he just didn't understand addiction. He knew people had addictions, and had an idea why they did, but Alan was lucky not to ever have any. He even had a pretty optimistic feeling that he couldn't. He felt as though what you revolve around your life is your own design, and if you want to constantly revolve yourself around alcohol, drugs, pornography, or in this case your own self-image, it should be rather easy to give up. He was, therefore, the most unconsciously critical when it came to the addictions of others.

He was also critical of people that kept him on the phone talking about the same thing over and over again. He was numb from her dialogue, and without realizing it, he removed the phone from his ear, looked at it, and pressed the 'end' button. He did this methodically and slowly, and stared at the phone in his hand taking it in.

She probably stayed on the other end of the line talking for the next five minutes before she realized he hung up. Alan thought that she would try to call back, but he was pretty confident that he could get away with not answering and telling her that the batteries on his cell phone had died, therefore he couldn't answer. Truth is, he was just sick of it.

He turned the ringer off, looked at the computer, paused, and began to type. He wouldn't stop. The words splashed down the screen, a waterfall of ink on ivory. He typed fast and determined, writing and writing, desperate to find his personal literary merit. His eyes filled with a shifting blur of creation, and the muses sang to him so loudly that they overpowered space, and his ears rang with passion.

• • •

"In the midst of a cement wasteland, among the mortar, cinderblock, glass, and air conditioning like a mid-west late-night empty supermarket, a man and a young woman dined on pancakes in a cheap breakfast restaurant next to the interstate. The layout of the restaurant, the waitress, the town, Tom Jones on the speakers, reminded him of the work Frank Lloyd Wright did that no one liked. What's new pussycat?

The sky was a blue sunny side up egg that baked the pimped out cars and discount superstore warehouses that lined every centimeter of the earth that wasn't covered with pavement. Here the people made the little money that they had at these warehouse stores, and then went on to spend it at the other warehouse stores. The heat that made the whole town look like a desert apparition made him dizzy. It made him feel empty.

"Want another O.J.?" he asked the young woman.

With a mouthful of syrupy pancakes, she looked up to him and nodded her head. He looked around the empty sixties game show set of *Let's Make A Breakfast* for the waitress. She was modeling, rather, cleaning off the shiny thirty-year-old industrial coffee maker that was behind door number one. When he got her attention, he pointed to the empty glass on the table, suggesting that this contestant couple needed more juice.

"How's the pancakes?" He asked.

"They're good."

The waitress brought over the juice. Up close, she didn't look like a grand prize model at all, but more like a heartbroken and weather-beaten cigarette widow in her bowling league outfit. Her big yellow name tag read 'Rita, serving you since 1992.' As Rita departed back behind her stage-like counter, the young woman took the last bite of her two ninety-nine value breakfast. She puffed out her cheeks, sat back, and patted her belly.

"I feel like I just ate a hockey puck..." she exclaimed.

"You always say that. Are you working tonight?"

"Yeah."

"I thought you didn't take Saturday nights anymore...That's when Mike works. You need to keep as far away from that sleaze as possible before I beat the shit out of him."

"I am covering his shift!"

"Oh."

She looked outside and exhaled like a blowfish. Always like a blowfish. The man looked down at the table, and noticed the shiny chrome mirror finish of the top of the saltshaker. It reflected them a million kilometers apart, and further as the young woman began to get up.

"Where are you going?" he asked impatiently.

"I have to go to the bathroom," she said as she walked off, holding her stomach.

"Please, don't…hold o-…Fuck."

He was sick of this town. This people. He is from the city, where people are looked upon as the celebrities that the culture out here strives to be. He was hungry for something. Hungry for home.

Outside, the thin and tall telephone poles stood desolated and dry carrying a network of communication to other bigger or crooked or pockmarked telephone poles, each discussing how they can become better telephone poles. Tall, thin, ignorant telephone poles. They didn't see the forest for the trees, well, they didn't see their existence in relation to the phones; they have never been out on the phone alone before. None of them even imagine being hit by a car and falling over, not even the pair that towered in front of the restaurant. That just can't happen to them.

"Hey, baby. What are you looking at?" she asked as she sat back down with new energy. She was happy now. She was finally clear and able to focus after all that breakfast. After her trip to the bathroom, she was finally clear and able to focus after all that breakfast.

"I can't believe they are building a *Chuck E' Cheese's* in the old rock club either." She said looking out in the general direction as the man. She was referring to construction they were doing in a strip mall across the street.

"Huh?" he replied.

"That's what you're looking at, right?"

"No…no, I was just looking at…at the telephone poles."

"Oh-kay…" she paused for a while in mid thought.

"What?"

"Oh, nothing. I never liked telephone poles. They all remind me of…well…a bunch of them all in a row…they're like crucifixes or something. I guess it was all that catholic school stuff they fed me growing up. You know what I mean?"

"Yeah," he replied, "I know what you mean."

As Rita returned with her small tray and retrieved the last of the dirty dishes, the man stared at the small, untouched glass of O.J. sitting in the middle of the desolate table. Small beads of sweat rolled down its side as it waited to quench somebody's thirst. It needed to.

"I've decided to leave," the man said to the young woman.

"Okay. Where do you want to go? The mall?"

"No."

"That movie you wanted to see-"

"I am leaving here. This town. You. I am going back to the city."

She stared at him in a dull silence. She was sort of confused, but moreover she didn't know what to say. In this game show, she hit her buzzer and didn't know the question.

"What?" she responded softly.

"I have been out here for a year. A year I spent with you. You said you would get better. You said this town would get better. It didn't. It just stays the same and it rots away. You just stay the same. You rot away."

"What are you talking about? I rot away?"

"Yeah, you rot away, just like the buildings and the pavement. Just like everyone and their shitty dreams. No one goes anywhere and they just take their depression and their problems and pump them into a few children or smoke them or drink them or...they all purge them somehow."

"I don't have that problem anymore."

"Yeah, I know you don't. No one here has a problem."

The young woman was silent for a little while. She stared at the man in contemplation. It seemed as if she knew that he had been suffering with the life he has lived away from home. She didn't though.

"Can I come with you?"

"No."

"What can I do?"

"When you met me I was just a guy who worked at a record store in the city. You were a pretty girl. We went out for drinks and you thought I was so cool. Then I came out here to be with you and I found out about your problem and...well, everything here, it's all been the same."

She didn't say anything after that. The young woman was just the expressionless cardboard cutout that the man didn't realize that he got involved with. There were now two models at this game show, both with an outer layer that was beautiful that showed off the fruits of just what someone with the right knowledge and skill could attain. The inside layer was a mess of electrical wire and cords, communications straight out of the glossy pages of *Cosmopolitan*. One, a college student learning how to become more successful than the other, a wrinkled model with yellowed fingers that just dropped the check off at a table at a chain restaurant in New England on a humid and hazy summer day.

The man pulled out his wallet and put a hundred dollar bill on top of the check. His last hundred dollars. He picked up the soggy glass off of the table in front of the two and drank the whole thing in one slow, methodical sip. The juice felt cool and delicious sliding down his throat as Ben Franklin looked on with pursed lips of disappointment and jealousy. Ben was parched, too. Hungry.

"This is it. I am going. Take this and get a cab back or something...keep the rest for yourself."

He waited for a response and, as he expected, he didn't receive one. She seemed to be staring down on the vinyl seat, waiting to be picked up and carried by the next man to come along. The man brushed his hand over his mouth, the stubble on his chin and cheeks making a raspy sound that made the girl's face wince. The man moved over on the seat, got up, and began to walk away. He weaved through the vacant tables and stopped at the fluorescent spinning pie case by the door to turn around.

As he looked around the musty room, he contemplated addressing something to the girls that would have an impact on their lives. The speaking of the one final word that would possibly strike an epiphany of some sort between them. Something that would persuade his girl to bring flowers to her parents, apologizing for her naive upbringing. For all the trips to the hospitals and clinics to fix what she brought upon herself. Maybe the waitress could also benefit from something. Just the speaking of the one line that would have her miss one night at the social club or the bingo hall to absorb some literature or a play. Or maybe that would just look like a corny exit of a character in a bad movie.

There was nothing more that he needed to say. This girl was good for him for the time he spent there. She consoled him when he got a flat tire. She put up with going to see his independent films that she didn't particularly care for. Her family was a blessing that the man didn't have the opportunity to thank enough. She was also a good lay. All these things were wonderful, he thought, but they were no consolation to the lack of progress and mutual knowledge the pair faced in their relationship. The only way he could truly cleanse himself of this society and situation was to leave, and he now knew this. He opened the door, looked around, and voted himself off of this show.

He got into the car, started it, and looked back inside to where he was sitting. As the girl sat sobbing, Rita approached her, sat down across from her, and took her hands off of her face. They held hands, and he could tell the girl spilled her guts out to her. They were communicating their life stories as their joined hands sagged between them. He imagined them staying that way forever and birds landing on their arms, watching the traffic drive by.

The man pulled out of the parking lot. He turned the radio on and a low-fi sixties emotional band droned on over muffled guitars. As he turned on to the interstate toward the city and felt the car pour its energy out to him, he felt good. He felt free and happy for the first time in a long while. He stepped on the gas, opened his window, rested his head on the frame of the door, and let the wind softly brush his face. On both sides of the interstate the man admired a collection of green, red, and yellow trees that formed a gorgeous, ever-changing abstract painting to anyone who had the opportunity to drive past them. He now felt as though he could go on and drive like this forever. There weren't any telephone poles for kilometers."

• • •

Alan opened his eyes and looked around. His head was resting on his arms, folded neatly in front of the keyboard on his desk. He snapped his head up when he heard it again. The phone was ringing.

A faint string of drool hung from his lip to a darkened patch on his gray hooded sweatshirt. He wiped his sleeve across his face, and then reached across the desk to the phone. He heard a tinkle and a thump as his glass of watery ginger brandy from fell to the floor and spilled in a neat line across his rug, the small melted ice cubes bouncing across the room. He took the phone and immediately pressed the answer button.

"Hello?" He managed to say.

"Hello, Alan? It's mum," she said hysterically. Alan felt an unpleasant warm sensation in the pit of his stomach. It was way too late for her to be calling, but when wasn't it? She would traditionally go to bed extremely early and wake up at an entirely inappropriate time in the morning and wander about the house for hours until a decent television show was on, or a store opened for her to go to and continue to wander around. Alan looked at the clock and it read eight thirty.

"Oh, hi, mum."

"Listen, Alan, you need to visit your father." The famous line. This was a commonplace conversation that always happened between the two of them. Whenever Alan's mother was feeling depressed, she would always tell him that he needed to visit his father in Florida. One of the times she did this, she had been crying, screaming about maggots being in the municipal trash bin at the house. Alan told her that the maggots were there probably because it was a trash can, and no amount of conversation would get him to go visit his father. It was his senior year of high school and he had neither the time nor the money to visit. His mother continued to scream, telling him that she wanted him and his sister to go visit his father in Florida so they wouldn't be around when she killed herself. To Alan, this sealed the deal and he wouldn't ever be visiting his father in Florida. As it stood, he had found the best way to deal with the requests as best he could.

"Sure, mum."

"Okay, because I was worried. You dad's lawyer sent a letter to my lawyer saying that I had kept you kids from him and I want you to go tell him that it isn't true."

"I understand." Truth was, he didn't. His father divorced his mother, moved into another home, never saw them or helped them out with anything, never showed up to any school plays, graduations, or anything else, and now he was just trying to get his fair share of the house that Alan's mother worked so terribly long and hard to pay for herself. Yes, that made perfect sense. Alan continued, "have you been taking your medication, mum? Going to your meetings?"

"Alan, don't worry about me."

"Okay, but you know how you get. You start to think things. I get worried about you. I don't want you sleeping your day away or getting up too early and worrying yourself to death." Ever since dad left, Alan has felt like he was the parent in his family, that is, when mum wasn't taking her brain candy.

"I'm okay, Alan...I have some errands to run. I just wanted to tell you about dad."

"Errands? Ma, it's...Whatever, I'll talk to you later."

"I love you, Alan."

"I love you too."

Alan hung up the phone and stared at the empty glass on the floor. He was always worried that she would start to drink again. She always would, off and on. What's worse is that she would also take her medications and be royally trashed at seven o'clock in the morning. Unless things were going spectacularly well in her life, she was always in some sort of mess. When they were still living together, Alan would find himself checking her breathing whenever he passed her sleeping somewhere in the house.

His mother had no social supports. She would surround herself with people who needed help more than herself. One man was a pothead who listened to talk radio all night while supporting her alcoholism, while the most recent as Alan could remember was a one armed man who was in a terrible motorcycle accident when he was eighteen and lost one of his arms. He walked around tilted off to one side as if a swift gust of wind would blow him over.

Alan took the remote control off of his desk and pointed it to the television, turning it on. He had forgotten that it was time for the hour of power, The Sacrosanctity Society's Sunday Special. The channel was already set, as this was one of the only programs he watched on television aside from another program he idolized, a bizarre 1970s British department store comedy that sporadically appeared on public television. Alan didn't like television because it seemed to have an effect on him that made him edgy and upset. He also often felt as though he wasn't accomplishing anything, and he often preferred watching films instead.

It is important to mention that Alan didn't watch these programs for any kind of guidance or spiritual fulfillment; in his opinion he was a rather secular and sporadically practicing Jew. He liked to watch because he wanted to see how others (specifically the conservatives who often appeared on the program) viewed the world, and get angry at their opinions. Just last week, for instance, they were rambling on about how gay relationships are spoken against in the bible and that everyone on the "wrong side" of the marriage issue would have it coming to them. For one, Alan thought, it says nowhere in the bible that gay relationships were bad, it was only sodomy that it spoke against, and everything else was implied. In many aspects of Judaism, in fact, anyone could openly marry – love trumped all else.

But this was America, wasn't it? This bothered Alan in the deepest reach of his soul. An apparently free society that allowed for every person to live in their own practice and beliefs, but didn't allow for their citizens to, because these people are apparently backed by God himself. In this degree do the ignorant voters of the country take the words of these television evangelists as their own. To Alan, it was sickening and depressing to believe that if the law allowed gay marriage, it would interfere with anyone but the groom and groom. Who knew what would happen if such a gay couple were walking in the park and sneezed on their baby? It might turn them gay, and what in the world could possibly be worse than that?

Charles Hobbeston began to speak, his words filling the one room of Alan's sparse apartment with words that moved his heart, his mind, and his feet.

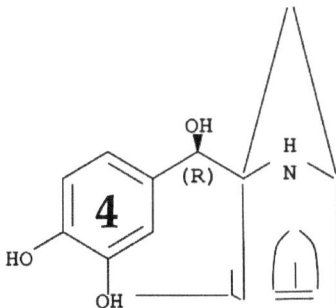

"...The laws of nature dictate that humans are constantly seeking peace, and the only way that we can keep this is through creating contracts. It is subsequently the establishment of these contracts that threatens peace and life itself because humanity is constantly seeking power."

Dr. Furman sat cross legged in his office, listening to Alan as he dictated his televangical experience to him over the phone. As he listened, he stared at his diploma on the wall and fingered a pen on his desk.

"So he says that we need to break away from our material values and take on a more natural existence. Our existence is only based upon what material possessions we own and how much money we have. Our existence is judged by that which comes with the ownership of such property, such as fear that it will disappear and one might resort to violence to obtain it. Now, he also goes on to say that the only way to free yourself of this is by believing in Christ and giving up everything and all the rest of it, but I sincerely think that-"

"Alan, where are you?" Dr. Furman inquired.

"Oh, that doesn't matter. So anyway, what I was going to say is that I have really decided to go back home once and for all and give everything up. Maybe finish school and become a philanthropist or Rabbi or something..."

"Alan, I really think you should come here and talk to me for a little bit. I know you are lucky you got a hold of me right after my monthly staff dinner meeting and it is kind of late and everything, but I will stick around so I can see you."

"But you don't think this is a good idea, then?" The sound of bangs and crashes sifted through the line, which made Dr. Furman annoyed because he couldn't quite hear what Alan was saying, and also because he was unsure of what was banging, and where Alan was.

"Well, to be honest with you, Alan, no, I don't. A lot of people have changed their whole lives for the worse in this way. The images and romanticism that you are dreaming about in flying away from where you are is a very common thing, but it is how we handle these things, Alan. It is one thing to think about it, and then examine your life to see how you could possibly make it better, but you are actually going to leave? I think you need to come see me and we can talk about this, face to face. We need a plan. Where did you say you were, again?"

"Sorry, I am at the bowling alley."

"What are you doing there?"

"Getting ready to leave."

• • •

Alan hung up the receiver in the small glass-enclosed foyer at Munson's Chapmansville Fun Lanes. Alan entered the bowling alley and strolled by the rows and rows of lanes, smelling the familiar wax and disinfectant spray in the air. Alan always loved the bowling alley; the vintage qualities always kept him in high spirits there, and the balls hitting the boards and the wooden pins falling created a familiar and erratic syncopated melody that made him feel like he was at the jazz rehearsal of the gods.

After listening to the evangelist speak about America's new society and how we all needed to live more naturally, he immediately packed his car with a few changes of clothes, a toothbrush, a bar of soap, a blanket, his cellular phone and charger, and some music. As far as where he was going to stay and where he was going once he got back to the city, he would figure it out. His first two stops that night would be a friend's house that he could contact if the need arose, and the bank the next morning to close his account.

Alan had come to the lane where Jane and her stocky brunette best friend Elizabeth were sitting at the scoring table. His ears were ringing when he sat down on the cold fiberglass bucket seat facing them. One thing that Alan was never able to do is seriously conduct any kind of a confrontation. He could easily do it to absolute strangers, but when it came to people he interacted with daily, he was in no way able to tell them off, even when they were severely wrong about something.   He was a wallflower.   Jane and Elizabeth sat silently facing forward, not making any kind of eye contact, until Elizabeth got up and looked into space in between them.

"Umm...I think I am going to the bathroom," she said nervously.

Alan and Jane watched as she made her way along the back wall that was papered in multicolored carpeting. Jane looked at Alan, and then got up, made her way to the alley, and began to violently toss balls down the lane. They bounced several times like solid billiard balls on a shiny cement floor before rolling on their own, and Alan actually thought that she would whip the next one at another bowler. She threw three or four hard, and none of them knocked any of the pins down. Exasperated, she turned toward Alan and sat down next to him weeping.

"What's wrong, Alan?" she asked.

"Nothing," he responded with a blank expression.

She stared at him. She searched his eyes. Alan was purposely acting somewhat depressed, and Jane was horrified and exasperated because she couldn't read him.

"Are you on drugs?"

"What did you say?"

"Nothing."

"No, did you just ask me if I was on drugs?"

"Yeah, you're acting really strange."

The whole bowling alley darkened around them, and everything went quiet. He looked into her brown eyes and analyzed everything that they have had in their relationship thus far. Alan had never done drugs in his life. Outrageous. With only a little bit of contemplation, Alan had come to the conclusion that his time as he had lived it in Chapmansville had been wasted, and there was no point to even argue about it.

"What the fuck?" Alan shouted. Jane jumped back in astonishment. She reached up and began pulling at one of the tendons in her neck.

"What?"

"Why would you ask me such a thing?"

"I don't know, you're being crazy!" she croaked. She began to pluck at the tendon. It looked as though she was playing some kind of bizarre instrument, aside from the fact that it looked absolutely disgusting.

Alan contemplated telling her that if she thought that he was using drugs, there was no way that she could possibly know him. He didn't want to; it would absolutely look like something from a trashy soap opera or the ending to an awful teen movie special. Alan was a lot better than making someone feel like they were living in a life that was something like that. He wanted to stop the cliché immediately.

"You know what? There is no way you could possibly know me if you think I am doing drugs all of the time." Damn, he thought.

"Is that what you think? Do you think that our relationship is just us not understanding each other? Why don't you just break up with me, then?" She was extending the cords in her neck harder and faster. She would pull it out in a bloody string.

"You know what? Since you have made everything so easy like you always do, I guess I will."

"Are you breaking up with me?" Alan thought about what she just said. Yup, it sure didn't make any sense. She continued, "you know what, whatever. Do your thing. I love you and nothing is going to change that, okay? I love you,…goodbye."

She made her way to the exit of the bowling alley, opened the front door, and tried to slam it behind her. The lights came back on and everything was back to normal in the alley, and Elizabeth made her way back to the seat she was in. She was watching from afar. She caught the whole thing. Alan imagined that it was her girl second sense that told her to leave anyway. She probably didn't have to go to the bathroom. The thought of her watching from a few meters away was appropriate. And creepy.

"So,…" Alan said.

"Yup." Elizabeth said and pursed her lips.

"You know that we've been having a few problems and whatever. I didn't want you to get the wrong idea about this. I am sure that she is going to try to make me look like an asshole next time you talk to her and whatever, and I just wanted to tell you what's up."

"Yeah..."

"So, umm... Basically, I decided to do this because she was too proud of herself, and there hasn't just been anything between us, you know? All we do is eat out and stuff. We never even 'do it' anymore. It has been like three months. But... I don't want to sound shallow. That isn't it, I just... I have shit to do. You know?"

"Yeah..." She just kept saying yeah, and Alan realized that she really didn't give a fuck about what he was saying. She wasn't listening. She was Jane's best friend, and no matter what he said, she would still think he was an asshole regardless.

This was certainly not how it was supposed to go. For some reason, Alan thought that this breakup would go smoothly and painless, and it didn't. He thought they could act like adults and just be civil about the whole thing, but that didn't happen. In fact, Alan had contemplated calling Jane on his way back to Boston and doing it when he got there. At that point, he wished he had.

"Let's hit the road," he said.

Alan and Elizabeth returned their shoes. They were going to pay the bill, but apparently Jane had come back in with the shoes to return them and paid it then. Elizabeth went back to the lane to get Jane's shoes while Alan left.

Alan took a right out of the bowling alley to where he parked his blue, and badly beaten hatchback. He walked around to the driver's side, opened the door, and sat down. He fondled his keys and put the appropriate one in the ignition. A familiar buzz sounded, but then he heard some sniffling. He hadn't noticed it, but Jane was in the backseat. She sat like a sack of flour in the backseat, and Alan's blanket was pushed aside to reveal his opened overnight bag.

"You have been seeing someone else, haven't you?" she said. She had gone from defensive, to raging, and now passively slumped. It was not the time to examine why she would think he was cheating on her, nor was it time to reassure her. It was only time to get her out of his car and go.

"No, Jane. God, why would you think that?" She gave him a look that teased him of his ignorance to her thoughts, and then she pulled part of a shirt out of his bag. Alan continued softly, "I am going home tonight. To Boston. I would never cheat on you, or anyone... I can't believe..."

"Well, what do you expect. I have no idea where this is coming from."

"What do you mean? We only spend a little time together, we never have sex anymore; you are always too busy for anything. You also think I am going to break up with you every five minutes. You say it for christ sake!"

"Yeah, but I'm not being serious... I am just trying to see your reaction - to see where we stand."

"Why the hell would you do that?"

"I don't know… I'm sorry. I love you."

"Well, I love you too, but I can't keep this up. That is dishonest and sneaky; that isn't love. That isn't want people who love one another do."

"I know, I'm sorry. I love you."

"Stop that." She started to sob more after he said that. He was referring to the fact that she was still pulling at her neck, but it worked on so many more levels. Alan continued, "I still love you, honey. I am going to continue to love you, but it is you who I love and not the way you have been acting recently. I feel like you treat me…like someone whose definition of love is a little messed up."

"Well, I'll change. Give me some time, I'll change."

"No, you shouldn't have to do that. We shouldn't have to be doing this."

"Can I come home with you? We can work it out from there! I will just stay there with you and we can live away from all of this! That will work, right? I want to sleep with you… You make me feel so safe."

"No, we can't do that."

"But, we can. It will be so easy. We'll just disappear and that will be the end of us both here. You are always saying how much you hate it here, so what difference would it make if I came? Least you could do when we get there is kick me out and I could live on the streets or come back here… I didn't realize just how much I hate it here, too, until yo-"

"Jane… I have to go. It's late."

With these words, Jane began to bawl. Her sobbing gave way to rivers of tears and a terrible cry that would break the strongest fortress down. What was important, Alan thought, was to be strong. Just open the door, and let her get out. Or better yet, driver her over to Elizabeth's car and have her help her out. He could just leave.

Alan turned the key and released his emergency brake. The little light that was on the dashboard that exclaimed "BRAKE!" just stayed on. That's great, Alan thought. Right before it is time to go, the car shits the bed and he can't go anywhere. He put the car into reverse, and released the regular brake in order to back out of the space, and the car reacted just as smoothly as it was supposed to. Evidently it was just the light that was broken, or not broken depending how you looked at it.

Alan drove to where Elizabeth was parked at the other end of the parking lot. She was standing by her car half-expecting that this would happen. Alan turned around in the seat, and faced Jane. She was still crying her eyes and lungs out, as if the absolute worst thing in her life had just happened. As Alan later learned, as a young woman who had never been dumped in her life it was one of the worst things to ever happen to her.

"Here's your stop."

Alan motioned to Elizabeth, and she opened the door. She reached her hand in for Jane, but she spilled herself out of the car and onto the wet pavement on her own. Rain had begun to lightly fall, making everything dark and shiny. Elizabeth closed the door to the car and they turned to walk back towards her car, Jane hanging off of her shoulder like a plastic bag filled with water.

Alan waited where he was, half waiting for Jane to turn around and dash for the car, wailing and gnashing her teeth. It would be just his luck that she would trip over something and he would run her head over, squashing it like a cantaloupe and burning it away with rubber into the pavement. That would be the perfect end to a perfect day. But she never came running back, and Alan wondered what was wrong with him to think such grizzly thoughts.

He turned the car towards the exit, and drove down the field of pavement. This particular parking lot not only served the bowling alley, but also served the New York Buffet and Mr. McGee's Party Center that flanked his small car on both sides of the covered earth that Alan traveled on as he left. The big domed halogen lights that hung in the air overhead spot-lighted the pavement in small halos that descended on his car and the wet pavement reacted like a pitch black void. It made Alan feel that he was piloting a spacecraft flying through the cosmos of a low budget science fiction flick.

Alan turned on to the main route that bisected the city. The rain pitter-patted the small car as it drove down the drag that was bordered by various businesses that once bustled with an independent energy, but they continued to stand rotting, with their defunct neon advertisements hanging over the street. Alan always thought that Chapmansville was a miniature and dying vision of the dreams promised in Las Vegas, and yet, the dreams were over a long time ago. They were now only stale memories. Alan realized that this was the end of the life of the city, and the end had no end, or end, or end. Even hope was rotten.

The interstate sign approached, and the rain intensified. The first sign he passed was for points northwest, including New Hampshire. The second had only one word, Boston. A synonym of home. As Alan began to turn his car towards the on-ramp, the contrasting brightness of the dark outside and the shining emergency brake light made him squint. At the point when he began to speed his car to join the empty highway, he was punching the dashboard, trying to shut that damn light off.

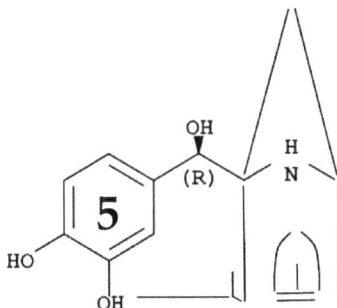

Alan sat outside of the tall blue-gray triple-decker in his small car. It took him an hour and a half to get to southie, and he was finally home. He sat outside waiting for a sign to see if anyone was inside, at which point he would call and see if Diana Quimby wanted to hang out with him. The rain had stopped halfway on his way to Boston, and it was a crisp, clean, and refreshing night. The city, freshly baptized by the cool rain, waited for Alan to step out of his car and be embraced in her comfortable bosom.

Diana's mother was an excellent example of a two-job, hard working, uncomplaining woman. Unlike many Americans, she didn't need to work so hard, she just did. It was almost as though she was trying to make sure she had absolutely no free time to herself after the death of her husband when Alan and Diana were still in high school. It made sense, almost; when people are alone, they begin to think, and this situation was no different.

Mr. Quimby was only fifty one years old, and he had just had his yearly physical, with absolutely nothing out of the ordinary. He was in great health. On his way to work one day, he had walked to the Broadway train station as he did every day, entered, and just fallen down. That was it. He wasn't on any special medication, he wasn't out of breath, and he wasn't worrying about anything out of the ordinary.

When he died, the family was absolutely devastated, but it was not visually apparent. The mere shock of the moment held the family in an absolute haze, and they were held in an almost trance-like state, smiling, and appreciative at the funeral like a row of delicate plaster figurines. Their loving husband and father had just left forever, and no one knows where he went. Thank you for coming.

Ever since, everyone in the family had their own ways of dealing with the situation. Mother worked, as did one of her brothers in China, and the other in St. Louis. Somehow the one in China managed to send her a small pet dog in the mail.

Diana exercised her personal reactions... First, she had gone to college at a prominent woman's only university in the city. Then she had tried to work with her degree, but wasn't able to. Now in her second year out of college she was a nanny during the day and a barrista at night, choosing to

take her mother's road to recovery. It was not immediately apparent to Alan
that she had ever finally gotten over the death of her father, even though it
happened almost six years ago.

A light came on in what Alan remembered as Diana's bedroom, and
then shut off just as quickly. Alan grabbed his cell phone and punched in her
number, hoping that it would be the same. He looked back at the house with
his finger on the 'send' button. As the streetlights illuminated the rain slicked
buildings, he thought it was funny how tall, skinny, and close together the
houses were. If a tornado were to ever hit Boston, they would all topple over
like dominoes; not breaking anything inside, but forcing everyone to happily
live in diagonally laid houses just a few degrees to the left. He pressed send.

Alan looked straight down the broad street at the homes, and how
they were lined up exactly for a kilometer or so down the road.   The
streetlights converged in the center of the horizon, highlighting an empty
street in an amazing glory. There was something about Boston that always got
Alan to feel wonderful at any given juncture of his life. This particular evening
that he left Jane and stole away to his home city, he felt rejuvenated. He was a
lover who freed himself from a repressive relationship of agony and stole
away to a secret and reliable long-term lover who had a great deal more to
offer him - his beautiful and comfortable city. Alan heard a click.

"Hello?" A familiar voice on the other end responded.

"Mrs. Quimby?"

"Yes, this is she…"

"How are you….This is Alan."

"Alan…Alan, how are you?"

"I am fantastic, and yourself?"

"Wonderful! I am actually on my way to work, would you like to
speak with Diana?"

"That would be fantastic, thanks. Have a good night at work."

"Thank you, you too!"

Alan wasn't entirely sure why she responded that way. It was a
common occurrence for Alan to include a personal response when bidding
adieu to a friend, and they always would respond with a "You too…" and it
would be totally inappropriate. This was one such instance. 'Yes, I will have a
good night at work, thank you very much?'

"Hello?" The voice on the other end answered. It was Diana, a
comforting voice that made him think of home. Alan remembered everything
about her. Her hair, her smell, the way she had a strange demeanor around
him as compared to other people. He also remembered that he hadn't talked
to her more than three times since he had started dating Jane. That was a long
time ago.

"Diana, it's Alan. How are you?"

"Oh! Alan! Oh my god, how are you? I thought you had fallen off
the face of the Earth again!"

"No,…no. I haven't. Just been busy you know, with work and school and everything."

"Like always. How is that going? Why don't you ever come to visit us?"

"It is…well, it's gone, I guess. I will come to visit a lot more, now."

"What? Great!"

"Yeah…So what are you up to?"

"Well, just about the same. Been nannying and everything else, and I-

"

"No, I mean right now."

"Uh…Nothing? About to change."

"Well, come outside."

"Oh my god! Okay, let me just get changed real quick."

• • •

Alan and Diana sat in the musty, all-night Someday Café in Davis Square. Technically they were in Somerville. Technically it didn't matter. The late night mocha-chess-players and the talkative espresso-debaters melted away along with the colorful walls and impromptu tables and chairs.

In this moment, there were only two, and they embraced their company over a steaming homemade caramel cappuccino that made them both feel as though they were enveloped in a warm comforter someone sewed for them – tailored them into a comfy bed that was absolutely perfect. Home. Where else could they go to possibly feel this? Well, to bed of course. Naked. Coincidentally, Alan needed a place to stay for the night.

"So, are you seeing anyone?" Alan asked.

"Wow. New world record! You lasted the fifteen minutes it took to get here. Amazing."

Smiling, she stared at Alan with her blue eyes. Was it that she was his mother, and that was why he wanted her so much? She was also her own mother. Her mother loved Alan. Her long blond hair fell on her shoulders. Her slightly crooked teeth reminded Alan of his personal commitment to the love of the inner self. She was adorable. She was radiant.

"Come on. Give me a break."

"What? How is your girlfriend?"

"Well, it is a long story, but basically we were fighting and a plane crashed into her backyard, and basically-"

"What? Basically, what?" She asked in a frantic tone. Alan didn't want to tell her the whole story.

"Well, I left her."

"And you come here?" Could she possibly read Alan that well? Did she have to be right about everything? No! Fuck her, Alan thought.

"I never knew you were one to pull that stupid woman shit."

"Whatever. A friend you haven't seen in almost two years and he swings by for a one night stand. That's good."

"I am not going back."

"Oh, I bet. And I also bet that you are just giving up school and you are beginning this journey of greatness coming back home."

Bitch. She was right. He was going to look like a complete asshole to everyone. One big walking cliché. Yeah, that was the point all along: become a literary bum in the city and not publish or even churn out anything. What was he going to do? Become a bartender who wrote during the day for the rest of his life? Never gets anything done? That sounded good; really promising.

"Yeah, Diana, that's it."

"I am not busting on you on purpose here, but I am worried about you."

"Don't. I'll figure this out. " The warm blanket started to get pulled off by an angry mother in the morning before school. This was a bad idea. Alan should have just gone to a random bar, picked up a random girl. Gone back to her place. That would have been fun.

"So...Hows work?   Your mother?" Alan asked, rotating the cappuccino cup on its mismatched saucer. Diana sucked her teeth.

"Great, thanks. Listen, it's late. We should get going."

"Oh, okay....Christ. I am here for ten minutes and the one person I think would take me in is blabbing on about how I am trying to get with her and she doesn't even want to hear any small talk. Nice. Fucking hypocrite."

"What are you talking about?"

"Only that every time we talk about you and I and how I have always wanted you in the worst way, you seem to forget about it. When I am with a girl for anything longer than a week or any number of other combinations, you start up this crap about me only wanting to sleep with you. That is nice."

"I never knew you wanted me!?"

"Wow, a breakthrough. I have only known you for...how long... Five or six years at least and if I start coming on to you, you walk away. If I have a girlfriend and it comes up, you are sure to mention that you have never heard of this before... Now it is kind of a little of both and you are still denying it."

"People change, Alan."

"Poetic. What after school teen soap opera did you get that from?"

After that statement, the pair sat silently. Alan thought about all of the times they almost kissed. All of the times after that where he wouldn't be talked to for a few weeks. All of the times that Diana had a boyfriend and became more apt to indulge in Alan. The one time they kissed, as a matter of fact, it was when she had a boyfriend.

Alan remembered. He sat in his bedroom of his family's house. He was still living there. He had not yet moved out to his apartment elsewhere in the city, and he was cleaning up after the party he had with his friends the night before. Diana was the only person left in the house from it, and she just approached Alan, pushed him on the bed, and began to kiss his neck. They finally kissed on the lips, and Alan thought it was everything he had originally wanted; the beauty of the moment highlighted by snowflakes falling out of the silence outside. When it was over, she cryptically said, 'that's dangerous,' and left it at that. It was never mentioned again.

As they sat in the café, Alan wanted to gauge how she felt about this whole situation. He tapped his foot nervously on the floor, feeling the hollow properties of the old wood planks. Alan broke the silence with the one thing that may just see how 'dangerous' the two of them actually were.

"I actually brought you here to say goodbye..." Alan actually wondered what the fuck he was doing. What would he say next, that he had less than two weeks to live?

"What are you talking about?"

"I was thinking that...I was thinking that since the world is going to be a wasteland soon, I should go out and see everything that I wanted to. I have heard there are really some beautiful parts of Montreal."

"You have lost your mind. Strictly between you and me, you need to see someone."

"Yeah; it didn't really work out."

"When are you going? Where are you planning on going?"

"I don't know yet. That's the beauty of it. I want to not worry about anything or be required to be anywhere for a change. I want to take some chances."

"Do you even have any money or anything?"

"I will...For a little while at least."

"This is ridiculous."

"Yeah, I agree." She was right. She had as many reasons to do this as Alan did. "But not as ridiculous as a friend not allowing me to crash at their house." They stared at each other for a moment. "Let's go."

As Alan drove her back, they remained silent. When did it become this? It certainly wasn't the last few years. They only talked in little bursts of enlightenment, only asking one another what they have been up to for the last few months or so. As it happened, they would only talk about that and that alone. There was nothing else to talk about.

Sitting in the driver's seat, Alan looked at Diana. She wasn't everything he always wanted. She was a mess. Sometimes she would actually say this, but it was obvious that she was only being dramatic; ironic even. Now, she actually was crazy. Alan was also crazy, so maybe they were made for each other. Yeah. Boston at its finest. Two flew over the cuckoo's nest.

Alan thought about what he was about to do. He has lost all connections in this beautiful city that he possibly had; all except for the fact that the city itself was his. He only had, by his recollection, about twenty five hundred dollars in the bank, which wasn't even enough to buy a first and last month's deposit on a place. Yeah, maybe it was time to disappear. It was time to disappear completely. See something new, go somewhere he has never been before, meet the people who make this country, who own its shops, who fight for it, and who make it 'Midwestern.'

They passed in front of Diana's house, and Alan pulled into her packed and narrow driveway as far as he could, actually letting the rear end of the car stick out into the broad road a little. He looked over at her and she looked back, her chin trembling. She began to cry. 'Bloody hell,' Alan thought to himself as he shifted the car into park and shut it off.

"I had no idea. I had no idea," she repeated. Diana was being a little irrational right now. She had no idea that Alan was totally in love with her, and it all comes out of him just wanting somewhere to stay for the night; or get laid. Whatever side of the argument you were on. Fuck the argument. Alan was getting tired.

"You really have to go."

"No. No, no, no. We have to talk about this. This is important."

"No it isn't. I am tired. I have to go."

"Matters of the heart are always important." Where the hell was she getting all of these trashy lines? Romance books? Television? All possibilities. Awful, awful, awful.

"This is your stop. Please leave. I really have to get some sleep." Truth is, it was late, and Alan's eyelids began feeling to him like cinderblocks. It was the coffee's fault. Coffee-

"No, Alan. No!"

Excuse me. Coffee always had that effect on Alan. In the morning it always kept him awake, but if there was one thing he learned in college, it was the idea that coffee put him to sleep after ten at night.

"Leave, Diana. I have to find somewhere to stay."

"No, come in. You can stay here."

"No, Diana. You have to go. This nonsense has to stop. I need to get some rest and leave." Alan was being very cold, which was very much unlike his character, he thought. There was only one other time he remembered being like this, and that was a couple of hours ago.

Diana was bawling at this point. She reached for the handle and pulled it weakly. She couldn't pull it any harder if she tried. It clicked open and she dragged herself out of the car. She didn't look back, and she wouldn't. She slammed the door, and made her way into her house. Alan tilted the seat back in the car, and stared at the roof. The windows were fogged up, and the way the light of the streetlamps came into the car was gorgeous. They were hazy glorious circles in a seventies music video.

Alan thought about what had just happened, and closed his eyes. He was finally free. Free of anything. He had no connections, no place to call home, and very few possessions. He was free. He was feng shuei in the raw, baby. He could go anywhere and become anything. He had everything he needed; a few changes of clothes, a blanket, his manuscripts. It was time to go, and he was ready. In a minute.

And a minute was all it took.

He drove over the West Broadway Bridge and made his way on to the

Mass Pike.

Driving ever so fast.

Driving faster than lightning. He was hurled through space and time as he felt a boom.

A terrible boom. His torso shook, and night became day.

The car started going faster than it ever had, the wind was driving now, pushing as it howled through the windows that were cracked and whistled in the gaps between the doors, trunk, and frame. In the rearview mirror Alan saw a mushroom cloud creeping towards the heavens, brilliant, taking up the horizon in his mirror.

Fear enraptured him, and he wept. The city was dying, his life. His tears were blood, the blood of Boston. A caravan of state troopers with their lights on was following Alan, and they passed. One stayed behind him, and Alan pulled over. He forgot why he was here. He didn't realize he was going too fast. He rolled his window down and the air burned going into his lungs. It was night again, and the officer walked up to the window.

"You're in a lot of trouble young man."

"I am?"

"You're in a lot of trouble young man."

"What?"

"That was your fault. The two pilots fell. They fell into your own backyard and died. Boston is gone…" Alan couldn't follow what was happening. It was happening so fast. "Step out of the vehicle." The trooper spoke in an almost scripted tone. He knew the lines, and he was like an actor who could only play one part; the part of the cold and calculated state trooper with the voice of a monotone computer program.

As Alan grabbed the door handle of the car, a white van drove by going at least a hundred and fifty kilometers an hour. The trooper looked in the direction of the car, and looked back at Alan. "Tonight's your lucky night." He put his hand on his weapon, ran back to the cruiser, and booked it. Alan rolled his window back up.

As he began to drive again, he began to feel sick. He bent over the passenger seat and began to vomit. It wasn't like it normally was, however; it was just water. Floods of water. So much water that Alan was running out of breath, and his ribs hurt. He was suffocating on his own vomit. His own water. He became dizzy, the water still spilling forth from his mouth and nose, filling the car. His heaving stopped, and he sat back upright, breathing in heavily as if he were in a swimming pool and stayed under too long.

He opened his eyes to see a dog running along with his car in the next lane over, being followed by an Army utility vehicle with a man in a black suit shooting out of the window.

The shooting was loud, and the dog couldn't outrun the truck. It was a beautiful dog. Maybe if Alan opened his window, the dog could jump in.

But the shooting was way too loud.

Rat-tat-a-tat-tat!

It was the words. Onomatopoeia.

Bang! Bang!

Bang! –

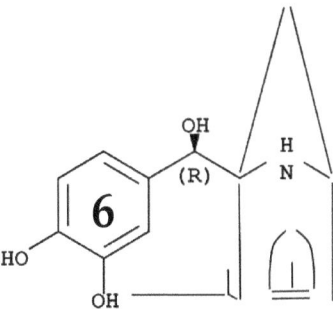

Bang!

Bang! Bang!

Light shone into the small car brilliantly. It took Alan a moment to realize what was going on. The banging continued. He looked at his watch. It was seven in the morning.

Bang! Bang! BANG! Maybe it was more like rapping.

It was his window. He lifted his seat up, and a dark figure hovered over the window. He rolled it down. A stocky man with black hair and a big bulbous and pockmarked nose stood over the car. He was still in the driveway. He had slept there whether she liked it or not. This must have been one of her neighbors.

"Hey! Buddy! Ya mind getting the hell out of my driveway?" He said, exasperated.

"Oh, sure - No problem. Sorry, I was sleeping."

"Oh, really? I couldn't fucking tell." Half asleep, one of the other things Alan missed was home's blatant sarcasm.

"Sorry, man."

"You can take your 'sorrys' and shove 'em in the tip of your dick as far as I care. Just move!" Alan turned the car on and slipped it into reverse, being careful to see if anyone was coming behind him.

"Get the hell out of here!"

The guy was still yelling, and for no reason this time. Alan put the car into drive and began to go.

He drove up West Broadway, and over the bridge where he picked up route 93 South. First stop would be to the main office of his bank fifteen minutes away in Quincy to close his account, then off to the mall in Braintree to buy a notebook computer, and then hit the closest branch of the auto club to get some free maps and discount coupons at hotels if the need arose.

• • •

Alan sat at the counter of the small Grille And Eye diner in Weymouth. It was a very small town that sat sandwiched between Braintree and Quincy just minutes south of downtown Boston. The diner sat maybe fifty people at its busiest, and today sat only one. Alan was eating a breakfast of two eggs, wheat toast, and spicy grilled potatoes; as he ate, he sat tinkering with his new notebook computer.

It was the biggest purchase he had ever made outside of his car. It was shiny and smelled fresh. The plastic was cool, and felt nice under his fingers. This machine's job was to exist as a tool; a tool that will carry Alan into the next phase of his life: bestselling renegade author. This is how Alan justified his purchase…it was half of his savings that, when withdrawn, totaled twenty-one hundred dollars.

Alan had one thousand fifty dollars left over to his name, and it existed in varying degrees in his pocket, shoe, and in his car. Alan would definitely need more money than this, especially if he wanted to continue to travel in this country: which was why Canada sounded so good. Regardless, it was time to go down south, view America, maybe even meet his dad again in Florida.

What Alan wanted to see most of all was the fields of grass and wheat that were apparently endless. You could drive for kilometers upon kilometers, hours upon hours, and not see any more than fields and fields of corn or wheat. Shades of green and gold, flowing by so fast, like pastels on the canvas of his passenger side window. That was somewhere down south he knew, and he had to find out where. That would be beautiful. Amber waves of grain.

Meet his dad again. That sounded so cliché, even though it became a cliché in his own head. The last time Alan saw his dad was the year before he graduated from high school. That was about five years ago at his count. His dad had paid for the flight and Alan went down with his girlfriend, who had never been on a plane before. It was hot, and the only thing that Alan really remembered about the vacation was the grass and the gated communities.

The grass in Florida is a lot different than the grass in the northeast. It was hard, and it stuck up like the blades of scissors. Alan had mistakenly tried to walk on it barefoot. Because it hurt, he retreated to the pavement, which then scalded the bottom of his feet.

The houses. Those were interesting. You couldn't get around or visit anyone unless you knew them. All of the houses in Florida were part of communities of twenty-five to fifty homes on small blocks that were surrounded by a giant fence. A guard's booth with electronic gates was the only way in or out. Alan thought about a prison as the pulled up for the first time, and felt more secure outside the gates than he did in. If the gates were to keep criminals out, but everyone lived within their walls, weren't the criminals actually being kept in?

He would always wonder what his dad did with his days. As a man who was too sick to leave the house, stricken with any number of clinically fabricated diseases to make the doctors more money and hand out more pills, he couldn't do very much. What was interesting to Alan was, as a man who had admitted that he was dying over and over again, he was doing pretty good for himself since he had been doing it for at least the past eleven years.

Alan opened up the word processing program on his laptop after he got all of the registration and setup of the laptop out of the way. He had spent the last fifteen minutes plugging his name and address information into the computer, and it was now officially his. The blank page on the screen was familiar to Alan. It stared at him virginous and pure, awaiting the flow of creativity to electrify its ones and zeroes. There just wasn't anything to put in.

Alan had taken his knapsack in with him to put the laptop in when he was done, but also because it contained hard copies as well as digital copies of his writing. He unzipped the front pocket, retrieved a disc that had 'Loose Nuke' written on the top in permanent marker, and stuck it in the drive on board the laptop. He continued on to copy all of his previous work onto the hard drive.

Alan had to send some of his work in to get published. That was a priority. The time it took for the documents and other information to get onto the hard drive seemed like an eternity, but that may just be because there were other things on the disc that were being copied like videos, music files, porn. Yeah. It was going to be lonely on the open road. Alan wished he smoked so he could say that out loud and take a long drag of his cigarette. "Yeah, I'm lonely," he would say in a gritty and dry voice, "It is just tough on the open road." Maybe that is another thing he could do. Take up smoking. Or not.

It was done. Alan asked the waitress for his bill, took the disc out, and closed the laptop. He slipped it into his bag, and as the waitress walked over to him, she watched the TV without even acknowledging Alan's presence. The morning news was on, and the newscaster was talking about the hazard posed by the enormous sport utility vehicles and their increasing volume on the roads. The bill came to six dollars. Alan left ten, and zipped his bag up.

Retrieving the bill, the waitress unknowingly grazed the disc on the counter, and it fell to the floor. Alan leaned over to get it without getting off of the stool and it felt enormously heavy as all of the blood rushed to his hand and head. He almost fell, but he steadied himself on the floor.

"Investigators think they may have found a link to the crash that happened just the other day in Chapmansville, Massachusetts to one that occurred in Harper, Louisiana today." The television reported. Alan swung up.

Bump. He hit his head on the corner of the counter, and stars spun forth from the back of his eyes. As he sat up, he was rubbing his head, watching as the report unfolded on the screen. Another man in a suit dominated the shot when Alan could regain his attention.

"...and it seems as though a sectional in the rear of this particular aircraft, the rear elevators, can jam in the down position in certain extreme circumstances. This is caused by a sudden change in the pressure of the fluids that make the instrument work, such as a quick push of the yoke in any direction. We, the FAA, are currently in contact with the company that makes the aircraft, Grodina, and beginning today all flights of this model aircraft are grounded until further inspection." The shot quickly jumped back to the newscaster.

"This news from the FAA comes after the findings of the investigation in Louisiana, and the recovered flight data recorders in yesterday's accident in Chapmansville."

Alan had to leave. The news made him jumpy. It always made him jumpy. He began thinking about all of the things that could kill him today: the eggs, the stool, the car, the other drivers in the other cars. It was too much. The news shows it to you in easy to digest thirty minute segments really, really fast. If the news shows one what could kill them, and it doesn't kill them, the anxiety of the news will.

Alan slipped the disc back into the pocket of his bag and walked outside. It was deliriously bright out, and he shielded his eyes from the sun. He walked down the street and to his car. The curb was unnaturally high, and he had to take a half-meter drop before he could go around his car to the driver's side.

He threw his bag in the backseat, turned the ignition, and shifted it into drive. He drove for about two minutes to the highway. The on ramps and off ramps were situated on a rotary that was planted in a big circle underneath the huge overpass. Alan turned on to the rotary, and from the direction he was going he passed the first on ramp. That one goes south, he thought. He drove around some more, passing the off ramp and a street that led to the mall where he bought the laptop, and passed the on ramp that went north. That one goes north, he thought.

Alan passed, and passed, and passed. He remembered reviewing the maps the auto club gave him, trying to figure out where he was going. But that was the beauty of this trip. He didn't want to have anywhere to go.

This one goes north, this one goes south.

It wasn't as if he were deciding on something as trivial as what to drink, a martini or a lager. This wasn't the end. The idea that he didn't know where to go was the whole point. Absolute freedom. Alan, turning the wheel slowly, putting his blinker on, had made a decision. The small blue hatchback, full of ambition, imagination, and explosive energy, shot forth as a cannonball onto the highway. Alan's heart pounded with romance and heat, his arms and legs trembling before the machine and its perpetuation of speed. He had no fucking clue where he was going...and that was okay.

Part II

Summer Song

Thou wilst bring forth what to Earth
And drive it to the ground
For what you haven't sacrificed
Will soon surely be found.

But do not underestimate
That struggle with the dark
For surely the journey that lies ahead
Will make an albatross of the lark.

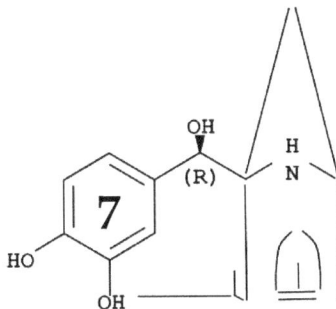

The tiny car darted and spun, sped and thundered, pushed and pushed ever forward to its indeterminable fate. Behind the wheel of this tiny car, Alan Levy felt protected and safe as the tiny cockpit ushered him through a wilderness he had never seen before. He could hardly control where it would bring him. Next stop Hartford, next stop Providence, next stop New York, next stop Philadelphia. The possibilities swam through his mind like a fantasy of a lover. Romantic and passionately he would face each new place, new culture, and new person.

He was only into his trip one half hour, and the experience of simply having nowhere to be was exhilarating. His heart pounded honestly and true, and in syncopation to the music that filled his car. Alan hadn't thought about the importance of bringing any music with him on his journey, but if he were to, the soundtrack of his life was already in the car, pushing him, driving him. Boxes containing the music was strewn about the cabin as it always was. Bostonian rock band names swam around in the CD boxes, and their music swam in the air.

The speakers screamed with the passion and heart of someone that was average. The average and the underdog, and all of the passions and feeling therein. The song that was playing was about being alive, and being dead. About being creative, and about partying. The song that was playing was about a man at a party who spent his time in a tree, and by the end of the party decided he would come down and become a born again Christian. He thought of The Sacrosanctity Society, the host Charles Hobbeston, and thought of why he was fascinated with the program.

Why did Hobbeston do what he did? Why did people believe his sincerity? Was he being sincere? Why did they give him their money? For what? To become better Christians? To heal or be blessed? What if they didn't need anything in return, like the people who donate to a charity? Did they want to buy something, like stock in their own faith or belief? Did it make it more real?

Or what about the people whose faith was perhaps not any form of Christianity when they were captivated by Hobbeston? How did he have the ability to reach through the television to speak to so many different types of people and convert people that send their money to him? Buying stock in their new belief that was so obviously true! The man reaching his hands through the television told me! Alan was captivated by this, and also by the sincerity that he honestly wanted to know how to do this with his writing. How can the same energy, power, and charisma be translated into the written word? He would love to meet him, talk to him, know him as a human being and a businessman.

Alan found that driving was extremely therapeutic. With the music pounding, no one could hear him talk to himself. He thought that no one could see him talking or singing along to the music, but he didn't care. He just did. He danced in his seat and smelled, but didn't care. The breeze swiftly blew on his face and he was happy. The stars bounced off the car and Alan bounced in his seat. The only thing that would make him happier was the rain pounding on the car, the car driving itself to nowhere in particular, a glass of wine in his hand, and his laptop in front of him.

That, Alan thought, would be gorgeous.

But cars didn't drive themselves, you can't drink and drive, it wasn't raining, and the next time he would be able to open his laptop would probably be at a corporate truck stop fast food joint. The perpetuation of his work in the coming weeks wasn't going to be smooth, and four hours into his ride as he filled up his car's fuel and watched the price tick up at a gas station in Maryland, he suddenly felt like he was falling through space. He became scared. He learned that at almost forty dollars a fill he would need to stop for a month and find some work. He did the math in his head as truckers stared from their rigs, and his heart sunk. If he were to travel to Vegas, he couldn't do it without some transient work and a bed to occasionally sleep in.

When he was finished paying, he sat in the driver's seat. He sat in the moment. His windows were open, and the hot afternoon air gusted through the car. A hand appeared on the frame of his window.

"Hey, son. You okay?" A moist breath smelling of stale breakfast passed by Alan's nose. He looked up and didn't say a word. The man continued, "You lost?"

"No, well... No. I'm just thinking." The man looked unkempt and made Alan uncomfortable. He wouldn't ever approach this man if he were even in dire need of help.

"Okay... It's just. Well, son, it doesn't look good for you. You look upset. Where are you going?" Alan was really nervous. He had been in his own head all day, and what right had this guy to barge in?

It wasn't until Alan answered that he realized it was the wrong answer, "I don't know."

"Here, take this, it'll get you to Virginia." The man produced a map with a road club logo on the front. "At least you can stop there and, I don't know, there's nice people there." It was wrinkly and stained with what Alan hoped was catsup. The man disappeared and Alan was left with a map of the southern part of the east coast of the United States. He turned the car on as his cell phone rang.

It was his mum calling. Without reason, Alan answered the phone and then immediately hung up. He shifted the car into drive and peeled out of the gas station, almost hitting a few cars. He continued south on route 95 with a tank full of gas and a head full of anger. He didn't know why he was angry, but he had a headache, and fuck that guy!

Fuck him and his Virginia map, Alan thought as he watched the scenery float by. Everything was the same as Massachusetts here! Everything! The foliage, the people who think they can just come up to you and talk to you! Mum! Stop calling! Can't a guy live here? Can't a guy just go off and write like a normal person? Christ!

Fuck him and his Virginia map and fuck mum, Alan thought as he weaved in and out of traffic, going much too fast. People are too uptight, and have no sense of harmony with themselves! They just walk around not trying to make anyone's life better. They just walk around and act selfishly, selfishly, selfishly. No regard for others or their lives. They might as well not even exist.

Fuck him and his Virginia map, fuck mum, and fuck everyone in the Northeast. He headed toward downtown Richmond. He needed to hear someone with an accent or a dog and feel something for people. He needed to feel like he belonged. He needed to feel like people were treating him nice for a change.

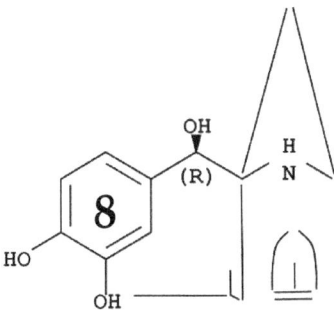

Alan pulled into Virginia Beach, Virginia the next day at eleven in the morning.

When he arrived in Richmond the night before, he had gotten in at almost eight or nine at night and stopped because a headache was eating his brain like an apple, and he had thought it was because he hadn't eaten anything all day. Alan spent ten dollars on a burger, a beer, and a tip. The bartender was attractive, tall, and skinny, with dark brown hair that shined in the overhead lights.

"So, you know anywhere where a guy could get a bartending job...just for a couple weeks?" he asked.

"You aren't from around here," she flirted. Alan didn't respond. "I can only tell you that down by the beach is a good place to go... Most of the people in the city here have been bartending at the places they are at for years. That's all I can tell you... All the places on the beach have an open work policy. The bartenders are only around for long vacations, or they are fired for some reason. Most bars and restaurants are independently owned and they pay cash, just because the turnover is so fast." While Alan wasn't here for it, she was acting like she wanted to be picked up. It was probably for some flirting and making eyes, and most likely a bigger tip. Alan could not leave a bigger tip.

"Are you hiring?"

"No."

He thought about when he tended bar back home in Boston at Bourbon's. He was there at least a year before he got on bar, and even then, it was only because he was good. The others were there for years, and years, and years. It was time to be street smart in this new environment; to strategize on how he would at least gain something from meeting his first southerner. Her accent was pretty hot, he thought.

"What are you doing after work?" he asked.

"Fuck you, asshole."

He was right.

It was no surprise that he didn't get laid that evening in particular. Considering he needed a place to sleep, and he didn't have to pay the parking meter until six in the morning, his parked car three blocks away from the bar was as good a hotel as any. Alan scoured the city for something to do for the rest of the night, and wasn't impressed, so he slept.

Her advice was fantastic, Alan thought as he drove into what he thought was one of the most beautiful places he had ever seen an hour or so after waking up. Virginia Beach was kilometers of sands, tall trees, and fresh air. Alan wasn't a beach person at all, but this beach was gorgeous. So gorgeous in fact, that Alan parked his car on a sandy street and rifled through his bag in the backseat for some shorts that he could swim in. He found a light pair that were certainly appropriate, tossed them on, locked his car, rolled up the windows, and ran the two blocks to the beach.

As he ran, he smelled salt, the wind flowing around his face like fresh bedsheets. Seagulls danced in the morning sky, and Alan could see in the distance a group of surfers that had to have been up since six in the morning to come out to surf at what was seven thirty in the morning.

He ran into the warm water; it splashed up into his crotch from below. He felt like a dog jumping in, felt the waves on his back, tasted the salt, and felt the sand rushing at his feet. At that moment, Alan realized that beaches in Virginia beat any beach he had ever been to in New England. The air was cool and the water warm, there wasn't anyone else on the beach, and everything just felt wonderful.

But that didn't really last, because as Alan got back to his car and dried off, and then got together his laptop to go back to the beach and do some writing, there was an influx of beachers that accumulated and arranged themselves with their cars, their coolers, and their kids. Alan still went down to the beach and planted himself on a beach wall, but the sun became hotter and hotter and the breeze started to blow sand in his computer. He figured that there really wasn't anything to write about anyway.

Alan had figured that he would go back to the car, take a nap, and find a job when he woke up. With gas and eating, Alan had already spent a hundred of his dollars, and he needed some income as soon as possible. He laid the seat back, tuned his radio to the first AM religious station that he liked. It was easy to find, just by tuning for only a couple of seconds; there was a tremendous amount of religious radio in Virginia. He covered himself in his towel, and dozed.

● ● ●

Alan woke up choking on the air in the car. It was an hour later, and his mouth was dry as hell, and his body was soaked in sweat. He had forgotten to roll the window down. Alan started to roll it down, but the metal on the hand crank was so hot, he thought he burned himself. The voices echoed in muggy fuzziness from the radio speakers, which Alan slapped off immediately.

He swung the door open, got out, and started to dry himself off with the towel a second time. An old couple, obviously going to the beach, passed him by looking at him quizzically and almost paranoid. They were holding hands, but as they passed, the woman let go of the man's hand. With one hand on her stomach, she reached up to try to grab her hat as it was blown clear of her head. The gentleman escorted the woman away from it as it landed on the ground, and they started walking twice as fast as they were before.

Did he look hideous? What was with these people?

Alan looked into the rear view mirror. He looked fine, aside from his hair. With a few minor adjustments, he was ready to start looking for a job. He locked his car up again, and walked back down towards the beach. When he was swimming he noticed the downtown was not so much in a centralized location, but all along the coastline.

The first bar he stopped in was called the "Fuzzy Beaver." They weren't hiring. The next was called the "Horny Buffalo." Not hiring. Also not hiring was the "Underground Scout," "The Coronado Pub," "The Border Grille," and "The Southside Slut." The "Cheap Mother," had no postings. Neither did "The Foggy Floor," "The Nazi Aunt," "The Sailboat Hammer," "Dirty Sanchez's Place," "J & G's Pub," "The Evening Screw," and "The Buttress of Virginia." There was a Chinese place hiring, "The Virginia China Eatery," but Alan didn't like the atmosphere of the place. That and the sign out front read "The VA China Eatery," and if read incorrectly, would suggest more services then he was willing to offer.

Alan was hungry, and he walked into a small dive that had a sandwich board out front advertising the cheapest roast beef sandwich and the cheapest drafts in Virginia Beach. At a total cost of three dollars, Alan was in. The bar was full of young women, and it was no surprise that the bartender was making his rounds and working the room in flirts and compliments to boost his tips. He was a young, blonde, rather short good-looking guy with what seemed like an explosively attractive personality to these women.

Alan sat down, and felt like he was imposing on a meeting he wasn't invited to. While he was waiting for service, he listened in on the conversation. Apparently, the ladies were on a volleyball team, and they were having lunch after their game. The bartender knew them all and it was apparent that he was also on the team. After the bartender was finished chatting and getting them all settled with their drinks and food, he approached Alan.

"What's goin' on!" He half shouted in his southern accent, like there was a huge party in the room. Several of the girls were talking to each other, and Alan overheard them admiring his good looks or his ass. Whatever they were doing, there had to be twenty or twenty five of them around the bar and they all had a thing or two to say to each other while his back was turned to them.

"What's up, bro. Can I get one of 'the cheapest deli sandwiches and drafts in Virginia Beach'?" Alan responded in a dull monotone that undermined the supposed party going on.

"Hell, yeah!"

And in less than a moment, the beer and the sandwich was in front of him. He ate it and it tasted absolutely lovely. The beer was nectary, cool, and wonderful sliding down his throat. Everything was great. The girls were nice to look at as well, Alan thought to himself.

By the time he was done eating, after watching a show on the television about a surfing competition, the bar had mostly cleaned out.

"How was the sandwich?" the bartender asked.

"It was a pretty damn good sandwich for two bucks, that's for sure."

"Nice... Nice. What do you think about Marcus taking the championship this year? Sucks, huh?"

"Huh?" Alan responded. The bartender pointed to one of the televisions still sporting the surfing event.

"Oh. Well, you know, I don't really know a lot about surfing. You surf?"

"Hell, yeah, I do! No surfing? That sucks. You're not really from around here, are you?"

"No... No I'm not, actually. First time..." Alan thought that this guy seemed pretty cool, and he felt like a loser for having to ask about the job, but it seemed like a shot. Besides, everyone always got a job at the last place they look, right? "I've actually been looking for a job all day. You guys hiring by any chance?"

The bartender answered in a confidant 'no,' but was obviously thinking pretty hard. "But, I do have some friends that work in some of the factories around here. I could probably get a job for you... Clark," he said, reaching his hand out, "Stetson." He sounded like a cowboy in a cigarette advertisement.

They shook, and Alan introduced himself. Clark told him a lot about the area. Bartending was a beach business, and it turned out that the same things were similar at the beach as they were in the city. There were a lot of jobs and a lot of money to be made, but when you came down to it, it was all about timing because the jobs have been held for a long, long time.

"You got anywhere to stay?" Clark asked.

"Well, I've been living out of my car, so I am fine in that-"

"No, no. Come stay at my place. That's stupid. You can stay in my spare bedroom. I have a two bedroom, and I hardly ever use the second one. Only if one of my old navy buddies comes to stay..."

"No, you don't have to do that, really."

"It's my pleasure. You can stay until you can get on your own feet."

"Well, I really appreciate it. I was only planning on staying for a couple weeks, anyway. I'm on a road trip. I just don't want to run out of cash."

"Oh, cool. Where you going?"

"Vegas." Alan hadn't realized it, but he just set his plan in motion.

He was going to Vegas. It was decided. Putting it in words, and sharing it with another human being made it more real.

"Nice. Awesome! A gambling man?"

"No...Just going to meet up with someone, that's all..."

"Relatives?"

"No...actually, you know Charles Hobbeston?"

"The TV preacher?"

"Yeah, him."

"You're a religious man... I like that. I've never been into-"

"Nope..." Clark looked confused. "It's for... For a book I'm writing."

"That's cool. A writer. Nice. My dad's a preacher in DC. If you need anyone to talk to in addition to Hobbeston, anyway."

"Yeah. That sounds good." There was a pause. He needed something to talk about. "So you were in the navy? That means you are at least twenty two...you look like you're nineteen and I couldn't figure out how you got the job. I was thinking of outing you so I could jump in."

"I'm actually twenty seven... I know. I always win those carnival games where they guess your age. They can't figure it out. If I am with a chick, that will win me a prize and get us going on a conversation on how much of an older man I am. Guaranteed."

"Nice."

"So listen - go do what you have to do, and I'll meet you up back here after my shift at six? I'll give my boys a call and try to find you a job."

"Yeah, that sounds great! You really don't have to do this for me. I am not even really sure why you feel the need to. How much do I owe you?"

"You seem like a nice guy. Just give me a couple bucks for the sandwich. I got your drink."

Just like that, Alan had a new friend and had a house to stay at. That simple. Alan shook his hand one more time, and turned out of the bar. The brightness of the sun shocked Alan, but he soon adjusted to it. It was a good day. Already a good day in a new place.

• • •

When Alan arrived at the "Vintage Raven" to meet up with Clark, he was already sitting on the curb outside talking on his phone. As Alan approached, he observed that Clark had an odd way of talking on the phone. He would stand up, brush and wave at the air around his head as he spoke, and shout. It was interesting just to see him stand and sit so often in the three minutes it took Alan to approach him.

Alan had spent the last five or six hours bumming around the city. He looked for a good coffee shop to do some writing, he scouted out the local library and sat down to read the local paper, and even walked the length of the beach to see where the more popular places that the beach bums visit. Oddly enough, as he walked down the strip and watched Clark in his bizarre dance ritual on the phone, his own phone started to ring.

Alan removed it from his pocket and the caller identification window said "Jane." It was only his second day away from everything that he ran from and he was already being reminded of why he ran in the first place. Who the hell was she to call him on his vacation? Didn't he dump Jane? Stop calling, you bitch! No. No, it was certainly just the female's response to loss, and she would get over it. There certainly wasn't anything that she couldn't get if she left it at Alan's apartment; she knew where the spare key was, and besides Alan had left it unlocked.

As he walked towards Clark, Alan had pushed it out of his head. Right now, he was just about survival and having fun. He had nowhere to be and nothing to do. He was ready for anything.

"...yeah? Yeah! Hold on..." Clark spoke into the phone and then changed his gaze to Alan. "What's up brotha!?! Hey, okay so here's the plan. –you still there Mike? –Okay, Alan, we're going to go down to the part of the beach that's mega party town because a bunch of my boys are getting together tonight. You can talk to them so can get you a job, and then just chill. I know you don't have any cash and shit, but I'll cover you... –HUH? Nonono, Mike! Mike, he's cool bro. Yeah, okay." Clark was back to talking on the phone.

Alan had never been one to party like a maniac. He didn't really even drink that much, but this sounded like a good time. But he was free now. Free from any responsibility. Clark said his goodbye and was off the phone.

"Okay, brotha, you ready to fuck shit up!? You ready!?" Clark screamed this while shaking Alan by the shoulders. No, he was never ready.

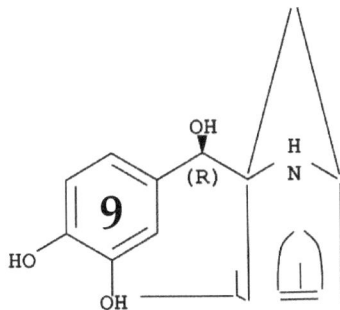

Alan had to have met at least thirty five tall, short, light, dark, amazing people in the first half hour of this night. The only strange thing was that they all looked the same. The ladies wore bikinis and the men wore boarder shorts without shirts. They almost couldn't be differentiated in the dim light of the bonfire on the beach, aside from some carrying guitars with string shoulder straps, hats, and the different bikinis that were difficult not to stare at given the endowments of some of the girls. Alan was ashamed that he could remember the names of the girls purely by virtue of how their breasts looked hanging in the various patterns of their bikinis.

After introducing each of the girls, Clark would have a story to tell Alan aside from the women regarding their sexual behavior. He had apparently slept with a good majority of them, and the ones he didn't recognize, he either didn't know or they were lacking in some department. It was simple. He was also quite the aficionado, constantly reminding Alan of the options he had upon returning to his apartment if in fact he did bring a girl home with him. It sounded nice.

"Dude, dude, dude; Jim. Tell this guy your story about the catcher," Clark said to a colleague in the business of excessive life.

"No, man, I can't," he responded.

"Oh, Alan, It is soooo good. This guy is a coach for a junior high girl's softball team. He has so many stories. It's a wonder that no one has given him shit so far for some of the stuff he's seen. Oh, man."

And Alan had heard a thousand stories just like this one. Stories about one guy throwing up all over a limo on this Passover trip Clark was invited to and making out with one of the girls right after, the story about the great sound they learned they could make with a beer bottle and the inside of their forearm, the guy that got arrested for breaking into a local high school and spraying all of the fire extinguishers all over the place – naked. They kept coming and coming, and Alan was learning that he really enjoyed this Clark guy. Really.

A tall brunette approached Alan and tapped him on the shoulder. She was tall and her hair flowed long past her shoulders in a straight line. Her forehead was larger than what one would expect a proportionate face would look like, but it didn't really make her look bad, once you got used to it. Her breasts were perky and small and the rest of her body flowed down to her slim hips and her long legs. She was hot.

"You went to Memorial in Windsor, right? Nick? You were the writer kid no one really talked to..." She was addressing him directly and distinctly. They had known one another practically forever, hadn't they?

"No, no. Sorry. But,... I am a writer."

"You're not from around here! What kind of accent is that?" she said, brushing the hair from her shoulder. Her hair was drastically different than all of the other girls on the beach; it was long and her natural color, without even a highlight.

"Boston, actually. I just drove down here."

"Really? That's interesting! I have relatives in Burlington, Massachusetts."

"Like the coat factory?"

"What? Oh, I don't know... You're funny. My name is Tessa... Tessa McGulligan."

"Alan Levy, nice to meet you." Alan looked over her body another time, and the ice cubes in her drink glowed in the light cast by the bonfire. "Looks like you're empty, want to get another?"

"Let's!"

They walked the fifty meters or so to the beachside bar, and Alan ordered them a Boston Lager and a drink, which had lemonade, raspberry liqueur, and raspberry vodka in it. It was a favorite of the house where he worked in Boston. Alan scanned the beach as the bartender made the drinks and looked for Clark. Alan saw his silhouette as he kissed a girl in the light of the bonfire and people danced around them.

"How much longer are you gonna be in town?," Tessa asked.

"Oh, I don't know. This is just a stop. I was planning on sticking around just long enough to make some cash for the trip. I bought a computer before I left that set me back a great deal. I was planning on just being able to make it on the cash I got, but I only have like five hundred bucks on me that has to last me until I get to Vegas. I am not even sure if I am going to go straight there. It would make sense from here, but... I don't know what I am doing. I'll probably kick around for a couple weeks so I can get a paycheck."

"I see. I'd like to see you again, that's all. What are you doing tonight?"

"I don't know. I am staying with a friend... He's over there. Clark?"

"Where do you know him from?"

"I met him while I was looking for a job this afternoon..."

Clark stumbled over to the pair, half running, sand spewing forth from his feet in the ground. A girl hung from his shoulder, a different one from the one he was with a moment earlier.

"Dude, dude, we're so taking this party over to my place. Oh, hey. Clark. I'm a friend of Alan's." He held out his hand and both girls giggled as

Clark tried desperately and humorously to gain composition to a certain degree. Alan looked over at Tessa and raised his eyebrows.

"Well... tonight's a good night to die. I'll go tell the girls I'm going with you guys." Tessa said. She turned and started to walk away and the girl hanging off of Clark went with her. They laughed and bounced as they walked away.

"Man, she is a HOTTIE! What do you think, dude?"

"I don't know, she seems kind of young, doesn't she?"

"Yeah, but come on. You know what they say. If there's grass on the field,..."

"No, I don't know."

"Play ball!"

"Oh, Jesus. Was that chick your girlfriend? She was pretty hot, dude."

"No..."

"No she isn't or no she's not your girlfriend?"

"She's not my girlfriend. My girlfriend lives faaaaar away, in Dover."

"Dover, Virginia?"

"No, north. Dover, Delaware."

"Oh... You figure if she isn't in the state, then..." Alan looked at Clark as if he was still trying to understand the situation.

"No, I love her. We've been together for like three years. We got a place up there, and a dog."

"So, why are you here?"

"Alan, I got to finish school and... All my friends are here. Listen, lets just forget about it and have a good time. I called up Stevie and Alex and they are going to come and party; and so is a bunch more folks. Lauren, Maggie, Sarah, Erin, a ton of people I want you to meet."

"That's a lot of ladies..." Alan smirked.

"And that never hurt anyone. Let's get you laid, brotha!"

When they got to Clark's house, there was an abundance of women. There were about twenty in all. Even Clark's friends Stevie and Alex, contrary to their namesake, were also women. In fact, including Clark and Alan, there were only four men. Alan supposed the numbers were in his favor, but at the same rate, the chemistry in the room was bizarre.

The apartment was a big, single-level home that had a lot of open space and high ceilings. There was a hip, modernistic feel to it, and it could be a cooler place if it weren't for the abundance of bar mirrors on the walls. There was comfort in the way everyone filled the room, however. Buckets of ice and beer were strewn about the room. Alan stood talking to Tessa. They were both strangers here.

"So, he's a cheater?" Tessa said.

"I don't know. Apparently. You said he has a reputation? That's what that girl talked to you about?"

"Yeah. Yeah... He's a popular guy. My question, and the question on the minds of a lot of the girls out there is why the girls all sleep with him knowing he's a slut?"

"I don't know. I don't even know him."

"Right, I forget that."

"Hmm. You're a really cool. What do you do with yourself?"

"Oh, it's actually really interesting. I am a secretary at the base. I am the secretary to the director of NICBDI... Nuclear Intercontinental Ballistics Deferment Initiative. I work for the guy that makes sure we don't get bombed in little ol' Virginia."

"Is that a big job?"

"Well, sure! There's a real lot of military bases here in Virginia!"

"I wasn't aware."

"Yeah. Well, that explains Clark. He was in the Navy; I imagine when he finished his term, he just stuck around. Hell, they're probably even paying for this nice place... Well, I imagine they were until that idiot president that started all the wars got into office years ago."

"Probably."

"Listen. I think we should go out back on the porch in the dark and you should kiss me and grab my tits. I think that would be a productive way to spend the rest of the night. That way, when you wake up next to me in the morning, I can get one of those more comfortable kisses... You know, the one where we're all warm and really close and we don't have to try as hard to impress one another."

Alan was shocked. He didn't know what to say.

"Okay." So they disappeared into the night and they sat in the moon kissing and feeling one another, only to stop for more alcohol and to find their way to the spare bedroom at four thirty in the morning. It was wonderful.

● ● ●

The next morning, Alan got up to go to the bathroom, and there were various bodies splayed about the apartment in various states of disarray. A lot of the girls that had stayed were huddled up with one another. The room looked like any room would in the morning... Any room in the morning in a nineteen-sixties porn.

Alan walked over to the refrigerator and opened it. There was a tremendous amount of juice in little cans, about a hundred or a hundred and fifty in all, and a ton of beers, but there was no food. Alan took one of the small cans of pineapple juice off of the door, opened it, and drank it all in one gulp. He grabbed another and walked to the large, open glass sliding doors at the back of the living room. He observed that the air was easy to breathe and felt good brushing around his body and through his boxer shorts. The small yard was an eyesore, leaves and overgrown foliage dominating every last square centimeter of usable space.

Alan turned to go back into the bedroom when he spotted a sticky note attached to the telephone.

"Alan, had to run off to work. I am sure you can take care of the women while I am gone. They usually let themselves out anyway. My boy Michael works over at the Stewart plant. Give him a call and he can give you work for the next ten days to cover a vacation."

The note ended with the number scrawled at the bottom and a messy "Clark." This was working out pretty well, he thought. He has a connection to a job, a woman and she was in a bed, and this all went down within the first twenty four hours of Alan's arrival in Virginia.

Alan returned to the bedroom and Tessa lay across the bed diagonally, making it impossible for him to fit. He lay down so his legs hung over hers and she tumbled over and moved up close to him. She whispered, asking Alan where he went, and he whispered back that he went to the bathroom.

After sleeping for another hour, they got up, got dressed, and made their way into the living room. All of the occupants of the living room had left sometime in that last hour. Considering there was no food in the refrigerator, they had to go out to eat. Alan had calculated that if they went out and ate breakfast at a small independent greasy spoon type place, they could both eat for around ten or fifteen bucks.

They chatted over pancakes. The conversation was not extremely active, and Alan was actually bored with it.

"So, who do you think is hotter... Mrs. Buttersby or Aunt Jesibel?" Tessa was referring to the two prominent corporate identities of maple syrups.

"I don't know."

"No, honestly."

"Well.. No, I am not answering that. It is stupid."

"Come on."

"No."

There was a pause. She looked down into her pancakes with a straight face, smiled, and then looked up again.

"So, what kind of stuff do you write?"

"Fiction. Literature."

"Cool, like... Science fiction?"

"Why does everyone automatically assume I write stories about fucking dragons or spaceships or whatever?" Truth was, no one ever said that to him. He didn't know why he swore. Alan slowed down. "I write reality fiction. Stories that could really happen."

"Oh."

"What do you do for fun? What would you do if you didn't need a job?"

"I don't know. I like clothes," she replied. Alan couldn't take any more Tessa for today.

"Don't you need to be at work or something?"

"Yeah... It's really easy to take time off. I don't even need to really call in or anything. I just can take a day off here and there. It makes up for the fact that I really don't take any vacations or sick time. It works out."

They were just about done eating and Alan thought it was time to get on the case of calling about that job. The only reason he stopped to begin with had nothing to do with a blow job. It was to get cash and get moving.

"Listen, I have a ton of stuff to get done today. Mind if I drop you off at your car back at the beach?"

"That's fine."

Alan brought her back to the beach and to her car, a sporty overseas lifetime-warranty maroon number. She gave Alan a hug and a kiss, brushed her hand across the front of his jeans, and said goodbye. Before she got into her car, she spun around and knocked on Alan's window before he pulled out.

He rolled it down and she gave him a little white card. It was her business card. On one side was her Department of Defense information in raised blue ink, and on the other she wrote her personal phone number.

"Call me Alan, I mean it."

Alan didn't respond, but waited instead for her to get in her car and pull away. Alan tossed the card on his passenger seat and pulled out of the sand strewn lot of cars. As he drove back to Clark's place, he thought about the night before and how the party was a giant orgy of beach life; it was a crash course on how to act, how to behave, how to look. It was fucking high school. It sucked, but it was also fun; Alan met a chick and got off. In hindsight it couldn't have gone better.

Alan pulled into Clark's driveway and shut the car off. Moving into the house, he tossed his keys on the counter and grabbed the remote control, turning the TV on. While he picked up the phone and dialed it, he surfed the television stations for the local cable station's Christian programming. Research.

"Stewart Industries, how can I direct your call?"

"Hi... I am looking at... Okay, I want to talk to Mike Baiden?"

"Plant supervisor's office. Extension 163. Thank you."

With a short hum and a few clicks, Alan met the voice of a kind man. He sounded short, and nerdy.

"Mike Baiden speaking."

"Mike, hey. Alan Levy here, Clark's friend. Listen, he said that you could hook me up with some work?"

"Oh, yeah, Alan. Hey, how's it goin?"

"Good, good."

"Heard it was a wild party last night!"

"Not bad. A lot of chicks. A lot of idiots there, too."

"That's Clark for you."

"You're the plant supervisor, good for you!"

"Well, sort of. I am more like the secretary to the plant supervisor. There are actually six of us, doing his job for him. But, I still pull some weight in Human Resources, so I got the perfect position for you. Short term. Our guy just left, and I am sure I can get you a thousand cash for ten days work. You can stick around longer than that if you want..."

"No, wow. That's great. I will totally do it. What will I be doing?"

"Easy stuff. Q.C. Basically... 'Quality Control.' Easy stuff, really."

"Nice. When do you need me?"

"Want to start tomorrow? You'll work though the end of the week and the whole next week, and by the next Thursday you'll be done, and have some cash in your pocket. We have a bank in house to deal with our smaller distributors, so you can pick up your money whenever before you leave."

"Nice. Yeah, absolutely. I'll be in...?"

"Seven is when we start work. We're between Clark's house and the beach, so you might convince him to get up with you and drop you off so he can go for a surf."

"Nice, okay."

"Well, I look forward to meeting you tomorrow..."

"Yeah, me too."

"Okay, brother. Gotta go make sure there aren't any machines blowing up. Talk to you tomorrow. Bring a couple IDs if you could too, okay?"

"Yup. Later, man."

"Bye."

The phone beeped as Alan hit the 'end' button on the cordless receiver. Turning his attention to the television, Alan found one of the Christian stations of Virginia Beach, which was now on its evangelical paid commercial programming.

It was an advertisement that had a man in a suit walking through the sands of the hills of Israel, talking about the urgent need to bring Jews to their homeland. It was said that millions of Jews lived in Russian Siberia, and were stranded and ignorant to the way of the true life they deserved in their homeland of Israel. They needed to go home, and live with their brethren.

The commercial was inter cut with depressed and old Russians, walking through the streets aimlessly and tired. They looked gray, beaten, old, and the loaves of bread they carried in their wrinkled hands were soggy and stale. But then, miraculously, when they got off of the planes in the sunny and gorgeous land of Israel, their frowns were forgotten as they sipped margaritas on the beaches of the Dead Sea, and prayed at the Western Wall, and were finally happy.

It didn't make any sense that you could send someone to live in Israel from Russia for a hundred and twenty five dollars and a family of four for five hundred. One could only imagine what they are doing with that money. Alan had a vision of this company investing in a giant bomb that would blow up everyone who was currently in Israel once they got everyone there, so then they could ask for money to bring the Christians home to Israel? He simply cold not understand why this company existed, and couldn't even understand what their game was. Were they just a glorified immigration service? Then

why were they asking for donations from strangers to bring people there
rather than the people who wanted to go there to begin with? Why was the
advertisements airing on a Christian station and targeted the Christian
market? It was incomprehensible.

The commercial ran for fifteen minutes, repeating itself often, until it
was the top of the hour. It was four o'clock in the evening. The station's own
commercials eventually came on, advertising everything from a catholic mass
to a music video show for Christian music. The programming was almost
identical to that in Massachusetts. The Sacrosanctity Society was on every
night, just as it was in Massachusetts, but in addition to the Sunday Special,
this station aired an editorial by Hobbeston for a half hour after the show. This
new commentary on Hobbeston's craziness made Alan feel electric.

Next up was a show called "Experiencing Every Day with Joy
Liedes." The program started with cool colors flowing around pictures of
Joyce hugging tons of people and waving her bible around in the air as her
speech had no audio under the music. The music had corny words, along the
lines of...

> *I see it now, my new day has come,*
> *I can't believe there is nothing to be done.*
> *My heart leaps up and my feet are halted,*
> *As I am lifted by the power of the exalted.*
> *I am so happy that the day is mine,*
> *There is no longer the pain of sin's sting*
> *I am Experiencing...Every Day!*

Alan started to watch the program and listen to the words of this
woman. She started the sermon with one sentence. For the most part, it
sounded like the sentence was a prelude to the sermon, based on a line from
the New Testament. She would wholly take that line out of context in
everything she said, and he could see this rhetorical approach being effective
with her audience. She was a professional.

For instance, today's talk was about the feeling that there was too
much worrying about how to fully represent God when doing life's mundane
chores. Alan thought that needing so much guidance and the necessity of
having people tell you what to do was ludicrous. Religion should be about
faith, love, and the opportunity for inner discovery regarding your higher
power to a level that you wouldn't normally reach without the presence of the
higher power. He understood guidance, but, this?

"You are at the supermarket, and asking the lord whether or not you
should choose the brown eggs or the white ones and then whether or not the
woman next to you is being a good Christian by taking the last package of
chicken shake. The lord wants you to live your life without any kind of
judgment and asking these questions. Do your shopping by only thinking
about the list and knowing that you are doing God's will by just living your
life and doing your chores. You will find that what you are doing, in actuality,

is making sure you are maintaining the vessel of the lord by getting the food you need. Need to go for a run? Do it. Need to wash laundry? Do it. Do these things without fear of judgment or worry that you are wasting study or prayer time. Need to wash your car? Do it, but don't go to the bikini car wash and expect your wife and the lord to be happy about it..." The audience cackled in response.

The camera often panned across the crowd with wide, sweeping crane shots that highlighted the majesty and power of so many people in one place. There were rows and rows of people in a stadium-sized arena all facing the stage, or was it a pulpit? It looked like a major league sports event, and Alan thought that if the place was sold out and each of those persons paid at the least $40 a seat for this event, Joy and her husband were easily clearing one and a half million dollars after paying for the venue and its staff. In fact, it would probably be more as they don't have to pay the pretzel and beer vendors for the day (as far as Alan knew anyway).

For the rest of the evening, Alan watched the station with his notebook open in front of himself. He took notes on the mannerisms of the different evangelists, as well as the whole of the discrepancies and continuity errors between what they said in the sermon. It seemed at least four times in the program they would say or read one thing, and then interpret it in the opposite or contradictory context of what they originally said. Alan recalled reading the New Testament and there being a theme of hypocrisy throughout the work, and it was apparent that if this was the Christian means to the end, it was certainly apparent on these programs.

Alan watched the Sacrosanctity Society and the new editorial that followed, and then watched the music program afterward. Alan programmed his phone's alarm for six the next morning. Falling asleep, Alan dreamt of the world. It pulsed through his being, and he thought about everything he hasn't seen and everything he needs to be, and everything he is missing. He was missing it. He felt vertigo, that where he worried and was concerned with such small things, that the world and the universe spread apart and flew far away so fast. There weren't even words to help correctly describe what he felt or saw in this dream... But perhaps, it was just 'falling emptiness.'

He had another dream, standing at the edge of a cliff. Spawning before him was a land that held the beautiful sights of the world. There was Venice, Rome, London. The Eiffel Tower was there, and the landscape of the moon. Singapore, Mexico City, and Tokyo. It was night in some spots, and day, and the beauty of it was gorgeous. There was a giant black pyramid in the distance, with a bright white spotlight shooting from the top. Alan realized it was Las Vegas. And there were hookers and druggies with needles in their arms walking the streets. Dirt and vomit spilled from the gutters and a stench filled his nostrils. And the sun came up and everything crumbled and turned to dust and blew away into a desert. He was dizzy.

As he fell from the cliff, the wind lapping at his ears.

He woke up the only time that night as Clark turned the television off. It was late, and he only opened his eyes to see it, and then closed them again. He drifted back into a dreamless sleep full of only blackness and comfort.

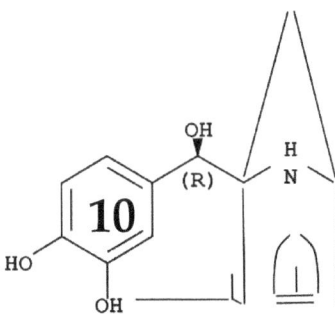

"So, did you get your dick wet the other night, dude?" Clark asked Alan. They drove with the windows down toward the factory, drinking in the freshest salt air Alan had ever breathed in his life.

"Oh? Well, I don't mean to toot my own horn but..."

"You got your dick sucked. Good for you. She looked like she had a good head on her shoulders."

"Yeah, hah."

Alan thought back to the night and how she looked hunched over his hips in the bed. She was like an egg fetus opened up at a science museum; naked, skinny, bony, and fleshy. He did what any polite guy would do and tapped her on the shoulder right before he came, but, in actuality, she drank every last drop of him and Alan felt better than he had felt in a long, long time. It was the best sex he had in a long, long time. He felt good in her mouth. He felt the need to keep this to himself, even though he anticipated Clark telling him everything about his night.

"You should invite her over tonight. It's Wednesday."

"What does that mean?"

"Porno Wednesdays, dude!"

"Porno Wednesdays?"

"Yeah, we rent a weird porn and all get together and eat and drink and watch it. Wednesday nights. Call her right now!"

"Okay...."

Alan reached into his pocket to retrieve his phone and his wallet that contained his card. He dialed. It rang and rang, and then finally a voice picked up asking for a transfer number. Alan punched in Tessa's extension and the phone sat dead.

"General Doniello's office?" Tessa's voice reverberated from the connection.

"Hello?"

"Hello, what can I do for you?"

"Tessa, it's Alan."

"Oh... Oh, I didn't think you would call me at work. You can't call me here."

"Sorry. Listen… You busy tonight?"

"No…"

"Okay, well give me a call when you're out. It is Porno Wednesday at Clark's. We're having dinner and drinks and watching pornos."

"Oh… Okay…" She sounded hesitant, and nervous.

"Just. It will be fun."

"I have to go Alan."

"Okay, whatever."

The line clicked and the phone disconnected itself. Alan sat in the car feeling the wind brush up against his face. Clark looked over at him…

"So?"

"I think she's coming…"

"Oh?"

"Yeah, it was confusing."

"Okay, whatever. Listen, you got my phone number if you need anything, right?"

"Yeah."

"Okay."

"…And we're here."

Alan looked up at the plain three-storied industrial building. There were no windows aside from the few in what was probably the front office that he was being dropped off at. Alan gave Clark a high five as he left the car.

"Dude, I'll be here to get you at four. I am pretty sure that is when this gets out. If you get out any earlier because it is your first day or anything, just give me a call."

"Okay, man. Later."

He closed the door. Clark almost peeled out, the harness on top of his car holding the matching surfboard screaming for release.

He entered the pleasantly air conditioned front office. The secretary looked up, and Alan mentioned his name. Another gentleman, stocky and tall wearing a tank top entered in behind him and began making his way through the heavy door with a small reinforced window.

"Bill, hold on," the secretary said to him. She picked up the phone and hit a button. "Alan Levy is here… Yup… Okay." She hung the phone up. "Bill, could you bring Alan here to sector 249?"

"Oh, come on! That is the opposite side of-," Bill complained.

"Bill, just bring him there."

"Fine."

Alan followed the man into the floor of the factory, and it was hot and loud. The machines resembled a giant spider, people scrambling around its feet. It extended high up into the building, and there was a man on top with a yellow hard hat shouting down to someone. Alan was led to the opposite side of the factory by following a thick yellow line in the shiny cement floor that resembled a sidewalk. Wisps of cotton or polyester spiderwebs shot out of the top of the machine and the man up there covered his face and started shouting even louder at the people below.

Alan was led to a bank of rooms that were haphazardly put together with drywall. Bill opened a door to one of these modular rooms, and let Alan in. The air was sweet, air conditioned so much that Alan thought he could see his breath. Directly ahead of him in the room was a conveyor belt, not moving, with flaps that hung down on each side. Alan assumed that they were for keeping the air conditioning in, but for what purpose? On the left and right sides of the small room were counters and six electrical outlets on each.

A tall, strong black man entered the room with neatly cropped short hair and a very tight red tee shirt on. He extended his hand.

"Alan, Michael Baiden. Welcome." He wasn't what Alan expected.

"Nice to meet you, Michael."

"Sorry I didn't come out to meet you right away. One of the machines broke down, so I have to be quick. Okay, quality control today. Just read the directions on the sheets here. Basically you will be taking the blankets from the conveyor and making sure they work. Plug them in, and as long as they are cool, write the lot and the product number on that clipboard. In about fifteen minutes, all these outlets should be full and you should be testing each level of the blanket."

"Okay." Alan looked next to the door where Michael pointed to a clipboard with a grid on it and a metal ringed pile of four or five laminated sheets nailed to the wall. "Sounds easy enough. So, I am just testing stuff…"

"Basically. Send them back down the line. If you get one that doesn't work, knock on one of your neighbor's doors. They will show you what to do. Only do the ones wrapped in plastic. The unwrapped ones were already done."

"Okay. What am I testing?"

"Right, sorry. Electric blankets. That is why it is so cold in here. It won't be that cold in a little while. You're an electric blanket tester."

"Oh."

"Any questions, just knock on the doors to the left or right of yours. You'll know it is lunch when the giant bell rings and everything stops. Umm… That is it. You coming to Porno Wednesday?"

"Oh, yeah, man. Totally. I am psyched."

"Awesome. See you then. I have to run."

"Later, man."

Alan liked the idea of working by himself in a small room. He thought that he might be able to get away with bringing in a stereo in. If he had one. He had a computer and could play music on it.

Alan took the clipboard down and put it on the counter, and he took the laminated sheets off the wall and flipped through them. The directions were exactly the same that Michael gave him, but the language was a lot simpler and there were pictures. He hung the cards back up and filled in the simple language on top of the sheet on the clipboard, and put it down, waiting for the fist blanket to peek its way through the curtain.

The conveyor belt hummed to life, and blankets came. Alan started work. It was strange, but by lunch time, Alan realized that he really couldn't remember anything that happened between when he started and lunch. Work at a factory was interesting. He never had to do it before, but the time literally melted away. When the bell rang, Alan followed everyone outside.

Most were smoking and everyone else lined up at the lunch truck. Michael approached Alan and told him that most workers had a tab and they took their lunches out of their checks, so if he wanted to get something, he could just give the driver his social security number. Alan didn't feel like eating. He walked over to a patch of grass out of the sun and decided to take a book with him the next time he had to work so he could spend his lunch reading.

Alan's phone in his pocket began to vibrate. He took it out and answered it.

"Hello?"

"Alan, it's Jane." Alan didn't think about looking at the caller identification before answering it. Idiot.

"Hi."

"What are you doing?"

"I am on break. Lunch break."

"That's cool. Where are you? Boston?"

"No, actually. I am in Virginia Beach if you would believe it..."

"What?"

"Yeah."

"What is in Virginia Beach?"

"I don't know. I was running low on money, so I stopped to work for a little while. That's all."

"Oh." Her voice sounded shaky. "Where are you going?"

"I don't know."

"I am working at the Collaborative in town. The one with the special needs people. It's good. I'm making like thirty five dollars an hour..."

"That's nice. I am an electric blanket tester. I am making a little over ten."

Alan didn't know how it happened, but Jane started blatantly sobbing on the line. Alan didn't know what to do. He listened. That is all he felt like he could do.

"I miss you Alan. Are you coming home any time soon?"

"No," he replied. Alan wasn't sure why she was calling. They were done and Alan was on his lunch break in Virginia. Well maybe, Alan thought, she didn't know he would be out here. But, what difference did it make? "Why are you crying? Don't cry."

"I'm not crying. I'm not upset."

"Oookay. Calm down."

"Stop telling me to clam down. I am calm. Shut up."

"Right."

"You know what? Fuck you Alan Levy. Fuck you. You just le- Just fuck you," and the line went silent. There was nothing but the blank noise of the open line air on the phone. Alan looked at the phone and then put it back to his ear. Sometimes the line could stay open for up to fifteen minutes before it actually broke the connection, and then the next time the person used the phone they were miraculously still there. Not really in this case. The phone went dead and the screen said that the line of communication was closed. After only thirty seconds.

Alan had hung up the phone on people before, but it wasn't often that they hung up on him. No. This time he was hung up on. But it didn't bother him. It bothered him more than anything that he picked the phone up to begin with. Next time, Alan thought, we must see who is calling before we answer the phone. That is why they put the caller ID on the phone.

• • •

Alan was sitting on a couch amid women and women and a couple guys sipping on a frozen margarita, biting into Hawaiian pizza with prosciutto and pineapples, and laughing his ass of with everyone else when the title screen came up that read, "The Tiniest Little Whore In The Old, Old West." If Alan got ten dollars for every word in the title, he thought, he would have a lot of fucking money.

The film opened in an eighties-looking Californian-style house and there was a character played by a little person in a little old-west dress. She was a little person alright. She came into the frame and was ready to have sex and make money for it. But the best part of this film was that no one else was dressed in the old-western style and there were no sets that suggested it took place in old-western times. But it got better.

It got better when she spoke. She was a little person and English was obviously not her first language. The poor lady. Her second and third were probably not English for that matter, either. She just barely put together the sentences that she used, and it seemed as though the words "Fuck," "Me," "Pussy," "Cock," "Yes," and even some of the ways that she moaned, were taught to her not even thirty seconds before they shot. As a matter of fact, by Alan's unconfirmed count those were the only five words she used, and those applications were few and far between.

Tessa was sandwiched in between Alan and another young lady on the couch and they were having a great time. Everyone in the room, totaling close to fifteen or twenty, were having a great time. Everyone except for Clark who was hiding in his room since the beginning of the movie.

Tessa got up and went for the kitchen, and when Alan got up to get some more pizza he noticed that she probably disappeared into Clark's room. Returning, everyone in the living room was having a blast, including Alan. At one point there was an almost unsaid contest when the members of the party first saw the little lady's genitals. It seemed that everyone in the room was doing their best to come up with a more vulgar and disgusting way to describe what they saw, and raise their drinks, holler, and laugh. While it wasn't of Alan's character to say anything, they were in a sense right that what they saw wasn't very pleasant. It was exploitation. Alan wasn't a connoisseur, but what this lady had was different, and it was probably closest to the name that seemed to have the biggest response so far, "Lady Rollins and her Diced Roast Beef Roll-Up." Disgusting.

Tessa had not returned yet, and the pizza was dwindling. Alan got up to get some more. He wasn't sure whether or not he saw Clark get up for pizza, he thought that he would get another slice for himself, another beer, and a slice for Clark and bring it into his room. He would throw in a tasty beer as well.

Alan grabbed a plate with a slice on it and a beer, and made his way down the short hall to Clark's room.

"Dude, you are missing the whole thing, man. This is great!" Alan saw what was happening in the room, and it was a whole lot of nothing. Clark sat at his desk and Tessa stood watching over his shoulder, diagonally three paces behind him. It was strange. Alan talked a little more slowly as if he was interrupting something, but it looked like there wasn't anything happening to interrupt. "I brought you some pizza and a beer... What are you doing?"

"Thanks, man. Working on a paper..." Clark responded.

"Oookay. Well... Don't you want to come out and hang with everyone else?"

"You know, I don't usually. I know. It is Porno Wednesday. Usually I just let people come and chill and eat pizza and drink beer. I don't usually partake because this is one of the few nights I have to do my work for my classes."

"Oh. Well... Come out when you can, I guess. You have classes?"

"Yeah... I'm taking some summer classes. On Saturdays. It goes like all day until five and then I go to work. It sucks, but usually it is an easy A."

Alan stood nodding for a moment, not quite sure why the two were together and quiet. He wouldn't mind if they were making out or anything, in fact he almost expected it, but you couldn't very well do that across the room from each other. Especially if you were a little person. That reminded him. Alan left the room, grabbed his pizza and beer from the kitchen, and went back into the living room. The seats on the couch were taken, so he planted himself on the floor.

The tiniest little whore from Texas was dressed again giving a man a blow job, but she was wearing the same dress. Alan was discouraged that the only thing that made this movie Texan or Old West anything was the one dress that they had her wear in every scene. Another little person came into the frame and started helping her out. The one good thing about her outfit was that it was made mostly of leather... Or fake leather anyway... It could be construed as western, if you thought real hard about it. Alan wondered whether or not any of the other guys in the room were getting any pleasure out of the video aside from the sheer humor of the whole thing. Alan sure wasn't.

When the movie was over, the party dissipated into a more cocktail-party atmosphere where people walked around and socialized. Music videos were playing on the TV and were a great addition to the party. Tessa and Clark eventually materialized form the bedroom. It turned out to be a pretty hip get together, and Alan had not realized the concept of the party and how great it was. The girls were horny and there were way more of them than guys.

Later in the night, some of the ladies had dissipated, and everyone was making out with someone. Tessa lay on the floor in front of Alan and her hips sat on top of Alan's legs crossed in front of him. Alan was pretty drunk, as he had also assumed Tessa was, and they were talking about some mundane detail of something in life. It was a stupid, pointless conversation, but Alan realized that her stupid, mundane conversations were a lot easier to deal with when he was drunk.

They were talking about bowling, or some aspect of it, and Tessa was holding Alan's hands. She pulled them up to her breasts as if there were no other people in the room. Alan didn't refuse, but at the same rate, it was strange behaving in this way in front of everyone. He figured that everyone else was drunk, so it didn't really matter.

Alan looked around the room and people were kissing. Clark had his hand up a blonde's shirt and Michael was watching as a girl was grinding against him while he sat on the couch. Tessa was watching Clark and giggling. Her hips started moving, and Alan watched her as she pressed his hands into her breasts with more fervor and energy. She was getting off.

Alan looked up at her and her eyes were closed. They were wrinkles in concentration and ecstasy. He wasn't sure what made him do it… If it was the alcohol, the heat, or the fact that it was turning into a junior high make out party, but Alan got up and left the room, Tessa's hips audibly hitting the wooden floor with a thump. Alan walked outside and sat on the front step, dizzy with a feeling that wasn't familiar, breathing in the fresh air that wasn't muggy with sweat and sex.

Tessa burst through the screen door. She immediately sat down next to Alan on the step and put her hand around him.

"What's wrong, baby?" she asked softly.

"I don't know. I… I just had to get out of there, you know? I'm sorry."

"No, what? Don't be sorry…" She kissed him on the forehead and Alan loved it. Its fading feeling felt cool in the nighttime air. She was looking at him. Her forehead looked bigger than ever for some reason. Alan looked at her and her innocence reached through his being and out the other side. It was her innocence, perhaps, that made the moment the most uncomfortable. He wasn't even sure what that meant, or what the feeling meant, but he asked her.

"How… How many people have you been with?" It was a valid

twenty-first century question that had to be asked. In fact, Alan had wished that he asked her this before they even saw each other naked. "I know it is a weird question, but I just want to know..."

"Like real boyfriends?"

"Yeah."

"Well, I have had three... But. Wait. Do you mean how many times have I had sex?"

"In a sense. Yeah, in a sense."

"Oh, jeez... You promise you won't think of me any worse?"

"Yeah."

"Zero? I'm a virgin, Alan."

Alan looked at her and he was puzzled. Her parents watched Charles Hobbeston for real, he thought. Tessa was nothing but a southern, country bumpkin that was ignorant to a lot of things. She probably didn't like the idea of two men or two women getting married. She probably voted republia- Well, she probably didn't vote at all. She had to eat meat at every meal, and church was a necessity in her life. Yup, that explained a lot.

"I see."

"Well, it isn't that I don't want to... I just haven't met the right person yet. That and I don't see myself doing it anywhere around here. Everyone lives in trailers and I want to do it somewhere beautiful... In a house overlooking a cliff, maybe, in a big soft bed. Yeah. Then I can take a hot bath after and feel lovely. Then have more sex."

"Right. So you have this all planned out."

"Mhmm!"

"Nice. Real nice."

"What?"

"Well, are you a real piece of work or what? Are you religious?"

"Thursday nights I do a youth faith gathering and I go to church on Sundays, yes."

"You go to youth group? Are you serious?"

"Yeah..."

"Your parents must be strict..."

"No, not really..."

"Did you know I am not really a church person? I mean, I am not much of anything, but I am Jewish more than I am not. Did you know that?"

"No... But you people are great! Oh, I like you so much more! I love the celebrations and the everything! Oh, boy. I was at a wedding of your people one time and I have to say, even though I am catholic, I really want to have a... Chuppa? Yeah, a chuppa at my wedding."

Alan looked at how she lit up and was so excited. She wasn't hot anymore. She wasn't even close. She was a little girl. A little, little girl and she was talking about something that she learned in her class a week or two ago. Yeah. He was willing to bet that she knew the whole dreidel song by heart!

Alan looked back at her deadpan and uttered the only thing he could think of at the moment…

"You people?"

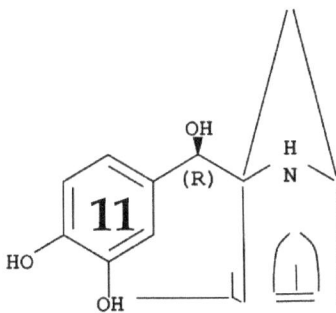

Alan worked for the next week without any kind of thought or perpetuation or feeling of time. He watched hours and hours and hours of evangelistic television whenever he had the time. He didn't know why, but he felt that the trash was somewhat therapeutic. There was nothing that surprised him. Every show was the same. He hung out with Tessa a couple more times, at her interestingly persistent requests, but didn't feel any more of a connection with her anymore.

She came to the next week's porno party, and this time spent the greater part of the film in Clark's room. By Alan's observation whenever he got up to go get more pizza or beer, she was doing the same thing she was the last week... Standing a few steps behind him and watching him do his paper. It was bizarre to look at; like a still picture. But it was real life.

The film they watched this week was called "Heffer Hotties," and by anyone's guess by the title, was about women who were blessed a little more horizontally than the rest of us. Alan wished he didn't hear any of the contributions of the naming game this round, and they really shouldn't ever be recorded for posterity. Alan was drunk, and found himself fending off the attention of two girls that were trying to kiss his neck at the same time, and were well aware of one another. Alan just didn't feel like the attention tonight.

The party was laid to rest, and Alan fell asleep by himself in his room that night.

The next evening after work, and after watching evangelical television all night, Alan found that he had fallen asleep when Clark woke him up.

"Dude, dude, hey."

"What? What?"

"Hey come here in the kitchen, I have to talk to you about something."

Alan followed Clark in the kitchen, and it was three in the morning - all of the clocks in the kitchen said it.

"Listen, I have to tell you this and I just want to do it because you are my boy and I don't want you to get pissed off or anything."

"What the fuck are you waking me up for? Why... Why couldn't you just tell me tomorrow?" Alan was still half asleep.

"Because, I don't want it to wait, and I didn't want to tell you in the morning. You know how people are in the morning..." He had a point, but it was the morning. Three in the morning.

"Okay, okay, what? I'm fucking tired, man."

"Okay. Umm... I have been seeing Tessa and I kissed her. I just... I don't want you to get pissed if we get together..."

"What the fuck?"

"Dude, okay, okay... I am sorry, man... I just-,"

"No, I don't care. I don't care. Fuck, is that all this is about? Let me go back to bed." Alan started to walk away, and planted himself on the couch.

The next morning, they got up and went to work like they always did. Nothing really changed until Friday swung around and Alan was working on Saturday morning. There was no sign of Clark on Friday night; all of Friday night. Alan last remembered staying up until two-thirty in the morning and Clark still not being home, so he went to bed.

The next morning, Alan got up and Clark's car stood in the driveway. Alan went into Clark's room and was about to shout "Why didn't you fucking wake me up," when he saw Tessa bare next to Clark in his bed. Alan tiptoed quietly out of the room and closed the door silently.

To himself, he waved his hands and tore at his clothes in silence outside the door. He was pissed. Okay, okay, okay, Alan thought. He paused. He thought a moment and a small pang of jealousy poked like a needle in his chest. This wasn't personal. He did tell him, but what was it about actually seeing it that made it all the more real? What was it that the woman in his bed, naked, beautiful and serene? What was it about this that made it personal? She was the first woman he kissed on the road. She was pretty. She was...

Alan, you need a ride to work.

He walked into the kitchen and called a cab company to come and pick him up, and drop him off at the factory. It wasn't very far, so with a tip he calculated it would cost him maybe six or seven dollars. He could bum if off of someone at work when he got there. It just made more sense than to take his car; fuel was so expensive and Alan had no idea how to get there. Even after a week and a half of watching Clark drive him. It also didn't make sense that Clark didn't think about Alan when he was out all night and sleeping with Alan's friend instead of driving Alan to work and going for a surf. Fucking guy.

The only problem was that, when it came time to wait the fifteen minutes for the cab to get there, Alan had a full fifteen minutes to think about the implications of what he just saw. He thought, okay, so you have Tessa, and she is with Clark. Okay. No biggie. But I needed to get to work today, and I have no way to do that, so I have to spend seven bucks for a cab. Ass. I can't believe it.

Alan sifted though the kitchen for breakfast, and he could only find a pack of gum. Alan did what anyone would do with it. He unwrapped all of the gum and ate it. He ate the first four pieces, and saved the fifth to chew.

And he chewed it… He chewed it sitting on the back of the couch with his feet on the cushions, shaking them with nerves.

The horn of the cab beeped. Alan jumped down off of the couch, and ran outside to get to work. When he got there, he was ten minutes late, and production was waiting. Gladly, Alan wasn't the only one late and his position allowed for late people considering there are two others with the same job. Also, one of the machines were broken, as they usually were in the morning. Alan wasn't even approached about it. The secretary that lent him the seven dollars for the cab wrote something down, probably about him being late, but Alan didn't think that it would go beyond that… Besides, he would get her back – he really had no intention to pay back the money.

The day went just like all of the others. Production was fast, and the time flew by. Alan loved having a factory job. He didn't have any conscious knowledge of the time as it went by, and he was usually only mentally tired at the end of the shift. He had plenty of time to think about partying or whatever he was doing on that given night. Today, he was thinking about what to say to Clark. Of wishing he kissed Tessa just a little bit. Of wanting her.

Alan had automatically assumed that Clark was a selfless and giving person, as there was nothing that would have suggested otherwise. That he could simply have concern for others without any concern for himself. He assumed Clark would think of Alan before thinking of himself when he went to bed that night. What a selfish bitch. A selfish, selfish bitch.

Alan sat outside at the end of his shift waiting for Clark to come retrieve him. Alan waited a half hour. Forty five minutes. He pulled out his little black notebook and started writing. He wrote with an energy that almost ran the pen though the pages he wrote at several points, and he was ready for business.

At what point does someone think they are the most important thing in the universe? Where does it come from? Where does the fire of self-centeredness start? Is the spark present in everyone inherently? Does it lay in America and our over-reaching feeling that we are the most important creatures on the face of this fucking planet? Or is it something deeper? Can someone bring it out of us like the horror of Pandora's Box? How does this happen?

Alan felt a tap on his shoulder and noticed men walking away from the factory in suits and ties. The secretary also made the effort to turn around and give him a dirty look. Alan turned his body and Michael was standing over him.

"You need a ride, brotha?"

"Oh, man… That would be so good. I have no idea where Clark is."

"Yeah. I have been trying to get a hold of him all day, and then I did, and I asked him what he was doing. He was like 'nothing,' so I said, 'Well, where are you?' and he just answered 'nowhere.' Honestly, Alan, sometimes you can't get that kid. I don't even think he gets himself…"

"Well, I can bet that he spent all day with Tessa… She stayed over last night. At some point they snuck in like bandits…"

"Wasn't that the girl you were dating?"

"No, thank you very much. She was a nimrod." Alan caught himself lying. Self preservation? Exercising his freedom? Trying to help himself get back to single life thinking? "She totally wanted my junk, but beside that... I just don't like the fact that they can't hang out like normal people and show that they were together. Clark actually woke me up at like three in the morning to tell me that they kissed."

"Weird,..."

"I know... And they were sleeping together this morning... I didn't have a ride to work. I didn't want to wake him up... She was naked right on top of the sheets." Why did he feel the need to share every detail? To cheapen it?

"I don't blame you... Well, come on, we'll get you over there. Think of it this way, you are only here for, what; two, three more days?"

"You got it."

Michael drove Alan home. Clark's car was gone and Alan had remembered that he was working, or in class... Last Saturday he had picked Alan up in between class and work to bring him home. No such luck here. Alan thanked Michael and went into the house.

Alan's phone vibrated in his pocket, and he removed it and looked at the caller identification that came up. He has learned a lot since the last time. It was Tessa. Alan felt heat surge through his chest and almost ignored the call, but he answered it. He needed to have a little chat.

"Hi."

"Hey, Alan, what's up?"

"Nothing." Alan picked up the remote control and pointed it at the television, turning it on. It was on a twenty-four hour news station. Alan put the remote down and spun it on the counter.

"What are you and Clark doing tonight?"

"Don't 'what are you and Clark doing tonight' me, honey." Alan couldn't believe that he used that comeback. He hated it. It was something his dad said.

"What?" There was a shake in her voice that was obviously that of guilt and hurt.

"Oh, well, I was going to go wake Clark up this morning to take me to work and it just so happens that I saw you sleeping with him. You know what, you are sick. Ignorant and sick. Did you not think about the time we spent together before you did this, or did you think it I would be cool with it?"

"Alan, listen, Clark said he didn't want you to find out. Okay? It wasn't me."

"What are you talking about? Clark just told me the other night that you guys were kissing or whatever. I don't care. Why are you hiding it? You snuck in last night like I was your mom or something. You can't come in like normal people? What... Did you stay outside until the lights went off?"

The other end of the line stayed silent for at least a minute.

"I didn't know you liked me, I just thought that you didn't like me? What about Jane?"

"Okay, exhibit a: I didn't like you. I didn't want you, but you need to know that you can't go around fucking a guy and then his close friend... Besides, what happened to all that shit about him being a slut? And exhibit b: what the hell are you talking about 'what about Jane?'"

"You have a girlfriend named Jane in Boston, don't you?"

"No... I have an ex in Chapmansville, Massachusetts named Jane... Where in the hell did you get that?"

"Clark said something about it... That, and there's a million calls on your phone to her..."

"Give me a fucking break. So? You aren't my girlfriend!? Why are you looking through my phone like a crazy, possessive one?"

"I don't know..." At this point she was crying. Anything to have a normal conversation with a woman that doesn't end in crying, Alan thought.

"God... Anything else you want to tell me?"

"... I have been over there like every night for the last week."

"What the FUCK? Are you a little kid, sneaking around so I didn't find out? Who the fuck are you two?"

She was crying hysterically. She started saying more, and Alan could hardly understand a word of what she said. Something Alan heard on the news station on the television that caught his attention...

"Shut up, shut up." He said. He turned the volume up with the remote. The newscaster spoke.

"...was called in last night at around nine PM. Authorities can't back up Hobbeston's claim, but it is certain that there is evidence that the police are not sharing just yet points to her disappearance being a kidnapping, and Hobbeston is considered not to be a suspect just yet. They are pleading that if anyone knows anything about the disappearance of Margaret Hobbeston to immediately call the Las Vegas Police or the FBI."

The woman talking into the microphone was outside of a fence with a good view of an expensive estate. Police cruisers were seen parked outside of it. The program immediately cut to the newscaster, another woman, in the newsroom.

"Once again, the wife of prominent television evangelist Charles Hobbeston, has disappeared last night from their home in Las Vegas, Nevada. The authorities say that evidence points to this being a kidnapping case, but they are not releasing many more facts about the case just yet. Margaret Hobbeston, wife of prominent television evangelist Charles Hobbeston, has disappeared."

Modern titles swept across the screen, "Missing in Vegas." Alan thought that they have gone a little too crazy with the labeling of big news stories, and the fact that they have scary music and sleek titles to accompany them make them really tacky. Alan assumed that some at the network thought it added a degree of seriousness to the story. Alan thought it added a degree of sleaziness.

After seeing this, Alan needed to get to Vegas. Soon. He had already wasted close to two weeks. This has become a mission rather than a flight of fancy.

"Stop, Alan, stop. I don't want to lose you. You're too good of a-" Alan interrupted the voice on the line, and hung up.

• • •

Alan woke up at the shouting of Clark, the clock on the bedside table reading three thirty in the morning.

"You little fuck. I fucking... Oooh I knew it. You jealous fuck."

"What the hell?" Alan couldn't even comprehend what was going on.

"Get up. Get out of my place. This is my apartment, I found it. If you don't like what I do here, then you can just leave."

"What?"

"I talked to Tessa and she was telling me that you said all this shit to her and you gave her so much shit about us being together... You are just jealous that you don't have her, that's all."

"I don't fucking care about what you do... God, you're cheating on your girlfriend left and right, no one could possibly count the amount of women you've been with... You're just one big bullshit artist. A fucking liar. Keep the bitch, I don't care, just don't sneak around your friends in the middle of the night not wanting to wake them up when you fuck. What the hell are you so upset about?"

"You're a disgrace. Get out of here. Honestly. And where's the spare key? What did you do with it? It isn't where I keep it! Give it back!"

"It's on the kitchen table... Why are you freaking out so-,"

"Get the fuck out."

Alan gathered his clothes in the middle of the night and walked outside to his car. Some dirty clothes were the only thing that he had in the house that was his. He tossed them in the backseat of the car, laid the back of the car seat down as far as it could go, and slept as comfortably on it as he already had a few nights before. Alan wasn't worried about how he was getting to work or what he was going to do with himself the last couple nights in Virginia Beach...

No... Alan could sleep in his car, and Alan paid attention to where the cab driver drove to bring him to work. Alan was worried about what a dishonest navy veteran in his late twenties was going to do acting like a six year old would do with himself in this real world, and how he would sound on his deathbed wondering what happened to his life. More than worried, Alan was happy that he had the opportunity in his life to meet such a complex person that he could probably use in his writing some day... A complex character that just woke him up at three in the morning for criticizing something he did with a girl Alan got head from once, and who isn't even his girlfriend, but who he is ridiculously possessive of nonetheless.

Alan softly drifted to sleep with the rhythmic sound of the trees swaying on the street outside of Clark's house. He contemplated, how could someone act discontent with the events in their life, and then feel the need to supplement it with sex, and alcohol, and parties. Supplement it with playing volleyball with girls in bikinis; and they themselves talk about how horrible he is, and in almost the same sentence he touts how good he is. Was this Midwestern? Was it?

Alan dreamt of words this particular night. The organizing of them into hierarchies and their respective position in his own considerations and analysis of everything he has seen so far in his journey and his life. Alan wished that he could print them out onto paper sometimes, on giant pieces of paper for him to hang on a wall and examine for hours. But in his dream he couldn't stop thinking about how technology wasn't there yet, nor would it probably ever be. The words flowed around in cyclical fountains and tides. The words glowed and felt good when he organized them in the dark room.

He hit the mark in this particular dream as he organized them in a hierarchy. That America was in fact one big social cosmos situated upon beliefs and ethics that were constantly evolving into horrid rotting corpses and walking material zombies. Was the Midwestern attitude of waste and consumption part of America, or was America in fact…

Alan woke up. He pulled out his small leather notebook and a pen, and put the pen to paper, and realized that he didn't remember one thing about what he just dreamed about. He flipped the pen and tapped it a few times on the notebook. He put it on the passenger seat and turned the car on.

Alan drove around for fifteen minutes, looking for something to do on a Sunday. There was nothing. Alan had no idea where any parks were or where there might be something to do. Alan thought about going to the library, but they certainly weren't open. He looked for the café, and he would plant himself there for the rest of the day and write. Then he would go to bed early, get up for work, and work until Wednesday, and hit the road. That was the plan.

Alan drove up to the café, and waited fifteen minutes outside for it to open. He read a little bit of literature on the area that was in a slotted sandwich board outside. Virginia Beach looked like a really hip place to be… A really hip place to be if you were into outdoor summer games and people walking around with bikinis and being fake all of the time. That wasn't Alan's bag, and he was glad that he was leaving. There was nothing more in the world that Alan hated than the beach and its strangers running around trying to impress each other…

Entering the café, he heard a jingle on the door as he entered. The oaky and dark atmosphere and the scattered bookcases with tattered copies of who-knew-what was exactly what he was looking for. It looked like so many of his favorite spots in Boston did. Hip. It also looked like there really weren't a lot of customers in Virginia Beach that liked this kind of place. It's rustic tones and old and tattered look about it was created with hand and chisel rather than ages of customers beating it into the ground.

Alan planted himself at a wooden table near the window, and paid two dollars for a refillable cup of coffee. Opening his computer, he felt a degree of grace and power being where he was. He was the coolest, most artistic being in the most immediate area, and maybe even the state at that exact moment. Alan was happy.

Sipping on his coffee, he started to write, and didn't stop until eight that night. He didn't write a story, or any plots. He just wrote words that sounded wonderful together that he could someday use in something else that he wrote. Words that when combined in the most strategic manner, would make anyone's heart leap or sink to the absolute apex in either direction. Words that when spoken aloud by any given college professor studying the work of Alan Levy, they could be analyzed for hours and hours and hours. Delicious hours. Hours of analysis, and hours of people saying them to each other as if they wrote them themselves; say them to win over someone's heart, or offend them to a degree that they would cut off all ties to that person indefinitely.

He wrote words that ignited a fire in humanity's heart: a fire of passion, melancholy, or loathing.

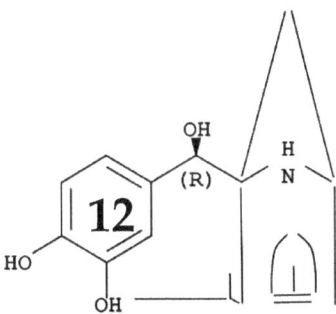

The last few days Alan spent in Virginia were an anti-climax. He worked, wrote, and slept.

Alan's working didn't amount to anything - he was working to just make some cash toward the end of his stay. His co-workers often invited Alan to go out and drink with them, but Alan was just stuck without money or the ability to pay, and the way that some of them looked at him after he answered suggested he was outgrowing his welcome. The writing Alan did had no purpose or excitement, and he hardly ate. He ate the occasional tuna sandwich, but besides that, he was pretty damn hungry.

At four in the afternoon on Wednesday, Alan walked out of the main office at Stewart Industries with eleven hundred, forty-three dollars and sixty-four cents more in his pocket, bringing his life savings in cash on him close to twenty-two hundred dollars. His pay was docked for the lunches and the seven dollars he borrowed from the secretary, and he felt like he was scammed. Luckily, it never came up to pay Clark for his time at his house.

While he pulled out of the driveway, Alan took out his phone and dialed Clark's phone number. It rang a few times, and then the answering machine picked up. As he headed for the highway, he did his best to improvise a message to Clark.

"Uh, Clark. Hey. Alan here. Listen, I am sorry about everything that went down the last week. It is my last day in Virginia and I am actually hitting the road right now. I am not entirely sure why you are angry or where you got the idea that I am so jealous of you. I just felt like – it seemed like you became a selfish jerk and was sneaking around behind me like I am a little kid. If you want to keep being friends, and I want to keep you as a friend, don't do that. Umm… I also wanted to thank you for everything. Thanks for letting me stay and taking care of me while I was in…" and that was when Alan saw them.

Driving down a two lane street, one of the last things Alan passed while in Virginia Beach on the right was a small independently owned ice cream store called "Carol's." Eating ice cream amid knee-high sea grass jutting out of the sandy embankment in front of the store stood Clark and Tessa. The moment they looked into the window of the hatchback piloted by Alan, Tessa spun around and hid in Clark's arms like a shy child in a restaurant when asked a question. Clark stood defiantly and looking brave, watching the car drive by; it was as if he was protecting Tessa from flying bullets.

Alan removed the phone from his ear and hit the 'end' button, not taking his eyes off of Clark for one minute. What was this man thinking? He could be ruining lives every second of every day and no one would do anything about it. At one particular party that Alan was at during his stay, he heard a story about a girl named Jessica that Clark was having regular sex with. One particular evening, Clark's long lost girlfriend from Maryland or Delaware or wherever she was from showed up at the party, and said something awful to the girl. Then Clark did the same. Five minutes later, the girl was on her way to the hospital in an ambulance, her stomach being pumped of seventeen over the counter severe allergy tablets and vodka... Four in any given amount of time were considered fatal, and only eight came in a package that was designed so it took a considerable amount of time to just remove one pill from its individual bubble packaging. She was determined.

The threat of any unhappiness or any hampering on his journey made Alan sick to his stomach. He had somewhere to be, and there was nothing that anyone could do to stop him. The car hit the pavement of the highway faster and harder than it ever had before, and Alan turned on the radio.

After listening for a half hour to several different religious radio stations, he was surprised that there was no coverage of the event that he had seen on the television a few nights earlier. The national public news stations also were devoid of anything related to the disappearance. It was strange. A prominent woman disappears off of the face of the earth, and so does any coverage of it. Did anyone care?

It was twilight. The sun set in the west as it always had, Alan's car driving toward the orange fireball descending into the highway hundreds of kilometers ahead. 'If I drove fast enough, and melted into the sun and vaporized, would anyone remember me?' Alan asked himself. As he pressed hard on the accelerator, he forgot the question altogether.

Alan drove, passing through several states that he had never seen before, and witnessing everything that he was owed. He spiraled through land rich with golden wheat stretching for kilometers and kilometers. He would drive for hours and hardly see another vehicle pass him. He would doze, the hazy street ahead of him feeling comforting, dreaming as if he were still driving, happy to be alive. It wasn't urgent in his head to stay awake. The streets were long and narrow without a car, tree, embankment, or pedestrian on either side of the street for kilometers at a time.

Someone later asked Alan "Weren't you bored? Seeing nothing but crops spanning before you on both sides for kilometers and kilometers and kilometers," and Alan answered quite honestly "no, it was one of the most beautiful things I have ever seen."

Alan passed through North Carolina, Tennessee, and Arkansas. And they all pretty much looked the same aside from the tuna sandwich he ate in Memphis. He passed a lot of interesting things, but mostly he relished in the simplicity of nothingness. If there was anywhere else that the art of meditation could have taken place, it would have been in the fields of the south. You could not escape thought and a peaceful osmosis while traveling in these parts of the country. It just wasn't possible.

As he turned north, Alan thought of his father. Alan could have driven south from Virginia just as easy to invite himself to his father's place in West Palm Beach. It wasn't a matter of time or distance or anything to do with keeping the boiler of the locomotive of his journey west stoked, no, it was more about whether he wanted to see dad. Alan thought about how he would react as the scene played out…

The door to a modest single level home in a gated community south of Orlando opens and reveals a slim and adventurous man. "Is that you, son?" he asks. The son, a fragile and underfed man of his twenties replies, "Dad?" They embrace. They embrace and it feels like the warmth of the younger man's soul is melting through his chest to the floor. Melting with the fire of years of neglect and finally revealing the atomic power of their mechanics; the fire of family…

A large wooden set of oak doors stand as a dot on the expansive and mammoth mansion. The carved marble above the doors read "The Levy Estate". Alan pulls a snakelike velveteen rope beside the entrance and a gong echoes somewhere in the distance behind the doors. A gaunt man in a tuxedo materializes in the doorway and he looks as though he was as old as the building, and shipped over with it from the United Kingdom somewhere judging by his accent. "May I help you young man?" he asks. "Yes, I am here to see my father?" Alan replies. "My boy, if you know anything about his household, Mr. Levy does not have any children of any kind. Didn't you see the sign on the gate on your way in? No solicitors. Now, take your candy bar sale elsewhere before I call the authorities." SLAM!

Alan pulls up in his tiny blue hatchback to a motor home somewhere in the everglades. It is run down and a brown muck descends form the corners of the building, their gooey entrails snaking about the small structure. A skinny woman trailed by several children and a fat baby resting in her arms answers Alan's repeated knocks. She speaks in a southern trashy drawl, "Honey, if you are looking for your daddy you can march yourself right across the street and look for him yourself. You know where he is." Alan runs across the gravel road and into "Evergreen Cemetery; A Mourning Community For The Dirty, Dirty Jews." He runs about the barren land, tripping over markers in the rain, his muddied jeans clinging to his flesh and stops at a gravestone that read "Jordan Levy, a loving father. Very loving. He had loved so much that he had illegitimate children all over the country that paid twelve dollars each to give him a great funeral that no one attended. April 15, 1954 – July 10, 2015." Alan wanted to reach his hands into the air, but a rumbling in his stomach prevented it. It must have been those enchiladas he had eaten at that run down Mexican joint up the road. Without anywhere to go, no woods or trees for a kilometer around on each side, Alan removed his pants and propped himself up on his father's headstone, defecating his waste onto the muddy earth like a dog.

It wasn't the time, nor was Alan in the capacity to meet his father again. It just didn't make sense. He called once a year, always a few months after the holidays, and always told Alan that his gift was on the way. That was never true. He wouldn't spend the rest of the conversation apologizing for lack of contact or anything else. No. He spent the rest of the conversation asking Alan when he was coming down to see him, as if with rent and school bills and no one helping him make his American Dream come true it made any sense to just up and disappear for a week. Or to bend to his desire for his son to come visit him where he retreated. It made no sense.

Alan pulled the tiny car over in the dust somewhere in the middle of nowhere to sleep. He dreamed, as he always did. He dreamed of what it would be like to keep driving through to the end of the earth until he melted into the sun and the stars. His flesh would purge the energy out of space so it shone ever more bright, his DNA and cells and tissue fueling the explosions and creation of galaxies and new worlds. His atoms would separate, and he would once again return to the stars.

He jumped into the fire before the world so as to give it only three more seconds to survive in its vast existence. His soul entered the pores of dignitaries and was ingested by flowers and daisies and lilies and orchids. He flowed into the earth as a nutrient and grew into a glorious and majestic tree. He towered above the world's landmarks and was swallowed by the meek creatures of the forest. Alan was all power and fusion. Alan was everything and God loved him. It was wonderful.

When he woke up, Alan piloted a tiny blue hatchback mouse as it scrambled north through its pavement and wheat maze. The mouse darted into a town close to the border that felt like home, close to the border of Missouri called Branson. It was bustling old town, full of theaters and attractions of the country music variety. There were cowboy-hat wearing men and Sunday dress wearing women. Everyone had a smile and the buildings looked old and down home country-like, but all with a fresh coat of paint on them. It was really, really nice.

Alan pulled up to a small deli that was in one of the many downtown areas that was brick with white-trimmed windows. A hanging sign above the door read "Stiller's of Branson." Alan entered the small delicatessen with a couple of booths and a counter for eating, but for the most part it looked like a convenience store. It sold chips and sodas, but you could also buy lottery tickets, cigarettes, motor oil, magazines, and anything else you could possibly need.

Alan sat at the counter and ordered his usual: a hot tuna and cheese sandwich with a cola. The store as a whole stood mostly empty aside from a few customers that would materialize in and out ringing the tiny bell attached to the door every time it sporadically opened. They would mostly enter for a soda, or a bag of chips, pay, and leave again just as quickly. The owner slid the plate down in front of Alan. He immediately dug into the chips and took a bite of the pickle spear. Alan was starving.

As Alan ate the sandwich, the delicious pulp sliding down his throat. As he ate, the owner of the restaurant watched him. He stared with a curious look, and Alan wasn't sure what he was getting at. Alan opened his mouth on several occasions to speak, but nothing came out. He felt a lump in the back of his throat.

"How's the sandwich?" the mild mannered restaurateur asked, concerned. He stood a hundred and seventy centimeters, had lightly graying black hair, and glasses. Behind his apron he wore a collared shirt and a tie, and Alan could tell he really enjoyed his job. His clean cut appearance was obviously concerned about how Alan liked what was prepared for him. The man was sincerely asking Alan how he enjoyed his sandwich. He really wanted to know how the sandwich was. There was nothing else to do.

"It's good. Fresh. It's a fresh tuna sandwich. My favorite."

"Good. Good. What are you doing in these parts? I have never seen you before and your speech is interesting…" The man's voice sounded like a southern movie star's echo in the small restaurant. Alan was immediately getting tired… Or something.

"Just passing through, my friend. On my way west."

"Huh. Excellent."

Alan was chewing and the lump in the back of his throat grew larger, and Alan was having a hard time holding up his sandwich. He was getting really tired really fast. Alan started to feel his breathing diminish and he looked around, the yellowed lights in the room creeping out of his peripheral vision. They were just static, now. Static running through your fingers…

"You okay, young man?" The voice echoed even more. It was encompassing the room and driving right through Alan's brain. It was going straight through him.

"I am… Fine, my driving. I have been driving and I, 'm just tired…" Alan breathed these words out with all of his might. He felt like he could honestly fall asleep right here and be comfortable. Alan sighed some more, "The sandwich, lovely, it is. I feel like…. It's funny how… To begin it all." The glass of soda fell to the ground. "I am clumsy. I f re an fa land. Not of… breathless. I'm so sorry…"

And Alan fell. He fell through clouds and he fell into the earth, gravity had no say here, but then it did. It hung on. Grassy plains spawned out from nowhere like a pop up book opening. Alan was dreaming again.

He was walking through these plains. There was something different here, though. The grass felt lovely on his bare feet and he was only looking to the sky. That was it. He was walking, but he was walking bent over backward so his feet were on the ground and were working, but his knees were bent at a forty-five degree angle, leveling Alan's upper body parallel to the ground. And there were more feet. Alan could feel them walking him on his back. There were twelve feet carrying him through the pasture.

Alan wasn't the only one there. He walked over to his mother who was lying, rather, walking in much the same manner. She was dressed in a large white cloth wrapped about her. The only difference between the two was that while Alan was being carried by twelve bare feet, his mother was only being carried by her own two, and she was constantly putting her hand down on the earth to steady herself. She was hovering... It looked like a magic trick.

Alan passed her by and he was sad. He wasn't sure why. Alan kept walking and kept walking and he felt a cool breeze start. It started from the center of his heart and blew around the globe. There was a sharp bite in his leg, and he looked down to see a small garter snake with one giant fang removing himself from his leg, and Alan watched as it started to snow. The breeze was swift and nice, and Alan felt the icy air radiating from his leg wound and his heart. It felt great. The snake turned to ash before him on the ground and blew away into dust.

Alan started to run, and wind blew the icy specks on his cheek and his chest. It felt rather uncomfortable. Alan ran and ran, his feet galloping underneath him. Alan ran, and he would have noticed if he had slowed down, but his feet didn't have the reaction time to notice that they had just run off of a cliff. Alan fell and fell, his heart pounding and racing. He felt like crying out. But it was a falling dream, after all, and these sort of things happen. As he felt the wind lapping at his ears and his adrenaline pumping, he awoke with a shake in a bed in Branson, Missouri.

He was cold. Colder than cold, he was shivering. Shivering under a deep pile of blankets. He was also sweating. This didn't make any sense. A man in a white coat sat beside him in a wooden chair, and the news was on. Alan was breathless.

"Hello there. You, young man, need to watch what you eat."

"What?"

"You are lucky that you ended up with Mr. Stiller. He is known to have the kindest heart in Branson, and he saved your life."

"What happened? Where am I?"

"You are a guest here at Mr. Stiller's home. I am Dr. Budz, and Mr. Stiller called me when he found you having passed out and shaking on the floor of his store. Originally, he thought you were having a seizure, however, it turns out that you are allergic to fish, and you overdosed on it pretty bad. I figured that out when I saw your face and took your pulse and blood pressure."

"What? I eat it every day..."

"I did some tests on your skin while you were out cold and tuna is the culprit. You have just gotten lucky your whole life, and you are lucky you were in the right place at the right time when you actually had your attack."

"What happened?"

"You had an allergic reaction. Your body went into what is called anaphylactic shock... parts of your central nervous system began to shut down. Mr. Stiller called me, and I ran down to his store with my medical kit, and in that kit was one of these..." The doctor held up a giant needle. "It is an ephedrine auto-injector. I administered it when I saw you in person and found out what was happening. I gave you a shot in your leg, and Mr. Stiller was nice enough to let you stay here... He felt that it happened at his restaurant, so why not. This one is for you. It is a new one. If this happens again, you can give yourself the shot. There are instructions inside… But please, no more tuna or fish or anything from the sea."

Alan was absolutely surprised. What in the world happened? Alan had tuna almost once a week, and more recently, every time he needed to eat. The nutrients and vitamins made it an excellent and healthy meal, especially considering he couldn't afford to eat as much now. The whole time he ate it, he was flirting with death. Excellent, he thought. Excellent.

"How are you feeling?" The doctor continued.

"Tired… I am still pretty tired."

"You are going to feel that way for a while. Ephedrine is basically adrenaline. I gave you a shot of the stuff your body naturally produces when it is in dangerous situations… So you will be tired. I am going to watch you for another hour and keep checking your blood pressure and pulse. It is almost back up to normal…"

"Thanks… Thanks a lot."

And just like that, Alan drifted to sleep again.

He woke up the next morning to the sound of opening cabinets and breakfast activities downstairs. Alan crawled down in his dirty clothes. The family was sitting down to eat. There was an older woman who was shuffling about the stove and looked very nice, there was Mr. Stiller whom Alan remembered from the day before, and there was their daughter who was easily the same age as Alan. She looked up from her empty place setting with an air of innocence. She was beautiful, and Alan enjoyed her gaze.

"Well, look who is up ladies!" Mr. Stiller said. He spoke with a wide-eyed enthusiasm. The two women turned their gaze to Alan, and they smiled. Alan felt as though they were family and he never met any of them to any degree. They giggled, and the daughter cocked her head in a sexy manner, brushing her long brunette hair behind her ear. She was at the prime of her life.

"I am pretty sure your name is Alan, right?" Mr. Stiller asked. Alan nodded and he continued, "This is my wife Joan, and this is my daughter Elle. My name is Jim. Welcome to our home, Alan. You can stay here as long as you need to in order for you get better and we'll take care of you. Anything you need, Alan. Really." They were all smiling at Alan, in fact, there was already a place setting for him at their table.

"Wow. Thank you. Thank you so much…" Alan responded.

"Now, move yourself on over to that seat there next to my daughter and we'll get some good southern breakfast on the table for you."

As Alan sat down, while he felt wholeheartedly comfortable and happy under the wings of these generous people, it was their generosity that Alan was receiving bad vibrations from. They were only too nice. The young lady to Alan's right started to speak.

"So, you had quite an episode there. What did it feel like?"

"It felt like I couldn't breathe, and then it just felt like I was sleeping."

"Wow. It must have been scary."

"Not really. It just felt like I was sleeping."

"Oh. So, where are you from? Dad told me that you were passing through, and you obviously don't have a Branson accent... Or any accent for that matter. You're from up north; you talk real fast."

"I'm from Boston."

"Wow." Alan knew that she was trying to flirt with him, but her one word answers were the flirter's dead end. She wasn't getting anywhere. "My mom makes the best breakfast in the world. Have you had a good southern breakfast yet?"

"Actually I have had nothing but a tuna sandwich a day for the longest time... So, no. The coincidence of being almost killed by the same thing I have been eating every day for the entire spring... it rather strange. It is going to be good to have a good breakfast. I am hungry. She doesn't put any fish in it, does she?"

She giggled a quick no.

"Okay boys and girls. It is time for a gooooooood breakfast! We have eggs and corned beef and biscuits and sausage gravy. There is cornbread and fruit."

And Alan ate. He ate until he couldn't eat any longer. He didn't even taste it, it was just a ridiculous wolfing down of food. Alan was out for survival, and even the family that he was staying with watched him in horror as he devoured breakfast. Alan went in for seconds, and he went in for thirds, and he finished everything off when he noticed that everyone else was done. Alan couldn't even keep up with the conversations going about the table; he was too busy stuffing himself.

When the massacre was over, Alan sat back as the mess on the table was cleaned up. It was true, Alan had never had a true southern breakfast. And he loved it. Joan Stiller stared down at him when she removed his plate and smiled.

"You know, I would love to have you at every meal...I really would. I hardly have to throw anything away...wait... I hardly have to clean anything!" Everyone laughed, but everyone but Alan laughed hysterically. Scarily, in fact. Then they all sighed in unison. The family then chatted as the mother cleaned. She did all the work, Elle and Jim chatted away, and Alan watched.

Alan lounged in the chair, and the conversation that revolved around him had something to do with the Elle and her decision whether or not to finish school. They discussed it, and the importance of it.

"You can't get anywhere in life without it, Elle. Anywhere."

"I know that, dad."

"Well, I have to go to work. So does your mother. Call them, Elle. I can't make you do this, they said they would be happy to make things work for you."

Joan folded her towel, and went down the hallway, Jim following behind her. Alan and Elle were the only ones left in the kitchen.

"I don't mean to pry, but what is the deal with that?"

"I don't want to talk about it, I am embarrassed."

"College is a waste of time, I dropped out too. You need to just go when you are ready for it, not when other people tell you to. I went to school with people who had careers and were sixty and you know what? The on-"

"Alan, I dropped out of high school."

"Oh." Alan considered the implications of what he just heard. It was almost strange for him to hear about anyone dropping out of high school. The only girl that he remembered dropping out was a girl named Rebecca who had twins, and even she returned after a year off. But if she dropped out of high school, and she could still attend… "How old are you?"

"Nineteen." Alan thought of Tessa, and immediately had a sneaking suspicion that he was a magnet for nineteen year old girls.

"You do need to finish high school, Elle."

"Thanks." The contempt in her voice was shattering.

"So… What do you do with yourself? I mean…"

"I work at the supermarket."

She didn't look like anything that made Alan leap and want to relish in her beauty anymore. She just looked like an ignorant, young, and selfish American brat. That is what they all were, isn't it? All of the women, men, and people of this rotten place were selfish brats. An epiphany rocked Alan's self. Alan looked up from his thoughtful pose.

"Are your parents still around?" Alan asked.

"No, they left five minutes ago, probably. They leave through the garage which is down a hall near their bedrooms."

"When do you go to work?"

"In an hour…"

"Do you think you can bring me to your dad's on your way? I have to get my car."

"Sure."

Alan spent his last hour in Branson writing the longest, most praising letter to the Stillers that he could possibly conjure from his still fresh English major psyche. It was lovely. Three pages of praise and thanks that he poured his heart into. For letting him stay the night, for not allowing him to die in their small deli in Branson, for the delicious breakfast.

Alan put it in an envelope and placed it on the dresser of Mr. and Mrs. Stiller, and grabbed his Ephedrine shot, and left the house with Elle. She was kind enough to give him a ride back to his car. The kindness of these people and the overall contrast of the selfishness of America was exactly what Alan thought of as he held the ephedrine shot in his hand, pressed on the accelerator, and shocked the little blue hatchback mouse into running out of Branson as fast as its little wheels could carry him.

Elements

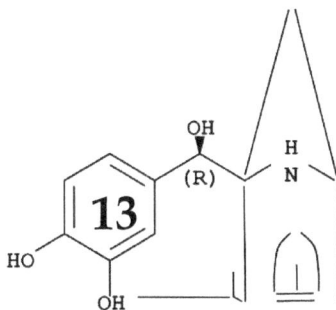

The Midwest was nothing as he had originally thought it would be. Alan only spent twelve days exploring the original destination of his journey. It took him two days to drive there, and two to get back down south, but the days that he spent there was, as a whole, uneventful and depressing.

Sure, his romantic vision of north central United States was simply a burnt out version of all of the white trash that lived in central Massachusetts, but when he got to the actual midwest there was nothing that could have prepared him for what he saw. It was a desert of desperation, the scorched earth looking like a war zone of decrepit industry and old appliances. Cars, washing machines, broken glass, dust, dying plants, and wandering animals were the mark that this version of humanity left on its land. The worst of it all was Michigan.

A state once considered to be wild and free, the birthplace of modern freedom thanks to the birthplace of modern industry, the state was exactly as its namesake had described it, sans the free part. Poor people wandered about looking for something to do with their time aside form being poor. It was truly a sorry sight. There was nothing about the area that had any redemption, aside from Iowa City where Alan had stopped for the majority of his layover.

Alan visited the University of Iowa, the home of the one thing that would get him through undergraduate school with any kind of a good grade, the Iowa Writer's Workshop. If you graduated from that particular program, you were instantly famous, published, recognized, and celebrated... or so it seemed. Alan spent most of his time in the library dawdling on the Internet and printing out copies of his manuscripts to send to publishers. No one seemed to ask him who he was or what he was doing there.

There was no metering or any kind of print counter on the printers, so Alan printed scores of his works and cover letters, and in the campus shop would buy envelopes and postage to markets. He dreamed of receiving checks in the mail, editors and publishers lauding him for his great work and what a contribution he was to The New Yorker, Paris Review, or The Atlantic Monthly. Alan dreamed of even having his name scrawled next to 'by' on the back of a greeting card at this point.

Leafing through a thick copy of the Writer's Market, Alan found almost thirty different publications that would be appropriate for some of his work. He felt nostalgic breathing the scent of library, and empowered as he stuffed the carefully worded manuscripts into large manila envelopes. He neatly wrote the return address; his mother's house on Cape Cod. Some day, he thought, not only will his work be forever displayed on a shelf for curious readers and scholars to pine over, discuss, and debate, but the radiating smell of indelible words on aging paper will be breathed in and become part of the living network of blood, tissue, and energy that powers the miraculous clockwork that is man. He will flow in a matrix of humanity, a scholastic Lazarus whose contributions to the greatest creatures in the universe will guarantee immortality.

But his goal those days was not just to waste a college's money that he never attended. He also researched the news on the Internet regarding developments in his next layover. He researched the disappearance of Hobbeston's wife.

As it turned out, there were no leads on the disappearance, and there was mention of a ransom note that suggested that the thieves wanted a grand sum of money. The date that the money needed to be given to insure the safe return of Hobbeston's wife was the second week of September. The fourteenth. It was confusing... Why would kidnappers want to hold someone for such a long time? With food, housing, the possibility of being outed. They could be caught in that time, they had to feed Hobbeston's wife, and historically if ransoms were paid at all, they were paid on the last day or later. This wasn't a very well thought out plan.

But neither was Alan's daily summertime visits to the campus library. After seven days of doing nothing but hanging out for the entire day on the Internet, printing countless pages on the school's paper on the school's printers, and living in the utter luxury of air-conditioned bliss, Alan was ejected by campus security after not being able to produce a student ID when he asked for more printer paper. They made him sign a paper that said he would never return.

Alan had found out some interesting things. One was that you could watch entire episodes of the Sacrosanctity Society on the Internet, and it was great considering the college had a high speed connection, and Alan had a pair of headphones and plenty of time. Oddly enough, the episodes that aired over the few weeks from when Mrs. Hobbeston disappeared leading up to the time Alan was watching them in the library, it was only reruns that ran and there was a new white trailer at the bottom. The words zooming by at the bottom of the frame were something along the lines of "We give thanks to all of our partners and friends in Jesus praying for the safe return of Margaret Hobbeston. Any leads to the story can be directed to the Federal Bureau of Investigations or any of the following telephone numbers... Prayer requests and donations are still being accepted on the Sacrosanctity Hotline 24 hours a day, seven days a week."

Another independent news station online reported the strange covering up of anything wrong over all avenues of the Christian media, including through the life of Hobbeston himself. There were a few canceled interviews, but for the most part they had already begun to tape new episodes of the Sacrosanctity Society, blatantly tiptoeing around the awful issue of his wife's disappearance. The particular news source he read most had an interesting commentary section; there were comments from readers that thought he very well may be guilty by not devoting all of his time to this, some thought he was keeping up his work to be brave, and some thought that if you believed in Jesus there was nothing to worry about.

Alan left and traveled to Indiana, Illinois, and Wisconsin, but was simply unimpressed in much the same way. The people were exactly what he thought he would find. Many were poor, unwilling to relocate and find work, and they all didn't like Alan. The only thing that Alan enjoyed about them was their unique accents that changed slightly every hundred kilometers. Their homes, cars, and everything else, just rotted, rotted, and rotted away. The states in the Midwest were one giant suburb. One giant suburb and one giant waste. What was coming from here, he wondered, what?

He stayed there for a shorter amount of time, and left the desolate and dreary Midwest. As he drove away, he was happy. Alan drove south following the same route he took north, but with a small detour east to remove himself from Missouri altogether and help himself get a good head start on the road to Vegas. He left enough of a detour to allow for some sight seeing. He started east again when he hit Oklahoma.

Alan was a great deal more impressed with Oklahoma than with its theatrical representation. He also was impressed that people were able to bite their tongue when he brought the musical up. The fields and fields of farmland was one of the most majestic things he had ever seen. Perfectly spaced rows of nature's production ready to be plucked and eaten right off of the plant. Alan had seen pictures that were taken from airplanes of this land, its glory reduced to squares and patches of a large quilt. It was even more beautiful here, on ground level.

Alan could see himself waking up every morning, and running. He could see himself owning a small house with a tremendous amount of land; he could wake up and take his dog out to play on the groomed grassy landscape. He could find a nice woman and make love to her under one of the giant trees on their property. They wouldn't have to worry about anyone seeing you because even the main road is kilometers away. He imagined feeling the rain beat you up, and then crying because there was nothing better than this. Nothing better than this lovely land that God made big and green just for him.

Alan passed through several towns on his way through Oklahoma without even realizing it. They just blurred by. But one of the first signs he did recognize was a town called Aline, Oklahoma. He was entering it just as dusk fully set in; the only lights illuminating the lonely highway were his own, and the orange crept over the lonely horizon. Alan was hungry, and he had decided that he would stop at the next eatery he came across. With all of the gas that he had bought on his venture north and the postage, Alan was depressingly already down almost three hundred dollars. It was time to be frugal again. At a rate of a hundred and fifty bucks a week, Alan would just make it to Vegas.

The dusty hatchback pulled up to an unnamed neon diner in Aline at eight thirty at night. It was one of the twenty-four hour joints, and Alan figured that he could hang out in the diner drinking all of the coffee that he wanted and write until he got tired. Pulling into the dimly lit parking lot, Alan figured that it seemed like a safe enough place for the night. When he was finished with his dinner, he could probably sleep until dawn without a hassle.

Alan entered as the door jingled a familiar bell, and it seemed like a busy night. Customers nonchalantly ate, some chatted softly. Everyone seemed polite, and the diner felt cozy. It smelled like must, bacon, and maple syrup. It was a nice place to be. Alan sat down at a booth and looked at a menu, the table and plastic coating on the menu were sticky, and he reconsidered going out to his car to fetch his computer. The napkin dispenser and the pen in his pocket would do just fine.

Alan studied the menu and looked at the variety they had. He wasn't used to wanting a variety, the desire for the Tuna Melt screamed at him. The menu almost jumped out of his hands, exclaiming "Do it, you idiot! You deserve this! It is only a tuna sandwich for crying out loud, why in the world can't you have it?" But alas, Alan had to settle for a patty melt. Much the same as a tuna melt, it was on rye with cheese and onions, but with red meat instead. Hamburger. Alan was all about trying new things, but he certainly did not like this idea one bit, but it was two dollars cheaper.

The older waitress approached him, and Alan ordered. Coffee was complimentary with any entrée at this eatery, so Alan was having coffee. As he sat waiting for his dinner, there was a loud eruption from the farthest corner of the restaurant. It was a small restaurant, and Alan tried to avoid his eyes as best he could while wanting to turn to keep an eye on the scuffle to avoid any projectiles. Alan couldn't translate what their argument was about considering they were talking so fast and all at the same time, but it was happening nonetheless. After a quick glance, he gathered it was a group of four men. They were all wearing baseball and trucker caps over long nappy black hair, and they all stood about two and a half meters tall, easily twenty stone each.

One of the men shouted swears in a southern drawl. The other men stood very close to him so that their noses were almost touching. They breathed at each other with flared nostrils. It looked stupid, but it must have been intense for them. They were either about to kiss or fight; Alan figured with their rotten breath, they weren't about to make out.

Alan's waitress approached them and told them to break it up. It seemed like she knew them because she was calling them by name… The man closest to Alan, Steve he thought he heard the waitress say, quickly stormed out of the diner. From the inside, Alan watched as the man got into his truck and started it up. As he was peeling out of the driveway, small pings and pangs of gravel hit the windows to the diner, and a yellow sack of potatoes looked as though it fell out of the bed of the truck and into the smoke it left behind.

"Holeeeeee shit, boys. That fucking asshole just bought himself a nice little present for him to find with his newspaper tomorrow morning." The ringleader of the opposing group remained indoors, and commented on his departure. Alan turned his gaze back into the diner as he said it, and the man started walking past Alan to the door at the opposite end of the diner. At the exit, he stopped and turned to Alan, his hand out to stop the other men following him. He started walking toward Alan, and Alan turned his gaze to his coffee on the table.

"What are you looking at, *faggot*?" Alan was right, his breath did smell. He looked down at Alan, his nostrils dilated to the size of large, round soup crackers.

"Well, I was looking at you and thinking about how sexy you are... You really are good looking... And I was wondering if you weren't doing anything – wait... why did you call me a faggot?" Alan wanted to say that... It would have been pretty funny... But he didn't. Instead he said, "watching you take care of that pussy," under his breath.

The other two with the guy laughed, exposing only enough teeth as they had fingers between them. The man himself turned around with a straight face and the other guys knew enough not to laugh. He looked back at Alan with red eyes.

"You better feel lucky that I have other shit to do than kick your sorry ass, you piece of shit."

Alan sat there and returned his gaze to the coffee until the men left the diner. Alan watched as they all stormed the parking lot, hovering around what fell out of the truck. It was moving. Alan hadn't realized it, but they were moving around what wasn't a sack of potatoes at all, but rather, a gaunt golden retriever struggling to stay on his feet. His coat was dusty and he was visibly hurt in one of his legs.

The main guy, wearing a flannel and an orange hunting cap, stepped on his leash that dangled loose from his neck. The dog struggled his head away from him without much difference. He pulled and pulled backward, the taut leash not giving way for an instant. At the same time, one of the other men wearing a sports baseball cap and what once was a white ribbed tank top, went to his car and returned. He retrieved an aluminum baseball bat with tape around the handle in one hand and a linked chain with briars on it in the other.

Knowing what was going to happen, Alan's stomach churned. He got up and ran to the counter. The waitress was taking his sandwich out of the window, and started to turn around.

"To go. Keep the change." Alan said, slapping a twenty dollar bill on the counter. He grabbed the greasy bag out of her hands, ran out to the parking lot, and jumped into the hatchback. He tossed the food in the back seat, and started the car up. The stereo was pounding.

Alan threw the car into reverse and slammed dust everywhere.

He was pointed toward the beat down defenseless animal, its audible screams tearing through Alan even though his stereo was turned all the way up shaking his mirrors throughout his field of vision.

He revved the measly engine, and a hand pulled a chain down toward the ground, hitting a living backbone, small needles tearing into flesh and fur. Blood spilled through a field of blonde and bone.

Alan hit the accelerator and tore through the parking lot just as the aluminum bat was raised. He was heading straight for the chain man on the left, and he did not let up. His car was the only thing that Alan had to defend the dog, smoky dust everywhere.

Alan missed the man, and the baseball bat was heard coming down onto the car. Glass and plastic broke and the definitive bang rattled the car. Alan pulled the emergency brake to try to spin the car around, but all it did was stop it in the gravel. In his rear view mirrors, he saw the two men approaching the car with a determined look on their faces, the other on the ground with his hand over his eyes. Alan was trying to disengage the brake as he saw the bat raised in the air again, and it slammed into the back window, shattering it to a million tempered pieces. It was raised again, and Alan did the first thing he could think of – slam the accelerator as hard as he could.

The dirt engulfed the air like ink poured into water. Alan could hear the bat hit the dirt, and coughing. The musty taste and smell of dry and sand clouded the air, and Alan took his foot off of the gas and got out of the car.

The dust was suffocating, and when it got in his eyes he focused only on what he heard. He swam though the cloudy air and could hear a huffy, different kind of cough. He found it. A dirty heap of hurt curled up like a lima bean in a sea of oatmeal. It wasn't moving. Alan reached down and wrapped his hands around the limp torso, lifting its dead weight. Alan was choking on the dust, and the animal easily weighed a hundred and fifty pounds. It might as well have been a sack of potatoes.

Alan carried it to his car, the dog's hips and hind legs dragging in the dirt. The dog moved, spinning around in Alan's arms, and it bit him on the face. Alan dropped the dog, and grabbed the leash, dragging him against his will toward the car. Alan grabbed his leash and pulled it into the car, then pulled his collar in, then pushed his rear-end in. He smelled. He was dirty.

Alan pulled his head back up to turn and get into the car himself, but he felt something hit the back of his head hard. The momentum pushed his face into the roof of the car. Rushes of energy shot down his back and into his arms, legs, fingers, and toes in waves and successions. Alan had a friend who played football that told him about these – shooters – and it wasn't pleasant at all. Alan fell in a heap onto the front seat of the car, and managed to push both of his feet into the chest of the man lunging at him. The man almost gained his footing, but just fell backward into the dirt. Alan couldn't tell which one it was. The music screamed.

He closed the door, and hit the gas again. He forgot the emergency brake was on, so he used all of his might to release it, and the car spun to life. In the rear view mirror, a pair of headlights emerged from the dust, and shook. They grew smaller as Alan sped away. They dimmed.

A moment of freedom and darkness. But the lights shook to life again. It was a red pickup truck, and it was closing fast on Alan.

Alan watched his rear view mirror and he pushed his accelerator hard as he could, the dog shivering on the seat beside him. There was no one else on the road going either direction, and Alan heard a bang. Looking in the mirror, there was another, sparks hurdling from a dark figure hanging out of the passenger window. Alan was being shot at.

"Fuck. Fuck, fuck, fuck. Why did I do this? Oh Fuck. Oh, god, please god, don't. I was doing something good. Don't let this happen, keep me safe. Please. Please please please. Oh FUCK!" Alan's hands were shaking on the steering wheel, and hit foot shook under him. His body pumped with adrenaline and fear. Alan didn't know why this was happening, and he doubted the men in the truck behind him did either.

Alan drove, and drove. The shooting stopped, but he kept his foot on the accelerator, the truck keeping a noticeable distance behind him. His heart pumped with more intensity than it ever had. Flight. Alan was running for his life. He stopped praying for salvation, but has since started talking to the dog.

"You know. I don't know why I did this for you. I don't know why you are so important to them. I definitely don't. I was being a good person, and now they want to kill me? Oh. Oh!" A shot rang, and the truck closed in. Alan was crying. He couldn't possibly go any faster! The car wouldn't go any faster! Oh, God, why don't you hear my call for help! Why? The truck closed within a meter from his bumper, but then it started to back down. It started to back down rapidly. Alan took his eyes off of the mirror just long enough to see another car approaching, passing him in the other direction.

The car passed, and he couldn't see the headlights behind him any longer. The truck disappeared from his rear view. But that didn't stop Alan. Alan kept driving. He kept driving, and driving, and driving. Alan would have guessed that the truck followed him and shot at him for an hour and a half, and yet he kept driving. Driving and driving, and driving. Dawn was impending when Alan took a right, and pulled over somewhere, and pushed his seat back, and fell asleep, drifting off to somewhere.

• • •

Alan woke up to a knock on the frame of the car near his window. Groggily he awoke, and remembered his car had less windows than yesterday. Instinctively, he whipped his hand around to the back seat and put his hand on his bag. It was there. He shot up, looked at the curled up dog next to him, and straight ahead. The morning light was harsh. Squinting, he noticed there was a red pickup truck directly in front of him. Fear surged in his abdomen.

Another knock, louder this time.

All Alan saw was a black stick sitting on the frame of the door.

"Son, you awake yet?" Alan looked out the window to a short, heavyset man in a green uniform with a dark green stripe running down the length of the sleeves of the short and legs of the trousers. "Son? You alright?"

"Yeah, uhh. Yeah, hi. What. I need to leave. The truck is…"

"Son, what are you talking about? Are you okay? The truck is what? I am officer Wight and that truck there is mine." Alan noticed a bar of lights on the roof he hadn't noticed the first time. "What are you doing?"

"I am… Driving. I just stopped to take a nap so I didn't fall asleep while I was driving."

"Son, you're looking pretty banged up and Cal MacArthur isn't really happy that you decided to park on his front lawn. So, why don't you step out of the car and talk to me and we'll get this figured out."

Alan half contemplated turning the key to his car and gunning it out of there. The odds were pretty good considering that they were in the middle of nowhere and that was probably the only cop in town who drove his own pickup truck. Instead, he opened the door and got out.

"First off, can I see some identification on you? Thanks. Now, I wouldn't have come over here for any reason had you just been sleeping on the side of the road, but truth is… Mr. Levy… Massachusetts? Truth is, Mr. Levy, with all of the terrorists going around and people on edge about things and everything, I have to investigate everything. Cal isn't about to press charges on account of his lawn, but…"

Alan looked behind his car. It had turned out that in the confusion of driving down a street and being neurotic and tired, and being shot at in the middle of the night… Well, he kind of forgot where the road was. Forgot by about a hundred meters. The cop had a point. This situation just didn't look quite right.

"Anyway, I have some questions for you… First of all, why are you parked on Cal's lawn sleeping?" Alan contemplated answering the officer truthfully, but he didn't feel like going into the details of last night's ordeal because it would open up a whole new aspect of needless conversation for this probably sixty year old man.

"Well, I told you, I was driving and I was tired, so pulled over to fall asleep. I am not really familiar to the area, so given the fact that there are no street lights and it was very late,…well, early… I don't know. I thought it was still the road."

"Where were you headed?"

"Well, I am going to… visit some relatives in Medford."

"Shouldn't you be farther north?" Alan held his breath until the cop responded. According to his map, in every U.S. state, it seemed as though there were several towns with names of cities in and around Boston. It was almost a sure bet to pick one. There was probably a Burlington, Clinton,

Quincy, and Canton if he mentioned it.

"See, I visited my dad in Florida, and-"

"Tell me... How long have you been driving like this?"

"Like what?"

"Well, you're missing a rear window and tail light. It looks like there are fresh dents everywhere... These stray shot holes. New. Were you in a gun battle, boy? You have weapons in the car?"

"No, and no. A branch fell on my car when I was in Missouri and I was waiting till I was in Medford to do the insurance stuff seeing as I would be out of a car for a couple days while it was fixed. It would just be easier there. The holes... Well. I don't know about any holes, but I don't really care. They have probably been there for a while."

"Well... Your story don't add up, but I trust you for some reason, kid. What's with the dog..."

"My dog? What about?"

"What's her name?"

Alan was at a loss. There was nothing he knew about the dog, and the condition he...well, somehow the cop knew it was a girl by a quick glance... she looked awful. What would he say? He looked around at the dog, but his eye caught a sticker on the bumper of the truck. "Celebrate Portsmouth. Two hundred years are *OK*." Witty. Cele!

"Her name is Cele..." It came out 'Sellah.'

"Cella? Like, 'my aunt Clara makes strawberry preserves in the *cella*. Boy, you are telling me the truth. You are from Massachusetts." The cop cocked his head in the window of the car and the dog miraculously looked up when she heard her new name. "God, son, she looks just as beat up as you... You beat your dog, son?"

"What kind of question is that? She's a sweetheart. She got into a fight with a bobcat." The cop considered what he just heard. Bobcat. Alan, you are a tool. The officer mouthed bobcat with a quizzical look on his face.

"I don't suppose you were beaten up by a bobcat, too?" he asked.

"No. Barfight. In Branson."

"Oh..." He paused for a moment, looked down at Alan's ID still in his hand, and continued. "Well, listen; I am going to take your information down. I believe you, but there's something about you that I feel isn't right. I'll fax it around the county, and if you do anything that is out of the ordinary... If an officer even needs to talk to you... you are going to be taken in and you'll be in a lot of trouble. I am also not supposed to let you go anywhere with your window like that, but you're only going to the next town over. Who are you visiting? I know just about everyone out here."

"Er... The... Johnsons?"

"Great family." Alan sighed in relief. He had never lied to an officer of the law before... Never really had to. But all he could think about is how stressful it was. "Small world. Well, have a good time son, and try to pull out the way you came in? I don't want Cal to change his mind about you. In fact, when you come back around here, I am sure he wouldn't turn down some of Mrs. Johnson's lovely apple turnovers."

"Sure... Sure."

"Take care. And get that window fixed and the tail light, will you? They'll have my head for letting you go if you get stopped again."

"Sure thing."

The cop made his way over to the door of his truck and got in. He flashed his lights and took great care in also managing to drive out the way Alan drove in. This was surely way too much stress for such a relaxed area, Alan thought. Everyone always talked about how courteous and kind and gentle the people of the south were. People always talked about how you shouldn't think they are dumb because they talk slower. Alan thinks that they are just out to get you. Out to get you all of the time.

Alan looked in the car, and the dog looked back at him. She was laying down, but she still managed to hang her head low and stare out of the top of her eyes as if she had done something wrong.

"You. You are a curse and a blessing. I could have gotten in a lot of trouble because of you, but you somehow got me out of it. Did we do anything, lady? No. But the suspicion was there and that is all that matters to cops, sometimes." Alan felt stupid addressing the dog, but she seemed to listen and stare back at him. She was interested, but she still looked like she did something wrong.

Alan opened the door to the car and as soon as he did, he saw the dog dart up and push herself into the seat and the door as firmly as she could. Afraid of something. Alan was puzzled. She let out soft whimpers at the very edge of speech. Alan sat, and turned the ignition to the car. It started up, but it looked like he was in desperate need of gas.

Alan held his hand out with his palm open to the dog, and a low moan escaped; almost a growl. It wasn't time to make friends, Alan thought. He would just drive with her and hopefully she would warm up to him. She has no one else, and Alan assumed that with her various wounds, she wouldn't make it on her own. Who knew what condition her legs were in considering the circumstances of falling out of a truck and getting mugged by a pack of trailer trash terrorists.

He pulled off the property, and pulled up to the road that he took to get to where he was - the one thing he could remember from the night before. He looked at his map. He calculated he was in the western part of the state. The sign at the end of the road read fifty one, and he was right according to his map. By his estimation, he had to go north until he just hit Kansas, and then head west through Colorado and Utah, finally running right into Nevada.

The destination and route was set. Two lonely creatures with running wounds accelerated on a lonely road, hoping to outrun their bruised hearts and weary souls. They were hoping to abandon them in the plains of Oklahoma.

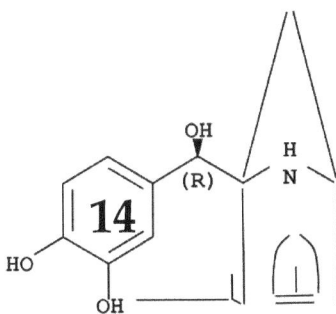

"...and of course it was no surprise that I had to leave. They were psycho, you know? Not to mention, the kid thought it made no difference whether or not he did the dishes. There would be a pan with eggs on it that he made, like, three weeks before, and it would sit in the sink for three weeks without him even touching it. It was no wonder that we were both getting colds all the time... I mean, even being in the kitchen..." Alan was shaking his head.

He looked over to the pooch sitting beside him and she looked back with the same degree of hesitation as before. Alan hadn't realized that all he needed in his life was someone to listen, and all of his stories of inattentive girlfriends and lame roommates were accepted with the same interest and dedication. The dog didn't understand a word he was saying, and yet it was immensely therapeutic just to have her there listening. Free therapy, and she never would tell Alan what he was going to do or where he was going was an unwise decision. She'd be there, with him. Eventually, there would be solidarity.

Alan thought back to the night before. He had forgotten, but in the midst of the drive away from Aline he shared his dinner with Sella while they were half asleep. He gave her half of his sandwich, and she hardly let his hand go near her face. She devoured the entire half in one bite, and was licking crumbs and grease off of the seat. Alan had offered her a few fries, and in doing so she would either bite the potato out of his hand so fast he was afraid of losing a finger, or, she would growl at the thought of a potato or a finger or a stick of anything even coming close to her.

She had her own wounds, and it seemed as though they were helping one another overcome them. He spoke to her as he drove on the highway out of Kansas and into Colorado. This was great, he thought. Absolutely great. Alan still had about a thousand dollars left, and he didn't feel the least bit threatened by his current condition. Driving was wonderful. This dog was wonderful. This dog was... Skinny.

Alan studied her, and hadn't realized it, but her skin hung off of malnourished bones. A brittle representation of her breed. Alan sunk in the seat and wondered how someone could have taken care of a dog in this manner. It was brutal - her scabs and her looks were temporary, but the wounds she would carry from here out were permanent. Alan felt his own bruise on his forehead from the frame of his door, and looked in the rear view mirror. A yellow and purple eggplant splotch rested on the forehead of a long-haired skeleton looking back at him. Alan held his hair back from his face.

"Who are you?" he whispered. His didn't recognize himself. His eyes were sunken and his skin was light, dry, and unkempt. When was the last time you were wet? Bathed with any conviction? Was it Virginia? No. Yes.... Alan thought of all of these things, and looked at the dusty dog next to him. When was the last time the dog went to the bathroom? Had water? Alan was living like a character in his own stories. Not only were the minute and mundane details of a man's daily life forgotten in them, but Alan was forgetting them himself. He hadn't even changed.

The wind, flowing in through the broken window of the hatch was wonderful. It whistled and flowed and felt comforting on the back of his sweaty neck. It was one reason that Alan forgot to do these things. The wonderful scenery was another. The drive to complete a mission... That was another. All these things. The wonderful journey. The journey to...

To where? People went on all kinds of journeys in their lives, for different reasons. Some are religious. Some are in the name of someone else. Others do it to gain something. Why was Alan doing it? He thought about it, and after about five minutes said aloud, "to see for myself how desperate the world is."

Sella's head popped up, and then she rested it back down on her paws. Alan was driving over a bridge, and under that bridge was water. Precious, life giving water. Clean water. They would go in that the water and bathe and shake and act like dogs.

Alan pulled around to a place to park on the side of the road. He didn't coax the dog out of the car, rather he left the door open for her to get out on her own accord. Alan made his way down to the river himself. It was in a valley, and the lush surroundings were not what he thought of when he thought Colorado. He always had the idea that it was a cold place year round where rich people went to ski.

The only thing cold was the water, and as he splashed in he opened his mouth and let the water flow in and out. The cool freshness was such a contrast to everything that he had lived. Sella slowly walked down the steep incline to the water, and looked at Alan, and at the water. She was reluctant. Alan had wished he named her that instead. Reluctance. That was unfair to her, though. She was hurt.

Alan watched as she stepped in. It was the first real movement he had seen since the episode in Oklahoma, and they have been driving for a couple days. She did get out of the car at a gas station to pee, but Alan wasn't paying attention to her gait at all to see if there was any bad damage.

She had a limp, and her coat was neatly streaked with brown... Her dried blood was the predominant part of her and if one had seen her from afar, they may have mistaken her for a rare breed of red on tan zebra. She limped herself in, and started to drink from the rushing tide. Alan had hoped that she would at least submerge herself somewhat so as to clean herself a little better. In a moment of inspiration, he waded over to the shoreline and retrieved a stick and threw it. All Sella did was look up at the stick he was about to throw, and when he threw it she bowed her head and took a few cowering steps away from the direction he threw it in.

She thought he was going to throw it at her.

Sella did bathe that day. The both of them did. Alan had originally worn his clothes into the water, but was stripping down as he felt they were getting clean. When Alan was completely naked, he walked over to Sella with his palms out in front of him, pushing an imaginary wall like a mime. She watched every move he made. He slowly put his hands out to offer nothing in front of her face. She smelled him.

Alan wasn't sure why, but the next thing she did was lick his hands, her raspy tongue scraping at his palms. She then put her face in the pillow of his palms, her muzzle pointed up to him. She nuzzled his hands like an actress would do in a mattress or pillow commercial. Sella exhibited the epitome of comfort. Contentment. The dog was Alan's. If she were human, she would have started to cry. Alan wanted to.

Alan ran his hand down her neck, her mane, her chest. The bones of her ribs and shoulders were chilling. Her flesh was furry rubber stretched to make a mechanical housing for a small, dehydrated drumming heart, dripping the blood it needed. Alan put his hand to his chest at that moment. He squinted at what he felt, and that was the same thing. The two pathetic and hurt and primal survivors rolled in the water, smooth rocks underfoot.

She stood her hind legs up, and Alan did his best to massage the pain out of her existence. He rubbed the dried blood out of her ear, he brushed it off of her backbone, and he lightly touched her flank, brown dry flakes falling into the current. Alan's hands looked like he had been gardening. He was only doing his best to sanitize. Fishing in the water, he cleaned her front paws, and washed her feet. Her left leg was damaged... She wouldn't really let him touch it, but it was apparent that there was something very wrong. Alan would wrap it in a tee shirt with a stick if he needed to - if she would let him.

They went up to the car, and in the windy hot summer air, they were able to dry off relatively easy without a towel. Alan had sneaked up to the car quickly and discreetly with his clothes in his hand, and grabbed a pair of boxers. The rest of the clothes would come, but first he placed the old clothes on the hood and the roof of the car to dry. It took no more than fifteen minutes. After that, they got in the car and drove off.

They were not traveling for more than ten minutes when Alan's phone rang, and he answered it.

"Hello?" a familiar voice on the line asked. Once more, he neglected screen the call.

"Hi, Mum. How are you?"

"I am good. How are you?"

"Good. What are you up to?"

"Well, this is a rather personal call, isn't it?"

"Huh?"

"Well, first you call me asking for my credit card number, and now you call me asking me how I am doing? What is to stop me from calling the police and turning you maniacs in? Huh?"

"Mum, you called me here. This is..."

"I did no such thing."

"This is your son, Alan."

"Right? Oh! Alan! Oh! How is your girlfriend?"

"Mum, I am... I don't have a girlfriend."

"Sure,... That is the same story. Alan, I want grand kids, and if I don't get grand kids I am going to fucking kill you."

"Mum?"

"No, Alan. No. I just. I want to have a full life, you know? I want to be full, Alan."

-Mum, have you been drinking? Have you been drinking and taking your pills? Do your doctors know this, Mum?

"Mum. Did you have anything to drink today?"

"Alan, don't start with this. I have a credit card guy breathing down my neck and I can't very well talk about this with you. And no, for your information, I have not. Besides, I am twenty-one. I can do whatever I want."

"That's good, Mum, and I don't mean to tell you what to do, bu-"

"NO YOU DON'T, ALAN. Jesus. Have you visited your father? When are you going to see him?"

"No, I can't. I am far away?"

"Well, if we stayed on Freeport Street, then we would have been okay. Now he is god knows where and you are a bastard son because of his floozies he is going around banging."

"Mum, he is in Fl-that is a different conversation. I am concerned about you, Mum. Are you taking care of yourself?"

"I am perfectly able, thank you, and don't try to change the subject..."

"Mum, it doesn't matter. That is all."

"I will tell you what matters. When are you coming to see me, huh? You are only a couple hours away, right? When aren't you working?"

"No, Mum. I was in Virginia when I talked to you last, and that was a month or so ago, remember? I am in Colorado now."

"Well, what in god's name are you doing out there? There aren't any nice Jewish Girls out there, are there? You know, Alan, I am really disappointed in you. You have never even dated a Jewish girl. If you only gave them a chance. I am telling you, they give great blow jobs, I hear - they do!"

Alan started to have a stomach ache. Not a sick one, nor a hungry one. One of the stomach aches you get when your heart feels like it is melting into it. Pouring hot molten blood into the pit of your stomach.

"Mum. Mum, are you okay?"

"Yes, I am fine. I don't need any more credit cards."

"Mum, it's Alan. You are talking to your son, Alan."

"A. d I am… you…always. Harassmen… tak-."

The line went dead and Alan didn't know where he was. While he was talking, and then after losing reception, he just kept driving. He spent the better part of the forty five minutes trying to call his Mum back. He just dialed and dialed without any regard for the bars on the phone that told him he had no reception. He pulled the car over and looked at the phone. There was nothing. Alan looked up for any sign as to where he was. He took a wrong turn somewhere, and he had no idea how this had happened.

He took out his auto club map and looked at it. He looked at the sign ahead of him that read "550." How did this happen? He was driving straight wasn't he? Back further, there was a bend in the road… Oh! Oh, no. Oh, what a waste. What an absolute waste. What a waste of time, and gas, and he had no extra money to blow on this idiocy.

Alan put the car back into drive, and started going straight until he could find a good place to turn around. He was looking at the map pressed against the steering wheel, and glancing at it occasionally. There was a berth in the road ahead, enough space for him to turn.

A sign read "Entering Purgatory."

"FUCK!"

He was lost.

• • •

At three in the morning it was no surprise that the giant ValuMart remained an empty library of American over consumption. It was a giant corporation that paid people half of the cost of living, and only provided them with enough hours so they could get away without giving them benefits. They were bloodthirsty and out for their own agenda, attacking art as if it were a deadly retail cancer by editing the books and compact discs it sold. If it was not in the bible, it evidently wasn't meant to be read or heard.

Apparently they didn't study the bible that well.

In any event, Alan wandered the desolate halls of merchandise in search of goods that would fill his belly and provide nourishment for himself and Sella. He carried a basket filled with a few small pouches of dog food, three litres of spring water, a few two-for-a-dollar sticky buns, some granola bars, and a package of road flares. He continued about the store looking for items of value on his journey. The store had to be a square kilometer, full of stuff that he absolutely did not need. Did anyone? Water, water everywhere, but not a drop to drink.

Alan turned a corner and was met with a wall of vacuums. Another corner brought him to magazines, and another brought him to blenders. One wall had rifles and another had darts. Alan stopped at the rifles, arranged in plastic sleeves on hooks. You could just walk up and buy them. Take them off of the hook, bring the gun to the counter and buy it. A gun. With bullets. Alan ran his hand down the smooth clear plastic. Its packaging offered an array of features and all of the practical uses almost invited Alan to a splurge purchase. He was on the open road, after all. Shouldn't he have some level of protection?

And then he had the epiphany. You could walk in to a ValuMart and buy something which only had one very simple mechanical desire: to kill. Simple as that. Or practice on targets in innocent sport, to see how good your killing ability is. Sure, there were knives and hammers and just about every Poirotian murder mechanism, but these guns had only one intentional job while everything else was simply a possible bystander in a murderous plot. But music? No. That had to be edited before it could be consumed by the American public, because who knows what someone would go out and do if they heard a swear or were offered a contrast to their religious beliefs or heard someone speaking their minds about authority. Speaking their minds about retail chains that ruined small businesses trying to make it and ruined the eroding lives of the senior citizens they employed in droves and made pray before the store opened everyday. They might go shoot someone!

No, they certainly wouldn't sell that album, but guns. They sold plenty of those and it made perfect sense that they edit the music and books or sell only selective video games. Because guns didn't kill people. The brainwashing of our youth did, and just by buying the wrong album or book or video game for your children would have a devastating effect on their development only after as little as ten minutes! That is right! A semi automatic weapon instantly materializes in their hands and they develop in a matter of minutes a psychotic mental condition that would take the normal child years to develop in bad parenting through abuse, neglect, or bizarre religious fundamentalism. They become a killing machine.

Alan turned another corner in the store toward the back. As he strolled, he came upon a man in conservative business attire sleeping on a mattress in a sea of beds. He looked sharp, and if it weren't for his location and his rosy cheeks, one would mistaken him for dead in his pressed suit and peaceful recline. Or a mannequin. He was just sleeping there, at three in the morning. Alan had wondered if anyone in the store had seen him there. The track record for ValuMart would easily suggest that if you sat in a chair for too long, or had a camera with you to make sure you are buying the right videocassette or film, or even tried out a bed before you bought it, you would be ejected. You are welcome to come spend your money, but don't take any pictures or try anything before you bought it. In that case, we don't want you here at all. Or your money. Ever.

What was strange about what Alan saw was the contrast of his black suit in the bedding landscape. The simple fact was, he wasn't just trying out the mattress, he was blatantly sleeping. Alan walked closer. He looked peaceful and happy. He was comfortable. So as not to wake him, Alan would have to tiptoe by so as not to disturb him. But, he soon learned that he wouldn't have to...

Out of the corner of his eye, an army of mauve smocked ValuMart employees marched down the aisle toward the bedding section. Alan watched as the manager (or so he seemed by his lack of smock, shirt and tie, and his apparent alpha-wolf attitude as the rest of the pack drifted behind him) walked up to the bed and started to shout in his most intense voice, which resembled a flamboyant upper-class dress socks salesman.

"Mr. Carson, you have to leave. The authorities are on their way," he said. Carson opened his eyes, sat up, and started his way down the aisles. There was no fight, or complaint. It was bizarrely routine. He was heading toward the direction Alan remembered the entrance to be. An entourage of mauve smocked employees escorted him away from the bedding section, and that was that.

The scope of the whole situation was interesting. A man slept in the bedding section of a popular, conservative department store, the staff of the store congregated to eject him, and then proceeded to do so after calling him by name. Not only that, but it was all done in a fashion that was interestingly fluid and routine. They have all done this before, haven't they? Might as well make it easier on yourself.

Alan made his way to the front of the store with his basket, almost running to catch up with the scene. He got to the rows of empty, unused counters, and paid for his merchandise. It was a lot less than he had originally thought, and looking at his receipt on his way out the door, it said he was in Cortez, Colorado. He only saw two things in the desolate parking lot. One was his beat up car with an obedient pooch in the front seat, and another sports car, black, with the four or five of the ValuMart worker people huddled around it. The manager was still shouting at the man in the car, and he was brushing it off. He started to pull away for a few centimeters, but the employees kept standing and moving in front of his car. He would hit the brakes again.

Alan quickly walked over to his car, opened the door, and sat down. Sella looked at him. Alan opened up the bag and took out two of the sticky buns and opened them. He fed one to Sella, and the other he munched on himself. The ratty processed dough tasted good, and Alan and Sella watched the strange events outside the car as they ate. Without hesitation this time, the car sped off and the small crowd beside it stepped back in offense. Alan turned the car on and looked at Sella who looked up from licking the cellophane wrapper from the sticky bun.

"Ready for an adventure?" Alan asked.

"I don't understand a word of English..." She replied.

They followed the black sports car for about ten minutes until it pulled into an upscale hotel. Alan parked on the far end of the well-maintained and well-lit parking lot, and watched as the man in the suit got out of the car without any luggage and made his way indoors. The hotel's main lobby, and almost the entirety of the first floor of the hotel was sleek and glass. Alan could see everything in the main lobby. It looked as though the man bypassed the front desk, and made his way straight to the elevators. Curious.

Alan continued to watch the hotel, and felt drowsy. He drank a few gulps of water from the jug, and then poured some of the water an old empty soft drink cup and let Sella lick it out, her muzzle tightly stuffed in the plastic container. As Alan fell asleep in the parking lot of the hotel, he smelled stale fast food and body odor.

• • •

Alan woke up to the sound of a rig making a delivery to the side of the building. The sports car was gone. Alan was going to go into the hotel to ask for directions to the nearest library. He wasn't sure why, but he felt obligated to stick around this small, hot city after the events of the previous night. Feeling his way around the tight cabin of the car, Alan opened the passenger side door and Sella got out. She walked over to the bushes and started to sniff around. Alan got out into the hot atmosphere of the parking lot and made his way to the lobby of the hotel.

He went through the revolving door, and his sneakers squeaked on the marble tiled floor. The air was shockingly cool and carried the light smell of pool chlorine. The building was cool and smelled clean. Alan started walking directly to the far end of the lobby.

"Can I help you?" a voice demanded from the desk. It was implied that he was really demanding to know what your business was there without being rude. That always used to happen to Alan when he was in high school in Boston and he and his peer corporate vigilantes walked around the Sacks Fifth Avenue and Neiman Marcus in Copley Square and knocked over a huge rack of clothes and made a giant mess as soon as someone asked if they could help them. It was their game, and it was also their statement.

"Uh, yeah… I was actually going to visit my friend Carson's room…"

"He is out right now. Is there anything I can help you with? What's your name, I can take a message."

"That won't be necessary."

Alan turned around and made his way out of the lobby. The wind and heat slapped him in the face as soon as the revolving door stopped spinning. Sella was back in the car and Alan closed her door. Obviously the people at this hotel knew Carson pretty well. Alan was going to stay in town and go to ValuMart and see if he showed up at all again. If the people were as rehearsed in kicking him out as it seemed they were, it would be silly not to assume that he would be there again tonight.

Alan spent the rest of his day at the public library on the Internet researching the story about Hobbeston's wife. It turned out there weren't any developments, and they are yet to figure out who the group was that took his wife and why. On the discussion board on the news website he was reading, the majority of the people commenting had a conspiracy theory or two, while others just had a comment about how brilliant these kidnappers were. Why would anyone kidnap the son or daughter or wife of a quasi-celebrity suburbanite that probably had little money, when you could kidnap a relative of a really rich person? A television evangelist... Hadn't been done, but the kidnappers were really smart, not to mention the fact that Hobbeston probably had a pretty plump insurance policy on his wife and if anything happened to her he would probably be doing fantastic for himself.

By seven that night, the library closed and Alan was starving. Alan drove to the ValuMart and went in to buy himself and Sella a real dinner. He bought a pre-cooked rotisserie chicken and brought it out to the car. In the lid of the plastic container it came in, he picked the meat off of half of the carcass and fed it to the hungry dog. She ate it slow and delicately, as if she was savoring every bite. It was strange to see a dog behave like that. Alan was the exact opposite, tearing the carcass apart with his fingers and teeth; drool and oil dripping from his chin.

Alan took the top of the container back from Sella, filled it with water, placed it in the foot well in front of the seat, and made his way back into the ValuMart. There were a lot of people in the ValuMart this time as opposed to when he was there the night before. The back-to-school section was drowned and inundated with carts and bodies. People fought over binders and pens and books; they worked quickly like bees so as to make sure there was enough for them. That was the new mantra of our world; not "America: Happiness Is Enough For Me," but rather "America: Enough Is Happiness For Me." And that was the problem: no one ever had enough. Alan took out his little black book and wrote that down.

He took about fifteen minutes finding the bedding section, dodging heavy women and heavier men pushing their carts through the high-towering aisles of excessive living and material escape. He pushed through power tools and tires, clothes and fabric, soft drinks and soft pillows. There was just so much stuff in this building, it was ridiculous. He found it.

Beds and beds and beds in rows of white clouds waiting for someone to purchase them. It was a soft, plush sea packed close together for inspection. There had to be at least fifty or a hundred there. Alan sat on the first bed he came to. It was a full size, good for kids it said, and it felt as hard as a rock. He tried the next, and the next. He needed something to do to occupy his time, and there was no sign of Carson. Alan took a walk to find the book section.

There was a small collection of books on the wall of 'literature' that didn't have something to do with the end of the world or Christianity or Jesus or God. They had a small collection of real books that one could buy at any given bookstore, so Alan picked up one about bees and went back to the bed section. Laying on another bed, an associate approached him and asked if there was any help he needed. Alan just replied that he was testing out the beds and may be there for a while. It seemed to be the right thing to say as the associate just turned around and left again, adding that if he did need any help that he would be in furnishings and to just press the red button on the phone on the pole in the middle of the bedding section to page him.

Alan read a chapter and then changed beds, read a chapter and changed beds, and read another, and changed beds. He was really enjoying the book. It was about a girl in the south during the civil rights movement who runs away from home with her black nanny and ends up at a honey farm that her dead mother had apparently visited. There were religious undertones to the book, but the book found a beautiful balance of secular and mystical.

Alan finished it, and thought it was wonderful and painful. It was exactly what Alan had wished he had written himself. Meanwhile, there was still no sign of Carson. Alan stood and returned his book to the reading section and then perused the magazines. Most of them had to do with homemaking or celebrity or hunting or wrestling or sports or cars. The ridiculous violent and homosexual undertones to the world of conservative life was puzzling to Alan. Why make the things you are interested one big double entendre for the things you despise? He picked up the only copy of the New Yorker, wondering how it got there in the first place, and made his way back toward the bedding section.

Grabbing a coke out of one of the many fridges scattered in the store, he noticed Carson laying on one of the beds from afar. Alan hadn't even reached the section and somehow this man was already asleep, as if he materialized out of the ether just to sleep in the ValuMart bedding section. This place, this town, this earth was so very strange.

Alan walked up to the bed and stood behind the man. He was tall, as far as Alan could tell. He was wearing the very same suit, and up close it looked brand new. His black hair was styled slick toward the back, but it actually looked hip on him as opposed to cheap and greasy. A swift breeze was hammering down on the man and Alan from the high ceiling, and it was apparent that an air vent was directly above them. Alan had no idea how to first communicate with this person. They were strangers, and one of the strangers was sleeping. In a bed. In a department store. He was certain Emily Post never covered this in her work.

For the most part, Alan was a shy man. He had trouble meeting girls and opening up conversations and starting things off. In this instance, it was even worse. This was a man that he had never met before, but he felt that he had to. This man had a penchant for getting kicked out of department stores, and he dressed nice and drove a nice car. For all Alan knew, he could be the stock broker killer... A man that sets up a gorgeous portfolio with someone's life savings, gets them to sign their account over to him, lures them to a big box big value department store, and then kills them.

"Carson?" Alan said, figuring that he had no money to invest anyway.

The huddled body nudged.

"Shhhhh-hh. Sh." It responded.

Alan sat on the adjacent bed, facing Carson's back.

"Carson."

He mumbled again in whisper, something that sounded like 'mother' or 'mothra.' In any case, he continued and it sounded a lot more like a response…

"It isn't time to go." This was plain as day. He sounded like a computer when he said it.

"I am not kicking you out. My name is Alan… I want to talk to you."

A long winded sigh emerged from the mass on the bed. He began to roll over, and he spoke as he did.

"I don't care about your image or your profit loss percentage. I don't want your bed. I just want-" He stopped short when he saw Alan; A skinny white man in his twenties wearing a rock tee shirt and jeans. Not a man in a suit or a smock yelling at him. Just a guy.

Alan studied Carson. He had the brightest blue eyes that he had ever seen. Like the sky. Alan almost thought he saw clouds blow by in them. His suit, something he couldn't take his mind off of, was neat. It looked as though it was made specifically so he could sleep in it, and yet it wasn't wrinkled or disheveled. It was perfect. Alan remembered why he thought he looked like he was dead. Dead at his wake.

"Why are you here?" Alan asked him.

"That is the question I wanted an answer to my whole life. Why are you here?"

"I am here because I want to know why you are here."

Carson paused. He looked at Alan and rolled over again so his back was facing him.

"Goodbye." He said.

Alan watched him. Even though he was being invaded and his personal space and time and sleep was being invaded, he fell back asleep. He was oblivious to Alan being there, to shoppers being there, and everything else. Just like that, in the middle of a ValuMart in western Colorado.

Alan lay down himself in the bed next to Carson, and watched his back for a half an hour. He watched his breathing. He watched as dust bunnies in the air seemed to waft nowhere near his suit, almost divinely keeping it from getting dirty. He watched as he felt himself get tired. He watched as he closed his eyes and drifted. Just like that, one bed over from a stranger in the middle of a ValuMart in western Colorado.

• • •

A hand reached down and snatched up Alan's arm. Confusion ricocheted around his head as he was brought upright and started walking amidst a circle of yelling voices. The only familiar one to him was Carson's amidst it all.

"Carson, you can't come back, we told you that." One voice said.

"Oh, poor bears!" Carson replied.

"...costing us business. We aren't a motel. There is a hotel right up the street, you understand?" another voice shouted.

"Oh, poor, poor bears" Carson replied again.

Alan's arm was being tugged and he was struggling to even stay upright. In the middle of the ValuMart he was being dragged, a throng of smocked employees drifting behind them shouting. They blew through the front door, and their cars were once again the only ones in the parking lot.

As if there was a way, Carson threw Alan's arm in the direction of his tiny blue hatchback, and somehow it worked toward getting him to stumble over in that direction. It worked so well that he stumbled to a good halfway point away from the confusion, just far enough to not have time to catch up with Carson. Carson stepped into his sports car, and without any hesitation it was running and he began to drive away slowly, the smocked employees parted, and then sped off.

Alan ran to his car and jumped in. It hesitated for a moment, but then caught a wind of power and started up. Sella looked over at him, and lay down on the seat with a sigh. Alan hit the gas and sped out of the parking lot just as Carson did, but hardly catching up. Up ahead, the sports car turned a right around the corner just as it had the night before. He was going to the hotel.

Alan had spent the next five minutes speeding through the streets, only a block or two behind Carson. He swung a left into the parking lot of the hotel, and was getting out as Alan pulled in to the parking lot and swung the car toward Carson. He stepped back against his car as if he was going to get hit. Alan pulled into the spot next to the sports car, shut the car off, opened his door, and got out.

"Why are you here?" Carson asked.

"I just want to talk to you... That's all."

Carson paused. He looked at Alan as if he was crazy. He was, but he surely wasn't as crazy as he looked at this exact moment. He was only maybe a quarter as crazy as he looked. The light from the spotlight illuminating the parking lot cast a luminescence on Carson that made him look as though he was a character in a film noir.

"Is that a dog?" Carson asked, pointing to the passenger seat of the car.

"Yeah. Her name is Sella."

Carson stared at the dog. He looked like he was about to start crying. He compassionately gazed at the skinny pooch. Alan would have given anything to know what he was thinking. What was he thinking while he looked at the dog? What was he thinking all curled up, sleeping in ValuMart?

"I haven't seen a dog in so long. Is she friendly?"

"She is just as friendly as she is hungry... So far, she has been hungry all the time, so it works out pretty well." Carson looked back up to Alan.

"Come on up. Bring the dog. You both look like you could use a hot shower."

They walked into the hotel, right past the front desk. The concierge looked like she wanted to yell about the dog, but resisted because of Carson. They took the elevator to the top floor, and got out in a long hallway with only four doors. Carson walked all the way down to the last door on the right, a big oaky number with gold trim and an ornate handle. A placard on the door read "M. Carson" in calligraphy.

The three walked in. They passed the bathroom, and Sella and Alan surveyed their surroundings. The suite had high ceilings and at least four or five rooms. Alan had no idea that hotels had apartment-sized suites, and this one, with a dining room, and two bedrooms was glorious. It was magnificent.

"This place is nice…" Alan said.

"Yeah, and it is pretty cheap considering I have a maid and all of my toiletries and amenities are taken care of."

"You live here?"

"Sure." The nonchalant attitude in his voice was strange.

"How much do you pay?"

"Monthly? It goes for about four a month…"

"Four?"

"Grand." He left the living room as soon as he said it.

It was no surprise that the place went for four a month. It looked like it, felt like it, and its total upper class attitude radiated 'four' a month. Why would someone allow me in here, Alan thought. I look like a street person, mangy and thin. I smell. Did this man realize he was taking a chance?

On second look, however, the room was empty aside from the provided amenities. It looked as though there was nothing for Alan to steal, even if he wanted to steal something. Who was this man? A shadow. He can afford to live in a hotel, but doesn't own a thing? He had everything, but hardly had anything? Why would he sleep in a ValuMart if he had such a nice place to sleep?

Carson returned to the room with a silk robe over his arm and a hand holding two tumblers of a whiskey-looking beverage. Okay. Alan got it. He was seducing him… He was seducing the…young…gaunt…homeless…dirty…smelly young man…and his dog?

"Here. I am going to go down to your car and take your clothes, and I am going to take these, and I am going to get them washed. Get in the shower and drink this. It will make you feel good…"

"What is it?" Alan asked as he took the robe and the glass.

"Benedictine and Brandy, a nighttime favorite of mine." Alan took a sip. The liquor was sweet and soft going down his throat. It tasted like scotch, but also like cotton candy. It was delicious. Alan had remembered it being in bars but never ordering it. A good sized bottle of it went for eighty dollars.

Alan handed Carson his keys, and he disappeared out of the room. Sella sat at Alan's feet for the whole show. Alan turned around to go into the bathroom. The door was open, and Alan went inside. There were about six dimmer switches on the wall. Alan turned them all up, one by one. There was a hot red light, track lights, and other lights in the wall that pointed up for no reason but to have some sexy light.

The bathroom was gorgeous. There was a giant bathtub, an open-air shower with two heads that had a frosted-glass partition to the rest of the room, and mirrors all over the place. The only thing that was missing was any evidence that a human being had been living there for any period of time. The towels were neatly folded, the soaps were wrapped in paper, and the only thing in the room that may have been added by Carson was a bottle of Paul Sebastian cologne next to the sink.

Alan drew a bath for Sella, and turned the shower on. The room was immediately steamy as there were no windows or ventilation; Alan remedied it by finding the dimmer for the fan. The water felt magnificent to the two of them. Considering that the last time they bathed was in the cold creek, this was heavenly. They were truly happy and comfortable in the water. With fresh soap, a razor, and towels, they were new. They were clean.

As Alan washed Sella, he noticed a lot of her wounds were healed up. As far as he could see, anyway. She was still ridiculously skinny, but it made no difference. She was clean. Clean and happy. They finished bathing, and they dried out. Alan hadn't realized it, but they were in the bathroom for over an hour.

Leaving the bathroom, Alan saw Carson standing by the bed. All of Alan's clothes were on the bed; clean and neatly pressed. He looked up to Carson.

"Thanks... Wow." Alan said.

"You're clean, your clothes are clean, your dog is clean. Now we have to talk."

"Great." He was trying to seduce him.

"Only one thing. You have to come with me..."

"Where?" Or was it murder him?

"To work."

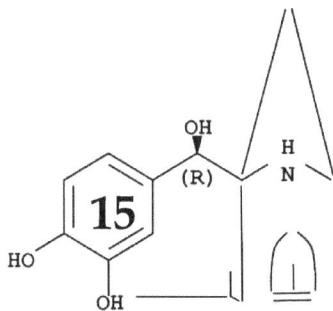

Alan had never been in a sports car, nor had he ridden over a hundred kilometers an hour in any kid of vehicle besides a plane. This was an interesting man. He had no concept of anything. He could have been pulled over and arrested for speeding and everything else, but somehow he couldn't grasp that. Either that, or he didn't care. They drove at a hundred and fifty kilometers an hour for at least twenty minutes… Alan had no idea where they were.

Carson worked in an office that was empty aside from the main room in the back that they were sitting in that had a huge oak desk, a filing cabinet, and some nice big oak bookcases with nothing on them. There were also some expensive looking leather seats. The rest of the large office really nothing in it. It looked like a dentist's office, without any…stuff. No furniture in the waiting room, no desk or files or shelves in the receptionist's area, not a thing in any of the empty rooms that would have the dentist chairs in them.

The first phone call at Carson's work came at four thirty in the morning.

Carson was talking really fast about numbers and figures. It made no real sense, but it seemed important to him and the person on the other end of the line. Without any hesitation, he ended the conversation by telling them that they would talk about it when the market opened. That is when he would have a better idea about what was going on.

"So, what do you want to know?" Carson asked.

"Who are you?"

"My name is Michael Carson. I was born in New York City. I go there by private jet every day and return to various places around the country every night. I have been coming here to Colorado every night for the past year or so, however. I am not sure why. I can usually do my business by phone or Internet. That is the beauty of my job… That I can take some time off whenever I want, do my job wherever I want. I can do whatever I want.

"I trade my stocks for a living. When I graduated high school, my dad gave me five hundred bucks. I decided to invest it instead of going to college, and now I have a lot more money. Plain and simple."

"How much is a lot more?"

"I have about... oh... a hundred and fifty million in accounts and stocks altogether."

"Oh my god." Alan looked at Carson, expecting a reaction, but Carson just remained still. "So, you fly from here to New York? Why don't you just live in New York?"

"It's just too much."

"...Do you go to ValuMart every night?"

"Just about, yeah."

"And you get kicked out-"

"Every night."

"Why do you do it?"

"I am not entirely sure. I go, and I feel comfortable all of a sudden. I feel like I belong, and I feel like I am okay to fall asleep. I feel like someone is watching me and it makes me feel safe, I suppose. You probably think that is strange."

"Do you have any relatives or anything?" Alan wanted to say, 'yeah, but only because you have all the money in the world.'

"No... They all died. Its just me."

"No friends or anything?"

"I really don't have time for it. Here's my day... I wake up at ValuMart when they kick me out. Then I go to the hotel and put a new suit on. I go to the airport and make it to New York by six or seven usually after they get my plane ready and I fly over there. I work until six or seven, fly back, and by then, we're talking eleven or midnight."

"Why do you keep working? I mean, with the money? I would stop at a million and probably be able to live the rest of my life." Alan was surprised by the absurdity of a man working so hard and not having anyone to inherit his trust or anything. He was surprised at the absurdity of having his own nonsense plan of a nonsense future and sharing it with this man who doesn't know him. It felt rude.

"I don't know why. I don't know. I really don't know why I just don't live in New York. I don't know why I don't sleep at the hotel I am paying so much for. I don't know why I go to ValuMart. I really don't know why I am doing any of this. It is just something to do."

And Alan supposed we all needed something to do. He watched as Carson feverishly made calls for the next few hours. He talked and talked and called and called and he worked so hard. For money that he didn't need. It was almost as though making money was his hobby, and he was very, very good at it. Alan had almost for a moment wished that he was a relative of Carson's. He would give him a lecture about how communism could really work in certain circumstances, and then Carson would cut him a check for forty thousand bucks to pay for college, and that would be that.

"Okay..." Carson said as he hung up the phone. He looked at Alan devilishly. "I have to go to New York anyway. Do you want to come?"

He picked up the receiver and dialed a number.

"Umm... No. No, I'm okay. I came so far."

"Actually this works out. We can drive to the airport and you can drive my car back. I can give you a call when I get back and you can come pick me up."

"Oh. Man, I can't... You want me to drive your car?"

"Yeah. Oh, it's no big deal, really. You can drive a standard, right?"

"Sure, but-"

"Then it's settled." Carson paused, pressed a button on the phone and a line opened, and he began to talk looking above Alan's head. "Hey Ronnie B! What's happening?... Good, good. Listen, I'm running a bit late today, but I am definitely heading out. Sure, sure. Okay, see you in five."

They went back downstairs, and the Colorado sun was just stretching above the fertile horizon on all sides of the plain brick office building. The sky was crisp and the clouds were clear; chiseled by hand. A larger influx of cars dotted the parking lot I the morning, as opposed to the zero that was there when they first pulled in.

They drove to the airport. It was a small municipal number - very similar to the one that Alan remembered from Chapmansville. Small single and double engine planes were scattered about the well-groomed airfield. There were three landing strips, two parallel ones, and one that slashed diagonally through the two.

They drove down to the airport and onto the tarmac without hesitation. The car pulled up to a large hanger where a shiny white Learjet was being towed out. It stopped, and a man in a very naval-militaristic uniform appeared out of the hanger with a hand-held box and an awake and happy attitude. He began tapping the box with a stylus as they got out of the car and walked over.

"Goooooood morning, Captain." The captain Carson was addressing looked up, and his face brightened when he made eye-contact with Carson.

"Good morning Michael. Is this a gorgeous day or what? Perfect for flying!"

"Sure is. This is my friend Alan. Alan, this is Captain Lindberg."

"Lindberg, huh?" Alan said as he shook the captain's free hand. "Was it almost predisposed that you become a pilot?"

"Actually, it seems that way, huh? My fathers name was Charles, in fact. He was a lawyer, though."

"Funny..." Alan replied. It seemed appropriate, but the men ignored him.

"This is a smart kid, isn't he? What's he even talking about?" Carson asked the pilot.

"Lindberg, Michel? Come on..." The pilot said. The quizzical face on the multimillionaire was rather depressing. Money didn't always mean brains... He looked smart, Alan thought. "He was the first... Wait, why am I even telling you this? Look it up... right, Alan?"

"Yeah!" Alan replied. Carson let out a hearty, inappropriately boisterous laugh.

"Always bustin' my balls, aren't ya' Cap?" Carson replied. He slapped the Captain on the shoulder, which prompted him to look at his shoulder in both an 'ouch' and 'what did you get on me?' way.

"Well, it looks like I just need to do a few more checks on our baby and I will think we'll be ready to go in fifteen?" Mark looked back down at the box and hit a few more things. On closer inspection, it carried the Learjet logo and it was a handheld computer. It was probably a wireless diagnostics tool for the plane. On closer further inspection, Alan thought, that is really, really cool.

"Excellent. Alan, want a tour of the plane?"

"Sure."

Alan had never been on a personal luxury aircraft, but upon entering this one, he instantly knew why people got them. It was a great deal nicer than most apartments and houses he had ever been in. It smelled like a batch of towels just out of the packaging; fresh, musty, clean, and new-plastic, in a pleasant way. He immediately wished that they would manufacture one of those little trees that would sit next to the 'new car smell' one on the rack. 'New plane smell.'

The plush beige upholstery on the floor was soft, and Alan almost didn't want step on it because it felt so lovely. The carpeting that was clean and made Alan think about eating cookies and falling asleep on the carpeting of his bedroom in Boston when he was little. A large plasma television was on at the front of the cabin piping financial news and stock quotes from a talking head. The seats were leather, and looked comfortable enough that they would actually provide a good night's sleep.

A gorgeous blond in a tight, revealing outfit walked into the cabin and placed a martini on a table that had two of the leather chairs facing it. She was older than Alan, but she was absolutely gorgeous. Between her tight body and the lovely outfit Alan was jealous of Carson, and wondered what services Carson was able to talk her into fourteen thousand meters above the Earth.

"Helena! How are you, sweetheart?" When Carson said her name, her face lit up with perkiness and sexuality. The air was thick with hormones.

"Great, Michael! Does your friend want a drink?"

"Alan, a martini?" Alan contemplated the idea of a potent drink like a martini at around eight or nine in the morning, and decided against it. Besides, he wasn't sure how soon Carson would hand the keys to the car over.

"Noooooo, no thank you." Was he being rude?

"Well, here's to prosperity!" Carson said, looking between Alan and Helena several times as he tossed the beverage back. Helena grabbed the glass and walked between them into the back of the aircraft. Carson whispered to Alan, "she's a firecracker, isn't she?"

"Oh, yeah," Alan said in a breathy fashion.

"Come on, you have got to see this." Carson walked Alan to the cockpit. All of the dials and controls looked brand new and futuristic. All black and several computer screens wrapped around two cockpit seats. It was glorious and new.

"I have been taking flight lessons so that I can get my license and learn to fly this thing, too. It's awesome, isn't it? I figure I paid a good chuck of cash for it, I might as well learn how to use it."

"It's the best, Carson, really."

"Why do you keep calling me that? You're my friend, right? Call me Michael."

"Okay. I guess that is the first name I heard, so it stuck."

Carson looked at him with a confused smile and a tilted head. He reached into his pocket and fished around. He produced a shiny thick key ring that only had three keys on it and one chrome keychain that simply said *Let age approve of youth, and death complete the same, R.B.* on one side, and *for M. C.* on the other.

"Here's my keys... If you need to go and take a nap and whatever and my place, they shouldn't give you trouble this time. Besides, your dog is up there and everything and you'll probably need to take her for a walk. If they need to call me to let you in, just tell them to, but considering they already saw you with me, it shouldn't be a big deal."

"Okay."

"Alright. Hit the road. What's the number for your cell?" Carson produced a pad of paper, where Alan wrote down his phone number and turned around to leave. He descended the stairs leading onto the tarmac, and proceeded to the sports car. Alan just leaned against the car as he watched the pilot enter and Carson pull up the stairs leading into the cabin. It looked as though they were preparing to leave, so Alan decided to wait to watch them take off. A small fat car with only an open-air driver's seat tugged the front wheel of the plane onto the landing strip, and the engine roared to life.

Not a minute later, the craft slowly drove itself off toward the furthest point of the runway. It rumbled for a moment. Then, it careened down the strip with amazing speed and deliberate grace. It didn't need very much of the tarmac as its front and rear wheels lifted off of the ground easily at the halfway point on the runway. Just like that, Carson was headed for New York and Alan leaned on a sports car that was worth more than he had made in his entire life.

The car that smelled like fresh upholstery and shampooed carpeting when he got in. The odometer read only four thousand, three hundred, and ninety seven kilometers. It was practically brand new and there was no reason that the car was so sparse on kilometers unless he had just bought it less than six months ago, or he just used it to travel the five square kilometers between the ValuMart, his office, and the hotel. Alan thought the latter was more true. Alan held down the clutch and turned the key. The car roared to life and Alan was on his way.

After finding his way back to the hotel and taking Sella for a walk, Alan laid down on his bed in the suite and fell asleep. Sella lay at his feet. The sound of this lavish apartment surrounded him, the air conditioning whispered like cash rustling in a bag.

• • •

Alan picked Carson up at the airport, and he looked tired. Bags hung under his eyes, but his suit looked brand new again. Alan inquired about his day as he drove them back toward the hotel.

"Oh, it was a bore. I traded all day and it looks like I have made a lot of money. One trade slip I signed was for a stock I bought at two and three quarters a share and sold at seven. That's a jump, and taking into consideration that I had about twenty thousand shares... well, I did pretty well. What did you do with yourself?"

"Slept... That is about the extent of it. Your apartment is wonderful, really."

"Thanks... Nothing bad about sleeping. You looked like you needed it pretty bad when I first ran into you. I thought you were one of those soulless ValuMart people." Alan wasn't sure what he meant. Did he mean an employee?

"Tell me something. How do you get your suits so damn clean and fresh looking all of the time?"

"Oh... Simply put, I buy a new suit every week and have it dry cleaned daily, that's all. My week-old suits I wear when the new one is getting clean, and anything older I donate."

"So, there is no trick to making them look new? They just are?" Taking into consideration that it was new, Alan thought about this man and his method of living. In any normal circumstance he would chastise this man for being a wasteful and ignorant American, but then again he didn't drive a giant truck that ate up fuel at a ridiculous pace, he didn't buy things for himself or others driving up the materialistic need that we all innately hold, and he didn't really own anything. He just spent a real lot of money, and he did it because he could.

What Alan still couldn't understand was why he would spend his nights at ValuMart. That was still unapparent to him. There was nothing that would otherwise suggest that he had to do what he did, Alan thought. Did his mother or father die in one? Was he there to be taken home in much the same fashion? Did he work there when he was younger? Was this a statement? A beacon to all of the other employees that they couldn't make it out someday, even if they wanted to leave? It simply could not be that he felt comfortable under the watchful eye of the obsessive-compulsive consumers that walked the aisles buying up as much as they possibly could.

Alan pulled the car down the street that the hotel stood on, and Carson instantly was surprised that they were heading in that direction.

"Where are we going?" Carson asked.

"I just assumed that we would be heading-"

"Don't assume, get back on the road. This is when I go to the store." He said it so sadistically and with such an icy look in his eyes that he was almost scary. Alan turned the car around, and they were back on the man two lane highway that would lead them to ValuMart. It was only eleven at night, a great deal earlier than Alan had found Carson at the store, and Alan had wondered what reaction he would get considering how early it was and the store would probably be busy.

As they pulled into the parking lot, his prediction was not entirely fabricated out of thin air. An abundance of cars filled most of the pavement, and Alan had to park the sports car a great deal away from the door. He wasn't sure why, but he felt the tingle of fear at the bottom of his heart as he turned the car off and the two opened the doors into the hot evening wind of the lot's concrete plateau.

They walked toward the door, not really saying anything to each other. Alan wasn't tired, and he wasn't sure what he was expected to do once they got to the bedding section. He had only done two things other than sleep that day; one was take Sella for a walk, and the other was sitting down to try to write just before he fell asleep. When he woke up, the only thing written on the screen of his notebook computer was 'why can't you think of anything, you fucking moron? You'll never amount to anything.' Alan was ashamed that was all he could come up with after such and interesting last few weeks, but as a whole this entire trip was nothing but one big excuse to procrastinate the weight of a crushing writer's block. Then he went to retrieve Carson.

Alan wondered if he was depressed.

They walked into the store, and Carson knew exactly where he was going. Weaving though the throngs of shoppers pushing giant carts chock full of ingredients that make feasts for families that they will never finish with fatty children with sausage fingers that refuse to eat leftovers, Alan squinted at the lights beating down on them that sent breezes of incandescent horror to his eyes. Alan would never understand Carson, but he would try his best to as long as he could.

Entering the cloudy fields of slumber and comfort, Alan and Carson paused at the people, couples, and children scoping out the wares that they offered. There were at least four dozen. When Carson spotted a couple inspecting his favorite bed, he growled under his breath. Alan then observed something he hadn't noticed about the shoppers – there was actually an alarming percentage of crunchy hippies in the perimeter of the bedding section, and he wondered if Carson had spotted them too. Without hesitation, Carson drove himself right into the middle of the field of beds. He dove onto the back of a fat sheep, in the midst of the pasture the flock was grazing in.

Carson methodically lay down as soon as the customers were done looking at it. In fact, those same customers seemed to walk away slowly and take interest in bedding models far away from where Carson was. Alan walked over to the bed next to his and sat as he had before.

He surveyed his surroundings, and noticed one of the dark-haired hippie looking girls nudge another, and they both started walking toward Alan and Carson. She looked pregnant. Some of the other hippies also descended upon their space. About five in all did exactly what Carson did, flanking around the two of them, making a protective sleeping hippie shield.

Alan dozed, and he could almost sympathize with Carson for a moment. He did feel safe sleeping in ValuMart. He wondered as he drifted, what could be more secure than being under the watchful eye of everyone else?

• • •

Alan awoke to the screaming of the staff. He was confused, and unlike the last time, the ValuMart employees weren't screaming at Alan nor Carson. Alan's head cleared.

"No, you have to turn the cameras off and leave. You- No! You are not allowed to film here. I don't care what you have. This is private property!"

Alan adjusted his eyes and he saw the manager of the ValuMart arguing with a cameraman and newswoman from a news station, as apparent by the seven that was imprinted on a box housing the head of the microphone she was holding. The manager was almost getting pushy, moving his body as close to the cameraman as he could to appear to be physically aggressive without touching him. His daily entourage of smocked minions stood behind him as they always did. The news crew turned around and were escorted toward the door by some of the other employees, while the manager turned toward the bedding section.

"Okay party animals, this love-in is over, you hear me?" he boomed in an un-flattering, flamboyant tone. Several employees walked with him though the aisles and started to wake people up. As the hippies woke up, they began screaming and aggressively slapping the employee's hands off of them.

"You can't tell me what to do, get off me!" one screamed.

"What do you think you are doing? This is assault! I was trying to buy a bed here! I'm testing it!" said another.

For the most part, the staff was behaving relatively polite, but Alan assumed that was against the manager's better wishes. Considering Alan was already up, it looked as though the employee assigned to him simply went over to Carson to wake him up.

While the screaming of hippies was drowning out much of what was happening, Carson simply reacted the way he always had to this.

"Carson, let's not make this more difficult than it should be. You and your friends need to leave."

"I don't know any of these people."

"I am sure you're right, but you have to go, along with everyone else."

"How ridiculous. I don't even know what's going on." Carson was confused.

As Alan and Carson stood, Alan thought about how strangely Carson was able to make it through the sleep-depriving arousal without any trace of grogginess. By Alan's estimation, this was the only sleep that he got in his routine. It seemed to him that as far between as it was, the moments of sleep that Carson did get was sparse. So sparse that even a couple of hours of sleep under the fluorescent lights, on the edge of being awoken by the staff, were simply imperfect.

The two of them stood and began walking toward the door – but they were escorted by several of the hippies that were struggling to hold off various members of the ValuMart staff. As the staff ridiculed him and implored that he not return, Carson only continued to say the same things that he had every night. It was surprising that they weren't already standing in the bedding section at all hours of the night, only to predict when Carson would arrive so they could promptly remove him. While it was probably difficult to gauge when he would arrive, it seemed that the fact he would be there night after night was the one thing that would always be certain.

When they exited the building, the pregnant-looking hippie was being interviewed by the news team that had been kicked out earlier. They filmed her screaming, raising her fist in the air proudly, high-fiving some other members of her posse. They also filmed her answering questions and making statements to the reporter. Alan couldn't hear what she said until they passed the scene with Carson.

"… without hesitation that we do something about the oppression and poor treatment of the staff with poor hours, pay, and benefits!" she yelled.

The reporter returned the microphone to her own face. "So your means are merely political in nature?"

"In a sense, yes. We are unofficially following the lead of Michael Carson who has been coming here every night for the past few years. He is a multimillionaire, and yet he sleeps here every night as a protest to his own selling-out as a corporate trading success story. Carson curls up as if he was the fetus in the womb of corporate America! He protests by posing as the bastard fuck-child of materialism and excessive capitalism!" The crunchy girl shook her fist to the screaming cheers of the rest of the crunchy folk with her.

Alan had stopped to listen, without realizing that Carson had almost broken into a run back to his car. He drove up, and Alan climbed in just as the cameraman turned his attention to the scene beside him. They screeched off, speeding through the parking lot and out onto the street.

Carson looked almost as if he were about to start crying, and his driving would have been considered insane if it weren't for his normal driving habits to which this was minimally different. They didn't say a word to each other, and hot wind gusted in through the open windows.

They were silent, except for Carson offhandedly throwing in, "I don't think I am going to work tomorrow." It was the only thing that was uttered before they got back to the hotel.

• • •

Alan woke up the next morning and walked into the living room. Carson sat in the chair watching the television. A lavish room service breakfast was set up on three trays, and Carson fed bacon to Sella piece by piece. She was as mesmerized by the bacon as much as Carson was by the television.

"Morning," Alan said, scratching the back of his head and yawning. Carson looked up from the television.

"Hi. You have to see this - they have shown it three times already. You know how the morning news repeats things a hundred times. I am sure it is coming on again." Carson sat in the chair as fresh and neatly pressed as ever.

"Did you sleep last night?"

"At the store, Alan, at the store."

"Right, but... you have been watching TV since we got back?"

"Yeah. Have some breakfast, it's great. The sausages they have here are something."

"Sure." Alan grabbed a plate of food and went into the bathroom. He ate his breakfast as he took a shower and shaved. He felt a full belly as he toweled off and made his way back into the living room. Carson was waving for him to come over.

"...local ValuMart last night prompts workers to ask for better pay, better benefits, and action. Mia Chaud reports..."

Much of the footage they began to show was of the hippies jumping and screaming. Apparently, many of the crunchy folk were ex-employees or people whose parents and grandparents worked for ValuMart. They were protesting; they were a force.

"There was an influx of protesters at the Cortez ValuMart last night causing what the manager of this particular store Dan DeSantos and town mayor Chuck Hanson are describing as 'madness and protest.'" Cut to the organic pregnant ringleader.

"Better Bennies, Better Pay! Carson says there is a way!" A chanting response. The small crew was growing to hundreds. Cut to a press conference. The store manager, standing behind a man who stood just as tall and really skinny with sagging flesh from the neck under a salt and pepper beard. Apparently he was the mayor. Microphones cramped the men on the screen.

"There appears to be a small group of people disturbing the ValuMart here in town, and I assure you we are going to get to the bottom of this. We don't want people to get rambunctious and disturb the shopping or work habits of any of the residents of Cortez or surrounding areas. There is certainly a misunderstanding, and if these employees and friends of employees really wanted change, they would certainly find a less intrusive avenue than by impeding on the way that Mr. DeSantos and the rest of the ValuMart

Corporation does its business." Cut back to images of the hippies, and to Alan's surprise, a blurry slow motion cut of Alan and Carson walking by the rally.

The newscaster continued, "the revolution happening here is run by these two men: New York executive Michael Carson, and self-proclaimed disciple Alan Levy. They haven't been charged with anything yet, but it seems that their protests have turned some heads in city hall and around the small community of Cortez." Cut to crunchy pregnant girl again.

"We are unofficially following the lead of Michael Carson who has been coming here every night for years. He is the singular voice protesting American sprawl. While he is a multimillionaire, he sleeps here every night as a protest to his own selling-out as a corporate trading success story. Carson curls up as if he was the fetus in the womb of corporate America. He protests by posing as the bastard (beep)-child of materialism and excessive capitalism!" Cut to reporter, standing in front of the ValuMart.

"We are not entirely sure how long this standoff will take place, but by the influx of cars here at the Cortez ValuMart, it is obvious that the Carsonian Movement has been going on for a while and is finally gathering steam. This is Mia Chaud for seven live. Back to you."

"Self-proclaimed disciple?" Alan asked, staring at the television.

"What is going on?"

"Is this why you would go there?"

"No... I went there to sleep. Didn't I?"

"So you have a following now. A following that has given you a definition and a means to what you do..."

"Oh, god. Oh. I. I guess I do."

"You know what I think? I think they have a point and you should just go along with it. Really."

"Oh. No. No, I have to do something. I have to go talk to those kids."

"Carson, it's a good cause. You have all the money in the world and you don't have to worry about paying for medicine and stuff... There are old ladies that work there just to make ends meet and they get no benefits or anything. Carson, I know this isn't the reason you go there, but come on, man..."

"I just went there to sleep; I don't... Can you bring me there?"

"Sure, I'll-"

"Now."

Alan, Carson, and Sella ventured out to the car, and Alan hadn't realized it until this moment considering he had been driving Carson's car the past few days, but the rear windshield in his car had been replaced. His car was surprisingly clean inside and out. His bag with his personal belongings sat clean in the back seat, and when they entered the car the chemical aroma of cleaning products wafted out. The only thing that may have discerned it from a new car from the outside was the bullet holes in the trunk.

Next to it, however, was Carson's sports car. It was irreparably destroyed. Windows were smashed, tires popped, dents, scratches, and the smell of some sweet fluid leaking onto the pavement filled their nostrils. It was completely wrecked. Carson walked over to it as Alan unlocked his car doors and opened them. He ran his fingers along the jagged edges, dents, and peeling paint that made it look like a giant, ugly prehistoric armadillo. Carson turned and walked toward the blue hatchback.

Alan wanted to thank Carson from the bottom of his heart, but it was obvious that he was not in the mood to receive praise. As Sella settled in the back seat and Carson sunk into the front seat, Alan could see something different about him. He wasn't sure if it was the panic across his face, or that the color of his eyes has changed to a gray, stormy day.

They drove to the ValuMart, and entering the parking lot it was apparent that there would be a problem. The sky was black, and the humidity could be wrung from your shirt. The parking lot was an entirely different problem.

Cars upon cars upon cars were piled up. Double parked, triple parked. It probably hadn't been that full since Christmas when people went down and bought everyone everything. That holiday was a true sign of American indulgence. Nonbelievers seemed to celebrate Christmas more than anyone.

Cars were everywhere; parked on the landscaping, on the sidewalks, and even down the road. It looked like a carnival or concert was happening at the ValuMart, pulling spectators from everywhere. News vans were lined up, at least twenty local and national crews, lined across the front of the building and curled around the back. Alan suggested that they park around back considering no one ever did, and they could walk around front or even sneak through the outdoor garden and nursery fence door.

They parked, and they heard many voices as they walked around the building. Carson's stress showed on his face. They stopped at the edge of the cage for the nursery, and tried it. The side door was locked with a bar handle that you would have to press to open it from the inside of the cage. There was a clear plastic guard that prevented one from pressing it to open the gate unless you were inside.

"Let me go around front and I will open it for you…" Alan suggested.

"No, let's just do this."

Carson led as they walked around the side of the building and began their walk toward the store's entrance. The side of the building was long, and every step closer to the front door left interesting yet dreadful ideas between the two of them about what would happen as they approached. At the edges of the parking lot, cameramen took videos of the front of the building. A mob was gathered at the front door. Alan was sure Carson had no idea that it would lead to this. Carson did had a point - what exactly was going on? Alan wondered this, along with trying to remember if he left the windows open a crack so Sella could breathe.

They approached the door, and were surprised they were able to wedge their way through most of the crowd. Until Alan was recognized. A hand grabbed Alan's shoulder and pulled him into the fold just as he watched Carson walk straight into the store as everyone gave him room; he was Moses parting a sea of people.

Alan turned to a hundred and eighty degree plastering of the night horizon by lenses and lenses and microphones. Immediately, there was a throng of people pointing cameras at him. Lights burned his eyes, and he didn't know what to do. The shadows holding the cameras and microphones all began to talk at the same time. It was confusing, eerie, and scary. Voices rose from the left and the right, and vertigo swept over him.

Alan walked backwards slowly, watching at all sides as if the cameras were predators ready to pounce on their dinners. He turned around and entered the ValuMart, stopping to notice a dayglow-orange sign on the door that notified the public that starting that evening this ValuMart would be closed and that they should visit the closest one in nearby Durango for all of the same markdown prices. Alan had always wondered why there were locks on the doors of twenty-four hour establishments. Apparently random acts of public outcry, protest, and demonstration was it.

The lights in the store provided more bizarre, dream-like vertigo. They were strangely half lit, as though the power went out and the generator-powered emergency lights were on. Only about one in five or six of the halogens lit the aisles and merchandise in small wading pools. In the back, there was a small spot where the lights were on and hazily leaking into the rest of the store: the bedding department.

Out of the silence, as he approached, Alan heard something strange. The store was mute, almost as if the lights also symbolized sound. As he walked toward the back of the store toward the section where beds stretched out like a pasture of slumber, what sounded like a lakeside cocktail party for waterfowl slowly entered his ears. Like a tide coming in at the beach, the conversation grew. Many people were talking, all at once.

As Alan approached the source of the noise, the sense of something strange enveloped his heart. It was the sense of danger and confusion. Dreamy. At the very edge of the aisle near the end of some shelving, just before you turned for the huge empty space reserved for the rows of mattresses, hundreds of bodies lay. They lay, sleeping, arranged in a perfect puzzle to signify the very edge of the outpouring of light. There was no one laying in the dark, only people laying as far over as they could before the dim remnants of glow touched their shoulders and ankles ever so lightly. They were curled so no one's head hit the floor, and there was no floor to be seen. Everyone had a shoulder, thigh, stomach, and ankle to lay on.

Alan got closer to the shelving and slowly peered around the corner. Hundreds were gathered about the area of light in much the same way. Carson stood in the middle of a bed in the middle of the crowd looking around him. It looked like a photograph. A man standing in a sea of sleepers or dead, signifying the rise of the strongest man symbolically standing above the rest that could just not make it in today's modern society. Sure that is what Alan would think if he saw it in a museum, however knowing the situation, it would symbolize a situation that was very much the opposite.

Alan tiptoed through the bodies, and while everyone looked as though they were sleeping, they were all very much awake and chatting. He found places to step, and as he edged closer to Carson, he heard not talk about what everyone was doing there, but rather, a dictation of grocery shopping from one, and how long of a drive it was from California from another. One spoke of the Internet site from where they found this gathering, while another spoke of a feminist play they saw a few weeks before. This was a cocktail party for the oppressed; the supporters of the underdog.

Watching faces as he tiptoed through crevices and spaces between bodies, Alan saw young, old, alternative, artsy, dark, fair, punk, and conservative. So many different people came to change the world, but the man responsible for all of this had no idea what it was all about. They came to change the world to something less corporate and something more humane. It seemed that everyone wanted this, even though there were a lot of people that obviously couldn't afford to open their own store or shop at an independent one with higher prices. It just seemed that this was what everyone wanted.

Ironically, it was through big companies like ValuMart that Michael Carson made his millions that he never seemed to spend.

As Alan made it within ten meters of Carson, he could see that Carson was talking to someone below him. He was talking to a dreadlocked man sitting on his knees, and by the looks of it, there was a line of others on their knees waiting to talk to him. In a store where Carson was always the only one laying down, the stark contrast of the current scene was dizzying.

Alan made it to the bed directly across from Carson. They knew who Alan was, and he was able to nudge his rear onto it, and listen in to the conversation. Everyone did.

His hands were on his lap facing the ceiling, his left hand laying in his right. A tattoo was burned into his flesh at the inside of his left wrist that said *bodhisattva* in an interesting calligraphic script, and another on his right that said *mitzvah* in much the same way. Alan had a roommate once with a tattoo of a ring of flames that went around his wrist, and he remembered taking pleasure in his roommate's recounting of his receiving them and how especially painful it was to get a tattoo there.

"...and she is working so hard and for nothing. She used to be a teacher, but when all of the layoffs came a few years ago after the president fucked everything up, she got canned. Michael, the lady is eighty years old. She came from a time where women didn't really need to work, and yet she did. She did her whole life, and now in order to pay for her medication and my grandfathers she has to work extra hard for next to nothing. That is why I am here. You're an inspiration." The organic man, covered in garments of hemp, sunk when he finished.

Carson looked down at him, his forehead wrinkled. He looked so absolutely drained and sad. He looked like ancient religious paintings that Alan had often seen at the Museum of Fine Arts in Boston; like a Russian icon of Jesus looking down at people from the cross. He had never looked like he was in pain or that he was suffering, but rather as if he felt so unbelievably sad for the people he was looking at.

"I am not going to tell you what to do…" Carson began, "but I will tell you that they want everyone to leave. I have come to sleep, and that is all. Considering you and I and the rest of these people have crossed paths, however, I will stand with you in solidarity and do my best to touch the most primitive wildness. By bed and board stands my duty."

Alan was now sure why he was so attracted to Carson, and that was because he wasn't as simple as he looked. It came now. His inspiration. The words under this immense stress. The lines that now flowed from his mouth was that of timeless poetry and literary genius. Whether or not he knew it was another story… He had no idea who Charles Lindberg was, and slept his nights at a ValuMart without any commercial, political, or practical agenda besides just needing to sleep.

The dreadlocked man bowed his head, and then crawled away on his hands and knees. Replacing him was a fifty-something woman wearing a simple flower print house dress and a large wooden necklace with nighttime imagery carved into the beads, a moon in a starburst the centerpiece of the charm hanging between her simple breasts.

Hours passed. Alan heard stories of children hurting themselves without any money or settlement from the store that hid behind their grand and well-paid lawyers, shoddy products that burned houses down, sweatshops in China, Indonesia, and Morocco. The stories he heard most were those of relatives, sons, daughters, mothers, fathers, grandparents who have worked their hands and hearts to nubs and black beating fleshy apparatus that wilted like a plum desiccated to a prune in the summer heat. Some cried their eyes out as they gnashed a story out to Carson, while some stared blankly and impassively dictated heartbreak. It was not always to Carson. Sometimes it was to no one at all.

With every story he heard, his face sunk just a little more. With every minute his frown became longer, and his brow aged years. It looked as though his flesh was beginning to run and ooze off of his skull bone at any moment like boiling the sloppy skin off already rotten tomatoes. And after every story that they heard, he gave the same response, "solidarity," "primitive wilderness," "my duty." Every time.

As the time passed, so did the stories and the people. There were no two faces that Alan had seen since the beginning of his arrival, and there were no two stories alike but in spirit, heartbreak, and anguish.

It was as if there were no end to the influx of people, and more were gaining in numbers and concentration. They were coming in larger numbers. As the sun set in the west end of Cortez, Colorado, the emergency lights in the store shut off. The only ones remaining were the ones in the bedding section. As the light outside of the only windows at the exits of the store dimmed, the crowd curled and fused together even closer, like a mechanical machine in the zero-gravity of space curling in to preserve the delicate instruments and tools from solar cold, debris, and the threat of over-exposure and the appearance of vulnerability. They were an organic machine.

After the lights went out, the room quieted down at a disturbing rate. The conversations subsided to a communal whisper. The hundreds of people who knew nothing of one another stopped to nap. While everyone had condensed even more, and there was an even larger moat of protection around Carson, Alan, and the current confessionalists, the feeling of exposure grew.

Just as Alan began to contemplate the sheer curiosity behind the absence of any staff members, managers, and other boisterous members of ValuMart authority criticizing the existence of one man sleeping in a bed in a twenty four hour department store, let a lone what may be close to a thousand participating in a sit-in unauthorized by the man to which it was named, a loud boom and a flash echoed off of the walls, aisles, vacuums, cereal, clothes, books, and people in the building.

Everyone's heads immediately popped up like a million prairie dogs protecting their homeland in a scientific and scratchy documentary from the nineteen fifties. Broken, dusty white plaster and ceiling tile cork fell, and curtained Carson in a blanket of white powder. He looked like a saint, or even a living statue street performer. Alan, and the rest of the Carsonian congregation turned their attention to the far end of the store where the boom originated. A shotgun was lowered among the shadows, and a dark mob of shadows silhouetted by a sprinkling of wooden posts aflame surrounded the peaceful protest.

There were men with torches, shotguns, baseball bats, tire irons, and megaphones. It also seemed as though the entire camera crew from outside had made their way in with them to record the happenings as they developed. At the front of the mob were various important men that had come to light in the last week as important to the ValuMart and tiny Cortez. The faces of those that had fronted the opposition were glowing in the flames. The store manager stood alongside the mayor, some other people in suits that looked just as important as the mayor, and a large group of bystanders that were the close opposition to the group laying about the floor. They surrounded the Carsonians in a large circle.

"MICHAEL CARSON, ALAN LEVY, AND THE REST OF THE CARSONIANS," the mayor shouted through the megaphone. "THE GENERAL MANAGER OF THIS ValuMart AND ITS STAFF, MYSELF, MY CABINET AND THE OFFICIALS OF CORTEZ COLORADO, THE SPEAKERS OF THE HOUSE AND THE SENATORS OF COLORADO, AND THE PEOPLE OF COLORADO DEMAND THAT YOU RELIEVE YOURSELVES OF THE COUP DE GRAS YOU ARE STAGING UPON THIS ESTABLISHMENT. YOU HAVE ONE HOUR TO LEAVE WITHOUT PENALTY; OTHERWISE, MANY

OF YOU WILL BE ARRESTED AND CHARGED WITH TRESSPASSING AND THE RETRIBUTION OF THE SALES AND PROFITS SUFFERED BY THE ESTABLISHMENT." The megaphone clicked off and removed from the mayor's mouth. Alan wondered how this man could even say these things. Weren't there cameras? Could everything he said be true? They were on private property. What was the mayor even doing there?

A sea of whispers flowed in waves around the group in stereophonic sound. It got louder and louder and the whispers felt like what an infrared video of body temperature would sound like; hot, fiery, and loud in some spots of movement, and blue, cool, and silent in others. It pulsed around them, and continually evolved. It grew louder and angrier. Moans and growls appeared, and the atmosphere perspired conflict. The dead were rising.

Carson raised his hands up slowly, a chalky ivory statue; the saint of business. The room hushed, and he stepped down from his plush PosturePlus pedestal, and as he walked, limbs and bodies moved away from his feet on their own accord, and then replaced themselves. The religious symbolism was killing Alan, and he wondered if everything in his life was somehow trying to tell him something spiritually. Yes, this would make a great story someday.

As Carson approached the mayor he opened his mouth. His hands were in the universal unarmed position, palms facing the aggressor.

"I came here to sleep and that is all. Considering I have crossed paths with these people for different reasons and they have taken my name, I feel that I have to stand with them in solidarity and do my best to touch the most primitive wildness in your hearts. By bed and board, my duty is to stand firm beside them." The same words, again. His speech was so soft that Alan slowly stood up on the bed to hear it.

What happened next happened so fast and was so confusing that even Alan had a hard time accurately writing about it in his journal later on. This action, his standing up on the bed, was misinterpreted somehow by the people surrounding the Carsonians. Out of the silence, a shotgun with a mahogany stock flew through the air and came back end first into Carson's face. The gun immediately discharged, and Carson's face was pushed even further back with the gun's kick back. One of the countless bodies shrouded in blackness behind them to fell to the floor. Crimson fluid immediately exploded from his nose as the gun continued its trajectory in the air, with syrupy blood arcing with it. A Carsonian safely caught the gun, and Carson's blood ran as cartographer's rivers down the white powder covering his body.

Instantaneously, the Carsonians stood, and both sides of the armies of industry and independence were at the razor's edge of war. Alan lept toward Carson just as the Carsonians were getting up. The throng let Alan through as he ducked below the shoulder height of the mob, shooting like a laser straight to Carson who was already holding his face in his hands. A four deep line of protection materialized in front of them. Alan grabbed Carson by the elbow and pulled with all of his might to the left, laterally forging to the back wall of the bedding section against the front line, quickly scanning for a door at the back of the store.

The silence broke to a thunderous and barbaric yell. Everything was a surprise; flashes lit up the darkness, and the feeling of heavy cans hitting the floor reverberated underfoot. Alan and Carson reached the back wall, and they were free from most of the maelstrom as the crowd pushed outward. Alan was searching for an emergency exit that he had seen... but where the hell was it? Alan stood from his crouch and saw it two meters away through the darkness. A hundred and eighty degrees of heavy smoke plumed in the air amid the crowd, and a thick sour and acidic scent touched his nose and his eyes. People began coughing just as Alan pressed the red bar that read "EMERGENCY EXIT." A piercing shriek cut through his eardrums.

The heavy metal door slammed behind them, and it drowned the sound of the alarm in perfect counter-harmony with the screaming mob in the background. They ran down an unknown concrete hallway. Their shuffling echoed off of the walls, and Carson's gurgling and coughing sounded painful. Still holding his elbow, Alan looked back at Carson running. A shiny, lacquered line of nail-polish-red spots connected the dots to their current position.

Alan opened some of the unmarked gray doors in haste as they moved down the corridor, checking their position in relation to where they were parked. As they closed in on the far corner of the building, Alan considered the strict possibility that nothing was to come of this. Corporations didn't bow to anything no matter how much protest and unhappiness they generated. If it wasn't cost-effective, they wouldn't do it. It also seemed that in this town, and in most states, ValuMart was in the back pocket of many politicians. Alan imagined that they donated giant sums of money to civic taxes and town officials. No one could tell them that they were wrong, because so many people shopped with them and worked for them. If nothing, they were giving back to the community with shitty jobs and great bargains. All of this was for nothing.

Alan slammed his shoulder into the last gray door before the corridor turned and ran the eastern border of the store. Outside, the air was muggy. To his surprise, there was no one in back of the store. To Alan and Carson's left was the small hatchback. Sella was bouncing around in the front seats, obviously shaken by something. The sixth sense of dogs, Alan thought. What amazing creatures.

Alan ran Carson around the passenger side, opened the door, and watched him hit the bucket seat like a sack of flour whose top that had busted open and bled all over the front of itself. He ran around to the driver's side, and Sella immediately climbed into the back seat. He started the car, threw it into reverse, and turned the car so that they faced the far end of the store. Alan figured there were less people on that side of the building as the door was situated more east than center.

They sped along side the building as Carson took his jacket off and used it to pinch his nose.

"How are you doing over there, brother?"

"I'm okay… I'm okay." He said. He was gurgling and his voice was painful to even listen to in its current state.

"Is it stopping? Do you need to go to the hospital?"

"No, No, I'm fine."

They reached the end of the building, and Alan pulled the handbrake as he cut the wheel right, sending the car into a sideways turn around the corner of the building. They thundered down the alley, trees on one side, building on the other, passing ever so fast. Upon passing the western edge of the ValuMart compound as they pulled away, they could see a piping excess of people with more torches and more guns and more cameras and more news trucks and police cruisers and police vans and more of everything. Spotlights from the cameras illuminated talking reporters, backs to the building. There were even tents set up. It was a modern witch hunt, and they were out to get the witches.

They met the bulk of the parking lot without any resistance. Looking back at the entrance, Alan could see some new fires smoldering inside the building through the glass doors. People outside shook their torches in the air. What a grand fuck-up this had become.

The car hit an island of concrete because Alan was concentrating on the store, and the front left side of the car jumped up over a splash of sparks.

Alan turned his attention back to driving, and they pressed on. The little blue hatchback heroically skidded out of the parking lot in stop motion stills, and into a voracious race away from the chaos and disorder.

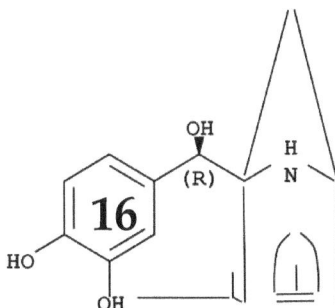

The hatchback hammered down the road north, and Carson and Sella slept loudly around Alan as he concentrated on their direction. Groggy, hazy, and sickly was the way the morning sun rose to the rear of the car, and Alan opened the windows and turned on the windshield wipers to remove the condensation from the car. The air was fresh, cool, and clean. His eyes burned as he gazed at the rear window, the sun illuminating its million beads of water.

Alan felt stale and gross for the first time this trip. In his seat, he sweat and smelled. It was as if he would have to peel his sticky clung clothes from his skin like a decal when the time came. The smell of fear and perspiration was thick off of his body, and it was uncomfortable to keep breathing the musky choking aroma. Just as he wiped his hands on the front of his pants where he sat, and considered the barren desolate plain of small brush trees that they seemed to have been passing for an hour, his phone rang in the central compartment.

"Hello?"

"Holy-fucking-Christ Alan, where the hell have you been?" a familiar voice on the other end screamed. It was Jane; such was the momentum of the last day that he once again forgot to look at the caller identification.

"What."

"You have been all over the news, and I hear that there was this giant riot and all of this going on and that you and this other guy were armed and holding up a ValuMart with a bunch of other people somewhere in Colorado, and then the whole thing caught on fire… Are you okay? I mean, what the fuck is going on with you?"

"Well… I don't know about that, but-"

"Are you okay, Alan?"

"Yes. Yeah, I'm fine… We actually got out of there before the riot started. Sort of."

"What were you doing there, Alan? Robbing it?"

"No, oh god no, we weren't armed either… I don't know who said that. The people that…" Alan was going to tell her the whole story, but he thought that it was probably best not to. "It was just a big misunderstanding, and a bunch of people freaked out, that's all..."

"Well, my parents were worried. They thought you turned into some crazy gay fundamentalist robbing department stores and killing cops and stuff..."

"I don't have anything to kill anyone with. Just my car and a bum dog that I picked up..." Alan looked over at Carson who was shifting around and blinking his eyes. Dry brown blood was crusted all over him, and some of it was already flaked off in flakes into his jacket and the car's upholstery. He looked like he was wearing some kind of black cape extending from his nose and over his mouth and fanning out from there all over his front. A blood cravat. He was waking up.

Was Alan becoming a celebrity already? Would he have to deal with the media contorting his life story into something that it wasn't already? At twenty-two that was pretty good, especially since he had nothing to show for it. Or was that his fifteen minutes? Fear shot through his limbs at the concept that nothing more would come of him aside from a story about a guy that apparently had an army hold up a ValuMart in Colorado once. With his gay lover, at least a decade older than him. Alan was that guy, and when recounted the story at the bar when he was sixty or seventy years old, he would just have to reply, 'I honestly have no idea who you're talking about...'

"I was worried too, Alan. I saw you on TV in the place, and then I saw it on fire... I... No, it doesn't matter."

"What?"

"I miss you Alan, I really do. The thought of you not around and getting burnt up in that... I would have been so upset. I was really worried. I miss you."

Alan wanted to shoot her down so much, and to tell her that she can't be worried. She never worried about Alan. She did when she thought he was changing... When he changed the balance of power in their relationship, she even thought he was on drugs. But it was not appropriate to do that. She sounded sincere, and for some reason that was a refreshing. Something he could believe in with her.

"Thank you," Alan mustered. Carson pulled the back of the seat up so he was upright, and he coughed. He wiped his nose a few times with the jacket, and sniffled. He looked like shit when he looked at Alan. Pursing his lip, he nodded his head once - the universal sign for 'hello' in guy speak. "Listen, Jane, I am going to have to go now... I think I am going to lose you. I am in the middle of nowhere."

"Okay, well, don't- uh- do me a favor and call me if you have a second. If anything else happens, I just would be happy knowing you are okay and happy... Alright?"

"Yup. Bye Jane."

He hung up the phone before he could hear any kind of response from her. Carson rubbed his head as Alan looked over at him.

"Morning... How are you feeling, man?" Alan asked.

"Like I have putty all down my throat. Dry. Headache. All the wonders of bleeding a lot for a long time. I'm shit."

"Yeah, I hear you. I have some water jugs in the back seat. You should drink."

"I will." He leaned back and took one of the jugs. It hit Sella's paw as he pulled it up and over between the seats. She bobbed her head up, and her neck chain jingled. "Sorry, dog. How long have we been driving?"

"All night; well, the handful of hours until it got light out anyway. But we should be coming up on a city soon. I passed though one, Monticello or something, but everything was closed. A real small place. We should hit a town called Moab soon. There have been signs, anyway."

"Okay. We should hit up a hotel and take some showers and sleep some more. You look like you need it pretty bad."

"Oh, believe me, I do. We should gas up and eat anyway."

And not ten minutes later, they entered the small, hot and fiery town of Moab, Utah and landed in a mid-scale hotel with enough amenities in the area that allowed Alan and Sella to get some sleep in. Carson showered, and went to find some new clothes while he bummed around in some he borrowed from Alan.

The sun was hot, and it felt great to Alan to lay in the crisp air conditioning of the hotel without any of the sticky and suffocating humidity the northeast and the south. Alan was happy and relaxed, the safety of this room receiving the most ample amount of his thankfulness. When Carson returned, he was carrying some bags and sat down to watch television until Alan woke up.

"What's up, man?" Carson asked as Alan awoke.

"Nothing… I feel a lot better though. Thanks for letting me sleep."

"Hey, it's no problem. Listen, I called my people and I think it is going to be best if I fly out of here somewhere on your way to Vegas… That's where you're going, right?"

"Yeah…"

"Well, there's a small municipal airport in Ely, Nevada and I already got my jet on its way out there. It's only going to be a little out of the way, but I talked to some people and you are only going to have to go south from there for a few hundred kilometers, and I'll give you some money for gas and stuff when we get to Ely."

"That sounds fine to me. You don't have to do that, Carson, but thanks."

And so they slept that entire night for the first time in a very long while. The next morning they left at ten after a continental breakfast, and then drove for the next four and a half hours through hot desert where there was nothing for kilometers. In silence they listened to the stories and entertainment afforded by National Public Radio along the way. Carson considered making a healthy donation to the organization as soon as he got his bearings back if only for the sheer enjoyment of what it had to offer.

The sun beat down on them, and the men pulled into Ely dehydrated and tired from all of the driving. The town was a dusty mess, the earth a dry fire bed of sand and stone. At the airport there was a little diner, and the two of them had a burger and some fries and discussed their situations a little more thoroughly and where they were going next. Alan talked about the preacher and Vegas, while Carson talked about becoming more active in his community and maybe taking Alan's advice and getting a place in New York. When they finished, and just before getting into his plane, Carson shook Alan's hand.

"I have to give you some credit, kid... You helped me get out of Cortez. Why did I sleep at ValuMart every night... I still have no fucking idea. But you know what? You helped me out, and I am grateful for that." The pilot came over and told Carson that they were ready for lift off and Carson whispered something in his ear. He nodded and walked away again. "I don't want to turn our goodbye into some cheesy thing. I just wanted to say thank you, and give you one piece of advice."

"And what would that be?" Alan asked.

"Money isn't everything, Alan. I have a lot and it hasn't gotten me a damn thing. I can be specific - safety, happiness, security, family. It takes many of us our whole lives to figure out what is important, but you have a good head on your shoulders. You are doing damn fucking good for your age, and I hope this writing thing and your research in Vegas gets you everything you want." He slipped on some aviator sunglasses and turned around. He made his way into the plane as the engine began to loudly gain in momentum.

"Michael!" Alan shouted. Michael turned before entering the plane. "How did you know all of that literary stuff?"

"Huh?!" Michael shouted back.

"I SAID, HOW DO YOU KNOW SO MUCH LITERATURE - WHEN YOU SPEAK TO ME?!!"

Michael responded, but under the oppressive noise of the jet engine it simply couldn't be heard. His mouth moved slowly. He was saying something sincere, and his smile was comforting. His face promised an intricate answer, only didn't deliver it.

Alan felt a tap on his shoulder and turned around. It was Carson's stewardess. He hadn't realized it until now, but Alan wasn't sure how she kept her breasts from falling out of her uniform. Regardless, she reached into her sport jacket pocket and produced an envelope with Alan's name written on it. She also produced a kiss on his cheek and walked toward the plane and up into the fuselage, pressing the button to close the staircase and waving at Alan simultaneously.

Alan watched the plane taxi on to the runway and quickly take-off into the air. Looking down into his hands, he turned the envelope over. "...but it sure helps if you need it, sometimes. Good Luck," was scribbled on the back. Alan stuck his index finger under the seal and tore the envelope open. Inside, the envelope held twenty crisp one hundred dollar bills, and the scent of freshly printed money wafted up to his nose. He didn't have to worry about money for a while.

Alan got into the hatchback, Sella waiting inside, and started the engine. Conveniently, there was a gas station at the small airport, so Alan fueled up and was ready for the final leg of his world tour. With simple directions, by the estimation of the gas station attendant, they would be driving for around five and a half to six hours south for the final leg of the journey.

"The key is to get there as fast as possible," the gas station attendant said to him over the map, "or else you'll go crazy without seeing anything for kilometers."

They set off, and the time as it passed was good for something. Alan reflected to Sella the torment and the torrent of his life and times. He shared with the dog everything, and wished that she could share her woes and anxieties and mistakes back at him. An inter-species desert road therapy group.

"I wish it had been different with Dad. He didn't even have a clue. I remember with one of the women he married after my mom, he made me the best man and the ring bearer at his wedding. Like, how fucked up is that? It was like I was the father of the groom giving him away to his wife... but... not because I was the son of the groom giving him away to someone other than my mom." Alan explained.

"I suppose on an Oedipal level it works, but... Wait. I still can't understand a goddamn thing you say. Sorry." Sella said.

And they drove and drove. The atmosphere and the surroundings of the desert were nowhere near as bland as the gas station attendant had made it seem. The swirling colors and variations of the area were simply magnificent. There were reds and oranges and other color schemes that were low on the color spectrum and made you feel just as hot when you looked at them as the way the hot wind felt when Alan opened the window to the car, rested his head on the frame, and pressed the accelerator as far as it could go.

One thing you could do out in the desert that you couldn't do anywhere else was a game with the rocks, Alan thought. That one he always played with the clouds. What does this rock look like? One looked like a slinky, another looked like one of those ergonomic baby bottles with the hole in the middle, and another looked like a really cool and giant desert rock... Oh, who was he kidding? The game sucked.

The air blowing in the car was so sweltering and dry that it actually felt a great deal better to simply keep the window closed. The air conditioning in the car helped a great deal, even though the recirculated air did get stale after a while. Alan turned the blower on as high as it could go. A sour, burning smell seemed to come from it, but it was better than keeping the window open and having to face the horrible air outside. The only thing Alan never liked about air conditioning was that it used up the gas quicker, and turned your fingers on the steering wheel to ice.

Three hours into the trip, Alan turned the radio on and heard nothing but static. He took the phone out of the center console and there was no reception, whatsoever. Alan was actually getting lonely, and just as he was thinking about it, the engine started to get louder and the tachometer on the dashboard was crawling quickly past five, then six, then seven thousand rounds per minute. There was a pump, sort of a muffled boom that made the hood jump on its joints, and thick blinding white smoke crawled over the windshield as the car slowed down and Alan estimated where to stop on the side of the road.

Alan pulled the lever that popped the hood up, and opened his door as the midday desert heat blasted his face and through his clothes. He walked around to the hood, and opened it. A billowing cloud escaped. The smoke cleared. There was nothing visibly wrong with the car, but one knew better that in such complicated machines it was never a matter of something as easy as seeing something wrong with it. Alan had always wished it was as easy as that... Every time he opened the hood of a car he thought that maybe all he needed to do was pull a wild badger out of there. 'Thar's ya problem. Got Damn Badgah.'

All the belts were in place, and everything was still connected. It did all look rather old with strange unidentifiable mineral and metal deposits about the compartment, but age was never a deciding factor. He removed the oil dipstick, and the oil level appeared low, but nothing the car couldn't run with. He checked the coolant and other fluids and everything was low but okay... Everything looked fine, so Alan tried the only thing that made sense at the moment, and that was to give starting it a shot.

He went back to the driver's seat and sat down, put the key in the ignition, and turned it. Absolutely nothing happened at all. Nothing. No click, no beep, no start. The car was dead.

Alan checked the phone again to see if there was any luck with the reception, and there wasn't. He could start walking to the closest gas station or something, but that wasn't a good idea considering he didn't know where he was. There wasn't going to be any this far into the trip. They were in the desert. He would just sit. That was a good plan.

So Sella and Alan sat. And they sat. They waited in the tiny dead blue hatchback for any sign of life. They sweat. They waited. Nighttime came without seeing anyone, and they began to get cold. So terribly cold. Alan wrote help in shaving cream on the front and rear windows of the car and curled up with Sella in the back seat. It was see-your-breath cold, and it was the desert. What an ironic place, Alan thought as he fell asleep.

The next day started out like a dream. The car was immediately stifling when they woke up, and Alan and Sella choked on the thick and hazy cockpit air. The shaving cream on the windshields looked like yellowed, filthy, dry, melted sour cream running down the glass. They had to start moving or else they would be draining all the time and energy they had left if no one came. Alan shuffled through his bag and threw the unimportant things he wouldn't need into the car. He focused. He packed water, some extra clothes, his computer, and the rest of the food they had. Alan was sure he was making a mistake, but he figured that he could die in the car, or he could take his chances and see how close he could get to civilization.

They started walking on the dirt road, the sun beating down on both of them. Alan took one of his t-shirts and made a turban out of it. The road, their walking, looked exactly like the cartoons portrayed walking in the desert in the heat; a hazy and vibrating sun baked the land, everything distorted in the swirls of its radiation. Lakes and pools of watery material floated across the plains and the road, beckoning for a refreshing virtual swim.

Alan was not sure why people had such problems in the desert. It really wasn't that bad. It was hot, and the sun was brutal, but it wasn't as excruciating as everyone always made it out to be. That was the first day.

As the days passed and the pair of dust-laden wanderers got ever more dehydrated and tired, they started to feel dizzy and horrible. Alan would pour piles of dust out of his shoes every half kilometer, every small pebble was an extra toe to which there was no room in the shoe. Sella's tongue was a long piece of wet leather dragging on the ground, the earth acting as a further anti-perspirant for her tongue.

At night when it was cold and they slept, Sella would curl up on top of Alan, sharing their heat and keeping them alive. Alan had a dream about a giant red flying wolf with wheels on its feet, coming out of the sky to help them. In the morning, Alan and Sella saw vultures lazily circling about in the sky.

They were hungry, and deciding that he couldn't hold the heavy bag any longer, he took it off of his shoulder and placed it on the ground. He removed all spare clothes and he contemplated the cosmic purpose for his losing weight. The water was mostly gone aside from a half liter or so in one of the jugs. He removed his computer and shoved it in between his back and his pants. It was heavy, but it would hold for a little while at least, he thought.

Both Alan and Sella's stomach were growling. Sella was tired, so very tired. At one point of their journey, her legs began to buckle under her as they walked. Alan was moaning and holding his stomach. Sella looked into Alan's eyes, and almost jumped in. Dogs are brilliantly smart and loyal creatures, and in the middle of the desert road when her legs couldn't hold her up any longer, Sella lay in Alan's path.

Alan looked at her body lying laterally in the sand at his feet. Anyone else would think that the dog was simply exhausted. Alan watched her as she lay, the thin burlap flesh stretched over her ribcage moving up and down as she breathed, and her eyes constantly looking up to Alan and then back ahead to the desert planes. She was offering her flesh to Alan as a sacrifice to his well being, and wholly understanding the consequences. She was a rabbit jumping into the fire so that the others may survive.

Alan knelt down in the bright fiery sun, and pat Sella on the head. She would have been mistaken for crying in any other circumstance, and she truly looked as though she were if it weren't for the fact that the pair hadn't had any water for the last twenty four hours. Alan looked up. The buzzards were rapidly lowering their altitude.

"Why, lady; why are you doing this?"

"So you can survive where most don't. Your golden heart is shining and you need to raise your lowly arms to the sky and shine... And you will."

"I thought you didn't understand English..."

"I am awakened." There was a certain degree of fear in her eyes, but it was also a look of authority.

"I can't eat you, lovely girl. You have no meat on your bones and you have the kindest heart of all. This sacrifice is a sacrament to that." Alan felt a rumble in the earth. This surreal moment was ending fast, without a means to get there.

"I have to, I am told." She said.

"Get up, Sella-Lady. Get up." The dog stay where she was, and her eyes closed. "GET UP!" and nothing happened. Her breathing slowed and her fur began to melt bloodily off of her bones and her organs spread onto the desert floor and stained the ground she was deteriorating on. Liquid ice-cream flesh ran, and when it hit the earth it crackled and jumped like butter on a sweltering skillet. It happened so fast.

Alan stood and stars shot from the back of his head in front of his eyes, and he felt like he was falling for a moment. Sella was just dust now. "GET UP, GET UP, GET UP, GET UP!"

The rumbling in the ground was worse, and he kicked Sella's dusty bones while his brain swam circles in his skull. The fluid was draining out of his eyes in bubbles like an office water cooler. From the crackly vertebrae and ribs where little bits of fur were hanging over like melted Dali clocks. A small patch of flowers rose from the ashes of Sella. Alan wished that he had eaten her like she wanted him to before she dissipated into flowers and nothingness.

The rumbling was earthquake-quality now, his brain bouncing groggily and dry in his head, his tongue cracking under the weight of his parched mouth. It felt like the cracked earth he was standing on. The camera-lenses of his eyes were vibrating and moving in and out of focus while he saw the edges of the film and their backlit eyelets for the teeth of the camera appearing at the edges along with black frames flying by. If Alan didn't straighten it out soon, he thought, the film would stop and the powerful bulb at the back of his head would burn right through the delicate film.

He spun around, and the sky opened up so in the middle of the day, the blue sky parted and he saw a hole of nothing but the blackness of space dotted with shining diamonds peering through. He had no idea when the world ended before his eyes that it would resemble shoddy early special effects, the distortion of the sky looking unprofessional and stretchy... As if the team behind this creation only nudged the sky so that it squished together rather than going through the effort of painting a new sky...

From the hole in the sky very far off in the distance, a dark mass appeared and ran out in great droves like a fast black, liquid cloud. Was it bees? Was space falling to the Earth? What the fuck was that? Alan's heart beat faster and he grabbed his laptop out of the back of his pants. With the quick flip of his fingers, he released the hard drive from its still housing in the bottom of the computer, and pocketed it. He dropped the laptop and the bag and everything else and started to run.

Looking back, the large mass touched down on the desert floor, and was taking over the entire horizon. When the light of the sun touched the mass, Alan could see that it was a great tower of rushing water pouring from space. He slowed down his running, his blood pounding from his heart and up through his neck. The fluid was gaining, a giant plume, a tidal wall, coming straight for him.

From the distance, it didn't look horrifically bad, but as it gained distance and speed, taking over all available avenues of escape, the giant curling wave gained in size as it got closer, and Alan could only watch in awe as he felt fiery heat being sucked into the wave's energy from behind his body and his ears. The sparkly dips and white crests of the water were mesmerizing, and why would Alan fight it? All he wanted was water.

It was moving at hundreds of kilometers an hour, and Alan only had time to hold his arms out, take a deep breath, and embrace the water when it slammed into his body. In the arms of the sea, he felt like he was in a womb, the muffles of the rushing water, it's 'tanks' and 'burbs' and 'clops' on his ear reminded him of a tape Mum used to play to help him sleep when he was little. The water was a savior to his exhaustion.

As he tossed and tumbled in the currents, his body rocked around in weightlessness, he felt the need to breathe. Opening his eyes, he saw the silvery ebb of the wave coming at him just as fast, the rush of bubbles tickling his eardrums and his nose. Alan felt his weight return to him, and his back attacked by the hot afternoon desert sun.

He pushed up with his arms, and was above water again. The landscape was changed, the dunes of the desert rising from the water like giant turtle's backs baking in the sun while their arms and head lay below water. Where Alan stood, he was knee-deep in the water. He reached his hands in and scooped up a handful of the refreshing liquid and brought it to his lips. It was crunchy and salty, probably from the earth, but it was refreshing to feel it slide down his throat. As he drank more and more, he felt his belly fill with air and rocks and lots and lots of water.

As Alan peeled the layers of soppy and heavy clothes away from his chest, he watched in the distance as one of the dune-turned-islands moved a little. Alan stopped his movement and straightened his gaze again, just to make sure. He waited. Stared and waited. No, this was crazy; thinking one of the islands was moving. Yes, it was. Alan returned to moving his clothes around, and he started to take off a shirt. He threw it next to him and it soggily floated on the surface. He unbuttoned a pair of pants, and started to peel those off as well. Pulling his feet through the holes and as they floated on the surface away from him, he saw the mound of sand move again…

Suddenly, it moved up, rivers of the water moving off of it. Two strong legs materialized behind it from a crouch, the mounds of its rear end raising and glistening-wet in the sun. Its arms appeared, muscular, strong and plump like gigantic hams. The creature stood, almost ten or fifteen meters tall. Alan could discern that this creature was a female, and her head was that of a catfish, a giant eye staring directly at Alan.

As the creature walked toward him, its hairless body draining of water and its head cocked to the side so it could see Alan, the water quickly drained from the desert floor. Alan watched the water seep through the sand, and he felt something nudge on his calf. Sella stood again, and she hid shaking behind Alan's legs, her tail between her legs. The giant in the distance dove into the sand, sending a tall round wall of the element into the sky.

"It's okay Sella. It's okay." Alan said drunkenly as he watched the creature splash up in front of him. As it rose from the depths of the sand, Alan saw what looked like the Hebrew letters 'he' and 'yod' tattooed into its forehead. Alan stepped backward and tripped over Sella, as the creature stood directly over them. Sella ran, and Alan saw the creature reach its wet, clawed hand down and steadily grab Alan's legs at his thighs.

It raised him into the air, and as Alan anticipated the horror that awaited him as he was brought closer to the monster's mouth, he reached into his pocket and withdrew his ephedrine auto-injector; the one with the drugs in it and the giant fucking needle. He removed the activator cap on the end of it, held it like a knife, and plunged it straight into the creature's hand where it held him.

The sound of its scream, a deep, guttural, engine scream, rattled for kilometers and made Alan's ears defecate a hot liquid drizzling down his neck. The creature let go, the needle sliding through its flesh and remaining in Alan's leg, and Alan fell.

He fell and fell and fell, his heart racing and adrenaline surging through his arteries outward from his heart. His body and soul hit the earth and crashed through it like glass, and fell into darkness. The coolest, most comfortable non threatening darkness. He hadn't felt this relived, no, this saved since he left Massachusetts months ago. He exploded in color and energy, and melted into the darkness.

And as the darkness wrapped around him in weightless flight, Alan felt like dozing off. Black nothingness carried him into slumber as he fell through the endless chasm of his mind.

Part III

Fall Lament

The winds of change gust harshly
As the inspiration for life's living
Flows against the tides
Bringing reveries to the dying.

Do not hesitate to think
That what you have come here to do holds on,
Follows creation,
But etches the design of bastion.

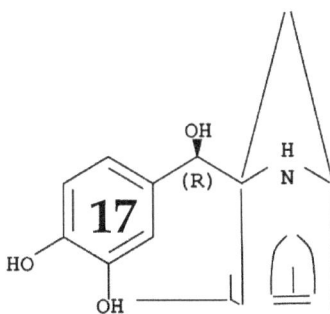

Swimming and swimming and swimming and swimming and swimming. Arms flailed and heart pumped. Air escaped, bubbling to the top. Alan was stuck in a womb. The surface was so close and it was easy to reach, the mercury floating upside down in valleys and dimples. A hand above and a knee cracked, the air clung to skin like a wet rag, icy wet rag; and a breath, a breath full of fresh air, shards of glass and metal rushed to the lungs.

From a clean, freshly pressed cotton bed in the intensive care unit of Moapa Valley General Hospital, Alan jumped up in and screamed in horror, inhaled and screamed, a vacuum of cotton sheet sticking to his body. His lungs were dry as a summer field of hay, shallow and hard to indulge in. Wires and tubes flowed off of his body. He was a jellyfish, delicate and frail, out of water. Silence, otherwise.

"Eripio. Hank Eripio." Across the room, a scraggly late middle age man sat with a book, staring at Alan in quiet astonishment. A dirty short-sleeved tan shirt with blue jeans and a belt buckle that said "Lone Wolf" in cursive and rhinestones. It was all so confusing.

"You know, ever since I got you down here, I have been really reading a lot," the man continued. "It's been fascinating, how much the library down here has. Learning a lot..." He trailed off. Then looking at the book, began to narrate part of it... " 'In an infinity of time, matter, and space, a bubble organism separates itself, maintains itself awhile, and then bursts, and that bubble is – I!' ...That is so beautiful. How are you feeling?"

Alan continued to survey his surroundings. Porcelain, glass, plastic, cotton, and latex. The room was plain, his bed and two chairs. One held Hank, and one held his clothes neatly pressed and clean. He didn't know where he was, who Hank was, and how he got there.

"Where am I?" Alan mustered to ask in a whisper. His throat was still so dry, every word sandpaper.

"You're at the hospital." Hank responded.

"Oh. And where is the hospital?"

"We're in Overton..."

"Where?" Alan's forehead hurt, as he was wrinkling it too hard, trying to understand what was happening. He relaxed.

"Moapa Valley? You don't know what's going on, do you?"

"Am I in Nevaahda?"

"It's Nevada, you're 'a' is like 'fall'...   It should be like the a in 'hat'..."

"What? What, what?"

"I could tell you weren't from around here. No one would be walking where I found you.   I thought you were crazy.   North-easterners say 'Nevaaaahdah,' It's Nevada." Alan had never considered the implications of his dialect on the pronunciation of Nevada. Alan never knew anyone gave a shit.

"How did I get here?" Alan managed.

"I picked you up. I drive a trailer six months out of the year. I am retired, but I still can use a little cash flow now and again. I enjoy seeing the country. So I am driving and I see you lying on the side of the road with a dog lying on top of you looking like he's about to starve to death. You were about eighty kilometers outside of the city. I said to myself, 'Hank, you got yourself a calling here. What's this kid doing here? His dog wouldn't be sitting here still alive if his body were sitting here for a week.' See, I was a little hesitant because your dog wanted to take a chunk out of me, and you had a needle in your hands, and it looked like you stuck yourself a few times with it... But it all seemed to make sense when we got down here and I talked to the doctors."

"What happened?"

"The doctors told me that you were severely dehydrated, you were sick with heat stroke, you were starving, and your body gave up. You were in the desert for chrissakes. You're lucky to be awake right now."

"Really..." Alan rolled over. It felt as though his body weighed six thousand pounds, every movement taking the most effort. His arms and legs were thin, thin, and thin. His elbows were nothing but a bulge in the line of his arm. He leaned over the bed and looked beside it. Sella was lying down and her head arched around backward to look at Alan and her tail began to wag, making a 'pink, pink' as it hit the bed's iron rods. She looked sad and as thin as Alan.

"I have been coming down here every day to stay with you. I figured, a man walking in the desert can't have much for family in the area and I have no one to take care of and not much to do. Catching up on my reading wouldn't be a bad thing..." Hank held up a weathered copy of Anna Karenina with a barcode and library shelving code on the spine. His thinning and wispy hair flowed through the breeze in the open window.

"Wow." Alan whispered with an unusual misunderstanding of what was going on. What had he missed? How was he here? Why were all of these people taking care of him? The IV needle dug around in his flesh, tugged on his skin, wishing to tear and rip. A strange man in a strange place sat with Alan and his dog. Alan began to drift, drift. His eyes were heavy, along with his arms and legs. Fluid warmth was creeping over his body like a tide. An echo approached from the old man...

"So, who are you, kid? Where, are you from?"

"What day...   What...   No day..." Alan breathed. Hi eyes were heavy. His head was cement... And then he drifted to sleep. He was comfortable.

• • •

When he woke up, daylight shone through the closed window. It was a pure, bright yellow fire outside his window. The air conditioner under it hummed and the clock read nine thirteen. Looking around the room, it seemed as though he was sharing the room with two other people, both sleeping, their machines behind them beeping every minute or so. It was two women, a lot older. Their tubes hooked up in much the same way as Alan's were.

Alan leaned over the bed once again. Sella laid and slept in the exact same spot that she was in when he last saw her. This time, she had two half moon plastic bowls next to her, one with water and another with a sort of granola or cereal. They sat as though they were untouched since they arrived next to Sella, a furry burlap sack of bones.

Alan lay back down and stared at the ceiling. The pock marked tiles looked perfect, as did the walls and everything else in the room. Absolutely perfect. It was good to be here. Nevada. He reached the destination, and he was alive. Everything in the room was shiny and perfect, plastic wrapped and clean.

A nurse walked in and began to do something to the woman closest to the door. There were no curtain dividers in this room, and Alan found that to be strange. There were usually the plastic patterned tablecloth curtains with the vent like holes running the length of the top and bottom edges hanging between the patients. In this room there were none... Not even the runners that they slid on to open and close.

"Water...please?" Alan mustered.

The nurse stopped fidgeting and turned around quickly. She was a really dull blonde, about thirty five who looked like she was probably more around forty. She walked slowly toward Alan's bed and he watched her as she came. The look on her face as she peered down on him was that of a victim in a horror film who is looking into a box or something and she doesn't know what is going to jump out at her face. She glanced at the clipboard at the foot of the bed quickly.

"Alan?" She asked.

"Yes. I would go to get it myself, but I am afraid I don't have the strength. And my stomach hurts." Alan said.

"Right away. Oh boy. Hold on one more minute." She walked into the hall and brought back a cart with a box attached diagonally to the top and pulled out a wand with a curly telephone cord connecting it to the box. She opened up her mouth and Alan did the same, assuming that it was what she was requesting. She inserted the wand into his mouth and disappeared out the door one more time. Alan wondered how they took his temperature as he slept.

The thermometer beeped, and as it did, the nurse came in with a doctor. His head was clean shaven in every aspect except for his eyebrows and a small patch of hair on his chin. He was extremely tan.

"Alan! Doctor Clarkson. Great to see that you're up. How are you feeling?" He spoke with an air that Alan was extremely fond of. His voice communicated that he knew what he was doing, and that he was smart, sophisticated, and hip. He made Alan feel comfortable.

"I am okay, I am just really, really dry. It feels like I have been chewing on cotton. I am also really weak and achy…"

"That is expected. You're a lucky guy. Three things saved you. That ephedrine shot you had on you, the trucker that picked you up, and your dog. You were found with a few problems… You were in the desert, and even a healthy person wouldn't survive out there. You're a strong guy."

Alan pondered what the doctor was telling him. He was a strong being. Alan wouldn't believe anyone who ever told him this. If he were strong, he wouldn't be here. He would be facing things back home instead of running away from them. Strong, Alan thought,…strong my ass.

Alan turned to the doctor. "So, what next?"

"Well, it looks like you have a temperature, but that is quite common for a person in your shape. We're going to have to do a little work on you before we let you go. Get you rehydrated and eating solid again. Dehydration is a serious condition, and you are going to be in a very fragile state for a while." He paused and looked down at a sheet of paper on a clipboard he carried in. "I am going to run down a list of things here and I want you to tell me if you had any of these symptoms now, or the last time you remember being awake and walking about. This way we can see where we are at and what we may need to do…"

"Sure…"

"What's the last thing you remember," The doctor asked.

"I remember being really, really tired. I felt a lot better when I fell asleep, but I don't remember doing it. I had a really bad headache, and I was really thirsty. I felt like the cartoon guys in the desert, crawling around whispering water… I wasn't crawling, but that's how I felt."

"When was the last time you took a pee?"

"Last time I remember, it was while I was at a diner, I think."

"Do you remember what color it was?"

"Oh, I remember that being strange… It was dark. Amber, maybe, light brown."

"Okay…" He scribbled something. "Now, what made you use the ephedrine on yourself?"

"I felt like I did when I had my allergic reaction. Dizzy and hard to breathe. Really dry. It just made sense at the time…"

"Okay, that works. You've raised some questions about the effectiveness of that, and I would refrain from doing that in the future. That was a dangerous risk, but it may have also been beneficial. We're going to look into that. That is about all of my questions. It looks like you were dehydrated and suffered some heat stroke. We're going to be bringing you some sport drinks that will rehydrate you quicker, so drink it as often as you can. You have been receiving fluids for the last week, and we have been watching you. What I would suggest you do is just rest. You're going to be weak for a while…"

"How long have I been here?"

"About a week…Six days." Alan hadn't realized it had been that long. He made it, and now he was just wasting time. "Do you have any questions?

"Yeah, when can I get out of here?"

"From everything we have seen, and we see this a lot, you may need to be here another week to get your health and strength back up to par. We just want to look out for you, that's all."

Okay, Alan thought. What's next? He looked around the room for anything that could possibly keep him occupied. He would sleep, eat, and drink. And that would be okay. A Television stared down at him on the wall ahead of his bed.

"How do I work that?" Alan asked, motioning his head towards the dark screened monitor. The doctor grabbed a cord hanging over the edge of the bed and handed a little off-white box to Alan.

"Right here. And actually there is any service you need on this box. Call a nurse, alarm, whatever you need. Anything else I can do for you?"

"All set for the time being…"

"Great! Well I will see you soon. I'll probably come swing by when we get the results of your most recent blood tests. Do me a favor and don't try to get up. A good seventy-five percent of people in your condition try it and they just end up falling on their face half the time. Call a nurse if you need something."

"Okay," and just like that the doctor turned around and left.

Alan turned on his side. His stomach still hurt, and he was still thirsty. He remembered the last time he was in the hospital a few months ago, and his stomach turned. He always thought that he would get more sick in the hospital whenever he was in one. The other people in the room with him didn't look too imposing on his health, but then again, who knows what they had.

He reached over to the box swinging from the handrail of the bed, his arm weighed down by theatrical sandbags. He swung the box around so that it was pressed against the rail to have some leverage as he pushed the blue 'on' button. It was so very heavy. He pushed, pushed, pushed the button with all of his might, and the speaker built in to the plastic handrail crackled to life with a woman talking about something to do with child support and the breaking of a door.

Alan rolled back over onto his back and watched the television as he put the voice to a face. It was a judge, an old woman, with a black robe and a white lace neckline on a bench talking to a plaintiff and defendant without lawyers. It was a small-claims reality court show, and it was just fine to pay attention to or not pay attention to.

Alan drifted. He is in an entirely new place at entirely new time and he didn't even remember getting there. Like a warp in time. It folded over and he ended up somewhere else with entirely new people. New people who, strangely enough, had no noticeable accents or wore funny hats or drank or did much of anything. Then again, Alan was only in Nevada for no more than a day. So far his experience of the state wasn't an extremely pleasing one.

With the soft talk of the courtroom singing a lullaby and the thoughts of new people and new surroundings, Alan fell into the arms of slumber.

• • •

There was a great deal of beeping. Beeping and shuffling. People talking, and a sucking sound. Sucking and gurgling. Lots of people working, doctors and nurses. Alan woke up and a large group of people with their hands up holding bags, shuffled quickly out of the room. They spoke kilometers of words that made no sense, technical words for things. A nun silently trailed behind them out of the room.

"That's too bad..." spoke a voice from the other side of the room. Hank sat in his chair with a new book, wearing a trucker hat and a flannel long sleeved shirt. Alan wondered how he could wear such attire in the desert, but he then remembered the bitter cold of evening. Something he will be eternally grateful to Sella for.

"Hello, Hank."

"Alan. You look better, you do! How are you feeling?"

"Oh, a lot better, but apparently I slept through the worst of it." Alan noticed the television was now off. He wondered what he was missing in the world. He was missing the news, the part of the television he hated the most. "Thank you, Hank. The doctor told me that you were one of the reasons I am here... Apparently a lot of people in my situation don't normally make it."

"That's why a lot of people don't do what you did, Alan. The desert's a mean place. You're just lucky you didn't get bitten by anything. That would have been the end." He reflected for a moment, and continued with modesty that Alan could tell he possessed by just looking at him, "besides, anyone would have done what I did. You can't give me any credit."

"Yeah... But no. Not these days. Not these days in America."

"You may be right. You may be." Alan heard Sella stand and shake off. The nails on her paws clicked on the floor tiles and she began to lap up the water in her bowl. She audibly finished it all and Hank watched as her tongue darted the dish around on the floor.

"Could you give her my drink? Just pour it in her bowl…" Alan said.

"What? No, that's for you."

"I can just get more. She needs it more than I do."

Hank stood. His air wafted over Alan as he stood up and reached over to his plastic cup, and it smelled like a cheap, musky drugstore cologne. He smelled like dad. It had a name like British Leather, and it came in a chrome liquor flask with a leather trim. Yes, like dad.

"So, who are you? What do you do? Where are you from? Where are you going? I want to know your story."

Alan pondered how he would answer this question. He has answered it so often over the last few months, and he noticed that it was his dynamic answer that defined who he was. Would he say wanderer? Crusader? Bum? He could define himself in so many ways now. He has changed so much in the past few months. How does one define himself in such a state?

"Well. You know my name at least. I am a writer from Boston. I want to see the country I live in, meet the people, scour the earth to see every-" Alan paused. This sounded so posh and passé. He sounded rehearsed. He sounded like he was traveling without a goal… a trip without a beginning and an end. But he is at the end – it could have easily been the end, literally. But this was the literally the current end, wasn't it? He got to where he wanted to go… Didn't he? Didn't he? Where was he? "I. I am a writer. I came out here to look for Hobbeston. I want to meet him."

That was the real reason.

"The television evangelist, with the missing wife?"

"Yeah…"

"What, are you doing an investigation or something?"

"No… I just watched him on TV and I want to meet him."

"You must be a very religious person."

"I'm not. Maybe I am. Not what he preaches, though, I suppose."

"Okay. I won't ask; I'm sure you have your reasons… So you were going to Vegas, then?"

"Yeah, actually. Did I get there?"

"We're about an hour and a half away… There's a bus a couple of times a day to bring people to work out there and there's also a couple a day to pay to ride, I think. That's probably your best bet. I am just telling you because I think that's why I found you. I think I saw your car broken down up the road a few kilometers. You made it pretty far, you know. Nowhere close to here, really, but you made it pretty far."

"Yeah, my car died. That's why I started walking. I was just going to sit there, but the car was brutally hot and my telephone had no service in the area. I figured I would be better off if I walked."

"That may not have been your brightest idea, and I only say that because of the nighttime… but you're lucky." Hank looked at Sella as he spoke, who had finished drinking and was now nosing the granola softly.

Alan thought about Sella, and how she probably felt like she owed

Alan a lot. She had so much personality. He thought about how if he had a dog that mirrored his human condition the most, it was that one. Then again, she could just be another dog.

A nurse entered with a jug of fluid and a thermometer cart. She took Alan's temperature and made a note of it on the clipboard at the end of the bed, and filled his cup with the drink from the jug. Alan realized he wasn't drinking sport drink at all, but rather, a beverage for infants and children that replaced fluids after bad diarrhea. Then again, it was probably the same stuff. Instead of a lightning bolt on the front, there was probably a stuffed bear, baby bottle, and pink pillow.

"Listen, Alan... Without a car and anyone out here that you know, I think that you should stay with me when you get out of here. You'll need a place until you can find a job and get on your feet. I know I shouldn't do this, because I hardly know you, but then again, I feel like I am supposed to do this."

"Okay..."

"You don't have to say anything now, of course; and you can say no, too. I know you have places to go; evangelists to meet. I just wanted to let you know that I would do that. I only live in a small trailer; whatever you want."

Alan has never really had anyone treat him this way, and he was taken aback for a minute. What did this guy want? Why was he doing this? Why were there so many questions?

Hank began to get up. He folded his book under his arm and stood up with a roar. "EEEaeaaaahhh... Well. It has been nice talking to you Alan; nice to have a new friend. I may see you tomorrow. I have been really enjoying the time alone being able to read in a really quiet place, so I won't hold it against you if you just want to sleep through my visits... See you tomorrow." And Hank reached down and shook Alan's almost lifeless hand.

He found the warm and damp encompassing of his hand comforting. It wasn't rough and wet; only soft and wonderful. He could tell that Hank was doing all the work, and was being careful not to break him. Alan had never felt more comfortable, but vulnerable. Alan had never felt this cared for.

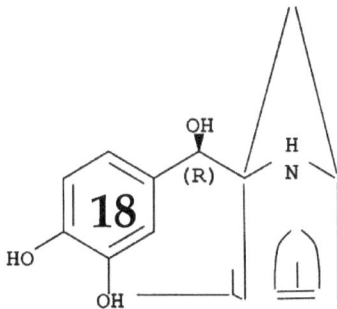

The next week for Alan was a trying one. He had never really been in such an incapacitated state. His limbs were weak, he was eating mashed food, drinking so much liquid and peeing it right out (which didn't make a ton of sense to him; he was dehydrated, wasn't he?), and wholly running on the time and direction of other people. Yes, this was pretty bad.

During this time, Alan was feeling inspired. The Reverend Hobbeston debacle was being brought up constantly on the twenty-four hour television news stations; the Reverend's shining face constantly pleading for his wife's safe return. It seemed as though his television show time slots were replaced with reruns of his previous shows. There was nothing new aside from a scrolling text reminder at the bottom of the screen asking for any information regarding the disappearance of his wife. His words, although old and already delivered, were just as powerful.

Alan was receiving a form of physical therapy. He learned to lift a fork again in a day. In four days he could write in his little black journal about his next short story. In five he had walked. At that point, they moved him into a smaller, two-patient room and he was hooked up to a great deal less instruments to watch his health. He had the entire room and his own bathroom to himself. It was nice. It was said that his digestive system was not entirely up to par, but he would be back to normal in that aspect of his life in upwards of four weeks. At least he could walk himself to the bathroom.

"Well, in four weeks I will have to bring you to get a nice southwestern steak, then. All you can eat." Hank responded to the doctor's news, and the doctor in the room turned his head toward Hank.

"Well, Mr. Eripio, I doubt that he's going to be able to eat as much as he wants." He looked back at Alan and continued, "It wouldn't be surprising to me if his stomach is the size of a tennis ball at this point. If it's any consolation, Alan, some good red meat would be good for you. I know you had said that your diet wasn't of the most carnivorous sort, but your blood and muscles need it; no matter how much you can't wait to sink your teeth into the meatloaf we throw at you here, you're going to need something fresh."

He was right. Alan thought back on it and he could only remember having a burger in Virginia, and that was weeks ago. The doctor continued,

"Listen, I am going to want you here for another couple of days, and then we have to kick you out. I know you were telling me that you weren't from around here, but I would suggest you set up a primary care doctor close by and then have them contact me to get your records from here. Are you going to stick around?"

Alan looked over at Hank. He had nowhere to go, as he was under the strict assumption that his car was totaled wherever it happened to lie in the desert, and he was totally out of money. Hank had a good heart, and Alan was lucky but at the same time puzzled that a random stranger would do this for him only because he was an older man who was bored. Hank nodded his head, looking strangely like a puppy looking up from the top of his eyes.

"Umm, sure..." Alan responded.

"Okay. Well, you're going to need to see your doctor every few days to keep tabs on your weight and blood pressure until you get back up to normal. You may be better off in New England right now, only because everything is so dry and hot out here, but we're going to have to work with what we've got. Just remember to keep up your fluids. You've been doing real well with that, so continue. I'll try to stop by before you hit the road, only because we're planning on starting you on some solid food before you leave and I just want to see how your body reacts to it. We are going to need you to have a couple of bowel movements as well. Otherwise, as far as I am concerned you are going to recover just fine from this and my job is done. If you need anything or you relapse with dizziness or really bad headaches, come by as soon as possible."

"Okay." Alan loved the way the doctor spoke. He knew absolutely everything in the world. The doctor turned to leave, but then paused and turned around one more time.

"One more thing, Alan. You aren't used to driving out here, and from what you told me this was your first time. I don't know if you know this, but there are quite a few precautions that you have to take when you're driving in the desert. They're fundamental, simply because there may be no people or towns for kilometers. You found out the hard way. When you are driving in the desert, toss extra coolant and water in the trunk; lots of water. Also, throw in a two or three litre gas tank. Those are my suggestions. The desert is just as brutal on your car as it was on you. Take it easy, Alan."

And just like that, the doctor left. Alan heard the jingling of Sella's dog chain as she stood up. The musty, skinny hound walked around the foot of the bed and jumped up to attempt to get on the bed. Her claws tore at the bottom of the sheet and she didn't make it. Once again she tried, and made it up, nuzzling in-between Alan's legs like she loved to do, resting her head on his thigh. The warmth and love felt wonderful.

"Hank," Alan called. He had returned to his book as Alan and the doctor were talking. Today, he was reading Salinger, one of Alan's favorites. He looked up. Alan was thinking about what he was carrying with him after he left the car, and couldn't remember. "Did I have anything on me other than my clothes and wallet and my black book? I mean, when you picked me up."

"Well..." Hank thought. "I didn't go through your stuff or anything. If you had it on you, it would still be with your clothes." He stood up and went over to the dormitory-style drawers built into the wall next to the closet. He rifled through them and produced the pair of khakis Alan was wearing. There were a lot of pockets, and the whole mess was really busted up and tattered.

Alan was hoping that, aside from the sad truth that he hadn't really produced much in the way of his writing was concerned over the last few months, his overall life's work was salvaged. He was hoping that he had taken something with his writing on it. Alan had sent the last of his hard copies off with his final magazine submissions.

The Velcro holding the pockets shut scratched open, and Hank produced some things that he placed on the counter under the mirror, but Alan couldn't see them. He had turned around and held up two little black rectangles. A small, dusty rectangular phone and a little black box the size of a cigarette case with various silver labels on it; the hard drive to his laptop.

"Oh, Hank. Oh, oh, oh," Alan exclaimed as he held out his hands. Hank approached his bed in wide-eyed curiosity and handed the two heavy plastic items to him. They were just what he wanted. First, Alan attempted to power the phone up, but it wouldn't on its own. It looked like it had been through a cement mixer, and Alan didn't really care. What he cared about, the hard drive to his computer, was in his hands.

It looked much the same way as the phone did, various rocky divots and scratches spotting the case, and a concerning dent of plastic where it would fit into the laptop made it look as though it wouldn't allow it to fit. Alan attempted to bend it down, and then bit it to force it, and just ended up making it worse. When Alan looked up, Hank had just been staring at him with an elderly curiosity.

"It looks busted..." Alan was rather disappointed, but he was happy with himself.

"Well, we can get it fixed, can't we?" Hank sounded exactly like he looked like he would sound. His voice was concerned and his question was ignorant. Older people, even after all this time around new technologies, still had no idea how it worked. Alan was afraid that the heat probably damaged it beyond repair.

"How hot was it outside when you picked me up? I'm just curious..."

"Oh, I would say around... Ninety-five plus at least, but it had to be more."

"Well, maybe not," and Alan looked back down at the little plastic box and sighed. "This is a delicate little thing. It has everything on it. Everything I ever wrote."

"I would love to read some of it." Hank was trying to be consoling, and yet, he was just making it a little bit worse. "Can we try to get it fixed? Where would you bring it?"

"Oh, a computer place. But not a regular small one. They'd probably fuck it up or something..." Alan looked up. He swore in front of an older, wiser person. He always felt uncomfortable doing that. He looked at Hank. "Sorry."

"Huh? Oh, don't sweat it. I do it all the time." Hank was cool. A realistic older person.

"We'd have to take it to a place that does data recovery or something. That's expensive. I'll probably just try to plug it into a computer and see what happens first." Alan fondled it in his hands, turning it over and over again, hoping that if he turned it over once the correct way, it would be miraculously fixed.

"I am going to hit the road, Alan. It's getting rather late. I have to work the next couple of days; have to make some runs between here and Flagstaff, but I will call in and check on you so I can come swing by when you get out." He pet Sella, and strangely enough, she didn't growl or make a noise like she usually did with people other than Alan. She was timid, and received the affection. Embraced it. He went over to the chair and picked the book up. "I will see you soon, Alan."

Before he left, he looked at the spine of the book. The bookmark was greater than halfway through, and then he placed it on Alan's lap. "Just in case you get bored." He said as he turned and finally left.

Alan examined the hard drive one more time, and then put it down. He picked up the tattered copy of *Nine Stories*, and examined it. Alan had never read this book before, but the familiar crackling of the poly-wrapped dust jacket and the musty smell of library paper made him think of home. He opened it, and began to curl up to someone else's story; someone else's story in the comfort of his own head.

• • •

Not two days later, Alan sat in the waiting room of the hospital with his own clothes on. He sat in a comfortable burlap-like blue bucket seat that was photocopied in neat rows around the lobby. He sat with his dog and a bag with the hospital's logo on it holding several jugs of blue infant liquid at his feet. He was writing in his black leather book as it rested on the Salinger volume on his lap that he must have read upwards of twenty five times over the last two days. He felt wonderful, and invigorated. He felt, for the first time in months, inspired.

'The concept: finding peace living in the creation of one's own hell...' he scrawled in the diary. 'What degree can humanity place themselves in such a situation and then expect to retrieve their sanity? Where can such things happen? Where are people the most vulnerable?'

'Possible settings: hospital, race track, an alcoholic in a liquor store, the field of war, high school...' Sella let out a huffy moan, and Alan tapped the notebook several times looking down at her. He underlined 'high school' twice. Alan's field of vision was attracted to a pair of dirty and tattered white tennis shoes on the floor in front of him, and brought his eyes up.

Hank stood in front of him with his usual belt, and a dirty white t-shirt. He was wearing a beaten 'trucker' style baseball cap that had an eighteen wheeled rig on it and said 'Dynamo, we distribute the world!' It really was where they got the name 'trucker hat'. He closed his journal.

"How are you feelin', man?" Hank asked. Alan had never been in a hospital as long as he had the last couple of weeks, and considering the circumstances, he was feeling a great deal better. He still had a light headache flowing back and forth in the distant realms of his head like carrying water in a plastic tote bin, and his muscles were a bit achy. Otherwise, he was doing pretty well for himself. A doctor was paged over the intercom.

"I'm doing alright, thanks. How have your missions been? Shipping anything exciting?"

"Frozen human heads, as a matter of fact." Alan looked at his face as he vocally delivered his cargo, entirely deadpan.

"Funny…" Alan said, as he realized Hank would be a formidable opponent to his sarcastic outbursts.

"I think soap…Or magazines. I distribute stuff for this center that organizes everything from cigarettes to toys, laundry detergent to chips. Sort of weird place, but if it is any idea, I can basically restock a drug store in one shipment with everything but the prescriptions. Big sorta place, high ceiling warehouse in an industrial park."

"Oh."

"I can bet anything that you're ready to get out of here. You have somewhere to go?"

"Well. To be honest, I was hoping I could still take you up on staying at your place. I don't really have anywhere to go, and I don't know anyone out here."

"Come on, then. Let's get back to my cab before the air conditioning runs off. You hungry?"

"Yeah, sort of."

"Well, I'll treat you to lunch."

And so it was. Alan stood up and gathered his bag. Sella automatically stood and the three walked through the edgy and bright hospital lobby and out towards the automatic doors. There were two banks of doors, and as they walked through the first, Alan could already feel the heat of the outside. The dust spotted the bristly carpet in footprints running into the hospital.

As the second bank of sliding doors slid open, Alan felt dizzy with the choking fire of the afternoon. The heat was dry, raspy, and brutal, and it had to be upwards of a hundred and ten outside. The breezy seaside city of Boston, even on the hottest of days would offer some relief to the sweltering beating of the sun's rays, but things were much different in Nevada. Alan felt dizzy and he saw sparks in the back of his eyes. Things were different in

Overton.

"Is it always this hot?"

"What? Hot? No, usually hotter. It is only about ninety three today..."

"It feels like a thousand." Alan managed to breathe.

"Are you okay?"

"Yeah... I'm only tired, that's all."

They walked in the dust of the desert. Alan felt lucky that he was wearing shoes, because he was sure the sand burned, and the little black spiky burrs in the earth probably weren't that pleasing to step on, either. Poor Sella.

They approached a mammoth truck that was at least three times the size of a regular car. The red giant was decorated in gold and cursive with Hank's mantra, 'Lone Wolf,' appearing in multitudes. Yellow lights dotted the rig in rows, and made it look extremely expensive and ornate. Two giant wheels sat at the front of the truck, and by Alan's count, eight at the back supporting a greasy and wiry slab of steel that Alan could easily assume would support the large part of the truck that housed the cargo, but now stood vacant and eager to work.

In order to enter the cockpit, one had to climb four steps and open a door handle that was a slab of chrome with a keyhole in the middle. When they got to the truck, Hank opened his door and climbed up. Alan went around to his side and Hank opened the door for him. It took Sella a couple of tries to climb into the rig, and Alan followed with the same degree of effort.

The cabin of the truck felt strangely brand new, and Hank didn't need to take anything off of Alan's seat before he sat down. For some reason, he had thought that truckers lived in some degree of squalor at all times, their trucks dingy and unkempt, dust settling on an immense pile of fast food bags strewn about the floor so badly that even the driver couldn't put his feet down. This was immaculate.

Alan studied his surroundings as the shiny black radio crackled and hissed slang and codes. There was another room behind the seats with a ladder that went up, presumably to a bed judging by the starch-white sheet corner hanging down. It was all very, very clean, and it smelled like a new car or new carpeting. That comforting new smell.

"You like it?" Hank asked.

"What, the truck? I've never been in one, honestly."

"I saved up my whole life to get a truck of my own, and this is what I got. I saved and I saved and I saved for it, hoping that I could get her and not have to use whatever my boss wanted me to. You get a better paycheck anyway and the way the taxes work out is wonderful, too."

"Hmm."

Hank turned the key and the rig roared to life. Hank reversed her, and they pulled out from where they were parked and toward the road. This was all assumed by Alan as there were no definitive lines or pavement. It just seemed as though people knew where to drive and park, Hank following the tire marks of burning through the dust.

"So, I bought her. Nice and shiny and new. That was about eleven years ago. All of the upkeep and engine work and everything I have done myself. She's got a good number of kilometers on her, but to be honest with you, I don't think that I have anything to worry about for a long time. She is a beauty." Hank was glowing. "I decided to spend all of my money on this here rather than a nicer place to live, so I apologize if you are cramped at all during your stay back at my place."

Alan responded, but not without studying the new landscape that he would call home. The musty trails cut through a barren horizon spotted with black brushy bushes and other random spots of vegetation. Everything looked dirty and filthy in contrast to this extremely clean truck.

"How much does someone pay for a truck like this?"

"Well, I don't want to go into detail, really. I wouldn't want to sound modest. But it was a lot; an extremely great deal of money."

"Oh." He had turned from proud to skittish, and Alan thought he would leave the conversation at that.

"Listen, I was thinking when I was at work today that you should come with me when you feel up to it. I think I can get you a job in the warehouse and that way you can start making some money and get out of here. I assume that's what you want, right?"

"Yeah, actually. That would be wonderful."

"Great. Oh, and another thing... I have something for you at the house. Sort of a 'get well' present." Alan felt uncomfortable. He wasn't even sure if Alan was staying with him a little earlier.

"Do you do this often? Save people who look like they're dead in the desert and give them gifts?"

"I do capture and rape nuns. There's no *real* count of the dead, but I have a map so I can keep track of them as I scatter them around Nevada like a morbid, desert Johnny Appleseed..."

"Yeah, beside them." Alan felt ashamed. Not only was he coming off that he was afraid that Hank was going to kill him and eat him, but Hank's sarcastic comments were light years ahead of Alan's in humor and scope, and Alan had yet to dish one out thus far.

"Then, no. I am just telling you. Remind me when we get home."

The rig pulled into the parking lot of a stainless steel oasis, and before he knew it, they were getting out of the truck to grab a late lunch. Hank reminded Alan that he could have Sella stay in the truck with the rest of the air conditioning, or so she doesn't bake, let her run around outside. Alan chose the latter. The three descended the cab and made their way towards the diner. Sella seemed to know to stay behind, and she sat by the potted plant by the door.

A neon sign above the diner advertised the restaurant, "Briner's Diner," in large neon holiness. They went in and the cool interior felt good. Hank automatically walked up to the bar and sat down, nodding to a patron.

Alan followed suit.   The place looked a lot like what Dan's back in Chapmansville was trying to look like. It was a classic diner environment that was a bit larger than one would have imagined from the outside. The dining room was maybe eight or ten meters by twenty. But then again, usually most restaurants are big when you eat at them, and when you work there, they appear a great deal smaller. Alan was studying his surroundings when Hank began talking to the waitress, and then nudged him.

"You want coffee, son?" He asked.

"Actually," Alan responded to Hank while looking directly at him. "I could really go for an ice cold coke." Hank nodded his head and Alan saw the waitress walk away out of the corner of his eye.

He turned around and Hank was studying a menu. Alan removed a plastic covered sheet out of the chrome holder that housed catsup, mustard, salt, and pepper. It was smudgy, which made Alan uncomfortable, but he studied the menu anyway. He wanted a burger. A burger with hot sauce. Alan looked up from the menu as the waitress put his soda in front of him. Immediately, strangely, Alan was attracted to her wrist. Her beautiful, beautiful wrist.

The wrist was attached to the fingers, where condensation dripped through the crevices. They were smooth, and young, and her nails were extremely well manicured and lovely. But the wrist. Oh, her wrist. It was elegant. She let go of the soda, and rested her hand on the countertop. Her flesh flowed down onto the platform, and her wrist resembled a dune of pale white sand on display in a glass box. Porcelain. The skin was like porcelain.

Who did the wrist belong to? A dignitary? A pop star modeling a wristwatch? No, no, no. This was a woman serving cola at a diner. Alan wanted, more than anything in the world at that moment, to hold that hand so that he may see what his wrist looked like next to hers. To kiss the wrist. Heat shot through his stomach, down his arm, and into his hand. Hot heat. Passion. He was passionate about that part of a woman, whom he never met, the part that must feel so insignificant to her. But it wasn't. Oh. It wasn't insignificant at all!

He wanted to kiss a wrist. Hold a wrist. Become enamored with the love and the beauty of a wrist. But not just 'a' wrist; *that particular wrist*. Haven't you ever seen a wrist? Payed any attention to it? Felt it in your eyes and your being about how wonderful the creation of such a mechanism is? No. Certainly not. And yet Alan would want you to. To feel just this. He would write scores upon scores about this wrist someday. Letters. Essays. Words put to paper. There weren't enough words. Certainly not enough words as to how absolutely wonderful this wrist was. Silky smooth with life giving pulse.

That pulse was within Alan as he watched. Stared. Why would he do this? In other circumstances he would see a man on the street staring inappropriately at the ground, or a bartender staring inappropriately at a customer, or a family staring inappropriately at a television, and judge them for what they do, and at this point, Alan just stares at the wrist of a waitress at a diner in Nevada.

"Alan, answer the lady..." Hank nudged him in the ribs.

"Oh, oh." Alan responded. He looked up at the waitress. He was immediately taken by her utter beauty and glory. She stood, not extremely tall, with short cropped hair that lay on her jaw. Her hair was what some may call strawberry blonde and her body was slim and simple. She wore the uniform open a few buttons and her body was almost screaming for Alan to jump across the counter. He had never felt in love like this. In love the first time... The first look.

"Burger! Burger. No cheese, medium, with Tabasco sauce. And fries." Alan responded while feeling his own wrist. He felt his vein pounding in sync with his heart that he felt in his ears. She was beautiful. She was amazing. She was Jaime. That is what her name tag said.

"Sure." She looked at Alan inquisitively. Her eyes held information that he would pay anything for, and the smirk across her face was adorable. She was amazing, and yet, Alan knew that if he wanted to speak with her, he would have to follow the sex laws of our universe. He would have to only say hi to her and half pay attention to her if he wanted to get anywhere. He couldn't call more than once in a three day period. And he would always need to be somewhere, somewhere not with her even though he will just spend the time alone. That is the way this system worked.

Her face was gorgeous. Her eyes, a pale blue, shone to Alan like a beacon. He thought that if it were nighttime, they would shine a reflection like a cat's if you looked at them the right way. He imagined how she looked when she smiled, when she laughed. She would laugh with her whole body. Her face would stay facing front and her body would buckle under her and look so terribly sexy. That is how it would look.

Oh, her mouth. Her lips were full and gorgeous and Alan wanted to taste them. He yearned for the opportunity. Alan could tell there were dimples on her cheeks when she smiled. Her hair bobbing the right way, just the right way, to make her look like a goddess. Alan's pretty, lazy afternoon, southwest goddess.

But it was time to eat. She was a stranger.

The food was delicious, and Alan spent the majority of the time thinking about the waitress. He only ate half of his sandwich and half of the fries they gave him. His stomach felt like an overfull water balloon, bobbing under its own weight with every move. He was stuffed and unhappy, and extremely tired. On the ride home, Sella ravaged Alan's leftovers in the back of the rig, and Hank didn't mind.

The three arrived at Hanks house, and there was no question that everyone was going to bed. Alan didn't get a good look at anything there on account of the darkness, but it was strange because it wasn't that late. Hank really hadn't turned a light on. He just pointed Alan to something soft to sleep on, and he curled up with Sella, and went to bed. Alan, Hank, and Sella ate like kings and queens that day, and Alan enjoyed dreaming that night about his meal mostly for one reason only: finding out that Jaime laughed just like he thought she would, and he was lucky enough to be there for it.

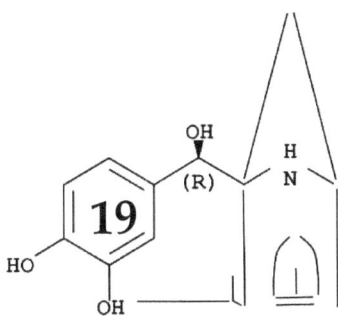

"This is your zone, zone 'S' for sanitary. You're going to be responsible for sending out all of this merchandise as it is ordered." The foreman yelled. He was the floor manager for the distribution outfit. He was a ragged older man with a graying mustache. He was shouting over a lot of noise, and Alan wasn't sure where the hell all the noise was coming from. Sucking, blowing, hydraulics hissing, slamming.

The two stood in the middle of a vast indoor warehouse that housed neat rows of corrugated boxes. Hundreds of thousands of corrugated boxes. Each aisle had a bright yellow letter spray painted on a pole, and Alan's was unsurprisingly 'S'. Attached to the pole was a vacuum tube machine. Going past all the aisles were a constant circle of hydraulic carts driven by older men. There were tons of numbers spray painted on the floor all over the place, and they seemed to coincide with the boxes they were underneath.

"Here's how it goes. You're gonna get an order, HERE," and he pointed to the vacuum tube machine. "You are going to take the slip and look at the numbers on it. Your numbers start with 'S' and they are under the boxes. There should be only ONE unwrapped pallet at a time with the cases above them. On top of that there should only be ONE opened box at a time. You will either get an order for a case or singles. Here's how you fill the order..." He pulls the order sheet out again.

"You will have a number with a decimal. The number before the decimal is the case number. This is what you will usually have to fill. You take it, and when the next cart comes around, toss the case on the pallet. The second number is singles. You will take the single smaller boxes out of the already opened box and put them in another already opened box on the cart. Easy?"

"Easy."

"Good. You look like a bright kid. Then you check the sheet off like so...There. Now take it back to the vacuum tube, toss it in, and hit the green button. That will send it to the next zone. After the carts are full, it goes to shipping where they quickly check the inventory again by assigning stickers to all the boxes, poly wrap it, and then ship it off. That's what Hank's truck does. We fill it up with about thirty to forty of these pallets and he delivers them.

Got it?"

"Pretty sure, yeah."

"Good. I know this is your first day, but you're gonna have to work fast here. This is a fast business and by the end of the day I am expecting you to have done what we just did about seven to ten thousand times. That's not strange. Some days its slow, and some its strong, but you just got to do your thing and focus. I am gonna pay you about seventy bucks a day, five a week, with a chance for overtime. You with me?"

"Yeah."

"Everyone takes lunch at the same time. Around one, and it is for a half hour. Most people bring their own lunch, but there's a van that comes outside if you need it. I'll be up there if you need anything." He points to an office attached to the ceiling with three flights of cast iron stairs leading to it. "There's also a radio on the vacuum. Just hit the RED button with the speaker on it and it will buzz me and I'll respond. Good luck, kid."

Alan worked and worked and worked. Filling orders and throwing boxes. Doing everything ever so fast. It was a rather easy job, but redundant and boring. All he did was run up and down an aisle and toss boxes on a pallet attached to a machine driven by a guy. Lunch was rather anticlimactic, as he didn't really talk to anyone, or even look at them, but Alan brought his journal to begin work on his story. The end of the day came quickly, which made Alan glad that he was working in such a fast-paced environment. The days in places like that always go fast, aside from the fact that the building was hotter than a Boston steam hole.

Hank was waiting by the shipping bay in his truck and Alan climbed the steps to get in. The two of them looked like callused dirty old bums, but only because their clothes were soaked through with sweat. It was three in the afternoon; a good time for an ice cold shower. They drove and drove through the musty streets of Overton, to Hank's home.

It stood one story and was as yellow as a flame, the roof being the first thing you noticed about it because it seemed as though it took up so much of the house's space – it looked like the burning sky was pressing down on it, a sandwich on a flat-grill. It only looked like it was four or five rooms, max, and there were strange trees that bordered it which stood like spires or needles, their height dwarfing the small house. It wasn't really a trailer, like what Hank originally called it, but it wasn't really a house. Then again, the Massachusetts definition of trailer is probably different.

"Listen, lets jump in the shower, and throw some dogs on the grill and have a couple of cold ones. Does that sound good?"

"Hank, I can't think of anything better."

And so they pulled into the gravel driveway, stepped out into the sweltering atmosphere, and then back into the air conditioned bliss when they entered the house. Sella jumped off the couch, and shook herself off, and ran straight outside beyond the men.

The inside was a neat little living room. The futon that Alan slept on the night before was a nice little plaid number on a really nice wooden base. In fact, it was one of the nicest futons he had ever seen. It was stained a burgundy that matched the coffee table, and at the top of the futon was a metal placard that had the manufacturer's name stamped into it, "Caulfield."

The living room breathed well, aside from the coffee table which took up most of the room. It was a cross-section slab of wood, bark and all, with a stain the same as the futon. It was tacky, but worked in the atmosphere of the whole place. There were speakers built into the walls, and a really nice TV hanging on the wall. A small, short hall led off the living room to the left with Hank's room and the bathroom on the end. On the right was the kitchen. Straight ahead was a divider with a pole to what Hank converted to a dining room with a huge window looking into the desert. Alan wasn't sure if the room came with the house or it was added later. He was just happy that the whole place was cool, dry, and comfortable.

"Okay, before you jump into the shower, remember I had something to give to you?" Hank said. He went to his room, and there was some shuffling. He took out a large corrugated box for shipping vegetables, and placed it on the table. It was heavy, and Hank motioned Alan over.

"Now, before I give you this, I have good news and bad news. The good news is this box is full of stuff from your car. I stopped by it on one of my runs." Alan didn't know what to say. On the very top of the box were his clothes. Clean, neatly pressed, and organized. He looked up at Hank.

"Oh my god, Hank, thank you. You didn't need to do this."

"It was no big deal, Alan, really, I would have passed it anyway."

Alan started to remove the contents of the box and his clothes were in great shape. They looked a lot better after a good washing anyway. Underneath the clothes sat his steel flashlight, his keys, his toiletries case, and his pillow all resting on top of his blanket. Under the blanket was his laptop. Alan picked it up and it smelled burnt. Not like it cooked in the car, which it probably did, but more like burnt electronics such as when a crappy ten dollar radio burns out. Alan wasn't surprised and it would probably have to be salvaged because to repair it would probably cost what the laptop originally cost.

"I took what I thought you might want or need. Everything else seemed like it hit the end of the road. The car, too, of course. I popped the hood, and it looked like your oil pan was dry and you probably fused the engine or something. Its dead, that's all."

"A lot of things are dead. Was that the bad news?"

"The bad news is that I took that little box from the hospital to a buddy of mine and it looks as though he can't do anything with it." Hank produced his laptop's hard drive. "I had to pay him a diagnostic fee, but, it wasn't that bad."

"Thanks, Hank. If I go home, or I end up in California at some point I am sure I can get the data off of here." Alan opened his laptop, depressed at the sight. It was banged up and extremely dusty. He pressed the power button and felt a little rock break under it. It did nothing. Alan sighed. "I really appreciate this. All of this."

"Go take your shower. I'll start dinner and then go after you."

Thank you. Thank you thank you thank you.

Alan went into the bathroom and turned the shower so that there was absolutely no hot water running. He took off his clothes and curled into his head, the cold water ran down the curves and bones of his body. It was in his head where he fabricated his next story. Words poured from his mouth and his hears and his heart. He was spent, but his words weren't.

• • •

"It was the semester that she was in just about all three of my history classes. I saw her everyday, and I can certainly say that my desire for her started then. Or not. I had seen her before, but she had only been there that year. She was new. She was amazing. Smart, sexy, young, tall. Everything that I could possibly want.

She wasn't like a lot of the girls in the high school. For a lot of reasons. Namely, though, she was a lot older than all the other girls in scope and maturity. She would always look at me with an amazing smirk that would drive me crazy, she always had a small feng shuei rock garden on her desk, and she knew everything. Absolutely everything.

I had first decided I needed to talk with her when I was having a problem with my grades. You see, I wasn't the best of students. I'm still not. So I sucked it up and decided that I would have to find some help. I took a chance one day before class, I don't often take chances, but it was the best decision I have ever made.

"Sarah?" I addressed. She looked up from her desk and smiled. That kind of smile that makes you feel bad, in a good way; the 'you shouldn't have done that' kind of look. "Sorry."

"Yes, Mr. Young?" She knew my name, and addressed me mister. That was good enough for me. I had never been awarded that luxury and it made me feel adult and masculine. A sophomore who was a sophisticated man. It sounded like a movie, 'The Sophisticated Sophomore.'

"I was wondering how I could get you to...you know...Help me with this stuff. It seems as though you know what you're doing. I would really like your help. I need to bring my grades up and...well, just 'get it.' I like history. A lot." I felt like I was blabbering away, but I seemed to have her attention.

"Of course! Absolutely! Let's see. The Academic Olympic Team meets after school every Wednesday. You could come to that and work on your stuff, and I could help you during it; or after. There's some days we could meet after school. I am sure we can meet in this room for a little while. They won't mind."

"Oh,...Oh wonderful."

And so it was. I didn't really have any friends in school. There were the few people, but for the most part I only had a terribly lonely existence. I liked to read... and movies. I worked part time at the movie store, and I was able to rent as many as I wanted for free; which was great because I could watch them all night.

I usually spent my nights alone. My dad ran a hobby store that sold models and role playing game cards. He would spend most nights not coming home until after eleven or twelve hosting games at the shop that people would pay in to with a chance of winning a pool at the end. Dad would usually take a cut of the profits of the tournaments and that would be the majority of our income. Mom died when I was young, and my life was basically spent fending for myself.

We didn't have a lot. We didn't really have anything. We had a small, three room trailer on the outskirts of Chicago that was considered to be almost the bad part of town by a lot of the standards of the other kids I went to school with. The big thing that really bothered me was that there was a strict possibility that Sarah would find out about it. She would, and then I would be just as lonely as I always am.

At any rate, I spoke with her again later in that day and we decided that we would meet at that Olympic meeting in the library the following week. It was interesting when I first got there. A lot of commotion and people talking to one another about various things. Sarah didn't come until the meeting started.

For the next hour and a half, we learned about the book Jane Eyre and all of the historical things that happened in it, as well as the significance of some of the symbolic events. At this point, I don't remember what was said in the meeting. Apparently, everyone got together once a week to discuss various things that would be on a test towards the end of the year. There were different parts of the test and everyone was supposed to study everything and win a victory for the school. Somehow we did very well at these tests, but I can't say anything about them. I didn't really learn anything in the meetings and I never studied for the big test - I never even took it. I was just there to do better in history...and to see Sarah.

After the meeting, she approached me and we started talking about the history stuff we were working on in class. I had never studied with anyone else before, and I assume that this would have been a great deal more productive had I not been staring at her deep blue eyes the whole time. And her adorable dimples when she smiled. Or her delicate hands. Or the way that her short, cropped hair flailed so nicely across the right side of her face just so... Just so to make her look edgy and smart. She was gorgeous. Absolutely lovely. Lovely defined.

She was trying to teach me about this Russian offense in some war where they allowed the other army to penetrate their defenses, and then attacked them with everything they had, leaving the other army slaughtered, wasted, and hollow. It was pretty messed up, I had thought, but then all is fair in war. All is fair in love and war.

Sarah smelled so absolutely wonderful. Like the spring, or fruit. Or the color pink. That was it. If the color pink had a smell, it would be Sarah, and I wanted to inhale her so. So much that she filled my lungs and I could siiiiigh her out again. It was a wonder, that. Would I feel as wonderful as she looked if I breathed her in?

"Could we do this again next week, then? Or sooner?" I had asked.

"Of course we can! Is it helpful?"

"I have never had anyone be more helpful in my life…"

I had gone to work that night feeling so wonderful I could not explain it. She was a woman that was helping me be something. She was perfect, and yet she knew not that I even thought so. But it was so better that way. I would screw it up somehow. Yeah. I would screw it up.

It was a Wednesday, so the movie store wasn't that busy. I spent most of the night watching trashy films that everyone loved – the non-masculine variety. I also watched one of the several adaptations of Jane Eyre we had in stock. That way, I could impress her with my knowledge of the book I had never read. It sat untouched in my book bag on the counter. If there was one thing good about this job, that was that I could sit and not do homework, still find out what I am supposed to know, and get paid for it. There was nothing wrong with that.

Something called to me while I was watching that film. I would buy a flower before school the next day, and awaiting her at her desk would be the flower. I suppose that was the beginning of the end in a sense. Yes. It would be a pink flower. A big one. And I thought that I would have to get to class before everyone else so it could be somewhat discreet as I would get a great deal of static and attention from everyone. Everyone that didn't ever pay attention to me.

So I did it.

On the walk to school there was a small convenience store that carried just about everything, and I picked a flower that would perfectly suit her. A large, pink daisy. It came just by itself in a small vase just plain and big enough for one flower, and a piece of twine with a tag on it. It looked rustic, and pink, and happy. I smelled it, and my heart felt it. It felt her, white hot, in my existence, my heart beat hot hot red blood. At the counter, I paid for the flower and took a pen from the attendant, and in my best handwriting I wrote on the manila tag exactly what I felt, "*lovely defined.*"

I got to class early, just as I had planned on doing, and placed it on her desk before she arrived. When she did, she looked around, put her books down, and moved the rock garden away from her books. She picked up the vase expressionless, smelling, and put it down again. From under her hair, I could see that she smiled. She was glowing. Her eyes were glowing. She was on fire, and it was because of me.

She went about the rest of that class the way she normally did. But I could not help looking forward to the next time that we would get together and study. After class, I walked up to her and asked when she would be willing to get together again. She told me that Wednesday would be good, but after school Friday she would be free at her house, if I wanted to go there. She just had to be there because of some kind of service person she was waiting for.

"Well, that's…Is that okay with you? I mean, you hardly know me." I said to her. She looked down at the flower and up at me, with that look again.

"Lovely defined? You know, anyone else who said that to me would be in an extremely great deal of trouble." Butterflies shot up through my chest. I remember looking around and there was no one left in the room.

"Yeah, well… You are just so-"

"See you Friday, tomorrow. Come meet me here after school and we'll go to my house together."

Everything before that afternoon, I couldn't possibly focus on anything. I spent the entire night Thursday listening to music. There was nothing productive in the least bit that I got done. No. I totally blew the night away thinking about it. And why? It wasn't a date… Or was it?

When my father came home, he was irritated. He always seemed to be. We all were. I heard him come in, and I saw his shadow at the bedroom door. He took his shirt off and sat on his bed. He turned around and looked in my direction.

"You up, pal?" he asked. He was asking through the words about a song I was listening to on my headphones of a guy who was singing about falling in love with the world through the eyes of a girl, who stuck around on the morning after, but then broke up with him. But he still loved her; wanted her to say yes to something.

"Yeah, dad."

"Go to bed, buddy. You got school tomorrow. It's…it's almost twelve thirty in the morning." It wasn't an order. It was a tired plea.

"I know. I know." I paused. I was thinking of something to say, and what had come out next was strange. I don't know why I said it, but I did anyway. "Dad, I might not be coming home tomorrow night… A friend is having a party and I might sleep over. I just didn't want you to get worried."

"That's alright pal. Just go to bed now."

"Night dad." Dad was the best at letting me do my thing. I could never possibly complain about him. No. He was a miracle in my life because he trusted me. He trusted my decisions and he really didn't think I needed any help out on my own. He rolled over and went to sleep, just as I did shortly after in my own bed. With a smile on my face, I touched the wall next to my twin bed and wondered what her hand felt like in mine.

The next day spun just as quickly, and I didn't pay attention to anything until I was waiting for Sarah to open the front door to her house, chilly in the winter Illinois air. The car in the driveway was clicking and tapping as it cooled off in the frost. We entered the house and it smelled magnificent. As fresh baked food does, the smell of home. Food smells, sexy patchouli smells, and pink wafted across my nose. Sarah dropped her keys in a dish in the hall on a long, thin table.

We continued on into the kitchen and it was immaculate and organized. Pots and pans hung from a rack on the ceiling, and it opened into the living room, clean and fresh. It hosted an off-white carpet and a clean and streamlined brick fireplace. It was nice. I walked into the living room and put my bag on the overstuffed couch, and sat, the plush folding around me in comfort.

The most striking things in the whole apartment was surely the artwork that hung on its walls. Thin and colorful portraits, abstract, made out of strategically and delicately cut pieces of paper in various colors, thicknesses, and textures. There were many of those, creative and striking. They hung everywhere. Along with those were comical hand-drawn portraits of bugs and bees, namely dragonflies, on parts of people's bodies. A belly button here, a pair of lips there. Asian woodblock prints also hung in the house.

"You want something to drink?"

"Those are really nice!" I said motioning to the framed pictures. I wasn't paying attention... Loser.

"They're all mine. Well, I made them I mean."

"Really? They really are fabulous!" I said. I turned my gaze to her, and she was holding up a pitcher of a lemonade-like fluid in a jug and an empty glass. "Oh sure! Sorry."

She poured two drinks and approached me. Placing them on the large coffee table, she sat down next to me, and placed her hands on her knees, and looked up to me in an excited way. She was wearing a black patchwork skirt and some nice tights. She was wearing a silk blouse, with horizontal rainbow pinstripes that showcased her modest breasts. I wanted to be in that shirt with her. Or out of it with her.

"So what do we have to do today?"

I looked around to my bag and opened it. It was empty. Among the commotion of the day and looking forward to this moment, I had not even thought to bring my books, or check if they were in there at all, anyway. I turned around to Sarah, looking at her in her empty house. The silence was eerie, and I thought to do nothing more than to hold her. I put my hand on hers.

"Where's your books, sir?" I felt so weird. I felt as though she was going to slap me or throw me or kick me out. All these things. All I did was hold her hand. She didn't stop me.

"I... It looks like I forgot them... I am such an idiot."

"I knew there was a reason that I kept you after school," and at that moment I felt truly like I was in a bad after midnight movie on the cable stations that didn't show any nudity, but came close many times. We had a lot of those at the video store since we didn't have an adult movie section. "Why did you give me that flower?"

"Because you're pretty. I don't know why. I like to see you smile."

"Hmm. You don't smile very often, mister. You know that? Are you lonely?"

"No... No, I'm not lonely." And so she was smarter than anyone I ever met. I hadn't realized just how lonely I was until someone asked me whether or not I was. Yes I was lonely. By the looks of the house, though, Sarah was too. I did the only thing I could think of. I kissed her.

One might tell me that it was a bad idea, and one might tell me that you should never do it, in the girl's own house, but at the time it felt great, and I had never kissed anyone like it before. I wasn't afraid of being caught, and if anyone should have, it should have been her. She immediately pushed me down on the couch and started rubbing against me.

I felt so fabulous. I certainly did. A woman, a creative woman, a woman with everything I ever wanted wanting me. She was wanting my flesh so bad that she couldn't just sit next to me like normal people do, no. She climbed on top of me, clothes and all, rubbing against me. She rubbed and rubbed, and she got off. Her body stiffened and released, and I can't blame her. I felt amazing.

The kissing was all I could remember of that moment. Her mouth tasted like candy, and I just wanted it to never end. I could have kissed her until the next morning, and as it turned out, before I knew it, I was being dropped off in front of my house at four thirty-seven in the morning by a girl I hardly knew. I was happy. Extremely happy.

I held my pillow as if it was her next to me in my bed that night. I wanted to see her, and I whispered her name that night. I whispered it aloud. I whispered it so much that I wanted to be, in my own head, the only person in the universe saying it at that moment. The person who holds the record for most consecutive spoken "Sarahs" of all time at five in the morning, or the most said in an hour ever. Speak Sarah. Say it, I thought.

I thought I would ask some divine being that I wanted this girl more than anything. That I would do anything for her. I would do anything for the chance for it to work out. I would do absolutely anything to have just a month of her undivided attention. A month to prove myself to her. It never works that way, though.

I had to wait until Monday to see her again, and on Wednesday, I went over her house again. She told me to put some clothes in a bag, and I did. I had no idea that I would be sleeping over in the middle of the week, but I did.

Sleep we didn't do. We spent the whole entire night rolling around in bed. I was in paradise. Kissing, caressing, making a mess. We were in a constant state of ecstasy, and I was the happiest I have ever been. She took me into her mouth, and rubbed me on her. I kissed, too. I kissed and kissed. I wished it could have lasted forever, and at five in the morning it felt as though it did. We had come so close to making love. We honestly did, but we didn't. She just rubbed me on her; among every part of her. It was a good decision that we didn't, but in the end, I wished that we had for several reasons, one being that we might as well have.

I stayed over there almost every other night, and dad didn't seem to mind. We were together for her birthday, and in the spirit for her artistic merit and our bohemian lives, I made her a card. A card with a giant slice of cake on the front. I can't remember what I wrote, but it was funny. She liked it so much, it hung on her wall.

I honestly fell in love with her, but she came to me one day with the worst possible news I have ever heard...

"We can't be together. We just can't do this anymore."

"Why? What?"

"I don't think I had to warn you about this. We can't do it."

"I don't understand..."

"You are... And I'm... Isn't it obvious?"

"Well, let's run away or something. Let's go to Niagara Falls, or Vegas... Cape Cod. Lets go somewhere where we can do this."

"You don't get it. We're... They're on to us. Just believe me."

"Who? What do they care?"

"Important people."

And I understood. I understood, but not as much as I needed to. I should have just left it at that, but I didn't. On a rainy Thursday, I walked to her house. The rain was ice cold and it dripped down my face and past my lips. It was icy cold, so terribly cold. My tee shirt had clung to my skin like a wet towel on a car and I was cold, cold, cold.

"Sarah," I screamed in the night, "You can't do this! You can't you can't you can't! You're everything I had ever had and wanted!" It felt cliche. She was going to call the cops.

Out of the corner of one of her windows on the second floor, the drapes were pulled aside and I saw her face. She was crying. That was perfect, and yet I didn't see the crying of a television show character. I saw the crying of a truly hurt person. She let go and the drape swung dead, the yellow hazy light behind it casting Sarah's shadow as she walked away.

Moments later, the front door opened and she appeared, slim and strangely tall. I had loved her smile so much, the crying was a stark contradiction of everything I ever wanted from her. It wasn't happy crying. I walked up the steps to her.

"Steve," she whispered through the rush of water. "Steve, I - " and I kissed her, because it seemed to be the right thing to do at the time, but it wasn't. It wasn't for me. A piece of my hair stuck to her face when I moved away.

"What..." I said, soothing it out of my mouth, mimicking the rain.

"Steve, I'm pregnant," were the words I heard. And the world spun and the rain stopped. I felt like I was falling down a dark, dark tunnel, but I was still in control. I turned around, and I wanted to take the knife out of my heart, but every time I tried to there were two more grinding in my organs. We never even had sex, and she was pregnant.

"Steve, go home. I'll take care of this. Just go home." Sarah said.

"No, no, no, no. Sarah, no. You can't just... We have to make it through - "

"We have to do nothing. We have to."

That was that. The door slowly closed, and she disappeared. I turned around and I ran. I ran and I ran and I ran. Ran faster than I ever had before, and the sky's condensation bounced off my body in armies of droplets. My heart pounded and felt like it was going to explode. Well, let it. Let it, I thought.

I didn't see her on Friday. When I bought her flowers on Monday, I didn't see her again. I just took them back at the end of the school day and I buried them alive in the field behind the cemetery. I wanted to see her so bad. To touch her face. To hold her hand again.

On Wednesday, I saw her. I stood next to her at her desk and waited. She spoke first, and didn't look at me, which was torture. It was torture enough to be with her and not to hold her or be next to her, but it was hell to have a conversation with her and have her ignore my gaze.

"Steve, I took care of it. There's nothing to worry about. Go have a seat."

"Sarah, you have to listen to-"

"Steve, go have a seat." The bell for class rang, and everyone was in their seats. She didn't sound like she was all put together, and she still wasn't looking at me. There was a soft thump and then the sound of a pebble hitting the floor. Sarah grabbed her forehead and let out an 'aah.' There were a few of the pebbles missing from her rock garden. Someone must have taken them before class. I felt like I had to stand up for her, of course...

"Who did that?" I demanded, looking out at the class. There was another soft thump and another. Three pebbles were gathered at my feet on the floor. Soft, supple pebbles that looked like they wouldn't hurt... But that was a bad assumption to make.

"Steve, I can handle this. I think that is all of the stones. Sue. Sue Mastenbrook, go to the office." Sarah said. Sue stood up slowly and gathered her things. She was guilty, it was obvious, but how did Sarah know? She was probably the least likely to do it. She was easily the most virginous and non threatening goody two shoes in the whole sophomore class. But teachers always knew somehow. Somehow they always knew. Sarah turned to me and whispered in my ear.

"I am the teacher here, Steve, and we can't very well talk about this. Besides, I don't want to. Go sit down, Steve."

"Well, what about the-"

"Go sit down Steve."

And I did. And I felt empty.

Sarah was in class for the rest of the week, and then we had a new history teacher. He was a hard ass. I didn't normally read the paper, but I had to because of the commotion. Dad didn't know about it, until the lawyers started showing up, but it didn't really matter because he trusted me to make my own decisions, and I frankly didn't understand what the big deal was about.

Sarah was fired within the next week. Well, the paper said she resigned, but we all know how that stuff goes. I had never really heard from her again, or seen her, until there was a poster in the bookstore downtown about a play in Chicago. It looked like Sarah. It was a play called "Corn and Awakening" whatever that meant, and it looked like it had some good reviews. It looked sad.

I missed her, and I never really had any kind of relationship like it again. I was happy that I could have, though. The state took her to court, but since I wouldn't testify and there really weren't any witnesses, they dropped the charges eventually because they had nothing to go on. Stupid thing it was.

I loved her, I decided. I took one of her creations one time from her house. A little number made of construction paper that looked like the silhouette of a girl with a flower dancing amid giant streaky reds and yellows and oranges that climbed toward the top of the frame. Yes, I loved her, but I was happy that my mind was made up and I could move on. I had to, no matter how empty I felt."

· · ·

Alan typed out the manuscript on a silent electronic typewriter that Hank had, and ate his hotdogs and drank his beer like a king. Hank told him that he wouldn't mind a bit of an advance on his first paycheck to make some copies of the story so he could send it out to some magazines. Hank said that he could pump out the copies at the office of the distribution center and that he would buy him some stamps when he was out the next day.

Alan was happy, comfortable, and appreciative. He asked Hank again why he was doing this for him and Hank said because no one ever did it for him. Alan had the last of his beer as he lay on the futon, and went to bed feeling like he was floating. Floating in his head and in his heart.

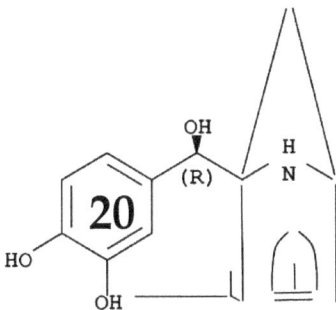

Alan simply worked almost every day of the week; simply had no time for anything else. Worked and worked. He was churning out and organizing products for everyone in the immediate distribution area of Overton. He was grateful for everything he had on his back, and grateful he still had a back. He was a machine.

Two weeks from when he started, on a Thursday, Alan received his first paycheck from the distribution center, and he was happy that he had something that secure for a change rather than working some cash-in-hand job that paid less. The check was for one week's work that included two days he was paid time and a half. In all, with taxes and other things taken out, his pay for two weeks figured around five hundred dollars.

The first thing after work that day Hank took Alan to his bank, Overton Trust. He opened a new account, deposited half of the money, and the other half put in his pocket. The bank was clean and smelled like a bank. Or a new car. Or a dentist's office. It was quite a distinct smell, Alan thought as he walked out and into the heat beating through his light clothes.

He climbed up into the rig and sat down after Hank did, and Alan immediately looked over at him and said, "To Briner's Diner!"

"To Briner's Diner!" Hank responded with a fist in the air, and they drove off, hammering away at the desert dust.

Tremendous amounts of dust coated and entered everything in the desert. Alan was constantly pouring sand out of his shoes whenever he had the chance. Alan stopped wearing socks. It was too damn hot out, and there was no point because your feet would end up getting more sweaty than it did on the east coast. All it did was make it more convenient for the little rocks to grind in your heels and turn the edges of your feet brown.

The desert foliage was fascinating, Alan had thought. They all resembled tangly briars or a mean king's mace ready to strike the wicked. They looked like they lived in the desert, mean creatures that didn't move. Mean creatures that would do anything for water; anything. Alan usually cheered Sella on for finding as many as she could to pee on when he would let her out. Her best record to date was a clean and vengeful thirteen bristly desert foliages, and while the urine was probably good for the vegetation and virility of the plant, Alan thought of it as a just punishment for looking so absolutely horrid.

They pulled up to the stainless steel mirror of the diner, and it seemed pretty empty, which was good for them so they could talk. After all, it was only four in the afternoon.

They entered and grabbed a seat at the counter. The men snatched up some menus and excitedly poured over what fare they would dine on that evening. Everything looked so wonderful, and Alan decided that he would care for a steak with his newfound wealth, thank you very much. Hank said he felt like pancakes.

"Then pancakes you may have, my fine gentleman!"

"Alan, look!" Hank whispered, and Alan knew right away what he was talking about. The restaurant froze, and walking through the threshold of a door was she, Jaime. Jaime, Jaime, Jaime. 'J'ai me!' It was the sexual and personal equivalent of everything that he felt he was made of. Fabulously the female equal of himself. Alan was excited. Alan was happy. Alan was complete. Alan was... Alan was heartbroken as he watched her walk out of the door.

"What are you having, kid?" Alan looked around and an older woman was standing in front of him. She was taking his order. Alan returned his gaze to the front of the restaurant and Jaime stood on the concrete steps to the diner. She looked as though she was waiting for something. Hank punched Alan in the arm.

"T-Bone and eggs... Medium well... over easy... wheat toast." Alan blurted, and just like that, Alan got up from his seat and made his way through the small diner and out the front door.

The heat blasted his face like pyrotechnics, and his eyes adjusted to the magnesium brightness of the outdoors. Jaime stood humming softly in a cute, light voice. She was carrying a hemp woven bag that slouched over her arms like a lazy pet.

Alan laid his hand on her shoulder. He hadn't thought his forwardness inappropriate, but it seemed as though it wouldn't matter. He was in a state of mind that already suggested that this would be accepted and that they already had some kind of connection. Or not. Her flesh was cool and comfortable. That was good enough for Alan.

"You're beautiful..." he said closely as he placed his hand upon her.

"Huh?!?" She turned around and removed one of the headphones from her ear. Alan hadn't realized that she was wearing them. Alan realized that he was crazy. This wasn't right. A new plan of action was in order.

"Who are you? Where are you from?" Alan paused. "Tell me your story..."

"Wow, umm..." She was smiling. Salvation lay in the utter shine of her face at this moment. It was heavenly. "Who are you?"

"Yeah... My name is Alan. I am here visiting a friend of mine and I just had to find out who you were. There's something about you that I like a lot, and I can't tell why." She stood watching Alan, nodding her head, smiling. Success. Alan had never been one with first words.

"My name is Jaime... Uh. Well, I am here visiting some people, also. I've only been here for a couple of weeks, but I had planned on staying for a while. My parents just moved here a year or so ago and I haven't seen them since. That's about it."

"Where are you from?"

"Oh. Umm, you know where Kalamazoo, Florida is? That's where I grew up. I don't know why my parents decided to move here. Usually people flock to Florida at their age... In any case, I think it is because dad found a job and he has been doing pretty good at it. Good money, anyway. I don't know."

"Huh. Interesting. What does he do?"

"Technology stuff. I am not too sure."

"Okay, what about dinner. Want to do dinner some night?"

"Are you asking me out?"

"I sure am!"

"Wow... Okay. Uh. You have a phone?"

"Yeah... Well, I am going to get a new one after lunch. It got busted up pretty bad. But I'll be able to call you. My number is long distance from here."

"Okay..." She wrote her number down on a Briner's Diner Guest Check she produced from her bag. Her handwriting was magnificent. It was a loopy cursive that made Alan yearn for something else from her. A car pulled up in the dust, the hazy curls of liquid heat reflecting off the hood of the car. An older woman with a medium build sat in the driver's seat with white hair and glasses. She smiled and waved.

Jaime folded up the heavy card and kissed the small packet. She handed it to Alan and Alan looked at the packet. The lipstick mark started back at him. That was hot, Alan thought. That was very, very hot.

"Well, looks like Bettie calls," Jaime said. "I can't wait to hear from you, Alan."

She turned around and got into the car. Alan opened the precious packet that he held. Inside, written in beautiful handwriting was "Chicken, Let's play!" and her phone number. It was wonderful.

As the car turned around and left, an abundance of dust kicked up and Alan was left tasting it in his mouth and his eyelids. This was upsetting, but Alan was already used to it. He turned around and made his way back into the diner. Hank sat, eying the steaming food in front of him, waiting for Alan's return.

"Hank, you shouldn't have waited. I was just out front talking..."

"I know, but it was the polite thing to do."

"Just eat!"

Hank didn't touch his food yet. He was staring at Alan and smiling devilishly.

"No, wait... You make a new friend?"

"Sort of... Come on-" Alan said as he cut into his steak, "I may be lost, but I still have to play the game, you know?"

"Oh, I know." Hank smiled.

Alan pulled the steak into his mouth and he thought that there couldn't have been anything that could have tasted better in the entire universe. Hank started to eat once Alan started. The food and the moment were wonderful and there couldn't have been a better apex to the last few weeks. Alan reached into his pocket as he chewed and fished for the bank envelope in his pocket. He had to give Hank some money for the last few weeks for food and rent or something. He was certain that Hank had some bills to pay. Or there was something he could use the money for.

"Did you know that Overton is known as 'the lost city'?" Hank said, making conversation.

"Hank, I have some money for you... I feel like I need to reimburse you or something..." Alan handed a balled up stack of twenties to Hank. He was chewing on a wet mouthful of sweet pancakes.

"Alan, I am gonna pretend you didn't do that. You need that so much more than I do." There was such a negative resistance and selflessness that Alan actually felt ashamed. Where was he? The self-centered personality of America was so unapparent in this man. An air of discomfort rested as a cloud over Alan's head. Who the hell does he think he is?

"I said, did you know that Overton is known as the lost city?"

"No, Hank. No I didn't." Alan replied.

• • •

Alan called Jaime the next night, and they decided that they would get together on Sunday. In two days. Jaime had said that she knew of an art museum that was close by. It was a contemporary little art place that was owned by some lady of affluence who had an obsession with collecting unknown contemporary art, and she did so in her gigantic stone house until she ran out of money and died, leaving it to the people of the area to curate her collection postmortem. It sounded perfect to Alan.

Alan had worked on Saturday, and on Sunday he picked a tee shirt out and a pair of jeans out of the remainder of his desert attire. They were the cleanest of all and also his favorite. After his shower, he put them on with a pair of boxers with flames on it like an antique roadster.

Hank had a friend in his neighborhood who lived about three quarters of a kilometer away. Alan had talked the neighbor into letting him borrow their car for the night. In return, he would wax it and gas it up for them so they had a relatively new looking car when he got it back to them before he went to work on Monday morning. After discussing where she lived, Alan asked Hank for directions to her house. It would be rather easy to find, Alan had thought, considering that there were really only a handful of streets in the sparse Overton.

When he hopped into the musty car that the owners had called a 'prehistoric boat,' Alan took out his new cellular phone that he had bought after dinner on Thursday. He was waiting to use it until then because he was waiting for it to get a full charge by virtue of what the salesman had told him about the pickup towers in the area; but he also wanted to use it as a prime accessory for his outfit to show the lady that he was top notch. Unfortunately, the mint-case sized mechanics of the new phones of the time didn't seem to do that second concept any justice.

Alan started the car, and shifted it into reverse out of Hank's driveway. It crackled and popped the hot gravel under the visually piercing shiny chrome of the wheel wells. It was still light out enough to see the laser reflection of it on the surrounding desert dustbin. Alan looked at the phone and the first thing he did was dial his own number, to get his voicemail. As he drove, he listened.

"Hey, this is Alan. If you could leave-" Alan cut himself off by pressing the pound key which opened up the password prompt. He was afraid of what he was going to hear.

"You have eleven new messages," the mechanical woman on the line informed him. "Your mailbox is one hundred percent full. You may have missed messages. Delete messages to free space in your mailbox..." there was a pause. "First new message;"

"Hi, Alan, it's Jane. I know you told me to leave you alone and not to worry about you, but after your scare there when you were in Virginia, I don't know. I really care about you, Alan. I really do. I wish you would let me come with you and take care of you. Oh, god. I sound pathetic, don't I? This is ridiculous. Could you just call me, Alan? When you have the chance? I would really appreciate knowing you're okay. We haven't talked, really. I want to know-" she was cut off. The woman returned, "To delete this message..." and Alan didn't even give her the chance to finish her story. He knew the drill.

"Next Message... Hi Alan, it's Mum. The insurance company is still calling me and I am trying to figure out what to do since I don't know where you are. They are getting impatient. Call me Alan. Call them, too. Their number is... Let's see. I have their number here. Hold on a sec. Eastern Massachusetts Alcoholics Anonymous meeting schedule. No that's not it. I have a sheet here from. No this is from your grandmother's funeral. No. Bill, bill, bill." Alan absolutely was always driven crazy by his mother's vocal ramblings on whatever is in her immediate vicinity. Why in the world would this happen. She is just wasting her breath and- "Okay, Alan. Sovereign Vanguard Health Insurance, TCM, Boston. Primary care Doctor Liu Casa... Remember him, Alan? What a great guy he was, huh? I bet he would love to see you. Here it is. Okay... The number you need to call is 555 – 6500 and your member number is, TCM – 11792688-" Alan pressed the delete button before his mother could even finish.

The next three messages were similar in scope. Well, similar in painfulness, anyway. His mother calling again asking about some random artifact she couldn't find around the house but was looking for on a whim, a credit agency asking about Alan's student loan bills already. Had it been six months? No matter. Finally it was a state trooper asking about a warrant that they had out for Alan. Transporting an expired inspection and registration on a car over state bounds and if he could call to clear it up. Alan thought that he would love to clear it up. The car was dead, and very missing. Alan had no idea it was found in Nevada! Someone must have stolen it!

"Next message, 'Hi Alan, it's Jane. I was just-.' Message deleted... Next message, 'It's Jane again.' Message deleted. Next message 'I am worried about you Alan. Your mother doesn't even know where you are and I heard from someone that you got into another accident or you were in the hospital again. Please Alan, I implore you, call me. Please. I love you. I' Message deleted. Next message, 'Hey, dude. Its Clark and Tessa in Virginia. We're having a birthday party. Just wondering if you're in the area. You should come out, man, it would be aweso-' Message deleted. Next message, 'Hey, Alan, it's your mother. Where are you? I am worried. I want to know that you're okay. I hope that if you're in trouble or doing drugs or anything that you would tell me. I would come and help you. I would. You mean too much to me. You're probably doing drugs somewhere, Alan. Call your mother, will you?' Message deleted. Next message, 'Alan, it's Jane. Please call me. Call me. Call. Me?' Press seven to delete this message, press nine to save it in the archives." Alan pressed nine. "Message will be saved for fourteen days. There are no more messages in your mailbox."

There was something different about that last message. Her voice sounded like despair, and sadness. Broken glass rolling like oats on Alan's sticky heart. Why did she care all of a sudden? Why did she care all of a sudden out of nowhere? This was ridiculous, and saddening. Could she be that pathetic? Go on. Go be happy. Why the fuck should Alan have saved that message? Why the fuck did any of it...

But that was when he saw her. Jaime sat on the concrete step of her one level house that looked a lot like Hank's. In fact, Alan would not give a second glance to it and would have walked right in if Hank had dropped him off there one day. It was just a tad bit bigger, which left Jaime in perfect, off-center harmony with the scene.

She stood up in a brown, ankle-length flowing and light Indian print dress and a shirt that was black velveteen and had a bow in the middle of the V of her shirt. She didn't have large breasts, but from the distance, Alan had seen what cleavage she had was magnificent in the dry desert air and could tell she wasn't wearing a bra. She was beautiful. She was beautiful. She was beautiful. The perfect creature floated to the car with a small pocketbook. She walked like she was the only human on earth for Alan, and in slow motion looked like a supermodel. Alan shut the phone off, stuck it in the cup holder in the center console, and reached over and opened the door from the inside.

She sat down on the leather seat and it made an unpleasant noise, and they laughed. She reached out to close the mammoth passenger door and it sounded like a baboon's howl, and they laughed. She looked at the radio with a puzzled smile, her dimples turning Alan on in the roots of his soul, and they listened as a southerner crooned half-assed-

> *And my baby she looks at me like I'm a Dixie, Dixie,*
> *Then as I drop her I say that, "I'm a fixie, fixie"*
> *And in our house all day, we just lovie, lovie,*
> *Lovie all night long, and then I sing it again*

And they laughed. She called him a 'Dixie, Dixie' and he said watch out before he 'fixie, fixies' and they laughed all the way to the museum. They talked about wine and movies and cheese and literature and they were happy. They were fantastically happy.

Alan had never seen a place like this before. It was in such stark contrast of all of the buildings he had seen so far in Overton and in Nevada, but he wasn't sure if they were still in either. The landscape was the same, but out of the sea of sand and burrs rose a castle of a place; a mansion of stone and mortar.

Around the museum was a lush garden. An oasis with desert grass and sculptures with identifying placards sticking up next to them, dotting the landscape stretching for at least a hectare around. Alan wondered how this place stood where it did with its grass and trees and sculptures and beauty. It was fantastic and lovely. They parked the car among others in the beautiful parking lot, went in, and paid the outrageously reasonable admission of four dollars.

At the museum they saw an exhibit called "The Inferno of the Ordinary" that showcased works by people from all over the United States painting pictures of things that you would see everyday but not pay any attention to. Alan recognized some of the paintings of Boston, and reflected upon them with a nostalgia that no one else there could. One was a painting of a hot roast beef stand that stood in front of the old prison on the Charles River. Alan always heard stories from his grandmother that when they would screw up an order, they would throw the sandwich over the wall of the prison in the yard and you could hear the guys scrambling and fighting over it. It was macabre, but it was home.

Jaime spent a long time staring at a painting of a group of sheep that were on a field in front of a fence. It was ordinary, but the strangest thing was going on with the perspective in the picture. There had to be a million fields and hills and houses and barns all squished up together. It was interesting because, somehow, it felt as through you were diving into the picture way too fast, passionately taking absolutely everything in.

They walked around the museum, most of the other exhibits appearing to permanent or semi-permanent. It was all contemporary and fabulous. There were sculptures of animals that didn't really exist, but looked so unmistakably real. Paintings of people's faces that were grotesquely large and gorgeous paintings of rainforest with one little thing wrong with them, such as the feet of a dead body peeking out from under a natural fern or a pile of large, gooey spider eggs in the crook of a tree with a pair of fangs leering down from the top of the fantastical portrait.

It was wonderful and fun. Fun and wonderful. Jaime and Alan talked about paintings and they talked about politics. They looked around at pictures and they looked within themselves at what kind of reaction they did have and what the artist probably wanted them to. It was great.

And then Jaime said...

"I think we should go for a walk. It's time for a snack..."

So they left after an hour and a half and they were happy, but there was more art to look at outside. They first stopped at a row of pipes of different sizes fastened to a rack of wood. There was a small bucket attached and Alan grabbed two thick sticks that were inside. There were no instructions of what to do, but it was obvious. Alan turned around to Jaime to hand her a stick, but she was just closing up what looked like a black film canister with a white top, and put it back in her purse.

"Here, take this, you, and eat. Just stick out your tongue." And Alan did. And Jaime's hands were in the sky with two little pieces of paper with stamps of monarch butterflies on them. Her hands lowered and one of the stamps she put on her tongue and one on Alan's. It tasted salty and oaky and like stale orange juice all at the same time as if it was shrinking up with pins and needles on his tongue, but he kept it there nonetheless, his eyes still fixated on the sky for a moment longer.

The sky was so gorgeous. It was glorious. Dusk in the southwest, Alan had decided, was certainly only the work of God, because there is no force other than an all encompassing force that could create something so absolutely wonderful. So absolutely fucking wonderful. Ripples of reds and oranges and... Oh fuck, Alan thought, this could not be any more perfect.

Jaime's hand reached over to one of his holding one of the sticks and he dropped the other. Together, they tapped out a tune that was awful, but then wonderful once they got the hang of it. Alan's only sense of music was what his own tastes were. He liked it, but other than that, he had never played an instrument. In junior high, he tried to play trumpet, but he sucked at that...just like everything else.

When they were done playing, they followed a trail that led them through sculptures made of tail ends of cars and piles of junk held together with chicken wire. White plastic piping creatures battling with hollow bronzed orphans running from the overpowering political machine, dresses trailing in the wind. But Alan started to feel like he was floating above it all, and Jaime started to pull him towards the grass.

Alan was watching his feet and he was walking in a jungle of grass, pushing the blades aside as he crawled through the forest of greens. He looked over the tall grass and the sculptures were dancing with each other, and their hips were bouncing, and they were having just as great of a time as he was. They were passing balls, and running with him through the thickets. And Jaime turned to Alan and motioned for him to sit in the grass, and as he lay down, the grass shrunk and he stared up at her face shining at him upside down, the ripples of clouds shooting away from her head making her look like an angel of heaven.

She kissed him, and the kiss lasted forever, and it felt like her face was melting into his. It was fresh, wonderful, and erotic. She was pressing against him and her tongue became part of his and her jaw wrapped around his head. They kissed and they kissed and they kissed and melted in the grass and it was wonderful. When she pulled away, their lips were still connected, and she rolled over and lay opposite him so her head was against his and his shoulder. Their heads and shoulders fused together and they were a perfect line.

The sky in all of its colorful glory sped by at hundreds of kilometers an hour and there was sunrise upon sunset. The sky was a work of art that could not ever be seen in a museum. The world was. The sculptures danced and darted and the sky flowed and purged and exploded. Fire rained down and heat swirled and love banged at the door as sculptures danced and partied around the bonfire that was Alan and Jaime.

Speeding by at gale force were rivers of blues and violets, crimsons and neons. Paint oozed across the horizon and flowers bloomed before his eyes like fireworks exploding into the night. He felt fur in his hands and he lay in a waterbed of clay, no, wine. Happy to be alive and in such a wonderful place. Look, that phoenix did such a funny thing through the hoop, and he burned to sparks and ash and was gone! Ha! And Alan was again happy to be alive and in such a wonderful place.

And Alan realized that he had taken a substance that made all of these things happen.

And Alan realized that he had never had a better time in his life. Love was flowing out of his ears, his nose, flowers erupted out of his mouth and his fingernails, and color and light exploded from everywhere else.

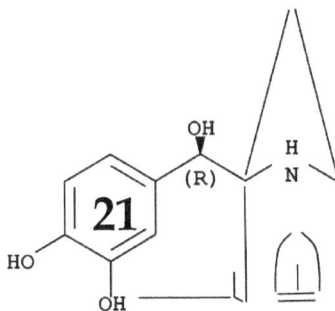

When they came down from their high, Alan and Jaime were shivering in the lawn of the museum at four in the morning, dry as hell. They sat up, hugged, and got close as to share their temperature. She let out a high squeal that made Alan think about being in bed at home. Comfortable.

Dew hung off of the strangely fertile land. Slingshotted through the back of his consciousness, he was so small and the drops of water on the blades were so huge at the same time. He watched the drops sit on the vegetation, and holding Jaime ever so close, the ultimate hugeness of the universe was so clear to him for just a moment. It was all night long, as it were also, and Alan had wished that he had thought to write some of it down before they came down and fell asleep... Maybe he had. With whatever preparation he had, it didn't matter. There was a whole black canister of psychedelia in her purse, and there was no end to where they would go with it.

'Oh, the holy art of making love under such conditions,' Alan thought, 'on the edge of both death and birth at once.'

The two vibrating and shivering creatures held each other in a vast space of dead land. Trading nuzzles and waxing xeric and caloric energy. They were machines, only basing their own purpose on their own existence; to feel, to keep active, these machines were not to do anything but concentrate on keeping one another warm, alive, and safe. Could anything be more beautiful? Could it? Perhaps it could not.

How did one relish commentary on such a wonderful night? The burned out children, satellites in a sea of dust, lay in an oasis silently. Alan wondered if they were both looking at dew. He wondered if they were both looking for something to say. What would be the first thing? How would Alan open the channels of communication between them?

"You are so very lovely..." Jaime said first. She hugged him tight again, letting out the tiny squeak that she had the last time they embraced one another as closely. Alan laughed as softly and as deeply as he could, magnifying the moment's reality and his own masculinity.

"And you are amazing..." Alan replied.

They rolled among the blades of the wet grass, their bodies freezing, and yet emitting an intense heat like dogs do sleeping on tiled floors. They stood, and Alan felt the earth teeter beneath his feet. White fire crept from the sides of his eyeballs for a moment, and the world flashed as he stood on his two feet; but it passed. Aside from light vertigo and starry eyes, there were no obvious side-effects of his night of consciousness-altering chemicals.

Jaime immediately took Alan's hand in hers and they silently made their way to the parking lot. Under a light in the parking lot, the car was covered in a haze of a million tiny globes of liquid from front to rear. The giant hulk looked at the pair, its radiator grill smiling to them in between two glassy eyes. Alan remembered that he would have to wash and wax the behemoth before returning it to Hank's neighbors. It was almost good that they stayed out all night, as Alan now had a few hours before they needed it back and he felt awake enough for his early morning endeavor.

They stepped into the vehicle, the harsh buzzing dashboard expressing the audible equivalent of the icy plastic seats they sunk into. For the ride back to her house, they really didn't say much of anything... Alan just turned the radio on and the two of them listened to the station that was on, the happy and ridiculous country music of the night before just pumping through the stereo now as a sad early-morning lonely wanderer. The car sang to them its songs of lost love, whiskey, and shotguns.

Alan pulled into the driveway of the house that belonged to Jaime's parents. She shifted her gaze from out of the window into the desert's loneliness and back to Alan. Alan held his gaze; he looked at the delicate fold of her skin and how it flowed down to a graceful goose-pimple ridden shoulder. The shoulder slumping down in frilly fabric exposing her simple and thin arm... The arm bent into a forearm, and then released ever so gently into a wrist. The wrist. The wrist was what brought him to her in the first place; only the simplicity and unnoticed beauty of the human female wrist.

She smiled, her perfect teeth and silken lips showcasing the dimples that drove Alan crazy.

"I don't know about you, but I had a great time..." Alan said. Jaime hid her face in her shoulder and nuzzled it, and Alan felt alone only a meter away from her. "When can I see you again?"

She looked at him, her eyes sparkling in synchronization with the sparkle of the glitter she wore on her chest that Alan had only just noticed by the dashboard light. "I had a great time too."

"Well, then? What are you doing this week?"

"I am working today, and tomorrow I am packing... I am leaving for about a week. I won't be back until... Next Tuesday or Thursday, I can't remember which my flight was on."

Alan was offended that she had chosen this week to take a vacation. How selfish, how brash, how... Well, how very smart of her. As Alan had such a tendency to fall head over heels with any girl that he set his sights on, this was a perfect opportunity to follow the twenty-first century's sex laws which stated in chapter four, section twenty-eight B, article six, that men must ignore the woman if they want them. The more a man can ignore his potential mate, the greater she will throw herself at him. This was perfect for Alan, as he loved to call a given woman's number on a given day every half-hour until she answered. This was devastating to his relationships because, in his more desirable or historically shorter relationships, that particular female had one or more roommates.

"Where are you going?"

"To Kalamazoo... I had this planned for weeks now. Visiting friends."

"Oh,... Well..." Where did one go from here, or better yet (in constant observance of the sex laws chapter currently in consideration by Alan), where did one go to avoid sounding desperate? "Sounds like a lot of fun... You'll just have to call me when you get back."

"Okay," she said, nodding with approval and the dimples in full effect. She leaned over the seat, the leather (or plastic... probably plastic) squeaking and shifting under her great ass, howling at the opportunity to serve such lovely flesh. She kissed Alan's cheek in a friendly way that was erotic and so wonderful all at the same time.

"I'll see you later, chicken," she whispered, and just like that she was gone. The door closed, and Alan noticed the hollowed out leather and how it expressed a burning void not only in the car, but in the atmosphere of Alan altogether. He was missing something and, goddammit, this girl was it.

Driving back to Hank's house, Alan ran his hand along the faux stitching and fused seams of the seat, holding his hand there, rubbing the concave hollow where Jaime's ass had been until there was no warmth left in it. As the heat dissipated, it was transferred inside of him as a fully encompassing warmth that he rarely felt in his life.

Alan pulled into Hank's driveway and spent the rest of the early morning hours washing and waxing the car as the red fiery sun of the desert crept over the horizon. Alan felt the heat and the warmth of the sun beating on him, and it felt like the radiation of Jaime and her skin and her wonder. Rubbing the white haze off of the car, he could only speculate how far this relationship would go. Their love and their happiness would be full of surprises and excitement. There would be no surprise that was too surprising and that wouldn't make Alan happy. He would have to compete with her! Who could be the most artistic and creative! Ha! What a concept!

Every spin of the rag that buffed the white cream onto the vehicle and every swipe that buffed the dry powder off made Alan think even more about her powerful hold on him; and every turn of his arm made him whisper her name...

"Jaime, Jaime, Jaime..."

. . .

"I miss you, Alan. I want you to come home."

It was with these words that Alan truly could have cared less. He was somewhere that he was getting by. He was with good people. He was practically in love. There was now, honestly, no place for Jane in his life, and it was just as easy to give up on her. He had a girl and he was getting by happily and quite well, thank you very much. Don't call us... We'll call you.

"Jane, I know you want me to go home... But I honestly don't see that happening. I am quite happy here."

"Where the hell are you."

"I told you, Nevada."

"But..." and she started sobbing on the other end of the line. It sounded like she was just told that she was just told that she had a week to live or that a relative wasn't coming home from war. It was a depressing sobbing. It was almost inaudible as if she were honestly holding the receiver away from her face while she cried or she was burying her face in a pillow.

"Jane, don't... Don't do this to me. I can't let you cry like this..."

"I'm not crying." It was a difficult effort to say it in between sobs, but somehow she managed to do it.

"No, really. It is tearing me apart."

"Why?"

"Because I love you Jane. I do. But I left for me and you are going to have to accept it. Especially considering that I am so far away and it is really not healthy for you to call once or twice a week and just cry at me." Alan was unsure why he had said this. Looking back at what he said after, he really shouldn't have told her that he loved her, but he also could have found a way to get her to stop the incessant and depressing act of her calling him that sounded a bit less like constructive criticism. The other end of the line was silent for at least three minutes.

A sniffle, and then a pause. "Did you meet someone?"

Alan looked off into the raspy billows of the futon's cushion in Hank's living room. He opened his mouth, considering consequence and backlash for whatever answer he produced. He could say yes, but that would make him a deserter; an utterly horrid human being who had no respect for between-relationship waiting times. If he said no, he faced more phone calls and what he hadn't predicted would be an endless battle for who felt the more regret in the shadow of their relationship.

In the end of the struggle for control of his vocabulary and line of communication to the girl on the other end of the line, he had in the end, chosen silence.

"I am;... I am going to go now, and I won't call you. You are-"

"No, Jane, I didn't mean-"

"No, no. I won't call you. You're right. Goodbye Alan."

The line was dead.

Alan's heart was the equivalent of what he thought it would feel like at the point in his life when he abandoned Jane. His heart floated somewhere between his lungs and safe behind a cage, floating in the liquid of discontent at the way things worked out.

A pop in his ear brought a brook of hot liquid, and it ran out as a remnant of his early morning shower. And that was all that life was, wasn't it? A buildup that you aren't even aware is taking place, a snap, and a hot molasses brook soothing out of a void that you never knew existed. It was that way with love, war, sex, violence. Love…

Alan reflected on his position, and while he gained a void in the release of Jane, the hope and horizon of Jaime was building. Who was she to make Alan feel bad? The degree of her selfishness of Alan was sickening. It was a weakness in the overall scheme of things! Why would she allow for someone to carry her heart across two or three thousand kilometers? She was let go.

It didn't matter one bit now. Alan had Jaime, and he was confident in their stroke of passion and happiness. He was enthralled, and he replayed every moment that they had spent together in his head. Oh, how wonderful it felt. She called him lovely and she called him chicken. They studied art. It was nothing less than spectacular, and to drink wine and roll in the grass, taking on only the figments of their chemically optimized imagination as reality allowed for explosions and fusion into the longest and most fantastical kiss Alan had ever enjoyed.

He thought about it as he packed crates of toiletries and tampons at the warehouse, and wrote it with his finger on the slippery latex finished wall of Hank's house. He would feel his own face to see if it reminded him of hers, and would run his hands through his hair as if Jaime were doing it. What would it feel like? Alan couldn't guess. But he could!

He could guess that if he saved up paychecks for a month, he could fly them both to Sydney or Melbourne! He could bring the two of them to the farthest corners of the universe! Oh, how wonderful that would be! To not have to worry about money, time, or what happened next! Jaime was Alan's utopia, and almost a beacon for his heart. It truly didn't matter what happened. He could just be happy moving with her back to Boston, crunching through the snow-ridden sidewalks of Newbury Street buying vinyl recordings of bands long forgotten and tasting a sloppy jimmy-ridden cup of ice cream! Oh, how ridiculous he and his wife would be; and oh how wonderful. She truly was Jaime! 'J'ai me!' Alan thought.

With the slide of the rubber runner of the door to the house against its frame, Alan's eyes opened in the dark blue room of early evening. He hadn't even remembered how he got there, but he was laying on the bed a few rooms away from the living room, his fingers in his hair.

A mass shuffled peacefully and tired through the sleepy house, the lights off and the shades drawn. The stillness and peace of the environment reminded Alan of sleepy late afternoon naps to recorded books and the whisper of simmering water. The steps approached the bedroom door.

"Alan?" The soft voice of Hank traveled on a dimmer-switch softness of a twenty watt glow.

"Yeah."

"You're up?," his voice still a hush.

"Yeah."

"Oh. How was your thing with Jaime?"

"Good. Good."

"You must have gotten in late... This morning you slept on the way to work. So it went well?"

"Magnificent."

"Wonderful. The craziest thing happened to me. Well, first, the Arnotts say thanks for the great way you buffed their car up – they thought it looked brand new... But, anyway, coincidentally they asked about you and I told them your story - briefly, of course - and then I mentioned the thing about Hobbeston. Wouldn't ya know it, Hobbeston is Mrs. Arnott's cousin. She wants to set you up with something with him..."

"Are you kidding?" Alan shot up.

"No, Alan."

"Oh...oh!" Alan pulled on his hair, and a smile stretched across his face in the room growing so dim that even he himself didn't realize he did it. What were the chances? What sort of cosmic series of events would have to come together to -

"Well?"

"Well, that is awesome, Hank. Thank you so much..."

"You're welcome. I didn't do anything; thank Mrs. Arnott."

"I absolutely will!"

"Well, I am going to bed. This dark house is calling me to fall asleep, and I had a long day besides."

"Goodnight Hank..."

"Night, Alan."

And without any degree of opposition, Alan fell asleep thinking of the cut grass, clovers, and kisses of less than a night ago. He thought about Jaime as he curled himself around a stray pillow and pressed his lips to it, humming himself to sleep, stroking his hand on the stomach of discount bedding and pretending it was her.

Alan would work for the next two weeks on a cloud. The days were long, but it passed like a dream, work only serving as the conductor for the candy floss fantasies wisping about his head. The boxes and boxes of product were only the mechanisms for Alan's goal: get through this day and the next, and Jaime will shortly be around. Every night when he went to bed, he wondered how the most wonderful gift that could be given to him came out this time of day; it was a new optimism and curiosity for the future that was closer than it ever had been in his life. Jaime was his future, and the future was illuminated by the residual sun spots in his eyes from the fireworks of their kiss.

Midway through the second week, Mrs. Arnott visited Hank to borrow some tools to fix their faucet at home and it just so happened that Hobbeston would be over for thanksgiving dinner in two Thursdays. He and

Hank were invited. She was also going to cook Hank and Alan some banana nut bread in retribution for lending her the tools. When she left, Hank had told Alan in confidence that she made the best bread in the southwest.

"Can you believe it, Alan? I mean... Thanksgiving, already?" Hank said.

Alan looked back at him. Was it Thanksgiving? Alan had been living with Hank for what only seemed like a month, and it was already one of the biggest holidays of the year. Yes... It was November. Alan had been with Hank for... Well, he figured he woke up in the hospital around the end of September. Yes. It had been a little over a month.

"Thanks, Hank..." Alan looked at Hank passively through the tops of his eyes. As Hank always carried himself slumped below Alan it was a strange sight to see the larger, bony man look surrendered and docile in front of the shorter stout figure.

"Alan, cut it out with that. Think of it this way, I am just a guy helping a kid get back on his feet." He paused, and looked up in the ceiling. These looks always brought his best introspection. He continued speaking slowly, and clearly. "I was reading a book, Alan. By a man who lost a son... It was all about how he had to live with burying him. His religion wanted him to bury him within twenty-four hours of his death... But he had him embalmed and he postponed it. He started to think about all that they didn't do and everything that they went through while he was still around. Truth was, his son was only nineteen, and his wife had already passed away. The story ended as his son was being lowered into the ground, but it was at least six months after he had died..." Hank pulled his mesh cap off of his head and itched it. He looked back at Alan as he replaced his hat.

"I apologize. I know that this is a strange way to tell you that... I just wanted to... Alan, you are a nice guy, and life has handed you shit. Now, I could have kept driving that day I picked you up; apparently people dump dead hookers all over the desert all the time. But there is something about you that is familiar. I like you Alan, and I hope that everything with you and Jaime works out, and I hope that you make it back home with her or you make it to Vegas with her or you keep going west until you hit Japan - but most importantly, I really want you to be happy, Alan. You are a good fellow. Maybe if you become rich and famous you can take care of me, but all I want in return is to know that I helped you out. There aren't too many people I have cared about in this life, and I am glad I could help."

Alan stepped backward, his hands on his thighs steadying his balance. Hank's generosity was his greatest asset. He was truly a selfless person. He was exactly what Alan thought America was missing. There were no more patriots or heroes: they were all played out by people that made millions of dollars a year in sports and movies and who volunteered and threw money around because there was really nothing they had to do with all of their time and money besides give it away. You were actually expected to feel bad for them if they became addicted to drugs. No, Hank wasn't like this. He was a hero. Alan thought that he would have been dead if it weren't for Hank.

But weren't there other heroes on his trip? Even though he resented Clark, he really helped him out... and then there was the family in Branson that took him in after his tuna fish episode. Come to think of it, Alan thought, while there were far more people on his trip that didn't help him, there was an alarming number of people that did. The others were really just extras in the adventure of this movie. Wasn't this country full of selfish, gas-hungry, materialistic capitalists? Where were the black hearts he thought existed? These American people were poor, unemployed, and depressed... Yet they helped him. Where was the squalor and horror that Alan thought existed around every corner? The closest he came to it was during his short trip to the Midwest... But... He really didn't interact with anyone, did he?

Alan looked into Hank's eyes. The tissue and flesh around the orbs was work beaten, soggy, and sloppy like the neck of a fresh store bought turkey. But his eyes were a vast sea of warmth and comfort. They spoke to him and embraced him, without anything further than their normal operational blinking and darting. They were the catalyst of everything Alan needed to find out about this world he lived in, and more. He needed to find out more.

Without further thought or any degree of hesitation, Alan threw his arms around Hank. It was a true and pure embrace that refused any complicated rules on how to act appropriately or what a socially acceptable standard was. It was just what needed to happen. Alan's eyes were closed and he felt Hank tremble in his arms. Hank didn't hug back; he just hung in the air, his balance mitigated by Alan's affection. Alan recognized the hush of sobs emanate from Hank's form in his chest.

They stood for what seemed like an eternity. Alan not only felt as though he truly wanted to be as close to Hank as he possibly could, but he also felt the pangs of loving respect for this man. This same man that saved his life, took him in, and fed him. Even though they stood for almost ten minutes, even when the hug seemed to last maybe too long, Alan felt it was his duty to stay there as long as Hank was crying.

"Oh, Harv," he whimpered, "oh, oh, how I miss you."

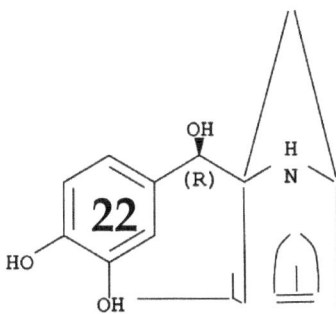

Alan stood on the porch of the Arnott's dusty ranch in the middle of Overton's hazy red thanksgiving landscape with his mobile phone to his ear.

"I really did miss you, chicken." Jaime's voice sounded so much more lovely than he had remembered.

"I miss you too, babe."

"Babe," she responded sarcastically.

"So, how was your trip?"

"It was great. I got to see all of my friends. Chris, Kate... I stayed over Kate's. They didn't have any extra room, so it is great - her parents always let me stay in her bed. She has a huge one. And Chris is a piano player at this hotel. He is so talented. I love him, I really do. He gets fifty bucks a night to play piano, and he is in this band, and he is also a waiter. It was just so much fun." Alan considered the hotness of this girl that he is totally in love with sharing a bed with another woman. Another woman who is also probably really, really hot and just as cool as Jaime.

"You'll have to tell me more. What are you doing tonight for Thanksgiving?"

"Well, my brother is here from New York, so we're here chilling out, drinking way too much; going to have some turkey. I should have invited you... You have somewhere to eat?"

"Yeah, I'm here at Hank's neighbor's. We're having Thanksgiving here, and their whole family is here. Hobbeston is going to stop by, apparently... Crazy coincidence - they are relatives."

"No way!"

"Yeah. I am kinda excited. I wrote down some questions I wanted to ask him, but I am not sure I am even gonna use them. I'll probably just going to shoot from the hip. But then again, I also want to maybe just schedule another time to meet with him. It is Thanksgiving, after all."

"You know, I think it is really cool that you're a writer. I couldn't imagine what it is like - just to be able to write. I have journals and stuff, but... I'm not sure. I could make them into a book sometime."

"You could!" Jaime rubbed her stomach on the other end of the line, and Alan heard a snake rustle in the brush nearby. "So, when do I get to see you?"

"Well, after this, my brother is going to be around for another day, and then we say goodbye to him tomorrow night. I have to work Saturday, but Saturday night I am free. I guess you can bank on Saturday night."

"Let's do it!"

"Okay!"

"Alright. I have to go, but give me a call with a time when you are ready to get together on Saturday, and I will make sure we have some wheels."

"Or I could drive."

"Whatever... Have a great Thanksgiving, baby."

"You too."

Alan pressed 'end' on the phone, and turned around into the house. It was a cozy little place. You first entered into the living room, which was connected to the kitchen by way of a bar that was bustling with holiday excitement. Everyone had a beer or a glass of wine in their hands. Mr. and Mrs. Arnott were bouncing around the kitchen, working on a portion of their project, and then leaning against the counter that they were at with the drink in their hands and their arms folded laughing at something. Hank just leaned on a counter and smiled while the extended family of the Arnott clan were bustling around and telling stories, the children chasing themselves and a dog around the floor.

It smelled like bread and pumpkin; it smelled like home. Alan went to the counter and took a beer, a very big beer, and opened it. Mrs. Arnott saw Alan and she put her hand out in a 'stop' or 'excuse me' gesture and made her way over to Alan.

"Honey, I have some bad news... I'm afraid that Tom called and he isn't able to make it..."

"Oh," Alan said, understanding she meant Hobbeston. "That... That is too bad..."

"I know you are disappointed, hon, but he does this every year. But I will tell you what I did for you. He told me that you are on the guest list for his sermon on Sunday and you are totally allowed to go, for free, and allowed to talk to him after the show. What do you think of that."

"Well! Well, I suppose that that is just a good!"

"Good. Now, let's have us a great thanksgiving, okay?"

"Sure, let's."

Alan joined the conversation and he heard some stories... The grandeur of these people's mundane and trivial lives was fantastic. They spoke decades of situations and happenings that utterly didn't matter to him, and it was good. They built the story of their lives in oral history and anecdote. It was exactly what Alan needed. 'This must be what family is like,' Alan thought

Later in the evening, just before dessert, Alan sat with Mrs. Arnott on the front porch of the small ranch style house as she slowly smoked what had to be the longest cigarette he had ever seen.   You didn't often see people smoke anymore in America; it was a rather old-fashioned and nostalgic activity that was mitigated by the horror of the packaging that required eighty percent of it be covered in photos of diseased body parts, birth defects, and widowed husbands and children grieving of photographs of the lost - women were statistically the only people who smoked anymore.

"So what brought you out here, Alan? You are different. Are you a relative of Hank's? He hasn't really said much about you."

"Hank saved my life. I would have thought he told you about this part..."

"No, I think I am the only person he hasn't told the story to."

"Oh. Well, I was stranded in the desert and something prompted him to pull his truck over and pick me and my dog up off of the ground, and take me to the hospital. Ever since then, he has been feeding me and taking care of me."

Mrs. Arnott laughed in a whisper, and clouds of smoke crawled a cloudy staircase toward the sky. She was very skinny, and her weight and skin and complexion was evidence of her compulsive nature this close up.

"That's Hank. His heart is the biggest one in the western hemisphere, I swear to it. You know what they used to say... The sun never sets on the British Empire? Well, the sun never sets on lives Hank touched; that's the truth."

"He's always been this kind?"

"Yes, but even more so since the accident with his son. For a man who has lost his wife, his son, and has nothing else to live for, I swear Jesus has entered his heart with even more glory and power than anyone else, and has justly picked just the right man. A kind, kind, kind, kind man."

"You're right..."   Lost wife and son?   Alan considered it briefly. "Compared to the rest of the country, Hank is a stark contrast to the rest of our so called brothers and countrymen."

Mrs. Arnott spun her head around at Alan and looked at him. She was confused, and Alan wasn't sure why. She had just spent the last minute talking about how wonderful Hank was and obviously that there wasn't anyone else on the planet as wonderful as he was...

"Well, I don't know what you're talking about," she said, taking a long drag. "There are plenty of good people here. Otherwise, why is my son and my daughter holding guns and shooting people on the other side of the world? To defend a bunch of selfish assholes? I don't know what you are talking about."

"I'm sorry... I didn't realize that - their cause is good, I suppose, but you can support them and not support the people that made those decisions, you kno-"

"Who are you?"

"Listen, I didn't mean to-," Alan trailed off. Mrs. Arnott placed her hands on her face and was hunched over. She was sobbing, and as she heaved, small ashes from the cigarette drifted down to the earth. Ashes to dust. Alan did only what he felt was appropriate for the moment. He put his arms around Mrs. Arnott and rocked her back and forth. A bright ember dropped from her cigarette down to Alan's leg and went straight through the fabric of his jeans. It burnt straight down like a molten needle dropped through a stick of butter.

Through his shirt, he felt Mrs. Arnott's breath escape her and sniffle.

"I... I just miss them so much." Her voice was muffled and sounded like a jazz trumpet player with the muffler on. "Every time the phone rings, I am worried that I am getting *the call*, you know? I hear about all these other mothers on the Internet and how they are dealing with their kids being away,... And poor Hank. Poor Hank. I wish I could protect them like when they were little and they thought I was *it*. I remember when they thought that *I was the world* and *nothing bad* would *ever* happen to them. *You have no right.*"

"Just stay strong..." It sounded like a greeting card, but it was all Alan could think of. "I understand."

"Dessert's ready!" Mr. Arnott called from the kitchen.

Mrs. Arnott stood up, the porch light highlighting her skinny body as she wiped her forehead. She couldn't have weighed more than ninety pounds, and it was clear that her physical stature closely mirrored her personal stability and susceptibility to environmental pressures. She wiped her eyes. She wiped her nose. The cigarette still stayed lit and stable in her hands.

She held the door open for Alan, and they made their way into the living room, and then the dining room. The crew was all situated around the grand table with black coffee and pumpkin pie in front of everyone. Even the small round kids table was waiting for Mrs. Arnott and Alan. They sat down, and everyone smiled at them.

Just as they did at the beginning of dinner, everyone held hands and bowed their heads. Alan liked the way that they said grace. It was silent. It allowed for introspection, the silent giving of thanks and observation any way that they felt necessary. Alan was almost ready to give the Hebrew prayer for bread, but instead, took the time to think about Jaime's legs, and how they must feel to have his lips on them.

The silence was broken by Alan's mobile phone. It started ringing, and Alan immediately let go of the Arnott's relative on his right side, pulled it out, and hit the ignore button. The caller identification read 'mom.' To save embarrassment on Alan's part, everyone already had their heads up anyway. Mr. Arnott decided to start the conversation this time.

"So, Alan, we all have heard a lot about you form Hank..." Hank looked up and smiled, and then looked back down and shook his head, "he can't stop talking about you! You are a writer, is that right?"

"That I am."

"What kind of stuff are you interested in? do you write like... Science fiction? Nonfiction?" Alan wasn't entirely sure why this always came up. Whenever someone figured out that he was a writer, they always immediately went to science fiction. Why was that?

"Reality fiction, basically. Literature. Stories that could really happen."

"His stuff is really great. I like it," Hank interjected.

Mr. Arnott continued, "So... Are you working on something right now? I mean, you are really interested in meeting Tom." Looking around the room, everyone was looking at him, smiling and chewing or sipping. It would be really hard not to deliver some kind of blockbuster response.

"Well... It really is just a - an obsession at this point. But no doubt these things usually turn into stories for me. I am just interested in meeting him, that's all. Take some notes, meet the people that are in love with him..."

"That's interesting. I was under the impression that it had something to do with your work..."

"Well. You could honestly say it does, I just haven't planned it out yet." Everyone just continued to stare, nodding their heads.

"I hope that you won't cast him in a bad light... Because if you did, we would feel partially responsible, you know."

"Sure... I actually was interested in this way before the whole thing with his wife happened. That is what brought me out here in the first place. Weeks, actually months ago I set out here to plan this."

"I wasn't even talking about the situation with his wife," Mr. Arnott replied. Alan looked down at his plate and sifted the contents of the pie around a little. "But that's okay. We have you in this weekend. I am sure you are excited."

"I am!"

"Good. You are going to be right up front. He always keeps a small section of the congregation available for press and you should be alone for the most part. He sees himself as the press does... As a bit of a celebrity... So he always wants to be considered as accessible as possible. He told me he wants to run for president one day. That will be interesting. That will make him the second person in his field ever to run for the presidency."

"Interesting. I'll have to ask him about that. Let's see... As far as what I am working on... Nothing right now, but I just finished up a story; probably the story with the biggest twist that I have had so far in any of my stories. It is about a high school boy that falls in love with a particular girl. She is really smart, and she's pretty and worldly, and she helps him with his homework all of the time. Well, she gets pregnant, and there's some nice religious imagery in it right before she gets an abortion. You don't find out until the end of the story that the girl that he was in love with was the teacher."

A fork dropped to a plate, and some of the people at the table looked genuinely interested while most looked disgusted. The kids table was also a rousing group of confusion, and there might as well have been a giant orange Styrofoam question mark hanging above it like a game show. Alan was hoping that the kids waited until they got home to ask their parents what an abortion was.

Luckily they restrained for the time being and Alan thought to himself, as he had countless other times in his life "you're a fucking moron." Apparently his northeastern conversations about literature and movies, no matter what their content, were not allowed anywhere but the northeast... Reality was reality, truth was truth.

"Okay," Mr. Arnott said. "Theresa, how is the flower business these days?"

Alan was immediately relieved that he was out of the conversation, and with good reason. Maybe, he thought, my big reason that I have such fears of other people and feel that they are rude to me is because they don't all hold the same open mind as I do. Maybe, he thought, it is me... not them?

No... No, that couldn't be it. There were several kinds of people in the world. There were the people Like Hank and the Stillers; people with a genuine spark of good faith and warmth in their hearts. To help without want or desire for reimbursement. Mitzvah, as Judaism called it, hospitality and good doings without a need for reward. These were your Jewish obligations; to commit as many random acts of kindness a day. Period.

But as his mother once said, the root of hospitality is hospital. Alan was never quite sure what she meant, but he came close when he met Sella in the dusty driveway of that diner earlier in his trip. He almost gotten the shit beaten out of him, literally, by the men that he feared were taking over his country. Selfish men with guns and bats and chains. Men that think they are being men by getting back at someone by killing his dog. That wasn't justice, but to them it was. They acted violently on impulse and had not a care as to what happened as long as they could keep their guns and get back at whoever killed their friend with their tiny militia.

Who was there more of? The city of Cortez, Colorado was full of them. Looking around the Thanksgiving table of these humble sheep, he could see that there wasn't a wolf here at all, and that the closest that came to it was... Alan was practically the only wolf disguised as a sheep around here. He hunted out sheep, and let them feed him and let them take care of him and for what? Where was his Mitzvah now? He hadn't done anything for anyone in a while, had he? Maybe in Cortez... Maybe in Aline for Sella... He didn't remember.

Maybe these big acts were enough to make up for it. Maybe.

Alan shook in his seat, his heart hot and the rest of his body cold as ice. The air conditioner was on too high. His heart felt like the fiery thorned muscle he so often saw in the religious catholic imagery... But it didn't hurt like usual, the fire with the barbed wire or thorns... It was just on fire this time.

The rest of the night went by uneventful. Alan just sat in his chair shivering, and the family warmly said their goodbyes. Alan was happy when he received the same, slow, familial goodbye that everyone else received. That was the part of the night when he was warm. Truly warm to the core.

• • •

Jaime's cat was pushing its paws into Alan's stomach, making a comfortable snuggly bed for itself as they sat on her comfortable futon couch watching a lovely French film.

It was Saturday night, and they had just decided to stay in and watch a movie. Alan pet the cat. It looked up at him with its sleek, loving face and its eyes. In the light, Alan could have sworn he saw flames emerging from the back of the feline's retinas... But animals' eyes were always the thing about them that Alan loved the most. You couldn't communicate with them any other way. They understood looks.

"What did she say?" Jaime asked.

"That is what bothers me. I have to try to get the number of her shrink or something... Mum is always changing her own medications... That is so dangerous when your mind is as fragile as hers is. She just said... Something like 'I am not happy, I am only elevated power, and that is not happiness... It is only less resistance' or something... then, 'oh, I hope I don't tragically outlive myself.' Oh, god, I hope she isn't drinking again. That doesn't work with her medication... Nope."

Jaime looked at Alan with a crinkled forehead that showed her true concern, but was also extremely, extremely sexy.

"What do you think that means?"

"Psssh. Fuck if I know." But in the back of his mind, he could never shake the thought. It was in his junior year of high school. His mother was standing in the garage of their home... She was looking at Alan, crying. He was on his way to work, and he had stopped to help her with the trash. She was holding the lid to the trashcan in her hand.

"Alan, ALAN!"

"What, Mum?"

"I CAN'T STAND IT! YOU! You need to- LOOK! There's MAGGOTS Alan! MAGGOTS!"

Alan looked into the trashcan. There was no trash. There were no maggots. Just the dusty bottom of a black barrel.

"Mum. What are you talking about?"

"ALAN! You need to visit your FATHER! I can't believe it. I can't believe it. Take the trash out. Take out the trash, will you? Oh, GOD!"

"Fine Mum. I will take the trash out more often. What's wrong?"

"There's maggots, Alan, obviously you don't take the trash out."

"I will, mum, I will."

Alan looked at her. She was sunk over the trashcan. She was looking inside, and saline was dripping from her eyes and her nose into the barrel. A barrage of 'tap' 'tap' 'tap' was audible. She huffed in. It was a beautiful day out, and Alan stood across from her, feeling dizzy in the moment.

"Aaaaaallllllllaaaaaannnnnn," she spoke low and long, making the moment feel like a horror movie, but in the beautiful daytime of Boston's spring. "I spoke with your father. You are going to visit him. You are going to see him next month... While you are gone, I am going to kill myself."

The surreal statement hit Alan, and it felt like a bad dream within reality. The kind that felt so real that you feel like you are in it. Normally, reality would sneak into your dreams, and everything would feel okay for a moment. But in this case, the nightmare was sneaking into reality. Alan looked down at her feet, and it looked as though there was some dust, maybe chalk, around her feet. What was that?

"Mum, what in the hell are you talking about? I am not going anywhere, I have to work, but I am certainly not going anywhere now."

"Well, that is what I am doing, Alan... Look at all these maggots! These filthy, filthy maggots!" Alan wondered if he knew that they would be living in her soon after she killed herself; and not the invisible ones she was looking at. Alan thought about these things now, especially since it helped take his mind off of the gravity of the situation.

That was over five years ago... But the horror of the moment was a lot to handle. He didn't have to worry about it on the futon with the cat on his lap, watching a French film, but really watching Jaime.

"I really don't know... and you know what the creepiest part of it was? She whispered it all. She whispered it really really slow like... Like I was listening to a seashell, or the smoke coming from a fire that was just put out by a bucket of water. Her voice was like smoke."

She reached over and put her opposite arm around him like a hug. The cat on his lap wasn't entirely amused, but it could be biting him and he wouldn't mind. The warmth of the moment was well received and he was happy.

The cat wiggled away from between the two of them, and jumped onto the floor. Its padding feet tapped its way into another part of her bedroom. Her bedroom was very interesting. One had to go down a very narrow hall with a couple of steps that turned ninety degrees around, and the first thing one saw was a living room with real wood paneling painted white. Then there was a short hallway off to the left with a closet and then her bedroom. There was nothing in it, really. There stood a bureau with all kinds of strange handmade knickknacks and natural artifacts, and photographs. There was a stereo on the floor, with an antenna going straight up and hanging from a coat hanger attached to the ceiling, which was in turn holding a mobile with dream catchers, feathers, and rocks hanging from it. Her bed, which was big and looked very comfortable for two... And a closet, stuffed with interesting historical artifacts that proved Jaime existed and roamed the Earth.

They sat in the living room in front of her small television on the futon couch, and enjoyed the moment.

"Ooooh, Onka, silly cat."

"That's the cat's name?" Alan asked.

"Yeah. There's Onka the cat, then there's Gizmo the cat and Moka the dog."

"Interesting names... Where?"

"I got the cat and the dog's name from a documentary... The title 'Onka's Big Mokah.' It was about this disappearing tribe and a guy accumulating pigs and things to pay tribute to this other tribe and also how modern consumerism has to do with it. It was the name of an album by the band Toploader that no one has ever heard of, too." She was looking for a response from Alan. He just shook his head. He loved how she knew so much... She wasn't book smart, but she knew so much; so many things that Alan didn't, and it turned him on. "My brother brought me the black cat from China, I don't even understand how he got it here, but I got the name Gizmo from Goonies; the movie where the dad brought the animal home one night from Chinatown?"

"Oh Gremlins!"

"Gremlins! Ha! I am so bad with names..."

"Hey, me too."

They turned their attention back to the small television, and watched the film. Alan looked over at Jaime and smiled. He reached his left hand over to her and slipped it under her right one. Out of the corner of his eye, he could see her look down at their clasped hands and smile. She turned her hand around on the sofa, looking at all of the possible angles of their intertwined flesh. Alan wasn't watching the movie at all, as a matter of fact, he had no idea what was going on... After a few minutes, she lifted their hands up between them.

"Hey!" she said.

"What?"

"What's this?"

"What, I can't hold your hand?" She pursed her lips.

"Why would you hold the hand of a married woman?"

Alan was utterly confused.

"I wasn't aware that you were married..."

"I'm not."

"Then, why would you say that?" She only looked at him. "What?"

"When I was down in Kalamazoo I went to my doctor, and..."

"And?"

"...and I am pregnant."

"Okay."

"I've felt like crap lately and I couldn't figure it out. Apparently that is it."

"Wow... How pregnant?"

"Ummm... About... Four months?"

"Holy crap! You don't look it at all..." Heat shot into Alan's abdomen. He didn't know what to say.

"I know, that is why it is so weird. It was strange to the doctor, too."

"Who is the dad?"

"Chris. My boyfriend Chris."

"Chris, the kid you saw in Kalamazoo? Boyfriend or husband?"

"Yeah, but... But he's not really my boyfriend."

"Okay,... Who is he?"

"The father of my baby, now, I suppose."

"Does he know?"

"Yeah. He thought we should get married."

"Oh... What do you think you should do?"

"Well, it's a terrible idea. I am not one to get an abortion. I - I am just going to see what happens. I mean, I think that's what I want to do. I told him that I really don't need his help or anything... I don't want to see him about this."

"You just saw him!"

"I know I did. I just figure it is in our best interest that we keep it friendly... That is where we had problems before. I think this makes it pretty apparent."

"Well, is there anything I can do?"

"No... This is good." She put their hands back down onto the sofa. The wind blew hard outside the small window at the top of the room. "Hey, you know what I think? I think that you should spend the night. That is what I think."

Alan considered the implications of this. His ears were hot. They rang with the consideration, 'You should spend the night. That is what I think.' He looked at her eager eyes. She said it with a nonchalance that was on par with 'this movie is great,' or 'I agree with you, ice cream would hit the spot!' Alan weighed his options. He had to get on a bus to Vegas at quarter of six in the morning. Maybe Jaime could drive him... But then again, he wouldn't get much sleep and he had to get his notebook and other accoutrements from Hank's house. He certainly had the option. But then again, he didn't want to give it all up. Alan remembered something about women that a friend told him once, 'Always keep them guessing, and they'll want you more and more by each day.'

"I can't, I have a thing in the morning. You can come if you want. I am going to meet Hobbeston at his church place for the filming of the show. Vegas, baby, Vegas!"

"Again? You aren't going to convert, are you?"

"No, no, no, I actually missed him at Thanksgiving. That's why I am going tomorrow, to make up for it."

"Sorry, baby, I have to work."

"That's too bad. Maybe we can do Vegas another time."

"I haven't even been there, isn't that sad?"

"Strange, yes; I don't know about sad. Then again, I would probably be sad if I never got to see it."

"Well, of course! That's the whole reason you're here, chicken!" Her dimples were amazing. Alan wanted to jump on her and kiss her and kiss her face and kiss her collarbone and kiss her arms and just take an hour and a half kissing every little section of bare skin that he could see right now. That is what he wanted.

He took his right hand. The one lonely on the sofa. He placed it on her cheek, and looked into her eyes. The passion of her asking if he wanted to stay. It was his understanding that men were not socially allowed to be this enthralled in a moment and a situation. That is what women wanted.

In her stomach was a fetus. They had taken drugs. They had drank wine. Yet, she was keeping the baby, and was going to find out what would happen? How tragic. It was apparent that she was going to lose the baby taking this into consideration. If Alan could have started again, he would have made sure that this didn't happen. He would have changed the outcome of the situation. He could have been the father, and they could have gone to Vegas to get married, and the birth of the child would have actually meant something. They could have had a son, and Sella, and a small house in the middle of the desert that they bought for a ridiculously miniscule amount of money, and they could have lived simple, and it would be beautiful.

"Jaime, do you want me?"

"You are wonderful. Of course." She smiled. The same smile that drove Alan crazy. This time, his hand was on her cheek, and he could feel her flesh for the most wonderful dimensions of heaven. His hand was the perfect size for her face, the grace of her skin, fitting like a gear in the machine of passion. He felt her say those words. He felt every elastic movement, and it meant so much more.

Alan moved closer to her. He moved her face closer to his. He had not yet kissed her, as much as me may have thought he did... He wasn't sure. But this didn't seem like the right moment. The wind blew dust into the windows, and it sounded like hail. No, this wasn't the way it was supposed to happen at all.

Alan took his hand and brushed Jaime's nose downward and she nodded her head downward and smirked. Behind her, the clock read three thirty-five. In the morning.

"Holy crap!"

"What?"

"Look what time it is?! Oh, man, I have to hit the road, baby."

"Okay," her more-than-understanding voice was a wonderful addition to the moment. It hung in the air, just like the moment would. It almost whispered the question 'where were we,' waiting for the next moment they would both be sitting in this exact location.

"Want me to call you when the bus pulls in tomorrow night? You are working in the morning or...?"

"I am working in the morning. Do you want to me to come and get you at the bus station?"

"Yeah, actually, that will be great."

"Okay. Well, have a good night. It looks like we're having a dust storm out there, so squint your eyes and drive carefully, will you?"

"Sure."

She hugged him, and kissed his neck. It didn't get old. They were very close to the same height and it was wonderful.

Alan turned around and made his way downstairs, past the dark dining room, out of the garage door, and into the sand-blasted environment. As he was driving home, Alan drove the borrowed behemoth back to what he thought was the Arnott's house. It was too hard to tell. The lights reflecting off of the sand made it look as if he were driving into a wall of flames; a fiery wall that morphed to the jittery contours of a fuel inefficient monster. The fire hugged him, and he thought of Jaime and her present situation, and thought of how it was so hard to know what direction he should be going in... But in the situation that he was in, he only felt as though the only thing he could do was continue enjoying her. Continue enjoying every part of her and do everything for her that he could.

Alan rolled the window down just enough for him to poke his fingers out into the chaos of the outside environment. It stung the skin. Pins and needles scraped his fingertips and he felt inspired. Inspired, poetic, and fabulous. He felt as if everything that he worked his whole life for came down to how he planned on spending it with Jaime. He could be a writer, and she could be a waitress, and he could probably be a waiter and a bartender, too, and they could live with the baby (but she probably wasn't going to have the baby, with the drugs and everything), and everything would be wonderful.

But there had to be some way to guarantee this. To guarantee a life that Alan was perfectly happy living in would be wonderful. The guarantee would start with Alan's heart. His heart forming anything that he possibly could form with his earthly efforts and would knock Jaime off of her feet, and pull her into Alan's orbit whether it be by virtue of his own doing or forcefully kicking and screaming. But how would he do that? What did Alan possess that materialized his heart and soul?

Then, he realized that that was just it. He reminded himself that he was feeling inspired, poetic, and amazed.

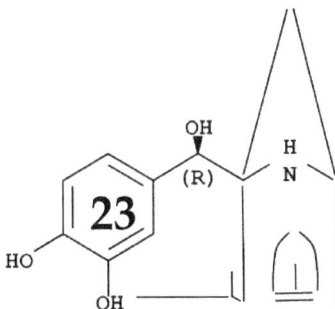

Penning the words sloppily on the small pages of his leather-bound notebook almost seemed natural and comforting to him. He would constantly look down at the scribbles and wonder what the implications of writing words in this indented and sporadic fashion were. Would he write anything that wasn't crap? Could he present this at any kind of poetry slam, or would it stand as a crappy crumpled up ball at the bottom of a shoebox? Oh fuck, he thought, this is madness; this is shit.

If only he had matches on his person, he would torch this whole mess. What a waste that he would soil his notebook with this crap. Crap crap crap. He should just stick to writing prose, but where the hell was the beauty in that nowadays? There wasn't any. No, he thought, and as if my writing was any good to begin with! He had no business with poetry.

Who is going to read over this stuff and be able to decipher all of the poets of long ago that he was ripping off! Inspired by Wilde and Woolf, he would be praised for his beauty and then found out and forever labeled as a charlatan! There was no way that he could purge his mind of the poetry of the past masters like Lowell, Plath, and Rich... The lines were echoing in his head, and the chances that he would come up with an original line were far less than the chances of totally slandering, selling-out, and making a fool of the fantastic!

He could just recite the letter now, and have a secretary type it out for him. He could prance around everywhere and scatter copies of the wax-sealed envelopes on the graves of the addressed artists like a demented version of the anonymous Poe toaster.

> *Dear Hall, Booth, Ginsberg, and Kumin; Wilbur, Merwin, Sweeney, and Richards; Attention Holmes, Davidson, Sexton, and Starbuck; I can't forget to mention Frost! Especially Frost! Please read on if you have the following names: Cummings, Alfred, Ashbery, Auden, Berryman, Bishop, Bly, Brinnin, Cardi, Conrad, Davison (Peter, Jane, or Edward, welcome to read on), Donleavy, Eliot, Fassett (S. and A.), Edward Gorey especially, Graves,*

Jarrell, Johnston, Joyce, Koch, Keough, Lang, Lurie, MacLeish, Macedo Soares, Middlebrook, Moss, Muir, Phelps, Poe, Pound, Ransom, Rich, Roethke, Roth, Salinger, Saxton and Sexton, Sissman, Snodgrass, Stevens, Sweeney, Swenson, Charles, Thommen, Valentine, Warren, Welty, Williams, Wright, Wyn, Yaddo, Yeats, and Zaturenska,

*I am formally announcing to you that I am about to **really** fuck it all up.*

Sincerely,

Alan Levy

Get those words out of my head, he thought with the passion that he first read them with! Get them out! They aren't helping, and they only contribute to a piece of crap that they have no place or right to be a part of! Fuck them! Fuck me and my shitty derivative crap! Fuck not trying to make derivative crap because it would just come out as crappy!

The pen hovered over the paper as the bus bombed down the desolate stretch of what was vaguely considered a road. It was so dirty that in the faint glimmer of the fluorescent lights at the bus station at dawn, one could hardly make out the giant blue "AmeriHiker" emblem on its side. Alan was sharing the transportation with a full house of elderly gamblers, the atmosphere of the bus reminding him of the scent of a public restroom that a baby had just been changed in. It was awful and noxious, and as a new patron of the sauna of incontinence, he wanted out. His only chance came in focusing on his writing. Sure, he had this to look forward when he got older, but don't let's start experiencing it before it was due.

Alan began to write four, five, six times. At times, it was simple, but his own harsh criticism out performed much of his poetry:

That   That I
Is The   Thought
Moment,   About,
The Wonderful Shape
Her Wrist Took
When She
Held My
Hand

It looked like a heart. How lovely! A shape poem that said so much! I mean, how often do people associate hearts with holding hands? When do you see shape poems anymore? What a cute and lovely little... Third grade project.

Alan looked at his creation wishing it never slandered the holy pages of his journal. He started again.

Hey Fantasy,
It's me!
Have I told you yet,
You're everything I want you to be
And-

"What the fuck is that shit?" Alan hadn't realized he said it aloud. Again, again, he put the pen to paper. He felt like he was his own kung fu sensei, coaching his own writing and focus.

Do you know how it feels
To be depressed like me?
She asked.

To feel the sting of love's
Lost away like a clump
Of sand
That drained
        Through
                Your fingertips?

That wasn't bad, but it felt like crap still. Yet Alan wasn't sure what poetry was all about. How did you know when it was done? Was this poem done? This piece of crap crap crappity crap ink on paper stepped in dog poo poo c-r-a double-p crap? He faintly thought that it reminded him of something...

Come on, Alan, go with something you know, he thought as he brushed some invisible eraser dust off of the page.

We have the same eyes, our style
And I want to talk forever
Talk forever and ever and ever

But you have a baby, a creation
And it is making you sick
And it threatens to ruin us, I fear

But you are so beautiful
And your lips feel wonderful
On my neck

It was no good, but it was something. Alan formulated a plan. He would write Jaime a poem today, and work on it every chance that he got.

When Jaime picked him up at the bus station, he would have it all ready to give it to her. A perfect representation of his soul and life's work on paper. What he was on this earth to accomplish. Would there be anything more rewarding than this?

The dusty AmeriHiker bus announced its arrival to Las Vegas, Nevada with a squeal of the breaks and a collective hiss of hydraulics. The doors squeaked open and the elderly women poised at ruining their husband's life insurance policy and grandchildren's college education inheritance slowly got up and collectively sifted through what sounded like a hundred plastic shopping bags and crumbs in each of their pocketbooks that were certainly twenty five years out of fashion. Bumping into each other and giving one another very non-Christian dirty glances and hard elbows reminded Alan that even at an older age, humanity was still just a big pool of flesh hungry sharks.

Alan made his way up to the front of the bus as most of the geriatric casino club had dispersed, and he dropped down the stairs and onto the sandy gravel. It was actually cool out, to his surprise; a swift reminder of the awful time he spent wandering the desert like a nineteen seventies television martial arts guru who, while Alan respected him very much, could not have prepared for the cold of the desert wearing what he did no matter what divine kung fu knowledge he possessed.

Surveying his surroundings for the first time, he realized that there may have been a mistake... A mistake that the rest of the senile travelers didn't notice. Alan stood on a dirt sidewalk in a part of town that reminded him of parts of Dorchester or Roxbury back home. Run down buildings and spray painted walls dotted a cheap and sleazy strip of bargain basement neon that only bordered wooden signs highlighting their shoddy construction. This wasn't Las Vegas, this was Detroit. But as he turned to tell the bus driver about his error, he had no choice but to watch him start to drive away.

Alan had to think up a plan. First he had to figure out where he was, and then he had to figure out how to get to where he needed to be by eight. Looking at his watch, he realized that he had plenty of time, and the only logical thing to do was to ask for directions. But where would he go to find people? His answer lay with the last of the silver haired slot sisters as they entered the seediest single-floored joint - a pest controller's ant trap transformed into a human-sized building.

The Royale Royale Casino stood in a part of Vegas that he imagines that many tourists got stuck in after making a sweet deal with a travel agent that they hadn't dealt with before. Alan felt more like a lost tourist as he enjoyed the sweet smells of stale booze and cigarettes in the air. He was glad that the cool, dewy air he was breathing was that of dawn and not dusk, otherwise he would have thought it smart to run after the bus. There was nothing to worry about, as it was apparent that the driver knew exactly where he was supposed to stop. With the looks of this place, Alan thought, I wouldn't drop my worst enemy off here... or my sister, or mother, or in this case, grandmother.

He stood at the restaurant shadowbox with lightbulbs in chickenwire announcing his location: *The Royale Royale Casino, Home of the 99 cent all you can eat Lebanese Cuisine Bar and the Largest Tahini Wrap In Vegas! Nickel Slots! Dollar Tables! Spend A Minute or Spend The Day!* Under the shadowbox was a small steel holder that held a stack of postcards that were old, chewed up, and covered in some unidentifiable organic human fluid. The pictures, the best Alan could see anyway, showed a retro looking place decorated in nineteen seventies decor. The printing on the cards looked as though they were last printed in the seventies as well; woodsy colors mixed with strange light fixtures and uncomfortable looking seats. But they were right; it looked exciting, modern retro, and edgy!

After entering, Alan decided that he would start the day off with a nice little cocktail. It was beyond his choice, actually. One of the cocktail waitresses brought him a short glass with ice in it and a caramel liquid in it. It reminded Alan of his Ginger Brandy he sometimes drank when he wrote. He didn't order it, in fact, he was more ordered to have it. He paid the skinny waitress with the sunken eyes a three dollar tip for her troubles, only because he knew she had quite a few. When he looked into the glass, he saw through the liquid onto the floor and realized that he was standing on a pamphlet. He moved his foot and bent down, staring into the eyes of a woman with giant breasts hanging out over a telephone number. 'I Love To Suck Cock!' it said, in front of a wall of fire. There were many of these glossy brochures scattered about the extremely run down floor of the casino... Some of them looked as though they were tracked in from outside; pits of sand dimpled them on the floorboards where only wisps of thread remained of the burgundy carpet. He needed a drink.

Yes, a nice drink. Alan could now say he was officially a member of My Lord's Greenwich Association. The Greenwich Association was the expression given to those who drank at such uncanny times of the day that they needed to calculate the Greenwich Mean Time in order to rationalize the pre-breakfast beverage. The Lord part was a rather self explanatory addition to the expression: a pun on English Lord and the thought, 'how many people can honestly say they have gotten trashed before attending church?' He sipped the mysterious liquid which ended up being a pungent discount whiskey. He coughed as it stung his throat.

All of the tables, highlighted by spotlights hung from the short ceiling, lay dormant. Seats fixed to the floor were upholstered with faux creamy green tanned leather. They sat empty, full of cracks and stress marks caused by years of neglect and pockets full of keys, or knives. Smoke hazily drifted midair, and the only activity in the whole place was the bartender and a lonely man sitting at the bar. Across the casino, movement was slightly decipherable behind a glass partition with different doors named "Bingo" and "Keno."

Alan sat at the bar. He plunked the shiny golden dollar coin he had in his pocket into the bar's tabletop animated slot machine. It was the first time that he had ever played any kind of gambling game; lost in the heat of the moment, he actually couldn't figure out how to work it. He just stared at it, sipped his drink, and dazed off. He needed to find out how to get to the church.

"Excuse me?" Alan asked the bartender.

The bartender was at the far right end of the bar, looking at the mirror behind the bottles. She stood tall, and had the same skinny, malnourished, drug induced look about her that the waitress had. Her eyes were baggy, and the puffy purple sacs of skin hanging below the yellowed orbs rested on more skin melting off of the bone. The mirror was strange; antique. In between the glass and the reflective silver was red foil webbing that sporadically coated the entire surface. One could hardly see through it. It looked as though someone took the mirror off of the wall, crumpled it up, dropped it in a bucket of red paint, and then flattened it out on the floor to dry before hanging it back up.

Alan didn't want to repeat himself. The place was so empty that just asking again would be ridiculous, and she certainly had to have heard him. Alan just continued playing with his glass and coaster on the bar to save himself from being rude. That was when the man hunched over at the end of the bar responded in a deep raspy drawl.

"She isn't going to hear you. She's deaf. If you need something to drink you have to flip that light switch over there." He pointed to a light switch on one of the pillars in the building. "She looks in the mirror because I think she doesn't like to stare, and I don't blame her."

"Oh," Alan replied softly. "I don't really need a drink. I just need to figure out how to get-"

"Get what, get what? If you're looking for drugs around here, this isn't the place to get them. You need to go over to the Lucky Shark if you want that shit. My father was killed trying to keep you jerks out of the north end here, so you can just get your ass out of here."

"Sorry, I didn't- I was hoping that someone could help me with directions..."

"Well... Sorry,... directions I can help you with." His tone was still dark. Alan so wanted to characterize the man. Man, at end of bar. Dark. Hair over his eyes. Could be anywhere between thirty and fifty. Dirty. Writer, looking at man. He is cliché, and ignorant.

"I need to find Hobbeston's church. The one that they film the services and the Sacrosanctity Society at..."

"Sandy here goes to the church every week after her shift. Normally it ends at eight, but on Sundays the morning person gets in early for her."

"Sandy," he said to the forlorn deaf woman, still staring into the mirror. She looked at him through the reflection. "This guy doesn't know where the church is; can he ride with you?" He didn't speak in exaggerated tones or any louder than normal. As a matter of fact, he spoke much softer. She looked over at Alan, nodded her head, and then returned to looking at the mirror. It was apparent why this man sat where he did. He didn't need to flip the light switch to get Sandy's attention.

Alan had wished it was as easy as that to get people's attention. In the cosmic universe you were either someone who could get people's attention by virtue of who you were, or you were one of the many people that had actually get up to flick the light switch. Alan wished that he could someday be the person who could get attention… Or at least get one of those old-fashioned devices that would allow him to clap his hands to flick the light on and off.

Silence registered throughout the casino only under the surface of the whirr of fans and clanks of ice bounced solitary off of the fake padded leather walls. Alan took out his black leather bound notebook and his pen and began to play around with the words on the pages. He wrote words that reminded him of Jaime, and what happened between them. The art they saw at the museum, the moments they shared, and words that reminded Alan of what he felt around Jaime: heart, passion, flame, heat. Pregnant. As much as he tried, he pushed this word from his mind, just as he tried to push the idea of a deaf woman driving him to church and attending a sermon. It wasn't that he was biased, but the idea in itself was ridiculous.

This was catastrophe. This was disaster. These words were everything that he had thought would send their world of caring and love falling away into the darkness. It was blatant prevention of their happiness and their hope for the future? How had this happened? She had not thought about this before she had disappeared? This child in her had made Alan's hope disappear! No. No, no, no. This was only the beginning of it, you see.

Alan began to furiously scribble words across the pages. He spoke them, and spoke them with the words he had written aloud. Some sounded too funny and too ridiculous to put in the poem. Drafts of the poem came and went, and lingered on the page. The whiskey whispered the soft words Alan had written on the page, as did he whisper them aloud as he giggled his way though the maze of letters and words that came and went like the imprint of a camera flash on your retinas.

He probably looked nuts. He probably looked drunk.

It was no surprise that when the time came to leave, he was completely oblivious to the deaf woman pulling his arm to take him with her. He pocketed his journal and staggered with her to her car. It was still chilly outside, and the tall, thin woman motioned for Alan to get in on the other side of the car. It was another large, antique vehicle; the kind with the spare tire displayed on the trunk. It reminded Alan of the gigantic vehicle that he had borrowed to take Jaime to the art museum where they tripped in the tall grass until morning. Dew beaded all over the white monster, and shook off like a pet after a shower when she closed the driver's side door.

Alan got into the passenger side, and as he sunk into the deep seat his ears hummed with alcohol and a faucet dripped somewhere distant in his head.

"Chande will some to you, get ready plead." The woman muffled through her disability, and Alan had no experience with it. Alan looked at her and she was looking at him and tugging at her seatbelt. She was actually beautiful, and he certainly couldn't have prepared for the way she had looked. He wasn't sure if it was the lighting or the awful mirror at the casino, but he just realized now that she was an attractive woman. She was clean, and her eyes spoke of virginous happiness – quite a contrast with what looked like harbored pain and broken dreams back inside the casino. He noticed she had changed, and was dressed in a light summer dress now rather than the work uniform. She was beautiful, and Alan had taken it upon himself to reevaluate his original ideas about her. "Pleade?"

Alan had realized that she was saying please, and wanted him to put his seat belt on. He nodded and smiled, breaking his deadpan drunken stare from her. He put his belt on, and she stared the car with a goose-pimpled hand, attached to a bumpy and fresh arm that reminded him of his mother's. The whiskey made Alan sleepy, and he drifted off; his head against the window, the engine's drowsy hum rocking him to sleep.

Alan's eyes opened ten minutes later, a soft hand stroking his cheek. Alan turned his head and the woman sitting next to him was looking down into him with worry, but when his eyes opened she smiled. Removing his head from the cold glass, a frosted halo of steam outlined where his head had touched the window. The woman unbuckled his belt for him, and worked it around his head as if he were a child. She turned to open her door, and Alan did the same.

The parking lot of the church itself was staggering. The woman had parked rather far away from the church itself. It wasn't a stretch of the imagination that, with the size of her car, she wanted to ensure that there weren't any accidents as she silently maneuvered the vehicle through the exiting traffic later after the service. It was so large. It looked as though they were visiting a mall, and yet at the center of the parking lot was the oasis of steel and glass that became a beacon of evangelistic faith and the financial power of mixing religion with fear and forcing it into every television in a persuasive country already on its sinful knees.

The burning asphalt radiated below them, and it had turned from the dull coolness of the nighttime desert to the blasting broiler of the daytime in only the short drive from the bar to the church. As they walked closer, they finally began to pass cars and campers parked in neat rows on the paved plains. The only thing the cars illustrated to Alan was simply desperation; they were rotting, dusty, scratchy, and old. The people who owned these cars were the people of hope rather than actualization.

Approaching the structure, a spidery and sharp instrument, Alan realized it was a great deal smaller than it looked across the parking lot. Even a great deal smaller than it appeared on the tiny screen of his television back home. There were other things worth mentioning; this glass theater with its spire that challenged the heights of the tallest casinos Vegas had to offer badly needed a cleaning. It was almost ridiculous how much this steel and dust-coated glass structure didn't resemble its video counterpart that appears daily on countless screens worldwide. It was small! Oh so small! The dust clung to the windows like webbed lint to clothes, and the steel network of the building, its supports that helped it climb to the heavens, had white paint that had peeled away to expose red, rusty dry wounds in the desert sun. The only majestic and magnificent thing about it was its inability to put any degree of awe into Alan's heart as it had so many times in the past... On television.

Was this where angels dined on the souls of the horrid and sickly after they traded in Hobbeston's stock market?

Alan's phone began to ring, and he immediately thought that he was happy this happened during their parking lot exodus rather than during the service or while he spoke with Hobbeston. He slowed down his pacing as he tried to read the tiny screen and shut off the ringer. He was successful in shutting the sound off, but he wasn't able to see who had called; he was too goddamn drunk. A hand reached over to his wrist and grabbed it and started pulling. It was the deaf bartender pulling him along. She was in a hurry. As they rushed closer, Alan realized that there weren't as many cars in the parking lot as he had originally gauged.

The size, magnificence, magnitude, and gravity of it all shrunk more and more the closer he got to his destination.

They arrived at the immense stainless steel doors at the front of the church and entered. Sand crept into the foyer from outside, and it either happened all the time, or no one ever bothered to clean it up. Bulletin boards on both sides of the foyer advertised Alcoholics Anonymous meetings and various functions held at the facilities: Bingo on Thursday, Sacrosanctity First Quarter Fund Drive in January, and under the corkboards stood a tall, lean table with pamphlets scattered on it in disarray.

Passing from the narthex through the threshold of the glass and steel doors, they entered the inside of the church which was bright and blanketed in a yellow hue from the dust in the windows. It also looked extremely small in the inside, and there weren't nearly as many chairs as they show on television. Not nearly as many cameras as one would imagine either.

Sweeping crane shots would fly over the crowd and magnify the giant scale and power of so many people in such a grand and prestigious building. But here, here lay no more than fifty to a hundred folding chairs, and two television cameras that stood idle behind the seats unmanned and without any of the electricity that a television studio would normally bustle with. Cords snaked back to the left of the nave's back wall to a small control panel manned by a bristly fat gentleman who was dressed awkwardly for church. On the monitors were the views from the two cameras, and on others were familiar scenes from the show, paused, a thousand people seen from above; ready to swoop in on the pulpit. There were no more than twenty five people waiting for the sermon to begin today, and the way the monitors looked, the cameras were positioned just right so that one didn't need to see the rest of the church to think that it wasn't full. The cameras made it look like what you were watching was real, and there honestly wasn't even anywhere else for the worshipers who were present to sit.

Alan thought when he arrived that there would be a sermon before Hobbeston even began, or even the rest of the service so that Hobbeston could be the headlining act.   Maybe even a band playing spiritual music that prompted the crowd to stand up with their eyes closed and put their hands in the air, palm forward, as he had always seen in the commercials for the Christian band of the month during the program. But the drum set on stage lay dusty and dormant, and the glass walls of the cathedral only echoed the bygone days of the church and what it had meant to follow Hobbeston.

As Alan and Sandy walked toward the three or four rows of folding chairs, she let go of his hand, and Alan stopped to look at her. She reached up and ran her hand motherly across his face, down his jaw line, and to the edge of his chin.

"Peace be with you," she spoke, almost phonetically perfect. Alan couldn't have said it any better. She turned, went down to the very end of the row, and sat down. She produced a beaten leather bound bible from her purse with bright yellow paper tabs jutting out throughout the pages of the volume. Alan had to find the place the congregation was supposed to sit, as Mrs. Arnott had described.

Alan slowly paced his way up the center of the aisle, and as he did, he observed the silent and reflective people in the seats. They each had a leather, floppy, oversized book in their lap with enough personal notations and commentaries in the margins that Alan could see them from where he stood. When he got to the front of the congregation, there were some reserved seats to his right with a yellow vinyl rope that draped across the plastic divots of the seat where your butt cheeks went.

Alan almost considered sitting there for a moment, but retracted his idea, as he would be the only one sitting there. He might be a blatant icon for Hobbeston to perform to, not that the video cameras pointing at him were any different. Alan turned to the rear of the room, and for the first time noticed the balcony seating above him, empty of course. Tucked away in the corner he saw the video production bridge from the front, and he made his way toward the inconspicuous felt wall.

Alan took out his leather notebook and pen and stepped up on the small platform.   Alan addressed the man at the intricate control panel. "Hello."

Without any stretch of the imagination, the man was busy twisting knobs and pushing buttons on the bridge and talking to an unknown receiver on the other end of his head-mounted microphone. Looking at it this close up revealed that more of the sandy grime and dust from the desert floor had crept its way onto the dials and buttons of the production bridge. You could tell which instruments on the panel were used the most by the degree of grime wiped away from it. The man turned his attention to Alan, said a final 'yes' into the head set, and nodded with the expression that demanded he was ready for whatever information Alan was about to present him with.

"I'm visiting the church today as a member of the press, and-"

"Well, the church seating for the press and for special guests is at the front of the left side of the church." His timbre was polite, but the delivery was curt.

"Well, actually, I was just curious if you would let me sit back here with you." Alan had just considered that he should spend his time at the service as an observant of not only the service, but also of the show itself. "After all, I would like to experience the service from every angle. As the live observer, of course, but I would also like to see what everyone sees on the telecast as well. I am sure you understand, these are vastly different."

"Well, I honestly don't think that the reverend will approve..." He reached down and clicked a button on a belt-mounted box that was connected to his headset. "Boss, the kid from the press is here to observe the service and he wants to know if it is okay for him to watch from where I sit... Uh-huh? Okay..." he turned his attention to Alan, "Alan?"

Alan nodded. The man looked down at the floor, concentrating on the conversation.

"Yup. Okay, no problem ... Okay I will let you know." The man looked back up at Alan. "Well, you check out. Pull up a seat – don't get in my way." Alan grabbed the one folded up chair that leaned against the back railing of the small command center. After a few more tweaks and checks, he continued, "so, you are a writer?"

"Yes, in a way." Alan could not really pinpoint what he was at this point. Wanderer. Black Sheep Son. Whatever he was, he was where he wanted to be since the beginning of his trip, however unimpressive it was.

"Well, I have a ton of stuff to do here. If you have any questions about what we do here, the boss tells me you can ask away." Alan thought for a moment.

Alan wanted to ask, 'so, you basically pull a smoke and mirrors production on the whole service?' But, "this looks a lot different from what we see on television," is all he could politely muster. The man at the bridge was already switching tapes around and adjusting buttons on long, sliding tracks.

"Yeah. Church attendance has been steadily declining - not just here, but at all churches. There are really few pastors out there that can pull in the crowds that Hobbeston used to have here. So, we make it look like there are many congregants in hopes that it will draw more visitors. His sermons are written by hand every week, however, and that is one aspect of this that remains a holy part of the production. Otherwise, we wouldn't have such a high number of viewers that we do; and it just keeps going up - especially recently."

"How many viewers would you say that you have for the Sunday service?"

"Well usually we are around a million, but in the last few weeks we have jumped significantly higher. Say,... Two or three million."

"Do you think it has anything to do with the disappearance?" The man did not respond, and in the void of sound Alan realized that he wasn't writing any of it down. He felt like a reporter or interrogator, drilling this man with questions in a cement room without windows, so desperate for answers out that he neglected to write anything down and his recorder was out of batteries.

"I can't talk about that. Not that I know anything anyway."

"Oh," Alan responded. The man uttered a few unintelligible figures into the microphone, and Alan just assumed to let him do his job. "Well, I will let you get back to your job. Just pretend I am not here."

"Okay."

Alan fiddled with his notebook and opened to his poem. After reading it over, and over, and over, and editing it to such a degree that the ink bore holes in the paper, he spent the next five minutes copying the extensive language to a fresh page. Rewriting and editing had left the poetry indelible on his mind, which made him feel accomplished as he sat in the back of the expansive room. He primarily wanted to memorize the poem and dictate it to Jaime, and he was already more than halfway there.

"Ten minutes." The portly gentleman spoke to nobody in his immediate vicinity, but to an unknown number of receivers on the other end of the microphone.

Alan was happy with the words, how they were arranged on the page, and confidant that his delivery would be semi-formal, sweet, and hardly hampering on the relationship that they now shared. After reciting the poem, Jaime would look at him smiling, and encompass her being around Alan, as she had never had anyone write a poem for her. How old fashioned; How Wonderful! She could only respond in the frame of love and healing and everything that Alan needed. Alan wanted to be swept off his feet and flown to a higher consciousness where any interaction from Jaime was manna that fueled his semi-religious experience with what heaven must really be like.

That was the way he felt around Jaime. She always would have something funny, interesting, and on point. She drank wine by the litre! Who drank wine nowadays, anyway?

His heart was jumping with the thought of seeing her, and it was absolute magic the way it felt to be in her presence. Even the air was different; sweeter and softer on the lungs, and tossed with the light aromas of compassion and rain and the electricity that flowed between clouds before a thunderous rainstorm. Ions. The kind of rainstorm that makes you sit inside thinking about love and how empty you feel, and wanting the one person to be next to you to share the cozy momentum of being shielded from nature's chaos. Oh, and to make love on a couch or next to a fireplace on the dark gray days of spring with the rebirth of the land and the downpours that were only snow flurries the day before, flakes landing on a paused existence of wilt and compost. That was the ultimate in human bonding and commitment. That was love in its most raw and elemental form.

The shiny stainless steel pen was heavy in his hand after he had finished writing, so he pocketed it, and read over the manuscript in his hands.

Alan was grateful that the small book with its brass clasp and leather binding resembled a scaled-down version of the giant bibles that the others in the congregation carried. No one would have to know that the only hymn that Alan was studying today was his own. Alan read the poem, he closed his eyes and visualized it, and then he read it again. These were the answers to his college anatomy test, and fuck if he didn't pass it this time, he never would.

"One minute…" The man next to him said. He started to feverishly press buttons and on one of the two biggest main screens in front of him, a paused number five faded in quickly when he pushed up one of three levers in front of him. "Thirty seconds…" On the other of the bigger screens, a man ran in from off of the main platform at the front of the church, made a quick adjustment to something behind the podium, and ran back off. Bars of lights next to the long, sliding dials on the big board in front of him began to illuminate now, and the man behind the bridge made sure they were all in the down position. Alan wanted to ask him what his name was, but he was almost positive that with his overweight, wide stature he would tell Alan to call him 'Tiny.'

The man flipped a switch and a red light turned on next to a box that said 'Satellink,' and then pressed another button and the numbers on the screen began to count down. He immediately responded to them in the microphone, "five, four, three, two, one; cameras are live and rolling." The big and bright digital clock at the top of the bridge read that it was still ten minutes of eight.

On the screen, the opening sequence of the television broadcast floated by, and Alan could hear from the big man's headset the music and dialogue that accompanied it. Helicopter aerial shots and pictures from lush and fertile gardens and palm trees were framed in the picture as they were every week.

"…for Sunday, December nineteenth, live from the Christ Glass Cathedral of Las Vegas, Nevada, this is Sunday Worship with Reverend Charles Hobbeston…" The title of the service flew by in a myriad of different languages, and then came applause from the audience shown in the picture. A roaring applause, thunderous, emanated from hundreds of people on the balcony and in the standing room only of the church as the camera flew over their heads to close in on the pulpit. The congregation in presence was not applauding, but Alan did notice that they were standing as he peeked around the hulking bridge. Just as the prerecorded Reverend Charles Hobbeston jumped out of the side of the altar, so did the real one, wearing the exact same suit and tie, casually walking and waving his way to the pulpit.

As the actual congregation sat down and Hobbeston stood at the podium, the applause in the man's earpiece continued, and the broadcast cut to actual live footage as Hobbeston raised his hand to acknowledge the invisible audience. While the man next to Alan was making short, unintelligible commentary as this was all going on, he did notice that he was giving Hobbeston a verbal timing signal, even though Alan didn't understand it. He also wasn't sure how the information was even getting to Hobbeston.

The cameras that were behind the current congregation also began to move somehow. After a slight jerk, it seemed that the cameras, attached to their heavy metal tripods lurched up slightly and coasted on a silent bed of air somehow. There was another camera or two that Alan had not noticed in the room; one on the balcony and one off stage that looked up at Hobbeston, magnifying his authority and size in the room. From where Alan was sitting, he didn't look the least bit as tall as he did on television.

"Good morning," Hobbeston spoke, and the fake and real audiences replied with a complimentary 'Good Morning' back. "Let us pray."

Everyone in the room bowed their heads including Hobbeston and the Wizard of OZ next to Alan. Alan did too, sneaking another glance at his poem, closing his eyes and reciting it in his head, and then opening them to study what words or lines he had missed. Alan had nothing to pray for. He was grateful he was here, and alive, and happy. He figured his god knew it, and he didn't want to jinx his relationship or personal standing by making unreasonable demands. No; he would just sit here and memorize his poem, thank you very much.

Hobbeston raised his eyes and met those of the congregation and of the cameras. Already, the man at the board faded in a toll-free number where people could call and make donations as they listened to the sermon. From a business perspective, they would start the selling as soon as possible without being too intrusive. Alan had a job once where his boss took him aside and told him the company was doing really well, and he owed it all to Alan. Alan had what had to be the most difficult and least important part time job in the organization, so he had replied, 'why?' The boss said, 'because we are all in sales.' Alan realized his boss was right, as the man next to him who was probably working for free, tweaked the message begging for alms on the bottom of the screen so it didn't go too fast.

"...And a wonderful morning it is! Welcome everyone to Sunday worship here at the lovely Christ Glass Cathedral, and everyone watching at home..." Hobbeston paused and looked down at the book on the pulpit. "In less than a week is the beginning of one of the holiest weeks in our faith. This week, our savior was born from the virginous womb of Mary and Joseph more than two centuries ago. He was visited by many, and then became one of the most famous people to ever set foot on this earth. These past few years have been particularly interesting and closely watched by observers of Christ as we gain more understanding of his life and times.

"Many people have differing concepts of Christ and they always come up in the next week more than ever. Some characterize this week as the holiest day of the year, while others characterize it as a time for them to display their faith in how much money they spend on gifts. Without a stretch of the imagination, this fever of spending grips much of our country, and people disguise the dollar and the material possession as the number one factor in their familial and interpersonal relationships. In a sense, that is what I would like to talk about today.

"Loneliness. The word has many definitions. My dictionary describes loneliness in its most basic meaning as 'being without company, or being cut off from others.' It also has some other meanings that are pertinent, 'desolate,' 'sad from being alone,' and the one I would like to focus on, 'producing a feeling of bleakness.'

"I tell you, I have had a great deal of loneliness lately, as you know. The Lord has absolutely no reservations in dealing with it, either. At the very beginning of the bible, Genesis 2:18, we read one simple line, 'it is not good for the man to be alone.' We don't need the bible to tell us this. The bible only reiterates what we already know, we are lonely creatures at times, and it is awful.

"Furthermore, I personally take a trip every week to Saint Aaron's Assisted Living Community here in Las Vegas, and I am constantly bombarded by the old and lonely. One nurse there regarded them as the 'poor lost souls of our day' who would end up in the nursing home 'just to die.' Of course, this is the most hopeless and sad and lonely times of the year for these people that are not lucky enough to be able to go and see their families or have them come and visit them. At a recent sermon I held a couple of weeks ago, I said to them, 'this is an assisted *living* community, not an assisted *dieing* community, so get busy living. I can help you. This is a community for a reason, if you are lonely you have nothing more to do than turn to your neighbor and your friends and build a network of love and compassion and caring just as Christ wishes you to. How do I know this? Because He says to in the Bible. Share your love of the lord with your neighbors and you will be sharing love between yourselves.'

"I had them open their bibles to Matthew 11:28-30 and asked them a simple question. 'When we are lonely, empty, and without any hope, what does the lord say we do with these emotions?' Of course, they all looked down at their bibles and understood immediately. 'Come to me, all you who are weary and burdened, and I will give you rest. Take my yoke upon you and learn from me, for I am gentle and humble in heart, and you will find rest for your souls. For my yoke is easy and my burden is light.'

"This time of the year is the biggest and most popular and exciting time for us, but by virtue of my illustration using those of us without the gratification of family and friends, it can also be the loneliest of days." Alan scribbled in his notebook 'the loneliest of days.' After doing this, he looked back up at the television monitors, more specifically the one showing what the actual broadcast was showing. Whenever the camera would sweep over the audience, you could almost not discern the gap that existed between the people that were in the pre-recorded video and the ones in the room. As a matter of fact, the front row that was empty was in fact full in some of the angles, and the way the cameras were positioned and repositioning themselves, you couldn't tell that it was actually empty. It was all a trick.

"…you have to believe that what we see is real. Christ is real. You are not wasting any time in exploring his life and his creation. When you are lonely this Christmas season, Christ will be your family. Christmas literally means 'Christ's Mass,' so how ignorant could you be to think that you need anyone else besides Christ in your life? Furthermore, what will buying people presents divulge about your relationship with them? That it is strong? Interesting that people begin to put price tags and shrink wrap and shiny paper on their relationships.

"Naiomi's neighbors tell us in 4:15 that Ruth, Naiomi's daughter-in-law, was more important to her, no, loved her and was more dedicated and selfless than 'seven sons.' Folks, do not materialize our relationships. They take time, sacrifice, diligence, not material possessions. That is the easy way out. God made us in his image to serve the purposes of this very fact. Just open the book anywhere - Proverbs 17:17; 18:24; Proverbs 27:17-19; 1 Corinthians 13:4-8; James 5:13-20. You name the place and the time and I can tell you what the lord said about this.

"Rather than give material gifts, show you care by giving in other ways. Donate to the Red Cross or even this Ministry in their name. Wouldn't that mean more? Most of us need no more than we already have. We are surviving after all, right? Give to those that need it more, or give to your church. Be generous, and give; give in the spirit of those that have passed and those that are coming into the world. A coffee bean grinder breaks, but virtue lasts not just a lifetime, but forever. Be a philanthropist to what your friendship represents, not just what it is missing. That will be the most fulfilling gift you can give." The fake applause rung through the earphone of the man sitting next to Alan, and it was obvious that while Hobbeston could not actively hear it in the room, there was some cue that told him to pause, which he did. He continued as the shoreline receded from the big man's headphone. In the room, Hobbeston succeeded in making it look like the extensive pause was meant to happen.

"As far as being lonely, do not let friendships go to the wayside. I say rebuild and forgive. Most of us have plenty of friends and plenty of relationships that we have only neglected or ended because of one reason or another. I say, good Christians, this makes you very unhealthy not only physically, but unhealthy in your relationship with the Lord. Leviticus 19:17; Let Go Of Grudges! Build Bridges!

"Continuing on, those of us who are wholly away from home, in a new place, or who genuinely feel as though you have no friends? I promise you, you have friends. In John 14:18, the lord said 'I will not leave you comfortless: I will come to you.' Even more promising is Matthew 28:20 when the lord tells us that as long as we observe Him, he will be with us at all times, until the end of the earth.

"The lord is with us at all times. Isn't that comforting? To take this even one step further, the lord 'healeth the broken in heart, and bindeth up their wounds,' says Psalms 147:3. If you are even feeling lonely, only think of the lord and he will come to rescue you from loneliness. That is what brings me back to the definition of loneliness that read 'bleakness and desolation.' To be bleak is to be dark, and you are the light of the world the Lord tells us.

"There have been some dark times upon you all. There have been bleak and desolate times for myself - there continue to be; but with a trust in the Lord, believing in the Lord, caring for the Lord, this is what brings about salvation from our darkest and deepest loneliness. Giving in the spirit of giving rather than giving in the spirit of want; that is what the lord wants from us. Take these things into heart this holiday season. Let us bow our heads once again."

"Was that it?" Alan could not help think of this question as after twenty minutes of what could only be described as unorganized biblical blathering, it was time for the final prayer. This show was over an hour long. Where was the rest of it? Alan looked over at the monitor, and a scene of Hobbeston that he saw in the first few minutes was still playing, and then faded to a scene where he was standing on stairs in an obvious shooting set that was set up to look like a house. And then it cut to pictures of an African nation and a Sacrosanctity Society missionary handing out food to starving people. This was a prepackaged, one size fits all, get on with your life after you receive your fast fed religious service! It was no more than a half hour long of nothing. Where was the rest of it? It was in the computer. It was regurgitated, prepackaged show, cut up in a variety of other formats and other clips ahead of time.

Hobbeston looked into the cameras and said, "have a wonderful, happy, and healthy Christmas." A light on top of the two cameras in Alan's immediate vision shut off.

"...and cut on the final live taping. Good job everyone. If the production crew could come for the remainder of the Sat-Feed, I would appreciate it. Make sure all mikes are off, staff, and Boss, hit your mike too." Hobbeston reached down behind his back and fiddled with something on his belt as he stepped down off of the stage to interact with the worshipers.

The man next to Alan was still very busy, and while Alan was enticed to get up and wander around the church and investigate its small unnoticeable imperfections, he refrained and waited for Hobbeston while he observed the men on the production crew interact.

The sun still shone brightly down through the muck on the windows, and Alan thought about home for a moment. He also thought about what it would be like to make this place his home, with Jaime. What would that be like, to just permanently relocate to Overton, or Vegas? Would he be happy? With the thought of Jaime, this idea did not seem without justification. What if she wanted to move back to Kalamazoo? What about Georgia?

They would live in the middle of nowhere, both working dead end jobs without saving any money whatsoever and they would live on a huge plantation that they purchased for a dollar to the hectare. Seeing her in a flowy, summer cotton dress pinning sheets to the clothesline while he drove the tractor across the immense land would make him happy; even moreover when he was finished with his work, sweaty and sun-burned, and he caught her in their bedroom listening to old jam bands from the early nineteen-nineties dancing about with a glass of wine in the afternoon. The way the sun shone though the cotton to reveal the shadow of her calves, knees, thighs, and sprigs of hair from where it all met without panties would drive Alan wild enough to make love to her right there on the hardwood floor.

She would go back to dancing while Alan pored a glass of wine for himself in the kitchen and made his way to the widow's tower at the top of a spiral staircase to write his novels and drink the night away happily with the wind blowing through the open windows and nothing to stop him from smiling, smiling, smiling. Jaime would sneak up and lay next to him, and they would sleep though the night under a blanket of nothing more than the stars and the moonlight, and a freshly sun-dried sheet on top of them; the stars tossing shadows of Goreyan creatures about the walls, and the wind rustling the trees outside. 'I haven't felt this happy in a long time,' Alan would remind himself.

He was staring off into the distant sky through the dirty glass as he thought about this. He recited his poem to himself in his head, and he realized that not only did he have it completely memorized from beginning to end, but he could now practice his inflection timbre, and delivery so that he could time it perfect for... When would they kiss? Afterward, surely, given the delivery was just so...just so absolutely perfect. Had they kissed yet? Alan recollected the only mental mention of it was when they took the hallucinogens at the museum, and he wasn't even sure that it had actually happened. Strange... They held hands, of course, but had they kissed for sure? He didn't know.

The worshipers had shifted and were loitering around a table with coffee and donuts laid about it. They were the exact opposite of what was shown of television, in fact, it seems the entire service was. It was shorter, devoid of dramatic music. There was no bargaining for alms and Alan hadn't realized until then the possibility of how short the service itself actually was. He showed up, watched a sermon, and everyone got coffee and donuts.

Alan hadn't noticed, but in his daydreaming of Jaime and the show on television as opposed to the live one he just witnessed, a tall, thin man emerged from the crowd. In one hand was a piping hot cup of coffee and in the other was a book. He approached Alan, and in a powerful but soft voice caught his attention.

"Brother Alan Levy, I presume," the blond man in white said. "My name is Charles Hobbeston, and I believe you are here to speak with me."

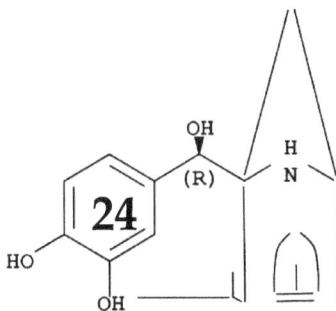

Hobbeston had led Alan through some hallways that connected to the church into a white office building behind the church. Sitting across from this man, Alan could not see the resemblance to the man he had always seen on television.

They sat in an oak paneled room with gold trim, hundreds of leather bound books, and leather chairs. The room was a lavish leather and gold centerpiece of any red blooded American man's office. The most notable part of the room, in a white suit, was Charles Hobbeston. He seemed nothing like he would have ever expected. Meeting Hobbeston was like having a relationship with someone for years, and then meeting their family and there was absolutely no possible influence on the acquaintance and who they were. Hobbeston was a specter of his televised self. He was a poor drugstore photocopy.

He was small for a man, standing a full head shorter than Alan. His flowing blond mane was, in person, just wisps of thinning yellow lint that looked like it was layered, stuck together, powdered, and precariously placed on top of his head. His stature was firm, but his handshake was clammy and soft. Alan investigated the man, and had no idea that this would be the meeting of minds, the same idea of what it would be like to meet with him as he watched him on television. He had no concept of it whatsoever.

"I am sorry if I was a bit forward in calling you brother, but my sister told me you were here because you are a Jewish writer, and you were doing a piece on faith, if I am not mistaken." Alan wasn't sure where Mrs. Arnott got the information, maybe second handed from Hank, but it sounded a lot better than 'I am writing a book about how fucking phony we are and how people have faith in us anyway.'

"Yes. That's an accurate assumption."

"Well, all Jews are my brothers and sisters. I learned a long time ago when I was studying the faith and the practice that we wouldn't be here if it weren't for the Jews. Jesus wouldn't have had such an impact on the human race. The world would be so absolutely different. I have read the Talmud and the Dead Sea Scrolls and even of the philosophies of Kabbala, and they have all strengthened my faith a hundredfold. For that, I thank you."

"Well, thank you reverend - although you shouldn't thank me, I obviously have nothing to do with it..."

"Sure, but in the same aspect, I get hundreds of letters a day from people thanking me for bringing them to Christ, and it is honestly a good feeling." Alan was not entirely sure that it was the same thing. In the small notebook in his lap he wrote one word, 'megalomaniac.' "So what are you here to talk about?"

"You," Alan responded. "I want to know what your day is like, what goes through your head, what exactly your faith is composed of, what your story is, basically."

"That is a lot of questions..."

"Sure, but that is the basis of my account of you. I want to know how you got here, if you always as faithful. I mean, of course there are going to be a lot of questions."

"Understood. Well first, let me give you this," He reached behind him and retrieved a glossy white business card from a holder with raised lettering and a unique die cut through the card of an almost calligraphic cross. It wasn't often that holding something, Alan felt the expensiveness and craftsmanship of it in his hands, but this was one of those times. "If you have a question for me, that has my office and home phone number on it. You are always welcome here Alan, and I will certainly put aside a half hour or an hour for you before I go on to tape my other shows if you give me a day's notice. I also would like you to come to the studio after this and watch us tape the Sacrosanctity Society if you would like. I am totally at your disposal for this project of yours."

"Thank you."

"Just make sure you don't lose it. The media vultures have been on to me quite often lately, as you can imagine, and I am not sure I can take much more of it." He said it so matter-of-factly and Alan was surprised that he had almost forgotten of his wife's disappearance. His wife was missing, and he was in a lot higher spirits than Alan could have been in the same circumstances. Alan scribbled 'wife' in his notebook also, so he didn't forget. "So, Alan, lets forge ahead with a couple questions for today, and we can save whatever we don't get to for the coming weeks."

"That would be fine..."

"Okay, so let's start with my story, 'my life story.' I outlined it shortly in several parts of my daily devotional book *In Gods Eyes, In God's Country*, and if I have a significant amount of time in the future, I wholly plan on writing an autobiography, but I suppose I can give you the benefit of the doubt that you have never read my book and that you know nothing of me besides my profession.

"In any case, I am sure you can understand that Christ has not always been in my life. In one form or another he has always tried to enter, but my personal agenda was never such that I could let him enter. I was wracked with self interest, personal ideals, sex, women, drugs; basically if it could be condemned by any form of our society, chances were good that I was into it. But I am getting a little far ahead of myself…"

He paused. Basking in the dark of the ornate room, Alan could sense that Hobbeston was almost comfortable and trusted the moment a little too much. Alan had seen this room on television before, and it was obvious that this wasn't so much of an office as it was a studio. There were no windows, but the high ceiling and perfection of the room almost lifted any claustrophobic feelings that are associated with a room without a view.

"I grew up on a veal farm in southern Indiana," he started after a big breath. "The air and the atmosphere outside was magnificent. Rolling hills, freedom echoing off of ever strand of golden wheat and every bark chip in the mulch of the towering oaks. It was gorgeous. But in our little home, a brewing and simmering catastrophe always teetered on the edge and brought my eleven brothers and sisters to the brink of insanity. Sure, that is a little dramatic, but our mother was constantly taking sleeping pills, and my father was a terrible alcoholic who beat her.

"It is awful to say, but we didn't blame him. It was a release of vengeance for the both of them, I suppose, the forceful hurt a release for my dad and the bitter pain under the hum of the Valium a release for my mother. It was so very difficult. We were poor; very poor, as was the case for farmers then and today in America. The real hurt for dad was forcing his kids to work the land, and then the machine of industry turning against him and his kids. Two of my brothers lost an arm, and one of my brothers and one of my sisters lost fingers in the mechanisms we used to till the land and slaughter the livestock.

"We were all wondering who was left to lose something, but what wasn't lost physically was lost mentally. To rear and raise the young and bulky animals, and then to slaughter them with a defective bolt gun at such a young age, no, to bleed them dry, upside down from their feet and to hear the deafening white noise of their blood on the pavement. Their suffocation. That was sickening. Sickening and unholy, and yet, we had become so desensitized to the process that it was just a job, which it was. The element of creation from the destruction of life; it was energy for others. Or money. Or a release of tension that harped on our brains that the meat and slaughter that we instigated was only a byproduct of our desire to feed a country… That was almost worth it… Or so we were taught to remind ourselves.

"When I was sixteen, I had decided to stand up to my father the next time he had beaten my mother. I remember thinking that if I was in any possible dire circumstance that I would never take it out on another human being, and it was myself who was either to blame or who needed to be punished. It wasn't until later that I understood that we should shed any ideas of retribution, and that compassion and humility was the road to the higher self. But that was after I discovered what Christ did for me…

"Father had come in from an auction where he went once a week to find new livestock for breeding or feed or whatever else he needed for the business. He came home empty handed, which wasn't entirely a surprise; it happened quite often, in fact. Well, this particular time, we had been running low on all of our supplies, and were living off of our own production. Again, it had happened before, and wasn't new to us. This time, however, it was different. The reason he came home empty handed was not because of disinterest with the auction's wares, or without a need for any of it. We needed it very badly. It was because there was not enough money to buy it. There wasn't enough money to buy anything. Feed, grain, cows, bulls, chickens, fat, suet… Nothing.

"He had come home depressed and upset for the lack of funds, but my sister started coughing, and the very last thing we could have afforded was medicine. He had his flask on him, and brown liquor rolled like tears under his chin and down the front of his neck. He was quiet when he walked in the door, but as soon as my sister started crying, he exploded, shouting and verbally hammering away at us as if it were our faults.

"When he had hit mother, it was the most forceful I had ever seen. She wasn't even expecting a shot from behind, but there his fist was hitting the back of her neck with an explosive momentum. She fell deliberately and without any sort of brace, like a marionette whose strings had been cut unexpectedly – what people mean when they say 'dead-weight.' She didn't move. That was when I thought I needed to take some kind of action.

"He stepped over her limp body and started to stagger his way to the basement, which is where he would always go to drink until he passed out. I snuck up behind him and tapped him on the shoulder.

" 'HEY!,' I had said. He spun around and grabbed my neck. His eyes, which looked like a bull, crazy with passion, red and large, stared down at me and burned through me with the searing white hot perpetuation of the brands we marked the livestock with. My sister was coughing again, far away, and another one of my sisters was crying. All of my other brothers and sisters made themselves scarce, as was the practice during these events.

" 'Listen, and listen well, you little twat, you will never come between your mother and I if you know what is good for you,' he said. He pushed me back and let go while I tripped over my mother's legs on the floor. He was walking away when I shouted again, 'don't touch her again or you'll regret it.'

"He turned around, grabbed my shirt, and pulled me outside. Taking another drink from his flask, he tossed it back in his pocket, started dancing around like a boxer does with his fists up, and asked me if I wanted to dance. Like, 'do you want to dance little man? Huh, tough guy?' In the moonlight he looked like a giant bulldog about to pounce on me. But he never did. He just taunted me a little more, and punched me once in the face. Then, he just stopped. He grabbed me by the shirt once more and dragged me to his truck.

"He swore the whole way into Chicago, murmuring under his breath, and then drank from a bottle he had under his seat. I remember the drive into town being a few hours, and then he just dropped me off. He said something about the niggers being able to straighten me out, and drove away."

Hobbeston paused again. He wasn't upset, it seemed. It was as if he recollected the whole thing nostalgically, or, at least introspectively.

"I suppose he figured I would make my way back home after the exodus and then keep my mouth shut and work for him, regretting the whole thing. But I didn't. I left the city and found another farm to work on, saving up some money, waiting for the perfect time to leave. I found it a few weeks later when I heard that my sister had died of the whooping cough. So I left.

"I went to Dallas and worked at a bar, back north to Michigan where I worked at a car factory which later closed, Wisconsin, Iowa City. I mixed with prostitutes and drug dealers, who I ended up making the most money with, but I also lost some teeth and almost died on more than one occasion.

"It was when I went to North Carolina where I found out that my mother had died. This was ten years after I left, when I was twenty-six. She would have only been fifty-eight, which was only almost two thirds of the average female life expectancy in the country at the time. I heard that the farm was sold, I was depressed, and I was taking more drugs than ever to fill the emptiness that I had in my life. I went to some friends to talk about it and they were no help, so then I went to a church for a meeting where I heard I may have some better luck for support. It was a twelve step program for drug addicts, and it really opened my eyes.

"I was taken in by my sponsor, and I really responded to the higher power aspects of the program. So much so that I started to really investigate Christ and his teachings. I began to attend Church services, but they weren't speaking to me. I went to Baptist churches, devotional churches, Jehova's Witnesses churches, and black churches where I was really well received. But it still said nothing to me. So, I thought I would begin my own church. After contacting my sister in Nevada, she said she would allow me to move in for a short amount of time while I sorted things out. I began my church in Vegas in a small, empty strip mall, and its popularity skyrocketed from there."

Hobbeston looked up at the ceiling. Alan thought about all that he had heard, and wondered how he had ended up the way he was. Was nothing important to him? He was lucky that he had never watched his mother and father fight. He didn't remember if they even ever had... But without any stretch of the imagination, he thought to himself about how selfish he was. How could he chastise his father so badly when his only crime was not doing anything, be it good or bad. Alan felt guilty that Hobbeston had not said a single opinionated thing about his father given the circumstances and Alan shot his mouth off about his dad constantly. He tried, it seemed, to only speak in truthful comments. He kept the use of any emotional language strictly to referring to himself.

"I suppose what I want to convey here is that everyone needs something to make them feel whole. In my opinion, the only way that you can feel truly whole with yourself and the world around you is with a common love and appreciation for Christ our savior. He knows you, and he knows me, and he loves us no matter what our race or origin or feelings or job. He will forgive us for our sins, just like he forgave my father for his, and his father before him." He paused, looking at Alan to say something next.

"Were you religious growing up?" Alan asked.

"Yes, we were, but as the economy bore down on us and as we got old enough to work the farm it was almost as if our survival took precedent over our faith. We were Lutheran growing up."

"What happened to your father and the farm before it was sold?"

"After I left, it was almost as if it started its gradual decline. My family got poorer and poorer, and dad was beating mom all of the time. I think it is safe to say that that was how she died; complications from a beating; or a broken heart. It is hard to say. In any case, dad moved in with my sister Grace after the farm was sold. Well, actually it was bought out by a big cereal company Nature's Mills, and they just paid the bank for it, so my family didn't get anything. Dad was sixty-eight when he died of a stroke in his sleep, six and a half years after my mother's death and only seven months after moving in with my sister. I didn't go to his funeral. I didn't go to my mother's either."

"That's too bad."

"Well, I was a mess and I didn't have any money to get there, anyway."

Alan looked down at his notebook, and moved his pen around as if he were writing something. He really didn't have anything to write, but wanted a moment to collect his thoughts surrounding the story he was just told.

The hulking mountain that hung over Hobbeston's head was surprising, but at the same rate wasn't. Alan had always considered the sharp and clean cut man to have a perfect upbringing that contained no heartbreak and nothing less than perfection. The man was in fact the very opposite. He was almost as dysfunctional and scarred as Alan was, and Alan could sense the very same pain that rotted in the pit of his heart in the rainy puddles of Hobbeston's eyes.

"Well, Alan, I want to make it very clear that I am going to respect your time that you spend with me. I know that you are here on your own accord, and without any idea of what your faith is or to what depth it extends in your soul, I will do my best not to impede on it. I support your ideals and certainly hope you will respect mine. That is not to say that I don't support the idea of your turning to Christ, but this will be the last you hear of it aside from your observation of my work."

"Well, thank you."

"It is the least I can do, literally. Now, I have to go get ready for my presentation of the Society broadcast in a while, but you can feel free to tag around with me and observe and we can get something to eat from the kitchen."

"That sounds wonderful, Reverend."

· · ·

It was dusk, and Alan sat across from Jaime in a bowl of stone with pillars of rock surrounding them that had been naturally eroded to form a natural rectangle. About sixty wooden benches were installed in parallel rows in the middle of the bowl, with a corridor in the middle of them, and they faced an installed wooden podium with benches behind it. Alan and Jaime sat underneath an arch of eroded stone on a blanket with a picnic basket and an open bottle of sparkling organic white grape juice and two glasses. It was a beautiful natural wonder surrounding them, and it was highlighted by the setting sun which hit the natural sandblasted structure with a phenomenon that caused the light to bounce up from the stone ground and dimly light the entire natural arena with a bright orange haze.

"Where we're going is a special place that I heard about from a friend of a friend whose parents came every Sunday morning," Jaime explained after she had picked him up from the bus terminal. "It's called the Chapel of the Earth, and the fiery sun at dusk and dawn, when the majority of the sky is still that not-so-much day and not-so-much night color, lights up the whole area with a gorgeous radiating splendor that is so amazing and spiritual. It's fabulous, it really is."

And here was Alan, at the point where he should be calm and composed, but he was spinning in the moment of truth. He had practiced his poem and recited it and wrote it and memorized it, all to come down to this. Jaime sat down in front of him on the cloth and she looked eager. Not happy, not like a person on their birthday waiting to see what the paper was going to show them when they tore it aside. No, she was eager and concentrated on Alan's mouth, waiting for the sounds and words to come out of it so she could drink them up. She was thirsty, after all.

Alan cleared his throat, and continued to hold his breath.

But there was no better way to unveil his newest creation. Look at the beauty and the magnitude of this situation! This was it! This was it! No, there could be no better place for this to happen, and Alan expected no less than jubilation and happiness to the highest degree of heaven after he was finished. This! This was it!

"*A Poem for Jaime, By Alan Levy*," he started. He sounded like a second grader at the head of the class reading a book report. This was already going downhill, but there were no brakes, so it was useless to try to stop. All he could do was take his frantic foot off the brake and steer this hulking machine.

"*In what presence of dust cover'd cacti*
we wander together, just you and I,
looking upon the fruits humanity makes,
digesting the colours, the scrapes, the lakes.

A terrible spark ignites among us,
A flame we don't particularly trust,
My heart continues burning inside me,
Oh! What future will there be?

We look upon a painting where,
The invisible flesh, their insides bear.
A gum-band of fire, two hearts become one,
Locked in a kiss, which never will be done.

As we talked, I learned of your intention,
To create this feeling, make us one invention.
And while you said you wouldn't cross that line,
I found your intentions to be like mine.

For I feel of you much the same way,
Never desired to someone, say,
'To leave your side I wish would happen, never,
I feel as though I have known you forever!

'We have the same eyes, our style, and thought,
and someday, forever, we'll decide to talk,
about nothing, and everything, for days and for months,
and maybe, just maybe, we'll kiss just once.'

But from whence inside a creation stirs,
A sickness that strikes, and purges, and whirrs,
Your future, and ours, uncertainly forlorn,
When, in fact, a child is born.

From lover afraid, but never known,
Their ignorance for such creation, shown,
In kindness to you, without knowing he flees,
He betrays the creator with infidelities

So, prove to me you love so much,
Whence from your eyes, your mouth, your touch,
You tell me how you've felt so blue,
And finally admit it: "I love you."

From blue to blue, or red to red,
A creation of fire will soon be bred,
The fire will burn and we will feed from,
The powers that conjoin our inner crimson.

And after all of this aside,
In my car, away we'll ride,
And feel the wind brush upon us full,
And realize that life is beautiful."

Jaime looked at Alan. She looked at Alan with eyes that were filled with something that he couldn't pinpoint. It was pain? No, happiness. What was it? Alan had absolutely no idea what was going on in her head, and he so wished, so wished that he could see inside of it. There was no evidence of any emotion, whatsoever.

"That was wonderful, Alan. Wonderful." She was smiling now, and it was almost a genuine grin. Her dimples were too much for him, and Alan wanted to leap upon them. If he had one opportunity to do anything, this was it. He reached over and took the woman into his arms, and she was solid.

He moved his face away from her cheek, and looked her in the eyes with his arms sill around her. The golden sunset's reflection on the rock brought about an amber glow to her face that no makeup or artificial colorant could possibly reproduce. Radiance was the only word for the moment, and Alan would commit the moment to memory with every effort of the reaches of his mind.

Why waste space with awful memories, when so many happy endings and new beginnings could replace them starting right at that moment. His heart was the ellipsis of his arms, holding her, his eyes was his spirit looking into hers, and his soul, their souls between them, splashing about and rolling around in the space between their flesh and bones and cotton. Rolling with the puppies in the grass of the first day of summer, or in the arms of a firefighter saving lives from a building, or in the bottle of champagne broken on the front of a ship with the cargo of a hundred thousand meals setting sail for the hungriest corners of the earth, or in the explosion of passion from a really good band, or in the chills of their audience. It was all there.

He moved toward her face, and she looked at his lips with determination, giggled, and moved in to kiss him on the cheek. She shifted away from Alan and climbed up to the ledge where the slope of the exterior of the rock sloped down seven meters to the other side where the desert began again. She lifted her arms to the sky and let out a scream of passionate joy and at the same time fanned her fingers like fireworks. She was glorious.

"Alan Levy! I Love You!" she shouted. It dissipated into the nothingness of the desert, like she screamed it in a room of pillows, and yet it was the greatest thing Alan could hear. Sure, she kissed him on the cheek which sent a message of 'hey, pal,' and yet she shouted that she loved him from the rooftops which was beauty in action. She spun around a few more times, and slid back to the blanket and sat with Alan.

"Tell me you have that written down for me somewhere," she said. Alan reached into his pocket and produced a wrinkled draft of the poem which spanned three pages because of the size of his little notebook. Jaime took them into her hands and smiled over them like a squirrel with a paper wrapper treasure in a parking lot. She was adorable.

"I am keeping this forever." She put the loose pages in her pocketbook next to the picnic basket. Alan was smiling, and watched her. Watched how her body curved and contorted to reach the pocketbook and how her legs looked in the breezy skirt and how her breasts looked and how everything here was so absolutely pleasant. She looked back up at him. "You memorized that whole thing?"

"Yeah, I did..."

"That is so lovely. I will cherish this, Alan, I honestly will. You make me really happy. It is so confusing." Alan wanted to ask her what she meant by confusing, but she was already on to her next statement as she unwrapped the foil on the sparkling juice. "So how was meeting with Hobbeston? Everything you expected?"

"Well, no, actually," Alan responded, "It was quite the opposite. He looks like nothing he looks like on television, the entire production of the service is a scam, there were only like twenty people there, and then he is really short. So we talk, and apparently he had kind of a crappy childhood like I did in a strange sense, and... Well, honestly Jaime, it was surreal. We are alike in some ways."

"Really?"

"Yeah, I mean, he's human. Celebrities, or people in the public spotlight get this strange aura about them, and then when you meet them, it is just so... so plain and nothing special at all. Sometimes you forget about that stuff, you know? He eats and shits and needs to have his makeup done. I guess his personality is so different than most celebrities is that he has such a solid ground and static belief in Christ, but most celebrities it seems like they are so strange and delicate every time you see them... They are always trying to perform for you, and why not? That's the business they are in. But it is strange to understand how they are when they aren't given something to read and things to say. They usually don't have anything to say, it seems."

"Trippy."

"Yeah, sorry about that; I haven't even met that many celebrities, but still, it is pretty strange how they are all pretty much the same, even when they are different."

She was sipping from her glass with a smile on. Nothing Alan had ever seen someone do before, and it was so unconscious on her part, but so attractive. It was amazing. She looked at him through the curve of the glass.

"Jaime, can I ask you a really personal question?"

"Is it about my sexual preferences or contraception habits or some other strange but useful question from a dating show, because if it is, I want to start thinking about some good bizarre answers to give you, you know? Like 'I like it only on top when you have a chocolate bar in your mouth and a red sock and a blue sock on your ears...'"

"No, although that would be a great conversation... No it is more about your faith. What is your faith, Jaime? What do you believe in?"

"Well, that's an awful big question..."

"I know, I know, but this is just something I was thinking about today. I am thinking that I am going to be really interested with what people have to say. You don't have to even answer me, I was just thi-"

"Oh, no, no, no Alan. I would be perfectly happy to share this with you, really. Honestly. But where to start, where to start." She was looking into the distant horizon. The long cottony gauze of clouds streaked across the sky horizontally, mixed with oranges and reds and blues, and it looked like it was a backdrop painting that a romantic artist painted to inspire just this conversation in a classroom of the cosmos in some distant universe thousands of years in the future.

"The big question," she began, "is God. Who is this God. Is it a man, or a woman? Big or small? Physical or ethereal? But I honestly don't think of that at all, really, Alan."

"You don't?"

"While I have no clear definition of what my religion is, and a hard pressed way to define my personal views on God, I can say for certain that God, or rather heaven resides within all of us. We see God everyday in the acts of compassion and virtue in the world. That is where God is. That is where I am. I feel that without a compassionate and humiliating outlook on my own existence, there is no way that I could possibly feel for another person or creature on this planet. And I do live with humility, and I do live with compassion, as best as I possibly can."

"That's beautiful. Where do you get it? It sounds Jewish."

"It is. It's also Buddhist. It's also Christian. But I can't stand the idolatry in those religions. I mean, would Jesus be catholic or Christian were he alive today? Of course not! He praised the simple life, pushed humility. But stepping foot into the lavish churches gilded with gold and statues of him bleeding from a cross would send him reeling.

"So, I suppose that my faith resides in the hope and possibilities of the chances that there are those with golden hearts walking on this earth. We are different than any creature on this earth, and yet we are so very similar. We have eyes, but when we see a mouse, the reaction is different than if my cat does. We have feet, yet our perpetuation drives us toward work, or the supermarket, while a doe's feet pushes ever closer toward grass, water, and solace. But what do we share?

"All that we share resides in what the doe's eyes hold after being struck by a car on the interstate. It is the same look in the eyes of a man in the same circumstance. Suffering. Suffering is the only thing that we share with beasts and creatures of the whole kingdom of Earth, and thus with our thought and higher knowledge it turns out that we are also the only species able to understand the implications of that look while others step around or leave the poor creature to die on the side of the road.

"That is where God exists, Alan. God exists in the moment of compassion where we understand what another is going through. God exists because in any sense of our understanding, our hearts, our hands, our minds are all fabrications of our consciousness and our universe is all that we have. Coincidentally it is all inside of our head. But when we feel pain, or we are able to help another in pain, we are one with that creature. We become a part of them because we know that it is us who will hurt if this creature is allowed to continue to suffer. Suffering allows compassion, and compassion allows God to exist.

"What's more? What is pain? It is a fabrication of energy that surges through our electric nerves that we feel when something happens. But what is electricity? What is light? Can we truly see it? Absolutely not. We can experience it through sight or feeling, but ultimately it is just faith that allows us to believe it is there. What keeps the electricity from falling out of our bodies or out of the sockets in the walls like milk? Who knows, but we have a certain degree of faith in it to know it will be contained. And those electric particles, and that wall, and your spine, and the air is all one. Particles pressing up against particles, pressing up against particles that whittles down to the smallest iota of existence, and there is no space in between at all. There is a connection between all of us."

Jaime picked up Alan's hand, and stood. They stood in the sunlight, their shadows casting a twenty meter shadow across the hardpan right outside of the chapel formation. She took his other hand and looked into his eyes. The azure brilliance, that was almost lit from within, shone on Alan like a beam and made him squint. It was hot, and burned to look at them.

"And here is where it all comes together, Alan." She held up their hands. "We are pressed together, as is our molecules at the smallest level. We are one now, but we always were, connected through the cosmos, there is nothing between us. Here I am, here you are. Here is Jupiter, and here is the tear you shed for your first girlfriend, and here is a grain of sand, and here is a billion more. Air between us is only more complicated molecules, moving and spinning and vibrating about. But we are here, and electricity in the most primitive and invisible level is surging through our veins together, now. And this is God. This feeling. This miniscule and invisible spark, and the atmosphere between us, which is really just more molecules, isn't between us at all. We are it.

"Love and Compassion, Alan. That is God, and it also proves the existence of that power which we could never, ever understand or comprehend with all of the knowledge in the expanses of the universe."

She dropped Alan's hands, and moved her hands up his arms. Alan kept his eyes on the brilliance and heavenly beauty of the horizon. Heavenly beauty. The horizon wasn't heaven at all, no not at all. It wasn't in the clouds, and it wasn't beneath them, and it wasn't on another spiritual plain. It was within them, and surrounding them at all times.

"So you are you saying," Alan began, "that your structure of heaven and God is a product of a design that resides within us and our actions?" Her hands moved their way up to his torso and his neck, as did her lips. She kissed his cheek, and then continued to kiss his neck and his ear as she spoke.

"Alan, heaven and God is within you at all times, and within your world and within your grasp. That is what I believe." Kiss, kiss, lip dragging up his neck. "Think of the absolute. A photograph, or a moment in your mind that stands out as a monolith, or several monoliths in your mind. That moment, or person, or teacher, or photograph, when you thought about it, when you absolutely positively thought about it, Alan, to the bottom of your soul would make you so happy that you would just begin to cry, and cry, and cry, and cry at how absolutely wonderful this life has been to you. Cry at what this person did for you. Cry at the moment and how happy you were even if you didn't realize it at the time. Cry at the care and attention to your personal well being and welfare. That is Heaven, Alan. That is God. That is the compassion and virtue that surges and drives our existence."

She was kissing his neck, and Alan felt her hands move up and down his arms, and his back. It was erotic, but he didn't have an erection or want sex or drop his inhibitions and listen to this call to nature. It was soothing. It felt happy and relaxed, like he was sleeping. He almost felt like he could sleep, were he not slightly aware of his surroundings in the back of his mind.

"Jaime, you. You are amazing. I have never known anyone like you."

"I have never known anyone like you, Alan." Her breath heaved on his flesh, and the breeze from her mouth and nose was magnified by the saliva on his delicate skin.

"It is unbelievable that you exist, and even more so that I met you," Alan said. He pulled her closer. There was no part of their bodies that weren't touching. The cotton merged with flesh and the air escaped from the cracks. Molecules melted and the two traded fleshy atoms and energy pulsed between their hearts and hands. They were one being in the middle of a desolate desert at sundown in the west.

Milky existence clouded Alan's mind, unsure of how to interpret his own feelings. He was in love with this woman, without a kiss, without even a stable understanding of who she was. But in the core of his being, this creature in his arms was one with him, and he could not deny any further drive to want her. This was her, this was the woman for him. Fuck the sex laws, and fuck the rules. Fuck the society and fuck the world. He would see it with her, and they would see it together for the first time, and for the first time Alan would live in his very own world in the scope of his very own mind. His very own mind, and his mind was him, and it was an illusion of the universe and God and compassion and heaven and virtue was surging through his veins when he said it…

"I love you, Jaime."

"I love you too, Alan."

They whispered it to each other and it sounded almost like a breaker crashing into the shoreline over its own perpetual drive. The hush. It was so natural, the statements with molecules and DNA of his own, holy fuck was he on drugs again, or what was this? This was what it was like, what it was like to fall in love. Screw the magazines or the movies, screw the songs or the poetry, nothing in the world could prepare him for this, and oh, oh, how he wished he hadn't said 'I love you' to anyone else before, for that was just embers on the pyre compared to the atomic destruction blown away from this very moment. Destruction. Or was it creation? Or was it creation resulting from the very melt of the moment?

"What do you believe in, Alan," Jaime asked. "What is your faith?"

Alan wanted to say he only believed in this moment. He wanted to say that so badly; this moment in heaven and in history. Judaism believed in the power of the moment, as it was a religion based on love. It was a religion based on knowledge. It was religion based on the flame. Fire was truly the first of the elements that one could not truly hold in their hands. An element that bonded, destroyed, created, and was so prevalent in every aspect of everything. There was no atom that was not conceived in the inferno of the sun; no atom in his body, or in his clothes, or in the grape juice, or the bubbles between it. In the glass. In the Jaime and her beautiful smile.

"I am Jewish, I suppose. I believe in everything you do. I honestly do."

"That is so very wonderful, Alan. Tell me more..."

And they sat. They talked, and Alan really understood something. His beliefs were not compassionate at times. Where were they? He spent so much time over the last nine months critiquing people, interpreting what they did wrong. He was being a bad human being, and in fact, there was no one on his exodus that did not treat him with a open heart and with open hands. He would have died in the desert. He would have died in the riots. He would have died after eating the tuna. He would have died if that plane was just six or seven meters closer to the house and crashed into it and sliced through his guts and his body with aluminum shards, gasoline, and bolts. It could have only been a matter of the breeze; been it so microscopically heavier than the one that was blowing the week before he left Chapmansville, Massachusetts, he would have been dead in the fiery cinders of a plane wreck.

Alan redirected his thoughts and his answers, and answered compassionately and focused. He answered from his heart. He answered the way that he was going to live his life from that moment on. He answered until the sun crawled over the dust and into a clay pot of water while the spectacle of the night took the sky over with brilliance and fervor, making a dark violet bed sheet for Alan and Jaime to get comfortable under until they left before the bitter cold infiltrated the extravagant Eden they constructed together. Alan believed that he finally found what he was looking for in these elements; the elements of life that the natural side of humanity searches for in every cycle of time since the beginning of its existence.

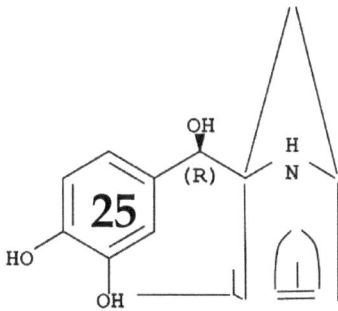

The Polaroid aura of a world that was constantly folding around Alan in a structured form was uncanny. He looked straight into the future, and while it was uncertain, he could not manage to grasp the idea that things were in fact going right for a change. Voices that were screaming from the back of his head toward the front that made him shy and weary of making any solid decisions, the same voices that made him feel half asleep when signing student loan contracts and dreamy when making decisions that he may not ever have answers for or solutions for were hushed at the moment, and Alan felt as thought he almost had forgotten how they sounded.

It was only three days since he had gone to meet Hobbeston and made a new world and new feelings with Jaime.

This day, he had a couple of things to do after work. Sella was lying across his lap, and sighed heavily through her nose as Alan made a phone call to Journey Airlines to buy Hank his Christmas present. Alan spent the last few days at work harassing his boss to tell him if Hank had any paid days off because Alan wanted to give him a vacation for Christmas that would allow him to get away, relax, and have a good time. When the representative picked up on the other end of the phone, Alan announced that he wanted to buy a roundtrip ticket, albeit an expensive one that for the most part would almost empty his bank account, that would allow Hank to pick anywhere in the country that he wanted to go within the next year, take a vacation, and come back without having to worry about paying for or scheduling the flight. He could pick the date, the place, the time, and get there and back without having to justify the cost. It was taken care of.

One thing that Alan always hated in America was Christmas. It showcased the materialistic, wasteful, unthoughtful, careless, and ignorance of his own country to the depths of everything that it was founded upon. Christmas was a joke to him. Every year he found a new and interesting way to boycott the holiday; only shop at stores with a definitive Hanukkah, Kwanzaa, and Ramadan display in different parts of the store (not just different shelves on an aisle end cap at the back of the store). No holiday music whatsoever. To boycott even if it was owned by a parent company run by an extreme right wing conglomeration that was careless for anyone that was anything other than white, upper middle class Christians.

Christmas time was debilitating for Alan and his personal situation. He was Jewish, came from a dysfunctional family who was lucky if they got together once a week for dinner, let alone able to share in the jovial family mess of national holidays. No. His girlfriend at the time's family felt obligated to get him gifts, and allow him to participate in their festivities. Because they did it different than everyone else, right? But it never made him happy. He was just the wrong gene in the chemistry of family. He always felt like Woody Allen did the old movie "Annie Hall," sitting like an Orthodox Hassidic at the table speaking in some guttural mishmash of Yiddish and lower Bronx Jew dialect.

In any case, he was able to buy people things without any selfish feelings or want for retribution. This was one part of humanity that Alan was grateful for, however, he was unsure of how effective the feelings of nostalgia, peace, and brotherhood were if they were only practiced by most of the population for this one day a year. No doubt, it couldn't be. Furthermore, most people acted in almost the opposite manner for the rest of the year, and that one month almost took on the opposite effect. Every year, Alan hoped that these countrywide feelings would carry on for the rest of the year just once. Selflessness. The one quality the country did not have aside from a few people that were considered heroes. The term was thrown around with such injustice since the happenings of that September decades ago that it almost has lost its meaning. Yes, everyone should strive to be heroes everyday, but they label others heroes almost as if they need not try to be a hero if they can point out who in fact is.

Sadly, it was even the wrong people that were labeled it. Sports stars, movie stars, religious leaders that made no sacrifice other than gaining the most souls for their side; political leaders who were misinterpreted as heroes and almost praised as gods. What had this place turned into?

The country needed to be baptized and washed ashore, but not literally. They needed a chance to be forgiven for all of the poor mistakes that they had made; given a second chance by the international community. Rather than think we were all right all along - rather than take offense to criticism - embrace it and look into why people would say that.

Alan was reminded whenever these thoughts braced his mind of a time, years ago, that Americans ignorantly thought they were making a statement by pouring French wine into the gutters and renaming French Toast and French Fries to Freedom Toast and Freedom Fries because they didn't want to say French anymore. Yes, it was effective, especially considering that there were many in the world who didn't have wine, and many others who recognized that by buying French wine and pouring it down the drain, they were just making room for more French wine on the shelves to be imported. Oh yeah, and French Toast was evidently invented in ancient Rome and French Fries were invented in Belgium, and both were evidently introduced to America by president Thomas Jefferson who gave them their American names.

Alan ordered the tickets and phoned his second operative, the Reverend Charles Hobbeston. Sella got up off of the couch, and clicked over to her food and water dish that was visible in the kitchen from the living room where Alan sat. She lapped the cool fluid as Alan listened to the phone ring on the other end.

"Hello, thank you for calling the Sacrosanctity Society offices, this is Tina, how may I direct your call?" a woman answered.

"Hello, this is Alan Levy, I am looking to speak with Reverend Hobbeston."

"Reverend Hobbeston is on the phone right now, shall I direct you to his voice mail?"

"Umm... Actually, would you mind seeing when he could speak with me?"

"I... I suppose that I could do that."

The line went silent for a moment, and Alan watched as Sella darted about the floor on her back, twisting East and West looking like a possessed elbow macaroni. She did this often enough, and Alan couldn't figure out why. She could be scratching her back, or just playing, giving herself a dizzying upside down view of the world that swished back and fourth making a launderette out of the living room. We all have our joys, Alan thought, and no one will even understand them.

The line came back. In the background, Alan could hear a medieval fax machine squealing to life.

"Alan?" Tina asked.

"Yes, I am here."

"He will speak with you, hold on one moment."

The line clicked over for a moment, and a familiar voice answered.

"Mr. Levy..."

"Hey Reverend, I didn't mean to interrupt, I mean, you could have totally finish-"

"No, Alan, no, I was just speaking with my son about a really ridiculous thing that has just come up, it is no problem."

"Are you sure?"

"I am positive."

Alan looked down at his notebook and investigated his options of this telephone call. Words stood out that he had scrawled on the way to work, or in the middle of working, or on his way home from work. Words that would prompt a vast explanation of what was going on and who had touched Hobbeston's life or some strange outlet like snorting cocaine off of a male hooker's ass in his wild days before joining the lord's service.

The words that Alan was currently investigating, scrawled bold and inky on the page were *saintly, adoration, devotion, heaven, energy, ascension, virtue, Eucharist, nine, faith, repent, and ultimate demise.* Alan was unsure of what he meant by some of these, and mentally scolded himself for not taking better notes for himself, but focused on why he wrote what he did and how to vocalize his answers.

"You are very passionate about your faith, Reverend, and I have noticed that watching you, you have never really touched on the ultimate demise of humanity. That is, what happens after we die? Do you share the apocalyptic visions that most people in your profession swear by? Another question, do you think that the general population of good Christians would not sin were they not told it was okay given the promises Christ threw around? Why not be devoted to living as a good human being everyday?"

"An interesting paradox, Alan, and I'm glad you brought it up. It is the greatest questions both of Christians themselves and of the people that observe them. I believe that I am going straight to heaven as I have Jesus Christ as my personal lord and savior. That is simple. All of my past has been wiped away, and why wouldn't I think it? That is what Christ says is the truth, and I am listening to him. He died for my sins. Tell me Alan, what do you think of death?"

Alan thought for a moment, staring at the black screen in front of him that made up the powerless television. He was seated in the living room on the futon, staring at it across the coffee table. Its matted surface reflected Alan as a specter in a mish-mash of futon and wall that was blurry and two dimensional. Alan never really considered what happened after he died. He knew something, but his ideas were never concrete.

"Well, I suppose," he started, "I suppose that I think about Peter Pan... Not the Hollywood sell-out cartoonie Peter Pans, but rather the Peter Pan conceived by James M. Barrie. When it comes to matters of spirituality, we have no concrete conception of it, and we are a lot like children. So taking that into consideration, I am going to quote a children's story in which Mr. Barrie had Peter Pan say his famous quote just before he died at the end. He said with a full heart, 'To die will be an awfully big adventure.' I believe that is true."

"Wow. I didn't know Peter Pan dies in the end... That's wonderful, Alan."

"Yes. Sort of. I mean, I think that I might just be energy, back into the earth and the solar system. Nothing more than that. Blackness. I think the hope is that I am not scared of it, or have any regrets."

"So you aren't afraid of what will happen when you die? That your sins will carry with you and you will go to heaven without expectation of the horror that awaits you in hell?"

"No,... honestly I don't reverend. I believe in one god and I try my best to live every day as wonderfully as I can. I strive to be the best person I can be... Why should I short change myself and live without compassion and virtue just knowing that I am going to be forgiven for being a complete jerk? I am not sure there is anything after this, so... That almost brings us to my other question..."

"Well, you are right. The truth is, the bible teaches us to be good. When I found Christ, as you remember my telling you, I was deep in sin. I was doing everything wrong and I was making a lot of mistakes. In my gut, I understood that everything around me was wrong. I did. But I made it a point to truly give myself to the lord. Since then, I have not committed any wrongdoing whatsoever.

"Alan, I am going to be straight with you. A lot of people that are in this country, in this world, are completely and utterly brain dead when it comes to their own religion. I don't need to tell you that there is a large percentage of Christians in America. Do I need to tell you that the majority of them do not go to church? No. I will be honest with you again. There are people out there that would rather you find Christ and convert than those lost Christians go to church. I am not kidding. Strangely enough, these are the same people that are defending their religion, voting for politicians because of their religious standing, and would die to protect their rights to have Christmas even though they have no idea what it means beyond Santa Claus. These are the jerks that go around and drive their giant cars and are careless and throw a blind eye to any other human beings, but they believe in Christ don't they, so why should they care?

"Alan, there has been people like this throughout history, no matter where you go, no matter what time, and yes, no matter what religion. Now, while my job is to get people interested in Christ like yourself who have him not at all in their lives, I am also interested in the born again Christian; for instance the Christian who has forgotten about virtue, who has forgotten about being a good person, et cetera. I am not just interested in you, Alan; I am interested in the welfare of all the rest of my own people. If they are truly invested in Christ, they aren't going to push it upon others or be the people that don't return their carriages at the supermarket. These are the people that are genuinely trying to turn their life around.

"As for the rest of the 'good Christians' in the world, Alan, I wish I had an explanation for you. I am embarrassed."

Sella was laying on the couch next to Alan, and he was running his hands through her ratty mane. He was surprised at how silky her mane was only after a couple months of some careful, loving treatment.

"What gets me," Alan started, "is that there are all these people that hate their religion, and know nothing about it, and yet will not journey to find something else. Or want to change it to their own agenda, but there is no room for that. Don't you find that strange?"

"I do, in a sense, but it is another one of those things, Alan. I would almost rather they leave the religion altogether and find something else instead."

"Do you mean that," Alan replied.

"No. But you don't have to be a Christian to erect a giant tree you pulled in from outside and put presents under it and make people think a fat guy is coming to put them there. It means nothing, anymore, but to a few executives that make a lot of money at the stores. To everyone else, there is magic. Magic supplied by money. Me, I spend every year feeding people here at the church. I spend every week here doing it; that, Alan, is the magic."

The phone beeped, and Alan looked at the screen. His mother was calling him, and the call waiting was informing him of this. He would call her back after this conversation, he thought.

"I understand what you mean, Reverend." Alan replied.

"Alan, I would like you to come to services next week. It is the beginning of one of the holiest weeks in Christianity, speaking of Christmas, not to mention one of the busiest services for the church. The busiest giving seasons of faith, of worship, and of bread."

"Okay, I think I can do that…"

"Are you going to need a ride, because I think that I can get a congregant to drive you that lives out in your neck of the woods. Give them the old 'Reverend Hobbeston really wants to see you for Christmas services' treatment. I am just kidding. I am sure that if they knew that I had someone who wanted to go to services out there they would help you out." Hank opened the front door, and entered the house without locking it behind him. He looked at Alan and smiled, his docile walk comforting to him. He made his way to the kitchen and Alan heard him begin to prepare dinner.

"I could just take a bus, I mean-"

"Nonsense, Alan, I will let you know. Well, listen, I have to give my son a call back and then go start taping the Society. If you need anything, call. It was nice hearing from you."

"You too, Reverend. Break a leg."

"Thanks, Alan," and with that, the call was over.

Shifting around, Hank called out to Alan as he always did when he was home at this time of night after he realized that Alan was off of the phone.

"How was your day, Alan?"

"Oh, it was good, nothing too exciting; packed a lot of tampons into a lot of boxes. How was yours?"

"Same as the usual. Want me to toss some dogs on for you?"

"Yeah, sure, that'd be great!"

"Okay, no problem. Hey, did you hear the news yet?"

"What news?"

"Well, it has been all over the radio for the last half hour or so. I know you don't usually watch TV unless you are watching the crazies, but, turn it on to the news real quick. The only reason that I think you would care is because of your project."

Alan reached for the remote control on the coffee table and Sella shifted to allow for it. He leaned back, turned it on, and Sella rested her head back down onto his lap. Alan switched it to the news, and there was a story about iodine and fluoride leaking into the water in certain towns in the northern part of the state, and then a sports story, and then the weather. Hank brought Alan in a cold beer, saying 'hot dog's holy cousin' as he set it down on the table.

Before a commercial, it was immediately apparent to Alan what Hank was talking about. There was a short quip about upcoming stories, but there was a helicopter shot of floodlights and police lights in the middle of the desert. When the news program returned, they explained that the remains of Margaret Hobbeston, the spouse of prominent prime time preacher Reverend Charles Hobbeston have been found buried in a shallow grave, twenty minutes from Las Vegas on the way to Overton, Nevada.

• • •

It was no surprise that Alan spent the majority of the rest of the night staring at various news stations covering the discovery. As soon as one station would stop coverage to make room for other stories, Alan would switch to another. And as soon as that was done, he would switch to another. He even switched to the news stations that he never watched, including the ones owned by a right wing family advocacy group and another that was owned by an extreme republican from overseas who tells his station exactly what to say and what stories to air like a third world dictatorship. Of course, he was allowed to do that, but it was puzzling that people believed what they heard.

Every station except for those with the skewed right wing agenda said the same thing; no suspects, blunt force trauma to the head, shallow grave, footprints and tracks virtually gone because of the desert's extreme winds. They did have some positive information leading to answers such as the desert providing an arid and dry environment which almost protected the remains of the late preacher's wife, they received the location from an anonymous tipster, and a written note was found with the body.

Alan was enthralled, and did not give himself an adequate rest whatsoever. When he got up, he only had enough time to brush his teeth and have a glass of water for breakfast. When pouring the water, he had another inspiration for a poem for Jaime which he scrawled into his notebook on the way to work, and then slept the rest of the way. He would give the poem to Jaime. He would give her everything.

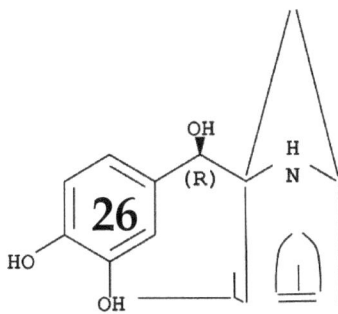

Briner's Diner was strangely desolate for three o'clock on a Tuesday, the cutlery tapping on stoneware sliced through the mostly silent environment. Alan took a seat at the counter and looked for a familiar face. There were only four patrons in the small restaurant, and it was rather steamy for an air conditioned diner in Nevada. Still, it was a comfortable escape from the blazing environment outside.

From a corner with a stainless steel swinging door, Jaime materialized carrying a large, rectangular covered steel tray that looked heavy. She fit it into a steamy hole on the counter, removed the cover, and stirred a solid that looked to Alan like mashed potatoes from where he sat. She still stood tall and slender, and one would never suspect that she was pregnant, especially as far into her pregnancy as she was. Of course, it seemed as though those who had no reason to be pregnant never showed it... It made Alan think of an extremely beautiful old French film where a woman who was speaking to her pregnant daughter of fifteen whose lover had gone to fight in the military, said "there is nothing that is not wholly beautiful of a pregnant woman."

Alan thought of this line as he watched her work and do her job; she had no idea that he sat only a couple meters away. His eyes were trained on her neck. His eyes moved slowly down her back like water, and then across her waist, and immediately to her wrist; the first thing that brought her to him. How lovely it was today, even more than it was when he first saw it. Elegance. 'She's the one thing that sets the world ablaze,' Alan thought to himself as his nose reached for her scent. She was glorious.

Alan held the index card with her poem on it in his sweaty hand. He didn't want it to be ruined. Scrawled on the card was a small poem in pencil. It was meant to be so simple, and say so much. He wanted to run up to her and give it to her, and jump, and have her read it aloud. They would be so happy, and the few people in the diner would reevaluate their own relationships, inspired by the public display of mutual, uninhibited joy.

"What does a guy have to do to get some service around here?" Alan said.

Jaime looked up at him and smiled. The smile was different than the one he was used to seeing, and it was strangely unpoetic and hollow. She looked like she was having an awful day. Her shoulders were slumped and her hand rested flatly on the top of her stomach, almost expecting the shelf of a pregnant stomach to hold it there. But it didn't, as she still looked thin. Alan was still curious about how she was pregnant, or if she even was any longer. If there was a baby in there, it was seriously taking up some prime real estate, pushing her stomach, intestines, and liver to the walls of her skin.

She looked at Alan as if she were waiting for him to say something. As if there was nothing for her to say. It was awkward, and Alan felt something awful in his stomach.

"How is your day, then?" Alan finally said.

"Horrible." She said nothing more.

"Oh, yeah?"

"It is awful. I have been here for hours and made twelve dollars. I am upset."

"I am sorry, sweetheart. At least it is just about time for you to get out of here."

"I suppose."

Alan did not understand the tone of her voice. He didn't understand why she seemed different and distant, and he had felt this feeling about someone before, but couldn't place it. Alan wanted to see her happy. He wanted to see her smiling at Alan as if he was the greatest and only creature on the planet with her, and she was surprised with something she had seen him do, everyday, even though one would think that they had seen it all. He wanted to see her without the wince on her face. Without her barbequed hand curled on her pelvis.

"I have something for you. A present." She cocked her head. Alan handed her the moist note card. It was simple, and elegant... as best as Alan could do.

It read, in Alan's minimalist hand...

> *When I woke this morning, and poured my glass of water,*
> *Two bubbles rose, and spun, and tossed in the current.*
> *They met in the center, and stuck,*
> *The center of a tumultuous vortex.*
> *In a moment*
> *They joined,*
> *And Formed One.*
> *and just as fast, disappeared completely.*
>
> *I thought to myself,*
> *"Isn't that wonderful?"*

Jaime looked up at Alan. She smiled.

"Thank you," was all she said. Alan had the feeling all of a sudden that she didn't get it. "Listen, I have to clean up so I can get out of here... Do you want a cheeseburger or something?"

"Yes, that would be good."

Jaime said something to the cook, and the grill fired to life, and flames shot into the air in the small service window. The sizzling and cracking of fat burning on the grill reminded Alan of Dan's.

As Jaime walked back and forth behind the counter, and placed the burger in front of Alan, and the catsup, and the Tabasco, and did her other chores, and cleaned the ice cream freezer, and bathed everything,... Alan wondered if she just managed to 'get it.' Had she managed to reach the transcendence of existence? He could not have made it any more clear at this moment. Under no circumstance could it be any clearer. They would live together, and love, and this child would be theirs, and everything would be okay. In the midst of this desert, where there were chances of death, and starvation, and dehydration, and any number of horrific possible outcomes, they had one another. They were satiated, and calm, and everything would be okay. Yet... Watching her, he felt as though there was nothing genuine at this moment. That while there was nothing to worry about, she was in the muddy, sickly mires of worry.

Honestly, she was probably just having a bad day.

Alan ate his cheeseburger quickly, and also ate the piping hot fries down. He thought about where they were going, and what was to happen next. There was no circumstance or outcome in his head that didn't sound wonderful. Alan thought that he might ask her to move with him; to go to Canada and get away from the bureaucracy and live somewhere where civil liberties still reigned free. Or Paris. Or Amsterdam. Alan wanted to disappear, and he was certain that Jaime did too.

That is what the poem was about. Why didn't she see that? It was about being free, finally. Having no chains or cares, not worried about school or bills. Alan was tired of his life and obligations being an anchor, and just wanted to go somewhere and be happy. That feeling of happiness,... oh, what a feeling that must be. This feeling, the feeling of being with Jaime, and the way Alan felt was true. His stomach totally told him that this was right. He was endlessly happy with her. They never ran out of things to talk about and reasons to laugh. And that was so good.

Before Alan realized it, Jaime stood behind him with her knit purse and a sprinkling of other cloth hanging about her body. She was magnificent, but her forehead made Alan concerned. He didn't even remember eating.

"Are you ready?" She asked him. Her voice was soft and passive.

"Yes," Alan got up from his seat and followed her. "Are you okay?"

"Oh, Alan. Yes. I have a headache, though. I have been throwing up all day, and I am a bit dizzy. I think I may have eaten something bad."

"I hope it wasn't a cheeseburger?"

"No. No." The door swung open and the pair exited. The heat was a mess, honestly. The kind that you became sweaty, and then your t-shirt hung off your skin, damp, and swung like a wet tee shirt you wore to the pool because you hated the way you looked – and then you hated the way you felt as well. Disgusting heat; choking and wet.

Jaime's mother's car sat beaten and idle just outside of the diner. The faux leather seats melted around their forms as they sunk into them, and the buckles stung their fingers, they were so hot. She turned the car on, pulled out of the driveway, and they shot down the dusty trail.

Their conversation was sparse for the ride. Pulling into her parent's driveway, she shut the car off and immediately walked over the side of the garage, took the dog leash off of the hook, and opened the door a crack to whistle for her puppy. Alan left the car, and the air outside felt like it was the same air that was inside.

They walked up the driveway to the street as Moka nuzzled every dead bush. There weren't any animals for kilometers save the poisonous reptiles that scavenged about silently, and it was interesting to see the dog work so hard to find the scent he was looking for. Alan and Jaime weren't talking, and it was unsettling to him.

"Hear about the reverend's wife?" Alan asked. He couldn't stand it being so quiet.

"Yeah, they found her body. That is crazy. The news is saying that the reverend was about to pay the ransom, too." She said it nonchalant and uninspired.

"Oh, I wasn't aware of that part."

"It was new today. There is a radio in the kitchen." They continued to walk. The dog urinated in drippy spurts and Alan wondered if he even had to go, or if this was a territorial fluid that he was pushing out deliberately. "Who do you think would do something like that?"

"I don't know. He was really nice, but by the looks of everything has a lot of money. That's probably all it was. Why they would do something to that poor woman before they got the money is beyond me..." Alan was staring at the hot dirt beneath his shoes as they walked.

"Jaime," Alan continued. He grabbed her hand as he spoke. "We don't have any money, you and I. We don't have a place to live, and we don't have anything. Let's just disappear. Let's go somewhere, the two of us, and no one will see us for ten years. Lets go to Canada. Everyone will say 'hey, what ever happened to Jaime and Alan,' and we will show up again, out of the blue, and there will be pictures and postcards of all of our adventures, and everyone will think 'boy, those two really were in lo-'"

Jaime stopped walking before he even finished talking, and looked into Alan's eyes for the first time since the diner.

"I'm afraid that it won't happen."

"What do you mean?"

"Alan, people look at me right now as the girl who you want to congratulate for being pregnant, but not sure if you should say anything because I may have just gotten fat. Why? Because there is no man in my life for the baby to have as a father, and I live with my parents, and it is a great big mess."

"Jaime, I wasn't aware that you were the type of woman who felt she needed a man in her life, but even if you are, I will be there for you…"

"I'm not Alan, I have just been confused."

"Why?"

She paused. She stopped looking at Alan and continued walking. The dog had been trying to sit down on the ground, but stood every time his ass touched it. The earth was scorching.

"Alan, you are the most genuine and amazing person I know right now. Being with you reminds me of home. It reminds me of the fresh air, being happy, the mist sprayers at the beach that make you feel great, the breeze… But… it isn't summer all of the time, no matter where you live. You have to get a job, and you have kids, and responsibilities."

"Yes…"

"Alan, I just don't know where you get all of this."

"All of what?"

"This… This feeling that you have to come in and save me. This feeling that you are in love with me… You aren't."

"What are you talking about, where is this coming from?" In the pit of Alan's stomach, he felt the heat, the raw sensation that comes from the sockets that your eyes roll around in, and the feeling that makes us different than any animal on the planet. It is acid and awful. It was horror. "Well? Two days ago you told me that you loved me. You shouted it in fact."

"No, Alan, I didn't."

"Yes you did. That was a direct quote; when we were at the chapel place you said 'Alan Levy, I love you,' and your arms were raised in the air and you kissed me." Jaime was looking away from Alan.

"I never kissed you Alan, and I never said those words."

Alan felt faint. Ahead in the distance a truck came toward them, barreling through the desert, kicking dust ten meters into the air. Alan needed to pause. He heeded to think about what to say. He was dizzy. He was losing this battle, and he didn't even know about the war. He was under a totally different assumption before they started walking this far; before they started walking at all. Alan looked back toward the house. They were no more than twenty meters from where they started.

"I am honestly sorry that you feel this way," Alan started, choosing his words carefully. "I never wanted you to feel like I was coming in to save you or that you felt I was making it seem like I needed to take care of you… I… I honestly just wanted to be with you when I first met you, that's all. It is rather unfair that you bring up your pregnancy, and it is unfortunate that you have to go through this, but honestly Jaime, I didn't even know about it until after I was here for a while. I know you can make it on your own, and I know that you can work things out, but honestly I had no intention to make you feel like this. I have really had feelings for you since I met you, and unless I have absolutely no idea how humans work, I thought you felt the same way…"

"I did," Jaime replied.

"What is all this about you denying things that have happened and everything else?"

"Because they didn't Alan!"

"Okay, fine. Let me put it another way. Have you ever wanted to start a relationship with me?"

She began slowly. "Yes, but..."

"But what?"

"I don't know, I am just confused."

"Okay. I understand." He didn't. He has been under the impression that he was one of the best things that she had ever come across. He felt as though he was everything to her. He thought that... He thought that she felt the same way about him. His phone began silently vibrating in his pocket again, and stopped. "Well, what do you think the chances are of us having a relationship? Do you think there are such chances?"

"I do, Alan, I do. I am just confused, and you need to be patient with me. Honestly I think it is just that I have never met anyone like you." The truck sped by and dust was kicked into their faces. The pins and needles of the sand along with the feeling of the dirt creeping into your shoes and under your clothes was getting quite old to Alan. "But I think there is a chance, sure."

Alan patted off his clothes, kicking more dust into the air.

"Well, then lets do this. I am going to pour myself out to you. I am going to pour every gram of my creativity and my work and my strength as an artist into you. I am going to do it all for you. Everything I do, I will do for you. Hopefully with the strength of my prose and weight of my words you will find something in there that is different than anyone else has ever presented to you. I am confident enough, in fact, to suggest that it will be better than anything that anyone can do for you in your entire life."

"I think we can swing that..."

"...and later on, when I am still shouting your name from the rooftops and in the pages of the world's publications, you can honestly say that I could have been the best thing to ever happen to you, and you wish it could have been different... I wish nothing less than regret from you if you fuck this up, because I will do nothing less than miss you from the bottom of my heart."

Jaime didn't respond at all. She dusted the dirt from her outfit, and looked as though she wasn't even listening paying attention to Alan. It was as if he didn't even say anything.

"Okay," she finally responded.

Standing next to Alan, she twisted the leash around her hand in loops and the hot leather popped against itself. Alan took out his mobile phone and looked at the screen. It read 'Mum,' and as he put it back into his pocket, he wondered how Jaime could feel so absolutely far away from him even though she was right there. The dog looked bored. They went in.

Jaime's mother stood in the kitchen with a glass of red wine, her hand hovering it about. The whirlpool inside the glass looked like the way her silver hair twisted and curled into a mountain of locks above her forehead, and Alan realized that it was almost impossible not to spot her without the alcoholic accessory.

"Hello, Alan," she spoke.

"Hi… How have you been?"

"Okay, you know. I've been busy with the house, and taking care of the animals." She spoke distantly. "Jaime, will you call your brother? I am trying to get him to come in from Chicago, and I'm having a tough time. I just want everyone together for Christmas - that's all I want."

"I'll do that, I'll do that." Jaime grabbed Alan and began to pull him towards the living room, and then up the three stairs, and then to her lonely room. The room was cool, light, and dry, and almost seemed illuminated from within – by virtue of its existence. Alan had since only been in during the nighttime, and its light breeze was refreshing and surprising for the brutality of the Nevada heat.

Jaime turned on her stereo, and the music of a piano player carelessly mashing the keyboard and singing words and words and words and words all next to each other and unintelligible came out of the speakers. However muffled the lyrics were, if Alan could understand them, he knew they would be wonderful, painful, and true. This mishmash of notes and vocabulary was almost comforting, and he really enjoyed it. In one song there was a trumpet, and in another there was an upright bass. Alan really wanted to know who this was. He was swimming in the music. The euclidean notes in space, in three dimensions, in confusing modes and scales and it all made sense and came together. Where am I? Alan wondered. Alan wondered.

Jaime was rummaging in her closet. She could fit into it if she wanted to. The closet was completely a gnarled contrast to her simplistic existence in the world. Only her feet stuck out from the mess of hanging clothes and possessions. There was a wall of cloth and fabric, but she knew what she was doing.

"What's your favorite book, Jaime?" Alan asked, looking around the room in its new illumination. He thought he would switch gears into something more simple as a contrast to the music, and their complicated conversation. Alan examined a small shelf with rocks, seashells, small hand-carved sculptures, and some picture frames that was across the room from the bed and next to the closet.

He had seen this shelf before, but never examined the photos. As a matter of fact, there were photos hung from the walls sporadically and ill-spaced around over her room, and Alan never bothered to look at them. They were accessories, after all. Accessories and background noise to why he was always really there, to look at and study Jaime. Why would he waste his time with anything else?

"What, Alan? My favorite book?"

"Yeah, your favorite book." She stopped rummaging just long enough to make sure she heard him correctly. She was rummaging again. Her toes curled, extended, flattened, and showed as much personality and concentration on the task at hand as her visage must have.

Alan turned his attention back to the photographs that he was so intent on studying. There was one with trees, light streaming in rays, and a string, several strings holding up a feather attached to a rock, and all of it swinging from the trees. It was a heavenly picture of improvised artwork in the middle of the forest. He wondered if they came across it and it hung there for generations, or if it was built by Jaime, or if it was divinely cast down as evidence of something greater than our poor humanity. The photo would clearly suggest just that, the lighting and the trees and the artifacts swinging were just so perfect – there was no wonder this needed to be saved for posterity. The dog came galloping into the room and stopped looking at Alan confused.

"Well, I really like... The Wind In The Willows; and I like Watership Down..."

Another picture on the shelf was of Jaime and another girl with sunglasses on. Jaime was behind her, and she sat on a street barricade on a bridge looking over a harbor. Her hair was cropped tight, brunette, and her face attractive and happy. Jaime's arms crossed in front of her neck and they were both laughing. One of Jaime's hands almost looked as though it was on one of the other girl's breasts. It was a sexy picture; innocent, and intriguing.

"Animal books," Alan replied. "For some reason I could have totally imagined that." And he was being honest. How could she relish in Tolstoy or O'Neill? She was simple, and that made her sexy.

The next photo on the shelf was a blurry picture, taken very close up, of Jaime and a man with a thick face and half of the dog's surprised face. Jaime's lips were smooching his face, and they were very happy. Laughing. Ecstatic. The picture was definitively imperfect, but happy. Happy in so many ways. His chubby face had a pencil line beard that extended from his sideburns and across his chin, and back up the other side to cover his head in short hair. Was this her brother?

As Alan considered that, he realized that there were no photographs of Jaime or her family anywhere in the house. Not that pictures of one's family taken at the local department store were anything to brag about, but the house was eerily bare of anything that would suggest a family lived there. There were more framed postcards than anything else in the house; an Irish pub here, an old fashioned man on an old fashioned bicycle, a cup of coffee on a table. Alan also realized that he had no pictures of Jaime. But maybe that was good, because he would stare at it, and stare, and obsess, and drown.

"That's Chris and I," Jaime said from behind him. He didn't realize that she had left the closet and was behind him. She had a thrown together pile of photo albums in her hands, and tossed them onto her bed, and walked over to her dresser. Opening the drawer, she retrieved a tank top, and Alan strolled around the room to look at the other pictures.

There was another on the wall, and it was Jaime, Chris, the girlfriend from the other picture, and an assortment of motley creatures all in different poses on a dock. It was humorous and intimate. One of them even had a plastic sword, and was stabbing another in the chest who looked a bit like Alan, but it was probably just the pose he was in.

"I have never looked at any of these pictures. It's funny, I am just noticing them." Alan was looking at her when he spoke, and Jaime pulled her shirt over her head. The first thing Alan noticed was that she didn't shave her armpits, and Alan observed that the light hair looked composed and combed before she put her arms down again to retrieve the tank top off of her bed. The second thing Alan noticed was her breasts. Devoid of any bra, they were small, polite, and plump. There were small purple lines next to her arms, and her nipples that were heavily defined against her smooth skin and raised in a plateau with purple intermittent spots that reminded Alan of the pregnancy.

He wasn't in the least bit turned on by the act, and was unsure of why not. Was it the frankness of the act? The uninhibited, blatancy of it? He wanted to jump on her, and kiss her, and it had nothing to do with that moment. He just wanted to kiss her. He wanted to kiss her then, and he wanted to kiss her in his heart and on his lips, and he wanted to kiss her yesterday and the day before. How would he know that he would feel anything when it happened? Would he?

But this was an image of intimacy, but not his. It was incidental, but everything he was observing was of a situation that he was slowly becoming devoid of. He was a bit actor in the background. He was the extra.

The radio crackled, and just like that her shirt was back on, and pulling it down over her belly. Alan noticed the purple stretch marks continuing down to her hips. His heart was heavy in his chest, and he turned his attention back to the wall of photos to hopefully exude the same lax attitude that Jaime had about the moment. No, he wasn't looking, but if he was, it wasn't anything he had ever seen before. Don't take any attention to yourself, Alan.

"I have more here, Alan, come look," Jaime said.

Alan sat on the bed, and they looked through the pictures, and leafed through the binders. In one group Jaime was in Prague, and in another she was among the Aztec ruins in Mexico. In some pictures she was singing, and in others laughing. She was everything that Alan wanted and more. Look at the adventures he could have, look at the wonder and at the sunny feeling. In one she was tan, and another at a topless beach. Her skin he had seen twice today, and it was the same thing. No sexual desire. No carnal reaction. Alan forgot exactly why he was enduring all of this. Did he want her? Romantically there was no question, but sexually there had been no reaction…

But had there been one romantically? Were they just selling out everything about their relationship? Seeing one or the other naked in a relationship was quite the accomplishment, even a beautiful thing, and yet there was nothing special about this moment. There were special moments before, though, and Alan doubted why he was having the inner dialogue he was just then. Things will happen the way they happen, he thought, and you should just be proud that she is so comfortable around you.

Another book that she pulled out was a scrapbook, and a piece of paper fell out of the bottom of it.

"What's this book?" Picking the paper up from the floor, she quickly opened the book and categorically placed it where it went.

"This is my life," she said. Where she opened the book to put the paper back was filled with little letters and pictures of her and a man. The papers were covered in scribbles of poetry and accolades.

"Was this a boyfriend?"

"No, a friend from back home."

"What was his name?"

"John."

"John," Alan repeated, leaving through the documents that Jaime had on him. There was poetry, letters, postcards. It was a very revealing package. "How long had you been with Chris?"

"I was with Toph for close to five years. We have known one another forever, it seems…" Deep in the heart of Alan he felt something. He felt a discomfort, as if a bone was out of place and needed to snap back in. Or did Jaime feel it? No one was sure.

"What ended up happening?" Alan asked, flipping the page. On this page was high school graduation. There were no family pictures, only Jaime and her cap and gown. There was also a picture of her mother with a glass of wine in her hand in a backyard.

"Well, we just needed different things I guess." She looked off into some distant universe. "…which is crazy that this ended up happening, I mean," and she trailed off, scratching the top of her inconspicuously occupied stomach.

Alan flipped another page, and there was another boy with other poems. He flipped the page again, revealing pictures of her and the girl in the other photo; another page with Chris; another with a boy and more writing. Alan considered that he gave Jaime some writing, and she didn't have any pictures of him. Alan would be a page in this book - a really crappy page that paid no homage to the fact that he existed and felt such an encompassing love with Jaime. Maybe it would be more meaningful, but maybe it wouldn't.

The poems were scattered throughout this book, and Alan was just another representative of what all these men were… Sad, hopeless creatures who fell in love with a woman who was in love with a man and didn't have the heart to tell the boys about him. Alan looked the pages up and down, and could only think that these people were only an indication of the reality of Jaime's collection of hearts. These were a girl's baseball card collection. Simply put, Alan had wanted to ask when these boys were in her life. Was it within the five years that she was with Chris? Were these just side projects of hers, an opportunity to gain the romance and respect of the first moments of love but without the burdens that she faced in the long term bore sleeping next to Chris?

"Jaime?" Alan was just going to ask. Alan was just going to ask about who the hell she thought she was doing this to these poor boys... And it was a good thing that they had such a good relationship, too, because he would be worried...

"Yes?"

"I am glad that you don't think of me as a place like you did with these boys. I am glad that you are so undeniably in love with me that you would do anything to make sure that we stay together and in tact... I am certainly glad that this is working out so well for the both of us because I can't imagine my being any happier right now." Well, that is what Alan wanted to say, anyway. That is what Alan wanted to belt from the rooftops and the hilltops, electrifying the dunes of Nevada and the rooftops of Boston. That is so what Alan wanted to say...

He wanted to tell Jaime how much of an impact she has had already on him. How much he is grateful for the support and the understanding of himself, how grateful he is for her. How he just wanted to tell her something he could never tell any other woman, 'Jaime, I appreciate you; I appreciate you so much,' and tell her everything. Tell her how he spent hours just saying her name in the dark at Hank's house because he liked the way it sounded on his lips and the way it made his heart feel when he said it. He liked the way it felt rolling off his tongue and onto his pillow like hot wax and leaking into his ears. He drew her name in cursive on the wall in the dark.

He wanted to tell her how beautiful she was, over and over again; how much understanding there was between them and how much she should forgive him for being so frank. But she would find the honesty beautiful and they would whisk away to Canada, or Mexico, or Paris, and never be heard of again. That was the plan, wasn't it? That was the plan.

And they would find a small pension or an apartment, and there would be a violinist that lived downstairs, it just so happens, and it would be wonderful. And they would practice twice a week with a man who played a harmonium and a singer who only spoke French and smoked way too much and had a very high voice for a man. That would be wonderful. And Alan could finish school as a writer, not a teacher because that is bullshit, and Jaime could study to be what she really wanted to be like a botanist or an opera singer and it would be absolutely wonderful as they cried every night because they were so happy for once. They would hold each other and weep for their happy, bohemian existence, and they wouldn't have any money, and the baby would never cry, and it would be just so wonderful because they all had one another.

But it isn't what Alan said. Alan just closed the book, and smiled.

"This is really nice Jaime... I mean, you have done so much."

"I know... I was thinking that I should put some stuff in here about you... I just don't know what to-" She took out the wrinkly poem out of her pocket and shoved it in the binding on the next blank page. "Here..."

"No, Jaime, you really shouldn't. I am nothing..." It was fucking offensive.

"No, I totally should. You have been a part of my life and I think you should be happy..."

"Whatever."

"Jaime?" Jaime's mother called up the stairs to her, sounding a little hesitant and weary. Not of anything in particular, probably just because of the beverage she almost surely had in her hand.

"Yes, mom?"

"Have you called your brother yet?"

"No, mom, I am going to..."

"Okay, I just don't want you to forget; Christmas is in a week, Jaim. This is important to your father and I."

"Yes mom." Jaime looked at Alan and waited until the door closed to the stairs up to her room. "I hate it when mom drinks. Dad, too. I swear that there isn't a day that they can not make it through without having a drink. I think they are alcoholics, but it is one of those things that they won't admit it. My brother was pretty bad when he moved to Chicago. There was three months where he didn't have a job and all he did was sit at home and drink all of the time. It was bad. I wish they could just go a week without a drink."

"I know what you mean," Alan replied.

"Listen, let's go downstairs and make something to eat... Then I will give my brother a call. Does that sound good?"

"Sure," Alan said, but he wasn't hungry. He had the burger at the diner not too long before, and this particular moment lent itself to not being too hungry for anything. This week has been like that, actually. Alan hasn't been hungry for a while, and his heart told him that he shouldn't worry about eating.

There was something about love that made everything else in the world seem so significant, Alan thought as he descended the staircase. There was something about a broken heart, however, that made you forget about everything else but the insignificance of yourself and how you would like to just waste away into the dirt. Yes, at this moment Alan was not hungry at all.

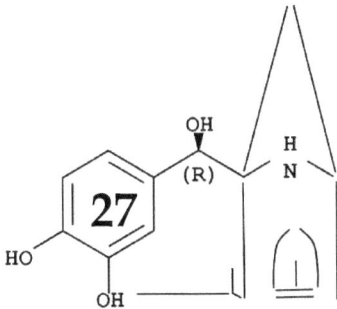

The brutal cruelty of the desert cold burned Alan's skin as he waited outside the back door to Hobbeston's church at six thirty in the morning.

It was Sunday, and he had set up another appointment to come to services. Hobbeston agreed to arrive earlier so they had more time to talk before his daily commitments. The morning was electric, and Alan felt strange about his surroundings. The world was pitch black, and the aluminum lamp over the door was covered in the winter detritus of paused natural existence; cobwebs and skeletons.

He pounded on the door for the second time. Beneath his feet, small improvised dunes of sand were swept against the building by a gradual dry breeze. It dispersed into pavement further away from the building. Wavy snake tracks plowed through the dust.

"Alan," the muffled voice from behind the steel door inquired.

"Yeah, yeah, it's me. It's freezing out here…"

The door resonated a loud clack as an elephant bolt was slid aside. The door creaked open, and Hobbeston stood beyond the threshold looking the worst Alan had seen him. He had tissue paper stuffed in the circumference of his collar, and his suit hung off of his body as if he had eaten a comical shrinking potion in an old cartoon.

"Come on in! It's a busy morning here," he continued as he led Alan down a cinder block hallway with high ceilings. "The week of Christmas is always a little chaotic. This is the time of year when we get a lot of our fund-raising done and we have to work extra hard to get a lot more souls on our side, you know?"

"I suppose…" They reached a door that Hobbeston opened for Alan. It was his oak paneled office, and the smell of maple syrup wafted out.

"Here, Alan, grab yourself something to eat. I am going to go get my makeup finished up and I will be right in to go over my sermon and we can talk…"

"Sure…"

"Actually, my son is around here somewhere and you should meet him. I will send him in… I am sure you could find something to talk to him about for your work." Hobbeston left the room, and just like that Alan was in his office with two large tables of fruit platters, carafes of juice, and large pans with torches under them keeping them warm. Alan investigated the wares. There were sausages, eggs, pancakes, syrup, bagels; anything you would possibly want for breakfast. At this point Alan was hungry, but he was almost relishing in his hunger as he didn't even consider taking any food from the table. He just took a glass, and poured some ice water into it.

Strolling around the room, alone, Alan took the opportunity to formally introduce himself to the world of Reverend Hobbeston. The oak desk, the shiny leather chairs, and the walls of books all made this office feel like Earnest Hemingway or Rock Hudson. The romance of this room's masculinity was intoxicating.

Alan walked over to the desk, and examined it. There was a modern looking phone, a pad of notepaper with the embossed logo from Hobbeston's business card, a pen, and other office supplies organized with an ordered and almost obsessive-compulsive placement about the desk. He turned to look at the books on the shelves that resembled a lawyer's bookshelf with uniformity, order, and leveled placement of intelligence and elegance.

Alan pulled on one of the volumes titled 'Philosophy and Thought.' The book gave way easily. So easily, as a matter of fact, that five other books on either side gave way attached to the first. Alan pulled the stack, and realized that they weren't real books at all but a professional theatrical piece made of plastic and ends of paper. They were so well made that Alan thought they were real even centimeters away with his hand on it. The underbelly of the apparently glued together stack was completely hollow, and the books looked as though they were just built around a plywood box without a bottom.

Alan put the stack back into their perfectly-fitting space on the shelf, and examined the rest of them. They were all completely the same, sans the ones that were written by Hobbeston himself. Each of those had their own shelf dedicated to twenty copies of the same title. Devoted to finding out what was behind this, Alan investigated that there were at least seven others of the same set piece with titles and authors like 'Marine Biology' by L. J. Silver, and 'Modern Existentialists' by O. Dog. Alan wasn't entirely sure that Hobbeston got the joke, or ever even examined them. Otherwise, the books wouldn't be there.

Alan thought about leaving behind something underneath one of the faux book stacks, as a surprise, but he had nothing on him other than his notebook and pen. He took out his pen, and flipping over one of the stacks of books, thought about something to write... He began in cursive - which he never wrote in – on the inside of the stack, "...and the melancholy fit shall fall. A. L., 20--"

He replaced the book, and turned back to the desk. He wanted to know more. He opened the drawer that closed above his lap, and inside there was a silver letter opener that looked like a dagger, but had a cross where the handle was. The insincerity of the symbol and catchpenny execution of the object was discomforting. He picked it up and placed the sharp point against his breast, straight at his heart. Yes, he thought, that would be bad if you accidentally fell on it. Accidentally.

There were papers with names and numbers on them, a menu from a local delivery restaurant, and a couple of old photographs that were fastened to very hard cardboard. One of them looked as though it was taken in the nineteen eighties because of the boxy style of the vehicle the family was standing in front of, as well as the style of hair, short shorts, and ringed gym socks. There was a tall young teenager with blond hair and he was standing with four or five other people his age, and two adults in overalls. They looked hot, but happy. There was a barn to the right behind them, and to the left behind them was a wide open field that seemed as though it didn't end.

Another photo was of a young Hobbeston, perhaps in his thirties. He looked a little scruffy, but in the middle of an engaging talk. His hand splayed above his head looked like it was in motion, holding an invisible orange. He was standing behind a pulpit, or podium, and there was a small cloth hanging from it with the letters 'NA' in a circle. Alan pocketed the photo and continued rummaging through his desk.

Suddenly the door opened and a man walked in. He was tall, blond, and skinny, with a very sharp pinstriped suit that fit perfectly. He was clearly just passing through, not expecting to see anyone. But when he looked up and saw Alan, he immediately froze.

"Hey, wait! Hey what the hell do you think you're doing?" He shouted.

"Oh, me, I'm Alan, I just needed-"

"Needed what? Needed what?" He briskly walked over beside Alan and closed the desk drawer with a slam. He was intentionally invading Alan's personal space, and centimeters from him. "Get the hell out of there."

"I just needed a pen. I was looking for a pen." Good save, Alan wondered?

"Pen, well, I have a pen for you, okay, but don't go snooping around!" He reached into his pocket inside his jacket and retrieved a black plastic pen with gold writing on it. It read *Jared Hobbeston, Esq.; Attorney At Law; 18 Heritage Lane, Suite 4; Chicago, Illinois.* "You are that writer kid. I should have known to tell him not to let you in here by yourself. Not that you would find anything."

"You are his son? Jared?"

"I'm his lawyer, and yes, I also happen to be his son." Alan looked him up and down, and he acted in the exact same way that he looked. He was biting, harsh, and his attitude was acidic. "Listen, what do you want with my dad, seriously?"

"I just have wanted to meet him, to get to know him..."

"What's this book you wrote?"

"I am writing a book about faith in America. What it means to be faithful. Of course, who else could I possibly pick besides your dad, I mean, he is one of the mos-"

"Don't bullshit me, okay?" His confrontational, acerbic attitude increased, and made Alan wince. "I suggest you run this book by me before you get it published, and if you need me to, I can get a judge to tell you to a little less politely than I am right now."

"Fine, whatever," Alan answered, knowing that such a book will never get published. Jared Hobbeston was leaning over him, teetering. Alan wasn't afraid of Jared falling, but he felt weightlessness in his own stomach.

Hobbeston entered the room. He looked powdered, clean, and orange - like the embodiment of exactly what Alan had seen on television; aside from the fact that his hair still looked like shit.

"I hope you boys are getting along..." Hobbeston said.

"Yeah. Yeah, we're getting along, isn't that right, Alan?

"Yeah, sure," Alan replied.

"Listen, let's grab a seat, get something to eat, and get comfortable. I still have a few minutes for you, Alan, and then you boys have to go out so I can go over my sermon."

Jared went over to the buffet and shifted around pans and covers and filled his plate. Hobbeston sat at his desk, and Alan sat at one of the chairs facing it. He paused, closed his eyes, and looked like he was meditating. Jared sat just behind and to the left of Alan with a small scoop of eggs and what looked like a huge pile of sausage patties. Hobbeston opened his eyes, looked up, and opened a desk drawer to remove a stack of papers. He watched Alan take out his notebook and uncap the pen Jared gave to him.

"What is your spiritual motivation, Reverend?" Alan asked. Jared's mouth was humming wide with egg and sausage just behind Alan. It was intimidating, and Alan felt like prey. He had to write down everything Hobbeston said this time to perform for his son. "Why do you do what you do with all of the cruelty in the world, if you don't mind my referencing your current loss..." Jared stopped chewing. Hobbeston was looking at his desk, making forlorn circles with his finger, pushing the silver pen around.

"Dad, dad nothing about mom, nothing about mom-" Jared interjected after a choking swallow.

"No, no, that's okay. I am going to have to get used to this, really." Hobbeston responded softly and slowly. "The question was not about your mother, Jared." He turned his attention back to Alan.

"What's your motivation, Alan? When you get up every morning, and you say to yourself, 'today I am going to make a difference, and I am going to do it sitting in front of a computer or a typewriter. And then I am going to send it to somebody who is going to give me a piece of paper that has a number on it, and then they are going to print out what I wrote a million times on dead trees or chopped up soy beans and people are going to read it and they are going to be really really sad or really really happy and then go on with their lives.

"I am a writer, also, as you know. I write and I write and I write and I never think that it is ever going to go anywhere, but I do know that I may take one or two people and make their lives a little better, whether by turning them to Christ or... or just by making their life a little bit easier, if just for one minute. That's what motivates me. My life wasn't always easy and I didn't always make the best decisions, either, but you know,... If I can help one person avoid the mistakes and the unhappiness of my life as it was before, I would.

"As far as the pain and the suffering and the inhumanity of the world... Well, Alan, it is always going to be like that, and we have to figure out ways around it, and strategies to make sure we don't make life like that for ourselves or for others."

He paused. He stopped spinning the pen on the desk, and returned it to its straight home. He looked up at the ceiling.

"I miss my wife, Alan. I miss her more than anything. I missed her since the minute she disappeared, and since the moment I met you, and right now. Jared does, too. I have been motivated by knowing that Jesus was in my heart and in hers, and that he would give me the strength to get us all through this. Now that it has ended the way it did, I just..." He paused again. "...I just have to trust it ended the way it did because it was god's will to take her home to Jesus." He was still looking at the ceiling.

"Listen, Alan, could I... Could I answer the rest of your questions after the service? I will make time for you. This is hard..."

"Sure, sure. I am sorry, I know you need to-"

"Jared, could you excuse me, too? Maybe talk with Alan for a little while before the service starts? You can get good seats, anyway."

He didn't reply, but put his fork down and stood.

Jared led Alan out of the room, and once they were in the hallway again wolfed down the rest of his breakfast. The lighting, or the hallway seemed to get darker as they left, and Alan felt bad he brought up the subject of Margaret. He didn't understand why people were constantly tiptoeing around death and grieving. Everyone died. It was almost the one simple truth of life for all of us. Ignoring it only prolonged acceptance of it, and some poor people never accepted it, even up to the point it takes them from their flesh.

There were already some congregants in the big room when they entered, and there were significantly more folding chairs set up around the room. The room was tightly lined with chairs for a small army of observance. Jared took Alan to seats in the back of the room toward the middle. On the balcony, a chorus was shuffling around. The choral conductor assigned standing spaces. The light of the morning sun shone through the glass, and the dirt and the support beams flickered danced on the heads and the shoulders of the singers.

"I don't know why you are doing this, honestly..." Jared spoke as they sat down.

"What do you mean?"

"I can't really grasp why you are here and doing what you are doing. What is this book about?"

"Faith in America..."

"Faith in America." He repeated the statement dryly. "So you thought you would come to the dirtiest and most fabricated part of the country to observe and meet one of the most fabricated religious figures? That's smart... Like I said, I don't understand your goal here."

Alan wasn't entirely sure what he should have said beyond that. He sat, looking at his notebook in his hands. Jared sat next to him with a smirk on his face and it was obvious that he was strategically choosing his words carefully in his head.

"I am going to be honest with you, guy. Dad is an asshole. I can't respect the man one bit - at least since what happened when I was younger. Do you know how he ended up in Vegas?" Alan shook his head.

" It wasn't because dad wanted to find some souls to save, no, it was because the first time around, the very first church he started and led and brought to the forefront was a complete travesty. It was a travesty because after mother had me and I had grown up a bit, dad had decided to start a relationship with a sixteen year old congregant.

"But don't worry, it was completely sexual; and at least it was a girl, I don't want you to gain more of a negative stereotype of any church from this... Are you catholic, or what?"

"No, no... Not," Alan responded.

"Yeah, me neither. I was obviously jaded the minute I had a conscious conceptualization of what Dad was about, what had happened, and why we were moving. Yeah,...when this information came to the forefront, we obviously had to leave town and all of my friends, and I have no idea why mother even decided to stay with him. She just loved him, I guess. She loved him so much, and it was his ability to mix his ambitious attitude toward the church with his uncanny ability to fuck everything up all of the time - *that* I think eventually killed mother." Jared looked down at his hands.

"Mother didn't die recently. Of course she was killed; she didn't just walk into the desert alone one day to get away from everything, as much as that is what she wanted to do... Her heart was broken and she gave up a long time ago, I think. You could tell by the way you spoke to her and it was always Jesus this and Jesus that, no matter if you were asking how she was or what she had been up to or if there was anything exciting happening; the way her glassy eyes were distant on television. They looked perfect, so perfect; and to the simple minded, I assume that they were, in a sense... The burning distance of the two of them, though. It was hard to be their son, so I just stopped. They wanted to play business, so that is the game I played with them."

Alan felt good that someone so close to Hobbeston could disclose who he really was, however, he felt betrayed that moment. He felt betrayed the moment Hobbeston told him about his past indiscretions, and now they were a great deal more magnified to the people around him – definitely to Alan. It was almost as if the character he had built in his head was just as human, just as incomplete, just as scattered as he had originally thought. At this moment he almost believed that it was more than he could have ever originally imagined in his head. The truth of the world was almost too bizarre and too fictitious for it to be real in any sense.

It worked this way in so very much. Love, sex, war. They all had what we believed to be the truthful side, but in an overall sense, they were all so unrealistically fictitious that there was nothing to explain the truth. Books written on these subjects only magnified the situation. Books on war that made you laugh at spilled blood and ripped flesh spread over a dirt street, a body pulled by a cord, a World War II bomber dropping nuclear weapons, obliterating cities and entire populations and races of human beings and animals and plants. It was funny, though, wasn't it?

Was this why Jared and Hobbeston didn't seem to mourn the loss of Margaret?

"So, you almost feel that the loss of your mother happened a long time ago? That is what makes it so much easier now?" Alan inquired.

Jared looked up at him from the floor, shook his head, and expelled a serious laugh.

"We're fake and dysfunctional. This whole country is, Alan. Don't forget it. The president and the materialism, the fuel and the waste, the paper bags and the sex, the prepackaged mess, *the appearance that everything is perfect and the selling of that*; this is the symptom finger, Alan. I mean, fuck, I make my living lying to everyone, don't I?"

"I suppose. Why are you your parent's lawyer, then?"

"Because money makes the world go round, Alan. It provides a more than stable allowance to keep the appearance that dad tries to put across fresh and alive. My existence in dad's life is almost the polar opposite of everything I have told you, but at the same level, is not the flower unaware of the deadly serpent beneath it?"

Alan was unsure if the misquote Jared was trying to use held any weight in the conversation.

The congregation was a great deal more populated, and seats were filling up fast. Conversations broke out among everyone, and the chorus had disappeared. The production crew was scrambling around the church making final adjustments, and it looked as though there were more cameramen today to operate the cameras that were normally unmanned, including the one attached to the crane that would probably provide Hobbeston with an audience and cutaways for the coming year's weekly productions.

"Do you come here for services often?" Alan asked Jared after a few minutes of taking in their surroundings. Jared sneered with a pretentious 'tsk.' While his response was expected, he was having a difficult time trying to find the next thing to say. It seemed as though everything had already been said.

And so they sat, basking in the early morning desert sunlight among what had to be close to a thousand congregants, waiting for the enlightening words to be spoken by Hobbeston. The chorus filed in, and the production started. It seemed as though they turned on every light, brushed the lint from every rug, and pushed the chorus to give their most polished performance, wherever in the world they came from.

After some whispers and shuffles, the chorus belted a triumphant gospel note from the depths of their souls and out of their throats. The serenade was spectacular, and the effect on the congregants was magnificent. Heads turned, hands pressed to breasts, and tears rolled from the cheeks of the truly passionate. Everyone clutched their purses in one hand and hymnals in the other, waiting for the moment that they could truly, truly prove their faith.

Careening to the pulpit, Hobbeston shot from the side of the stage with more bravado than Alan was used to in person and on television. He looked like a nineteen-sixties movie star: oiled up, over tanned, and ready to sign an autograph. As fired-up as his father was, Jared only shifted in his chair. The crowd applauded, and Hobbeston immediately grabbed the microphone from the pulpit.

"Good Morning, everyone!" he said, walking to the edge of the stage. He looked like a game show host. "Welcome to Christmas week services at the Cathedral. This week, over two thousand years and several decades ago, Jesus Christ was born unto this revolving soil in the universe and died no longer than three decades from it. Here we are, forgiven and ready to enter the gates of heaven because we are pure and have golden hearts thanks to the lord Jesus Christ, Amen!"

The congregation responded 'Amen!' with resounding enthusiasm.

"This time of year is one of our faith's holiest," he began, "and now, more than ever we need to spread generosity, brotherhood, and the words of Christ around the globe. Before we begin today, let us bow our heads and pray for those less fortunate than ourselves." The congregation did as they were told.

All around Alan and Jared, the congregant's heads were bowed down. They were praying, or so they made it appear. Without much of a stretch of the imagination, this room of good Christians were probably only at fifty percent of the prayer compliance. Full of broken thoughts, the rest wondered why Mrs. Evian wore that horrid dress to church, and others wondered where the Indian family came from, and what that awful smell was, and others were wondering how they were going to afford to pay their Christmas bills and how much they could afford to give today, and others thought about nothing.

Alan's college friends stopped going to church for this reason; the reason that a lot of people stopped going to church: they said it had become cliquey, judgmental, and very non-Christian. Alan would ask this of them; why, in the face of such awful behavior, can you simply stand by your religion and want to defend it so harshly. Defend it to the depths of your being. Defend it and its rules and its members and its cultish leaders.

Originally they didn't like the blacks... But the faithful persevered and had to start their own churches. In the face of hatred and bigotry and they still had faith. Faith, even in some of the very leader's recognition that slavery should indeed be legal, because the Lord wanted the whites to educate and lead the blacks to goodness like sheep.

No, they didn't like the faggots. The faggots would ruin the universe, and they weren't allowed in the church because the lord said they were bad and the devil's instruments for the simple-minded.

The church loved the disabled, though, because it could make them well again.

The church didn't like the Chinese, the Arabic, and the Jews.

The Jews. Alan was Jewish, and so was Jesus. How interesting that the church did not accept the faith of the very man whose philosophy their faith in god originated from. Then again, they ordained the buildings with expensive towering spires, and gold gilded every square centimeter. Yes, quite the appropriate homage to a man who died because of what he believed in, and that was to love and live with only the Lord in one's heart. He didn't need money, nor did he have any; only ears to listen to what god had to say. Imagine, a man persecuted for being a leader and nothing to show for it besides a following, and yet now he does need something to show for it. The sweetest price, death was, for him there was nothing further for him to give than the ultimate sacrifice, and today; today sacrifice was hard to come by.

Heads returned upright. It wasn't their fault, Alan thought. It was the fault of their culture, our culture, and being able to have anything, and being able to afford anything, and the feeling of invincibility. There once was a time in this country that people didn't feel so invincible, and they felt raped! So they went after the ghosts that caused the destruction, and it was quite the existential dilemma because the ghosts they hunted were ghosts that were created by paranoia and violation. From the ground it looked like they were making headway against the ghosts, or so they were able to made it look. For from space, thousands of kilometers away, the only thing you could see was green. And on that green there were little fleshy hairless animals. And those animals just could not take it anymore being peaceful and happy, so they started to hunt themselves. Nothing had changed, besides the fact that the little fleshy animals were more scared than ever.

"This year, I would like to remember the sacrifice Christ brought to us, and I would like to talk about sacrifice." Hobbeston began. "During the holiday season, many people mistaken generosity for sacrifice. Generosity is giving and giving without regard for cost. Sacrifice is giving when the cost is a great deal more than one can afford to give, and it gives more to another in such a way that it may change their life forever.

"I just read an old book about a man without a job and without money who gains a large inheritance from an aunt who had passed away. Rather than keep the money and spend it on material things, rather than give himself an easier life and try to make a difference for himself, rather than become a philanthropist and give it to his college, he had a much better idea.

"He bought two one way tickets around the world, one for himself, and one for his friend. They could make as many stops as they could, and they did. They stopped in as many countries as they possibly could… But they just didn't pick any country. He carried the great sum of money in his pockets and socks and underwear in cash. All cash. The countries that he picked were the poorest of the poor, the dankest of the dank, and the saddest of the sad. The money he carried, he distributed to the few people that would show him the kindness and hospitality that only he would fee was the most generous and abiding of it all, and to those people he would give money.

"Now when I say money; to you and I that speaks of paper that flows in and out of our lives like rain. Some of us in this room have too much; so much that they don't know what to do with it and they are generous. Others in this room have hardly any, and when the collection basket passes in front of them, they drop in only a dollar, and to them I say thank you because that is simply the absolute most that they could give.

"To the people in the story, though, this money was a great deal more. It was an instinct for survival. The dollar that even the most simple living person in this room would in fact mean to the person in the story that it was given to that they would not have to work for a week. Could you imagine that? A week? But the protagonist gave not one dollar, not ten, but enough to change their life so that they may never have to worry about money ever again. He gave them a life changing sum of money; a hundred dollars to one person in Africa, two hundred more in the wasteland of Siberia.

"What was even more beautiful about the story is that he expected no retribution for his acts, and why would he? The people receiving the money didn't know who he was, nor did they know how very much money that they were being given. They would the minute they arrived at an exchange of course, but they were indifferent as to what the paper meant that they were being given.

"Children, I ask this holiday season that you are generous and sacrificial. Do not go into the throngs and spend your money on junk and materials that no one could possibly thank you for enough. The surprise on their faces when they open the packaging is only temporary. Many things… The things that truly last in this life have nothing to do with those feelings. Give. Give like you have never given before.

"This year, do not give gifts that people can hold in their hands; give gifts they can hold in their hearts. Donate to a charity in their name. Tell them that all of the money that would have been spent on their gifts was spent on helping the poor, helping the independent medical and aid organizations bring relief to parts of the world suffering disaster, helping this church. There can be no greater gift than this. Let us pray."

The congregation bowed their heads and Hobbeston raised his hand in the air. Several of the congregants did the same.

"Lord, help us to bring salvation and harmony to the meek and the suffering in the world this holiday season, just as you have brought salvation and harmony to our lives. Thank you for bringing us into your heart and being a part of your life, and please do not hesitate to help us become more like you in every way that we humanly can. In Christ's name, Amen."

Hobbeston looked up. His gaze was immediately toward the back of the congregation, and he placed one of his fingers nonchalantly in his ear. Alan had never seen Hobbeston do this. As a matter of fact, Alan never realized that he had any kind of an earpiece in at all. He looked up at the choir. There was confusion in his eyes. He walked off stage, and the choir began to sing.

Alan looked down at his program. This special looked like it was at least twice as long as the regular program, there was an intermission, as well as time blocked off for songs where the show was dedicated to the chorus. Nothing seemed to point to this cascade of unfolding events.

Consequently, Alan had no recollection of watching the Christmas services before, so he thought it may not be that important that he was a little bit lost in the maze of what was happening.

Looking around, the congregants seemed quite happy. Flanking the aisles, basket-wielding men in white suits walked up the aisles and started to push the baskets attached to long poles down the aisles and collect money. Maybe this is how it happened, Alan thought. Chorus, collect money, and perhaps he could run backstage for water and a makeup touch up?

Alan's telephone hummed silently against his leg in his pocket. He reached down and pulled it out. He hasn't made any telephone calls in weeks, it seemed, and the small icon denoted nine voicemails in the phone memory. The screen on the phone identified the caller as Alan's Mum. He had to find time to call her later on, he thought.

His thoughts careened from his mother over to what the preacher was talking about. Sacrifice, in this day and age. What a horrible thing this was. Coming from Hobbeston's mouth, it sounded like the sappiest, sad, horrid, depressing slow piano music he had ever heard in his life. The man was spewing verbal diarrhea to a crowd of people that were the polar opposite of what he was trying to convey. What nerve did he have? What nerve?

Above, as the chorus began yet another song, Alan realized that the simple concept of the whole situation was hypocrisy. The man, who is solely driven by making money off of the faithful, being completely selfish and absorbed in the gaining of liquid assets, was asking his American congregants, on Christmas, to spend their money on the image of sacrifice and the image of charitable philanthropy. This same man - not only just a man, but a businessman; a magnetized and charged man taking these poor people's money for his own business – masked the charade in making them think they were doing good. But all they were doing was fueling this man's drive to become rich.

He picks and he pulls at their hair, and their wallets. Making their fear go away, making their hopelessness go away. The deeper their wound, the more their cash feeds the fire that will heal them. The more they give, the better they will be forgiven. If this world cracked in half it is certain that the prayers and cash flow to Hobbeston would only intensify, as if this holy man's progress and the hand of the lord they were financing could hold this planet together if only for one moment longer. Fire would tear through the pulpit, down a straight line, and parishioners would fall in the blazing pit. Even then, people would be throwing cash and wallets and purses at the front of the room. Why? Because they needed immediate salvation, and that is how they would get it.

The basket came down the row where Alan and Jared sat, and passed by Jared first. He made no motion to put anything in. He just continued to stare forward. The basket shook, as if it was going to magnetically pull the cash from Jared's pockets, but he didn't flinch. It passed in front of Alan, and Alan motioned as if he put something into the basket, but didn't. While he didn't have any money, he was a generous soul and he selfishly felt as though he could always find a better charity to give his money to than this one. That is what the sermon was about, wasn't it?

The chorus began another song, and Jared flinched, spun in his seat, and looked up at the balcony. He looked at Alan, and then stood. He walked in front of him sideways down the aisle, and then after clearing everyone in his way, he took a right and began to make his way past the money collector and toward the door that led to the backside of the building. Alan followed, and caught up with him just as he turned left to the hallway and to the door.

Jared reached for the handle, and turned it. He looked behind him to see Alan there, sneered, and then turned to push the door open.

The hallway, desolate the last few visits, was congested with suits and uniforms shuffling between rooms, looking at papers, carrying boxes, and speaking with each other. Police uniforms. The officer the closest to Alan and Jared was peering over a stack of papers in the threshold of a doorway. He looked up at them, and immediately approached them.

"Excuse me, you are going to have to leave, here," he said, manually turning Jared by his shoulder toward the door they had just come in. He shook it free and glared at the police officer.

"No, excuse me, I am Charles Hobbeston's attorney, as well as the attorney for this church. Do you have a warrant?"

"Yeah, as a matter of fact we do. Do you want to see the federal warrant, or the county one?" Jared's exhale indicated there was a degree of disappointment in the officer's response. "Let me take you to your client. He's with the one of the federal deputies that would love to show you our credentials."

They walked down the hallway, and took a right into the first room. It was a dressing room of sorts, lit only by lights that were around the mirrors. Alan first saw Hobbeston through one of these mirrors. Sitting in one of the barber chairs, his shoulders hung and his head was sunken down. It looked like it was detached, and it was going to fall into his lap. The halogen lights made his hair look awful. He looked up as Jared and Alan entered the room, and through the mirror it looked as though Hobbeston's face was plastic and beaten in with a brick, wrinkly and doughy. He looked exactly like a man would if he was about to kill himself, desperate and unkempt.

In one mirror, was Jared's face looking down at his desperate father. He looked much different through the glass. He looked down at his father with a sort of worrisome disgust, without any kind of idea what to say or what to do. In another mirror, angled so he looked stretched out vertically, was Hobbeston himself. The shiny sparkle of a pair of handcuffs reflected through the mirror into Alan's eyes, and danced about the room like a disco ball with a million tiny mirrors. It was glorious, and sad. This wasn't that kind of party.

"What happened, dad?" Jared finally uttered.

"All my love… All my love is leaving me."

"Dad, cut the shit." Hobbeston looked up. "Is it a tax thing again, or what? The feds are here AND the locals? I am going to go find the person in charge here and figure out what's-" he turned to leave as he was speaking, and just as he was about to run Alan over, was cut off by Hobbeston.

"It's your mother, Jared. They're here about your mother." Jared stopped. He squinted, as if the statement was cutting straight to his heart. Alan could also see in his eyes something else: that, perhaps it was not enough of a surprise to lead him to fall to the floor and start crying and gnashing his teeth.

"What about mother, Dad?" He turned to his father. Alan could not move. He was stone. The energy in the room was pushing the cosmic mercury ever higher. If anyone in the room teetered any closer to the brink of atomic tension, the mirrors would shatter in an orgasm of release and collapse.

Hobbeston looked over at Alan. He nodded his head up, and a painful scowl was born across his face. It was different than anything Alan had ever seen him make. Different than he had ever seen any human make. This wasn't just Hobbeston, but the face of a shattered human being, and Alan didn't mind it for the moment.

Jared grabbed Alan by the shoulders gently, and motioned him out of the room. Hobbeston sunk lower in the chair looking up at him. Bathed in the dim light, Alan watched as Hobbeston got further and further away from him. It wasn't as if he was being escorted out, but led by golden threads of innocence.

The next moment, he was in the hallway.

The next moment he was led away from the hallway and back to the main cathedral by impatient police officers.

The next moment, his feet carried him through the worshipers still clapping their hands in slow motion to the choral music and praising the lord.

The next moment, the brutality of the midday sun beat down on his face like the cindery pop of a campfire.

The next moment he weaved through the police cars and made his way over the endless hardtop.

The next moment he hurdled over to an air conditioned casino.

The next moment he stumbled around, looking for a payphone.

The next moment, he couldn't find one.

The next moment, he had a drink at the casino.

The next moment, he had another.

The next moment he chased himself to the bus station.

The next moment, he scrounged up a dollar and deposited it into a payphone.

The next moment, he called Jaime.

The next moment, he told her he was on his way back to Overton, and that he would be there in an hour.

The next moment, he was on a bus...

...and the next, he was asleep.

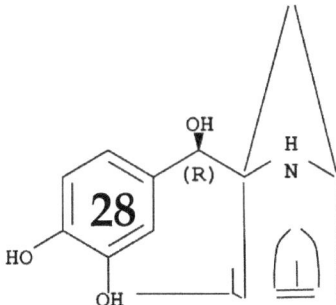

"Please hold on to it; Fuck, hold on to it, Alan."

Bombing down the dusty road, Alan and Jaime shot through the streets and the communities of Overton toward the hospital. Tears poured down Jaime's face, and she was driving with one hand and holding Alan's hand with the other.

"Oh fu-huck, Alan, this isn't right, this isn't right.. I know I am not goi-" and she sobbed uncontrollably. She stopped looking at the road at moments, wincing through the pain. Alan was afraid that they would get into an accident. A terrible, awful accident.

"Honey; Jaime, honey, just pull over and let me drive."

"No, no, there's no time, we have to get to the hospital. There is something wrong, something definitely fucking wrong. Oh God!" She screamed; emotional, physical, and utterly encompassing agony.

"Pull over, Jaime," Alan suggested again, and she did. Alan got out of the passenger side as Jaime slid across the long front seat. He walked around the front of the vehicle. He sat behind the steering wheel, immediately yanking the shifter down to 'drive.'

"You are going to have to help me get there... I haven't been since I was-"

"Can I just borrow your cell phone?" Alan looked over at her. His hand was in hers again, and she was squeezing it so tight, he could feel his own pulse. She was wearing gray lipstick; Alan had never noticed her wear lipstick before.

He took his hand off of the steering wheel and reached into his pocket. His telephone was damp with sweat, and he passed it to Jaime unaware that he wasn't looking where he was going. She dialed her mother, and Alan watched as she spoke. Her mouth trembled and her voice was shaky, but she didn't cry.

"Mom? Yes, I,... Well, I'm on my way to the hospital. What? No, Alan is driving. Something is happening and I am hurt. No... No, it's too early, don't be ridiculous. Alan is taking me. No, nothing happened... I just started feeling hurt and pain and... Okay, mom. I'll see you there. Thanks..."

The conversation was over, offering nothing less than complete misery for Alan. Jaime was asking her mother to help, and Alan being here for her in just this moment was not enough. It was immediately apparent that it could never be enough.

He leaned hard on the gas and the car strained to pull them down the dirt road. Alan began to think of the surreal nature of what was happening around him at this moment. His feet were rocks, his pulse drummed in his hand, sweat leaked through his pores, his heart beating magma blood ever so thick and heavy. There was a smell in the air. A rotten toothy smell from under bitten nails, and piano on the radio. There was nothing of this moment that was real; Alan felt drunk, floating above his seat.

He pulled on the steering wheel with his free hand like the yoke of an old fashioned airplane. He wanted this car to take off - to leave Jaime's pain, and to leave her baby to melt out of her and through the seat and through the floor of the car like molten ore. But it wouldn't take off, and even if it did no circumstance would change what was happening right now. It was a slow progression of these cascading piano notes falling like dominoes on the radio, unevenly rolling into the front seat.

Two turns later, and the car was idling outside of the hospital. Alan darted out and ran in for a wheelchair for Jaime. He grabbed one from inside of the automatic doors by a pole sticking up from it like a flagpole without a flag. Something about it seemed familiar – this entirely surreal, unnatural situation seemed familiar.

Jaime was crying as he helped her from the passenger's side and into the wheelchair. Alan began to wheel her into the emergency waiting room, but an ambulance pushed into the idle bay where the big car stood with its lights flashing. It sounded two loud horns, obviously in response to Alan's choice use of Emergency Room admission vehicle real estate.

"Alan, go move the car... I should be okay..." Jaime said with her neck craned around.

"Are you sure, I mean-"

"Yes, Alan, just go move the fucking car!"

Alan turned around, ran back to the car, and pulled out of the emergency bay searching for a spot. Gleaming into the corner of his eye from the seat next to him, three puddles of a clear substance reflected the afternoon light up into his face and onto the ceiling of the car. They swirled and ebbed around the deep button divots in the sofa-length seats. The fluid had a Technicolor film on the surface of it, just like a puddle in the concrete at a fueling station at three in the morning.

As he drove through the endless cars in full parking spots, the pooled substance stared at him, and he felt a terrible deep down sickness. Something was really, really not right about this. He quickly pulled into an empty spot on the other side of the building. There was a newspaper in the rear of the car, and Alan reached back to grab it and threw it over the oily seat.

A cool crosswind captured Alan by surprise as he exited the car; the breeze hit his face in waves. He locked the car, and walked toward the entrance. The last time he had been here he was recovering from dehydration and taken here under someone else's wing from the middle of the desert. Now, it was he who was taking another to the sanitized fluorescent halls of the Overton hospital.

Jaime. For some reason, even though they were only months apart in age, Alan felt as though she carried herself as a much more worldly and aware creature when even she didn't seem to have it all figured out. Here Alan was, walking into the hospital for a woman who was pregnant but who evidently did not feel the need even once to visit any number of doctors and specialists to examine her unborn child. Alan knew of many women who went a superfluous number of times to the obstetrician to check on the health of their baby, carrying around ultrasonic three dimensional snapshots of their squished and misshapen bodies in their purses. But entering her third trimester, Jaime thought it unnecessary to visit any of these doctors even once.

It almost seemed socially required to visit often and carry months worth of images, not that Alan agreed with anything that was ever socially required.

Jaime was still sitting in her flagpole wheelchair in front of a little to go window that had a sign that read "Triage Nurse / Admissions" above it when Alan walked in the door. Alan's shoes squeaked on the polished floors of the emergency room as he weaved among the rows of chairs; it looked more like an airport, Alan thought. Jaime was still holding her stomach, the triage desk empty and devoid of any evidence of a nurse being on duty aside from a laminated sign reading "Your Triage Nurse Today Is:" and "Linda" haphazardly scribbled in dry erase marker.

"Hey," Alan said.

"Hey."

"You feeling any better, orrr…"

"A little, I mean; it still hurts, and I think I peed myself, which is a little embarrassing, but aside from that… It's better."

"That's good…"

The two sat and stared at the empty triage desk like executives watching the numbers on an elevator. Alan was looking at the items on the desk… A pen, a hospital thermometer, a desk calendar with a lot of writing on it and the word "access" prominently spelled incorrectly with one 'c' instead of two. Jaime was looking at the matching framed motivational posters that adorned the rear wall of the office. One had an inspirational photo of an eagle in flight and said in big letters "ENDURANCE" and underneath "What it takes to be number one is a persistent outlook and a sharp eye for your goal." After fifteen minutes, just as Alan and Jaime had grown tired of their separate thoughts on the poster's shortcomings, a stressed young woman materialized behind the desk.

She was a heavy girl, with normal arms and legs but an unnaturally protruding midriff. She was the icon of America that no one saw in movies or on television; the genuine American article: stressed, young, studied hard with a dream and a focus, but no ability to look at her self in the mirror because of the feelings of inadequacy. She was the kind of girl that someone accidentally asked when the baby was due. She wanted to be like the love lost girls of the sitcoms and prime time soaps she taped and watched on the weekend... But she would have to be thin... She would have to live in Boston or Baltimore or New York or wherever her new group of televised friends lived... She would have to be done with medical school... In actuality, she would have to live her life in the way she wanted to starting today; but her parents probably wouldn't have that. There was her career, after all.

"Hello-there-what-can-I-help-you-with-today," she said quickly and hastily as she shuffled around papers on the desk, deposited them into some folders, and stood up walking them to a file holder across the room.

"Yeah, hi, we're here because Jaime here is having some problems..."

"Jaime what?" she asked, sitting back down behind the desk and looking at Jaime with a pen at the ready above a blue and white form.

"Jaime Gale."

"Okay, Jaime, have you been admitted to this hospital before?" She asked quickly again. If this was a take-away restaurant, the turnover would be unbelievable.

"No."

"Do you have insurance, Jaime?"

"No."

"Okay; just so you know we are legally required to treat you even in the event that you are unable to pay for services. These services can be rendered in any way that the doctors see fit and payment can be worked out after the fact. We would be happy to discuss this with you further if you need us to, and we also would like you to have the most comfortable experience here in the hospital, but we will need you to sign some documents that reflect your willingness to shoulder the costs of your stay. Do you understand what I have just told you?" She said it so quickly that Alan thought he would have felt more comfortable if he had just dropped a quarter into a table-side jukebox and allowed it to squawk it out to them regardless of whether they understood it or not.

"I understand."

"Okay, Jaime, what are your symptoms?"

"Well... I have a lot of pain in my stomach and I haven't been able to control my bladder apparently."

She nodded and asked them to follow her through the door inside the triage admission room. Alan wheeled Jaime to a table next to the triage desk that was outfitted with a thermometer that she immediately turned on and placed in Jaime's mouth as well as a sphygmomanometer, a stethoscope, tongue depressors, and other triage tools. She wrapped the cuff of the sphygmomanometer around Jaime's arm with her stethoscope just under it. She listened as she asked more questions.

"How long has this been going on?"

"Oh, for the last half hour or so; well, more frequently anyway. It has really been going on for an hour. I just peed myself in the car in the last half hour."

The nurse was looking at the stethoscope with wide eyes as well as the thermometer. There was a stretcher in the room that she looked at and then back to Jaime as she tore the cuff from her arm.

"Okay, Jaime, I am going to have you stand up and lay down on this stretcher here." Alan had to take a step back as the nurse pulled Jaime from the wheelchair, and help her up to the stretcher. Alan moved over between the nurse and Jaime's head on the disposable pillow. Her face winced. "Okay, Jaime I am going to pull your shirt up just enough so I can feel your stomach, and you tell me when it hurts."

"It just did…" she said softly.

"Okay." The nurse's hands delicately lifted the veil of cotton and began to just place her hands on her stomach, looking at Jaime's face. There were large, purple stretch marks on her belly, and the skin was taut, even though her pregnancy still did not show. The nurse's face darted down to the stomach only after a second, and Jaime moaned. "Holy shit; are you pregnant?" Jaime nodded, and the nurse darted out of the room the way she came, screaming the unintelligible name of a doctor.

Alan looked down at Jaime. Her hand was over her mouth, and tears were welling in her eyes. Alan wrinkled his forehead, just as an audible and mucousy sniffle projected from her nose.

"Jaime? Jaime? Jaime, it's going to be okay. It's going to be great. You are going to do great."

"No, it's too early. It's too early."

"Jaime, you are about to have a beautiful baby; you look great. You are going to do so great!" Alan kept repeating this phrase, but he was also aware that the look of astonishment and fear was gripping his countenance. He was worried, and he honestly hoped that it would not be too obvious. The sickness knotted in his stomach once more; it was what you felt when you were pulled over by a traffic cop, or just avoided a dangerous accident, or both.

"It's too early, it's too early, oh god." Barrels of tears poured down her face sideways onto the pillow. Alan wanted to say something to her. He wanted to say something that would honestly and truthfully make her feel better and make her strong. Today, Alan's purpose was to give strength and hope to an awfully frightened bird of a girl entering a world she had never entered before. A world she was scared of, or at least that took her by surprise as she had no feeling of entering it for another couple of days. Alan was scared.

"I love you, Jaime."

Alan had no concept of what he had just said or what weight it carried right now or why he was even saying it. He would have tried saying anything to rid the creature before him of the pain and anguish. His mind was crowded with words and phrases and greetings and goodbyes and all sorts of whispered and chain lettered sentences that brought the simple minded hope and sounded like Al-anon slogans. She reminded him of the dying deer left on the side of the road. Tears, fear, pain, and horrific uncertainty. What weight did what he said carry? There was nothing else to say.

She tilted her head and looked at him astonished; astonished but almost appalled. It looked not like it was a good surprise, but almost a wordless dagger with 'how could you' etched in the side hurdling toward his face. She didn't say anything, but she was no longer crying. Alan made her feel better, if only it was to take her mind off of the pain and to concentrate on making Alan feel like shit.

A dark man in a turban with a beard and a doctor's coat strode quickly into the room.

"Hello, Jaime, my name is Doctor Dave Vatche, and I am going to be your doctor today. Before we take you into the room, I am just going to ask you a few questions to determine if you are in fact going into labor or if we just need to watch you for a little while. How long have your contractions been going on for?" He had a clipboard and pen at the ready.

"For a few hours... I guess. I wasn't sure what this was."

"Okay, good, and how long have you been pregnant for?"

"I am in the third trimester, six and a half months or so..."

"Okay. Who is your obstetrician or gynecologist so I can get some information surrounding your pregnancy?"

"I don't have one..."

"Have you seen anyone? Only because this is important so that we may follow the correct procedures considering it is so early on..."

"Oh, my god," and she covered her mouth again, this time with both hands. One of the hands shot down onto the bed and grabbed a fistful of blanket and she screamed a muffled 'fuck' into her hand as her knees pumped up, curling in pain. She relaxed. "It is too early, oh god..."

"Okay, okay, okay, Jaime... let's get you something to deal with the pain and I will perform a quick-"

"No medicine, doctor, please. I want this to be as natural as possible." Doctor Vatche and the nurse looked down at her with the same wrinkled face as Alan had been looking at her with for the last fifteen minutes.

"As you wish. But we may need to for your sake – we may be beyond wishes and may be more concerned about your health and the baby's at this point. I am going to secure a room. -Katie," he motioned for Katie to follow him. He quickly turned around to face Jaime and Alan again. "Are you the father?"

"Well, no, but..."

"Okay, that makes the search for a room a lot easier."

The pair left the room. Alan looked down at Jaime, and she was wincing. He did the only thing he felt was appropriate and put his hand on her forehead. The muscles relaxed in his flesh. She was breathing heavily, her eyes straining sideways to look up at him. They just stared, and her chest heaved up and down. Her eyes blinked drowsily, and after a moment her breathing slowed and her muscles relaxed even further.

"You are so strong, Jaime; you're doing so well," Alan said. She just stared. Alan wanted to gather all of his strength in his veins and give it to her, but he knew he did the only thing he could in driving her here - even if it was only halfway. Alan's hand remained on her forehead, and he could feel her throbbing temples and the fire in her blood. It was boiling, gathering steam, and ready to gather all of the energy her body could muster.

The doctor returned with the nurse, and there was already another patient waiting to be admitted in front of the triage desk. He asked the nurse to attend to that woman, and asked Jaime if she was ready. She nodded. The doctor looked up at Alan.

"Sir, this might take a while, so we ask that you patiently wait in the waiting room where you came in."

"Okay... How will I know what-"

"I will come out personally and keep you posted."

"Fine... Good luck, Jaime, you'll do great..." Alan hated that he had used the word 'great' so much. Jaime twisted her body on the stretcher so she was facing Alan as she rolled away.

"Alan... I... I was a lot happier before I knew you existed..."

And she rolled away from him.

Alan turned out of the triage desk and sat in a cushioned chair attached to other cushioned chairs in the waiting room. It felt like the airport, he thought as he took his leather bound notebook out. He removed the pen and scribbled the only thing he was thinking at that exact moment, "I was a lot happier before I knew you existed."

He would have had to write it a thousand more times to understand what she meant by it, he thought. The ink smudged as her voice echoed and deposited feelings into parts of his mind he never knew existed.

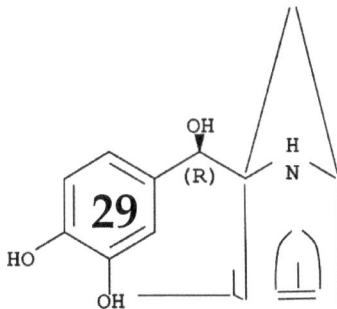

Crimson wove a thread about his mind as he fell into the deep crevices of the fable unfolding before him. All of the pieces fell into place around him as they happened and as they didn't – he couldn't even recall what was happening as it happened. The stench, no the taste of passion, no of blood in his mouth; the sickly bitter copper flowed in and out and beat like a heart; no of two hearts; no, of just one; no, of none.

There was Jaime's parents he recalled. There was also the turbaned doctor walking down a hall; he recalled seeing him several times. There was a very angry man with a pencil lined beard that shadowed his jaw, and there was an airplane, even though he wasn't at the airport. He recalled flying several times, and he recalled jumping. He recalled gasping for air, and gasping for breath, and gasping, gasping, gasping, the fire of absence in his lungs still stung.

He was watching it all on a fuzzy television with springs and wires jutting out from the old fashioned tubes in the back. Yes. But it didn't have a box and it was just wires coiled around the frosted glass, hung suspended by dusty springs that had ants crawling on it. The fuzzy picture tube showed Alan in the waiting room in black and white as Jaime's parents walked in. They had seen Alan sitting and reading his little black notebook and they went straight to the triage desk. He watched silently from afar, in this cloudy, dark room.

She was in the delivery room, the chubby girl said.

Six-A to be exact, the chubby girl said.

No, you could not go in, she said.

Because it is policy for that room and for the hospital that no observation by civilians is allowed in the theater, she said.

Are you the father, she asked…

No, the father of the baby being delivered, she clarified.

Well, than you will have to wait in the waiting room, she said.

Doctor Vatche is extremely qualified, thank you very much, and he will be happy to inform you of the condition of your daughter, she said.

And then the fuzzy screen panned around to Alan like a security camera, and Alan grabbed the armrests of the plane as it was taking off, wondering how Sella was doing in the pet compartment of the plane. He wondered if they checked her for bombs.

Doctor Vatche came down the hallway for the first time in slow motion, capturing the drama of an urban hospital in his lab coat and mask, but also capturing the aroma of an unmistakable spice in his tightly wrapped turban. He turned the corner and walked through the double automatic doors where he zeroed in on Alan to report the news.

She is doing quite fine, the doctor said. There is a bit of speculation as to what is causing the dryness, he said, but thanks to modern techniques it should all be taken care of; not to worry.

Jaime's parents were behind him and stood up.

How is she? They asked from behind the doctor, and the doctor spun around.

Well, she is doing quite well. May I ask who you are?

We are her parents. It was the first words they spoke since leaving the triage desk. The rest of the time they sat across from Alan, leering at him.

Above Alan in the airplane, the no smoking sign came on, as did the fasten safety belts sign. The plane dodged and darted vertically; it was certain as you could feel it in your stomach and on your ass as it bounced on the cheap felt.

There was a man that arrived at the hospital, to the great joy of Jaime's father. He shook his hand, and spoke quietly. He looked worried too, and it was a much more genuine look. He was the man with the pencil line beard across his chin. His name was Chris, as he was introduced to Alan. Just flew in from Kalamazoo, as a matter of fact.

How was your flight, they asked.

Good, he replied.

Good to see you Chris. We were really worried.

Yeah, well... it's important. He replied.

On the little television screen, Alan watched Chris sit next to Jaime's parents one seat away. He also watched him look at Alan with the same contempt of Jaime's parents.

The television beamed to Hank. Good, kindhearted Hank staring at Alan wide-eyed and mesmerized. He couldn't believe it, he said, he just couldn't believe it. Striking, he continued, and how did you get the black eye, Alan?

Then Alan was back in the waiting room. He was watching Jaime's parents; he was watching Chris; he was watching his notebook. Chris left. Chris came back with coffee for himself and Jaime's parents. They drank and laughed. They had stories to tell. What has he been doing? Where is he going? The dog has been great... really well behaved.

And then it was back to Hank. Alan remembers coming home and not feeling a connection anymore. Anymore to Hank and anymore to being here. He felt lost. He felt without purpose. It was Christmas and he remembered giving Hank his present after dark on top of the coffee table in front of the futon. He was watching the news and Hobbeston had been indicted the day before.

Hank was happy when he opened Alan's present.

He was very grateful.

And it was back to the hospital again, hours later, the turbaned doctor walked down the scratchy hallway. The small screen of the television made him look photocopied at each step, with awful resolution and streaks down the page; gritty and cheap. When he arrived in the waiting room, he began to address Alan again. Jaime's parents stood up immediately and pulled Chris into the conversation.

They had discovered something wrong with Jaime and the pregnancy. She had what was known as eclampsia, and it wasn't immediately certain how it would impact the delivery. Traditionally, he said, this disorder is characterized by high blood pressure and may explain the apparent absence of prenatal fluids, but may also be characterized by headaches, blurred vision, flu-like symptoms, and seizures that are traditionally like epileptic fits. The doctor then asked if Jaime had experienced any of these.

No, she hadn't, her father said.

Well, for future reference, Jaime should have visited a doctor at least a few times. The test we are conducting now actually determines if this diagnosis is true. Traditionally, the OB would perform this simple urine test and prescribe a simple salt, magnesium sulfate, to treat the disorder. The doctor said they are working on finding this out, and also adjusting the delivery to take this into consideration.

Jaime's father asked if he would keep them posted. He also introduced Chris as the father and made him shake the doctor's hand.

Alan thought, staring at the wiry picture tube about how young he was. About how young Chris and Jaime were. About how young everyone is, really. About how decisions in life could in fact be postponed, or rather care taken to ensure that things like this did not happen. Jaime's naive stance on this pregnancy and on their relationship cost what? Simply not knowing what was going to happen, Alan suspected originally, but was afraid it may have been more.

The screen cut to Alan again, being driven away from the hospital in the back of a taxi. He thought it was raining out originally, but in fact it was just the way the sand and dust had stuck to the glass of the cab… As if they hadn't dried it before tossing it into the brutal winds and fires of this hell's innate nature. It was either that, or his eye throbbing. It was either that or both of his eyes watering. He was sobbing for nothing more than Alan.

And then the picture cut again. It cut out for a moment, the screen blank until Alan hit the side of the television with a pang and rattled the wire protruding from the tube, holding it in place. There was Hank giving him his gift back, and Alan shaking his head. Hank put his hand on Alan's heart and said something to him. You couldn't hear it; it was ever so faint.

The hospital's halogen lights shone down again, and this time with determination but way too little contrast and brightness on the screen, the Doctor hurdled down the hallway the slowest he had ever done it to the waiting room. Alan watched the friction of his shoes give way on the corner, a shadow sliding like a ghost through the halls. He pushed the double doors open, and they bounced off of the walls just as the doctor made his way through.

But it wasn't the doctor. Alan should have known because there was no turban, but rather the flowing hair of a female. It was just so dark. Alan remembered in real life that she was clean, even though on this horrid screen he could see nothing, what the fuck, why does it have to be like this, where's the fucking antenna?

His eye felt cold; the one with the black and blue on it. It was cold because he was holding an ice pack on it.

The paper ticket was heavy when he gave it to the person at the desk. So was the dog's wire crate. It was going to cover it all, the woman at the desk said. Sella lay at his feet, and Alan really felt good that something loved and appreciated him as much. His bag with a few days worth of clothes that he bought while he was in Overton would do just fine. It wasn't as heavy as the dog, anyway. He was glad that something was taken care of for a change.

The nurse was hurdling ever so slowly down the hall and into the waiting room that she finally materialized between Chris, Jaime's parent's, and Alan as it played in the background of the other shots...

This time everyone stood. Everyone stood and gathered around the nurse, and the nurse spoke swiftly. Seizure. Descent. Rapid blood loss. Trauma. No longer conscious. Just wanted to inform them of what was happening. Currently a team was working on saving the baby while she remains stable and unconscious. As her parents, you were listed on her form to make decisions for her in the event of a problem. If in fact we need to, would you allow us to perform a caesarean even though it is against her wishes?

If you must, we would support it, they replied.

There was a horrible storm in Boston as the plane entered the city's airspace. It tossed and tumbled the aircraft about as drinks slid to and fro, drinks tossed onto laps, Sella falling off of her feet at least twice a minute. Hank cut his hand while slicing a pear. A pair of clamps with gauze fell on the operating room floor. The taxicab driver dropped cigarette embers on his slacks as he and Alan went over a bump.

As the sun rose, Alan, Chris, and Jaime's mother and father were taken into a room as the sun rose. Stark, raw light radiated in definitive bars across the room. Alan and Chris stood while Jaime's parents sat in the plush chairs. The sun that beamed in cut a hot line across Alan's ankles and he could feel the radiation through his jeans. Jaime's dad asked Alan to wait outside in a firm and rude voice. Could you wait outside, Alan, please.   Please.

I was a lot happier   before I knew you   existed...

He spent the majority of his time sitting across from Jaime's parents, when it was just the three of them, thinking about that line. I was a lot happier before I knew you existed... He would say it in different inflections, different dialects, different beats in his mind. I was a lot happier before I knew you existed... I was a lot happier before I knew you existed... I was a lot happier before I knew you existed... If he said it one way, it sounded rash and hateful. I was a lot happier before I knew you existed... Another way brought it a whole new meaning of passion and loss experienced by someone opening one's eyes in a way that had never been before. Iwasalothappier, before I knew, you existed... It was gorgeous. It was meaningful. It was cruel. He wondered what it looked like written in her handwriting. If he had that, he would make a scrapbook of his own. All it would be is a picture of Jaime, which he didn't have, and that statement in writing. All he had was a dinner check asking a chicken to play. And her phone number. Which he would later cherish.

He cherished that napkin in Boston like he cherished that line, savoring it in his mouth like warm chocolate and coffee and martinis and cigarettes. The bitter fruits of the most satisfying humanity has to offer. It was a lush sentence, dripping in the sweat and blood that fell from the delivery table that day.

The wail of another mother's cry came from behind the door of that special room. A wail that was so pure it was humorous. It was funny how she sounded, like a spasm of sexual energy. A huff, huffaw haw, ehweeze, wail. It sounded like a wild animal laughing, but it was really sad all the while because within the crack of the door, Alan watched the doctor sitting on his desk in front of Jaime's parents, her dad holding her mother as her body expanded and contracted with each sound that said everything. It was sad, in actuality. It was only funny for a second. Another wail of another mother.

This is how they mourned, Alan thought, it was powerful. Alan turned back and wasn't entirely sure what happened as there were two lives in the balance. As Jaime was an especially strong woman there could not have been anything wrongwithher, and ultimately with all of the technology, it is safe to say that babies dieeveryday all over the world. It has been that way since the dawn of humanity. This would almost be acceptable or welcome as there were no plans on how to raise a child, or even that the pregnancy followed the right procedures and preparations for birth.

On the other hand, if Jaime had died, there would almost be a triumph. A triumph of the humanspirit and a symbol of renewal and strength. A new life has entered the world and one that has barely begun was sacrificed for it. How beautiful.

Chris stormed out of the office and paused looking straight ahead. His gaze was unmistakably stern and the skin was taut. He just stared. Alan was to the right of the door, and for a split moment they looked at each other. Alan searched his face for any sign of any news. All Chris did was turn, and then spun back around with a fist dangerously hurdling towards Alan's face.

The powerful blastrattledAlan   straight to   the   floor, and
fireworksexplodedfromthesocket. He was down and a   s   le   ep.

The taxicab stopped in front of Hank's house, and Alan just went in.
He fell to the bed he had been sleeping on with a thud. It was the morning, the
morning of Christmas, and he hadn't gone to work. Hank was still in bed, and
he just wanted to sleep. He stripped all of his clothes off as he drifted to sleep
and slid under the sheets. The comforters stayed on the bed, and he curled up
in them. He twisted them around his body until he made a cigar, and then he
pulled the slack under his feet and over his face.

While he was knocked out, Alan had a dream   that he was
running to see Jaime. He felt something heavy in his hands, and he looked
down and in   his arms was his   mother's face. She   spoke to
him. She said   not to trip, Alan,   be   careful.   You'll   hurt
yourself.   Alan kept running.

When he came to, Alan was in a wheelchair and a nurse was holding
an icepack on his face. He was about thirty five, and had a gut and a goatee.
Hey,   he said, welcome back. There was a police officer standing behind
him and there was also the triage nurse in the room.

What   happened to   Jaime,   Alan asked.
They looked around and didn't know what he was talking about.
Would you like to   press charges   on the man that did
this? He left, but we know who it is and it would be just as easy to pick him
up at the hotel he is stay-

Alan cut him off. Alan asked   what   happened to
Jaime, again.

The nurse handed Alan his icepack and went over to talk to the triage
nurse. She came over and knelt beside Alan. She took one of his hands in
hers, and was a great deal more human this time around. She looked in Alan's
eyes. The television was cutting out, skipping, erratic.

Alan,   right?   Of   cour se. Jaime   and the baby,
after suffering   a difficult and trying   l abor,   have exp   ire
d .

Static shot down the screen and leak   edonto t he floor.
Exp   ire   d. Of cour   se, Alan said. Tha   nk you.
I a   mso s or r   y. Sh e r   epli   ed.
The offi   cer asked   again abou   t pressingcharges.
No, people   mourn I   n d iffer   ent   w ays, I guess
After a   ll was d   one,   Alan ask   ed him self a
nother t I m e ab   out wh   enh e co uld se   e on the str I   ngy televi sion sc
re en how it a ll c   ame abo   ut. Ho   w did he   end up in a
dodgyplane, caree   ning t   oward th e   ea st co   a s t a gain.   Back in M
ass ac huse tts.

        T   hisis w   heret   he st   ati   c was t   heworst,
h   e t   told hims   elf...
        I   t   was   n't   r I g   ht. Th   e be a t s, t

he t I m in g, n o th   in g w as   r ig ht ab   out the w   hole l
ot ofi t .

                                    No…… ButthesignalskeptremindingAlan…
                            AsHankputhishanduponhisheartandhanded
                                    HisgiftbacktohimwithtearsfallingfromAlans

            Eyes…
                            He said one thing…

                        Love is never wasted

            So a ll   Alan di d o   n th   e pla n   e was w
ri t   e th e phr   ase ha ut In g him ove r an d
ove r ag a In on the   bac k of t h e g I ft   tic   k
e t stu b w hich wou ld ha ve fl ow n Hank   an yw
h er e In th ec ontinen tal U n it ed St ate s , but he I
n stea d ga ve bac k t o A l an bec au s e It just ha p p
en ed to be enou gh f or on e pers on an d on e dog to ta
ke an emerg en cy fl I ght t o Bo s to n. Ala n wro t e, a
nd w r ote ,

            I was a lot happ   ier   beforeIknew youexist   e
d…
            I wasal   o   thap   pier   bef oreIkn ew   you
xisted
                was   t hap ier   before I knew you   existed…
                    was   th   er   ore I ew yo   e sted…
                        was   t   r   o   e o   e   d…
                            was   t   e   d…

            A   s   h   e   plan e was t o uch In g dow n, t he
te l ev is io n s c ree n was c o m in g back I nto f o cus. E ve ry t hing w a s
bec oming cle a r, an d f o r a br ief moment, it w as c erta I nly the work of
so meth ing else al together; some fo rce beyond Alan's scope of t he univ erse
and o f religi on. Everythi ng cleared up if only f or a moment. The television
clicked off. He had to take care of things.

· · ·

Two days after Christmas, just before New Years and just before work started up again, Alan really appreciated everything that Hank had done for him. He let him know on every occasion he had. Hank had been in contact with the Gale family, and they were truly grateful for all of the support Hank was giving them, and all of the support that Alan offered, even though they would have none of it.

Alan wondered what made her parents act like this toward him so. Did they feel that he had created a rift between her and Chris? Did they somehow feel that Alan was responsible for her not going to the doctor's? The belly punching contests didn't contribute in a good way, Alan thought looking back at it... But in all seriousness, he felt as though he was an inspiration if anything.

The last few days were somber between Hank and Alan, but at the same time refreshing. It renewed their relationship to be spending such a great deal of time together, not to mention that the beer and barbeque was almost therapeutic. It was easy to take their minds off of the morbid state of a mother and child being taken off of the earth.

Jaime had a small memorial service two days after she and the baby died. Alan and Hank attended the somber get together with wide eyes. It seemed to the world that there was nothing more tragic than a woman and her child dying during labor. In effect, it was extremely tragic, but it was also tragic that this entire thing could have been avoided if only she had visited the doctor and taken those salt pills. Or if she didn't have to have sex with Chris every time she saw him. Or if she had stuck with Alan.

Hank was wrapping a bandage around his finger with one hand, and juggling a sliced pear with the other. He was telling a story of himself and his cousin Ray when they were younger and something his father had done on the way to the dentist.

"So we are sitting there in Los Angeles... I was living in Los Angeles at the time, and this is before they redid all of the streets and everything... Like, this was back in the 1990s. So my dad is taking me and my cousin Ray to the dentist when this lady in one of those big, old fashioned truck cars that people that drove to work just by themselves everyday comes swingin' in to our lane and nearly takes our whole front end out."

"Okay," Alan replied, obviously amused. His cell phone was ringing in his pocket. He turned it on silent and placed it on the coffee table, continuing to listen to Hank's story.

"So he does anything that any red-blooded driver would do and that is lay on the horn, and start screaming expletives out the window. But dad takes it a bit too far, and pulls around the truck, and stays in front of it, going half the speed limit. If the SUV switched lanes, dad switched lanes. He was being a top of the line jerk. It was pretty funny, and worked out well because we were pretty sure the SUV chick didn't have any guns to kill us with. She was a pretty brunette and looked harmless enough, anyway…

"Well, we get off the exit that we could get off of - just so we could get off the highway, and we bolt it to the dentist's office just in time. We run in, dad pays the-" Just then, in the middle of the conversation, Alan's phone began to vibrate on the table, ringing again. He picked it up and did not recognize the number on the screen. Ignoring the call, he placed it on the table once again.

"-receptionist and then we wait in the waiting room. We get called in one by one for our checkups and everything is cool. My teeth and Rays check out great with the dental hygienist. Well, dad takes a longer amount of time than usual and…"

The phone emits a tone that suggests that someone had paged Alan, sending their telephone number straight to the phone. Alan picked the phone up, and looked at the number. It read '(617) 555-4170' a number from a Boston area code. Alan looked up at Hank as he continued his story.

"…anyway, to make a long story short, Dad walked out of there with three cavities, and an appointment for a root canal, all because why?"

"The lady with the SUV wasn't the dentist, was she?"

"She was!"

"Unbelievable, Hank." Alan tried to act surprised and amused, even though what the story needed was some fairy dust and a better delivery. Alan looked down at his phone, and asked Hank if he wouldn't mind if he called these people back. Hank shook his head, and continued to inhale a giant gulp of frosty beer.

Alan dialed the number, and Hank went out into the backyard to check on their lunch sizzling on the grill. The receiver rang a few times, and Alan thought about what he would do here, and what his next step would be. There was a state college in Las Vegas. He could get a job bar-tending or waiting tables and put himself through school and buy a car. Live with Hank. He could almost afford the car now… And then a woman picked up the phone.

"Boston Police…" she said.

"Yeah, hi, I just received a phone call from you, actually, but I am not sure-"

"Who are you trying to reach?"

"I… I don't know, exactly. See, I received about three calls from you in the last fifteen minutes and I-"

"What is your name?" There was a beep on the line. The caller ID window said that it was coming from the same number.

"You know what? It actually looks like you guys are calling me on the other line, here… So… I guess I will call back if I have any problems…" The phone just hung up without any farewell. Alan pressed the button that brought him to the other waiting line. "Hello?"

"Good afternoon, am I speaking to a Mr. Alan Levy?" a deep voice resounded through the line.

"Yes… This is him…"

"Hello, Alan, may I ask where you are right now?"

"Excuse me, who is this?"

"I am sorry. This is Detective Saint Germain of the Boston Police."

"Oh; and what is the purpose of your calling?"

"I will get to that…"

"Well, I am in Nevada right now; Overton. I have not been in town for-"

"-Are you available to talk, or are you at work?"

"I am available… What is going on?"

"Okay, Alan. This… This is pretty hard." His speech slowed down and it sounded like he was announcing a film trailer. "I don't really have any other way to tell you. Alan, your mother has been found,… deceased in your home. She had taken her own life within the last twenty four hours…"

"Okay,… what?"

"You mother has taken her own life, Alan. I am so sorry."

And that was where every thing got so fuzzy. It was apparent that the week's happenings were so terribly contorted because of that one sentence. Mum had taken her own life? Absurd! Does this man's story even add up, Alan asked himself.

"What happened?"

"She… She had mailed a letter to the police station with a key to the house and instructions outlining what happened. She also mailed your phone number to us. We went down there this afternoon and we're just now getting a hold of you. She did it last night, and must have sent the letter to us a couple days ago. Anyway, we had a small investigation, but that is what happened, Alan. I am so sorry."

Alan was staring between the bottle on the table, and the dog on the floor sitting behind the bottle. The focus shifted between the bottle and the dog, the dog and the bottle. It all seemed as though it was right there. What was right there? Nothing. Nothing. Wasted.

Hank entered the room. He entered the room with the barbequed dinner, and nothing else.

"Alan?" The voice on the other end of the line was agitated, and didn't want to be.

"Alan, you okay," Hank asked.

Bottle, dog. This is a bottle. The bottle is on a table. The table is made of wood. Under the table is a beating heart in a ball of flesh and blood. That heart pumped for another animal and her name was Sella. Impossible that there could be so much death and it could hit so close to someone all at the same time – funny wasn't it.

"Thank you detective. What do I do next?"

"As you remember, your mother wishes a traditional Jewish burial, but under the circumstances, it is my understanding that this will be difficult, so you are going to have to contact Koch Funerary Services… She has made all of her pre-need preparations there, and I can supply you with the number…"

The detective gave Alan the number, and then continued to give further instructions of how Alan could help when he got back. Alan wrote down all of the prevalent information, and hung up the phone.

"What's happening, Alan?" Hank asked as softly as his heart beat.

Alan spoke deliberately, softly, and slowly. "Well, uh… It… It turns out that… That my mother has killed herself… And… And I need to go home and sort things out." And then Alan's heart emptied. He cried and cried. He cried not only for himself, but for the burdens of life and the suburbs and for his mother and for Jaime's baby and her mother. He cried for his heart and for his future, and he cried for the past. He cried because he was getting older, and he cried for Hank and his son.

Sniffling in Hank's chest, he remembered the time when things were different. Hank was holding and stroking his head and it felt so well. It felt better and it felt like things were okay. It felt like home. Being held felt like home… Alan wondered if home felt like home any longer.

Hank let go of Alan, retreated into his bedroom, and returned with the envelope and the voucher for his two tickets anywhere; his Christmas gift. Alan wiped his eyes, and collected his sobs. Hank handed them to Alan, opening Alan's hands for him.

"No, no, no, Hank, no." Alan said, shaking his head.

"Alan," and pressed them in harder. "Love is never wasted."

Hank held him once more, and when he let go, Alan fell into an uncomfortable seat somewhere over the Midwest. It was three in the morning, and he couldn't sleep. He should have, but he didn't.

It was three in the morning somewhere over the Midwest, Sella lay in a crate bouncing with the turbulence, and a martini fell to the carpet. Condensation froze in the air in ribbons from the engines. Somewhere hundreds of meters above the earth, Alan thought about his journey and all of everything. Of the people and of the time. It was just under a year and he had been rolling with the pulse of a thousand horses at the speed of the same.

Perpetual heartbreak brought him back eastbound, and all he could think was that his time was wasted. It was three in the morning, somewhere over the Midwest, and his Mum was dead, and there wasn't anything anyone could do about it, except allow the east coast hurdle toward the fuselage and engulf them all at once. It was inevitable.

Part IV

Winter's Eulogy

It is best to define an epitaph
For those who land without their dreams,
Falling in the vacuum's senseless wrath,
And live beneath their means.

Frightened like a spider's sickly prey
You waste away your precious life
Throwing away chance, it seems at bay
Evil engulfs time in its ivy vine.

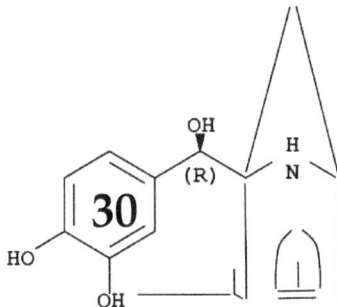

Alan opened the door to his family's home in Southie, pushing the heavy wood against an unknown obstacle behind it, and entered. Sella pushed past him and began scouring every square centimeter of the house for scents. Alan scanned the homestead. Rays of light beamed through the windows, reflecting stagnant weightless dust in the air.

It was nine thirty in the morning, and he had been in the car for the last hour and a half in traffic along the five kilometers to get to their house. In three hours he would have to leave for his mother's burial, which took place in four hours at a secular cemetery in Milton. Alan walked into the kitchen.

There were still dishes in the sink, coffee in the coffee pot, food in the refrigerator. He had heard that when people decide that they are going to kill themselves that there was some point where they began to give things away and tell people they were going to do it. Alan wondered if his mother did. Alan wondered if she had told anyone. Alan wondered if the funeral director knew that they had a family plot in a Jewish cemetery in Rockland. Alan wondered why she did it.

Alan wondered if he had answered his phone, or called her more often, or if anything would have made any difference.

The house looked pretty much as it did the last time he was there. There were bills and odds and ends piled up on the dining room table, the living room had a musty familial smell like the sweet scent of heat and sweat when he used to cuddle up and watch television with his parents and fall asleep. There was still the miswoven patch on the rug they bought at the junky overstock store in Weymouth, and still the dormant and dusty organ his catholic grandmother owned from when she was a beauty school tycoon before she lost it all. There was still a creek in the hardwood exactly twenty paces from the tiled landing of the stairs to the second floor, and the cracked ceramic and plaster of the tiles at the foot of those same stairs.

Alan walked up the stairs, his hand trailing along its old-fashioned cast iron railing. To the right was a large bedroom that mum would always let out to whatever surrogate boyfriend/father she was seeing, to the left an apricot flavored carpet trailing the hallway to the two bedrooms at the end. Alan's was on the right, and Mum's on the left.

Alan first made his way to his bedroom. Next to it was a bathroom that he had exclusive privileges to, not two steps form his door. It lay clean and sparkling, probably unused since he was last home and in desperate need of some attention by a plumber. The cabinets still held his various accoutrements that a young man would need; razors, a dried up wrinkly bone of a stick of deodorant, some old yellowed allergy pills, and a bottle of cheap drugstore cologne that Mum would always buy him, 'Kayak.'

He had his own little life and his own little world here, and he thought to himself that it would be interesting to watch the mirror like a movie showcasing all of the impressions his twenty years looking into it imprinted on its reflection. There would be tooth brushing, a fight between a mother and a son, an intimate shower with his first girlfriend that no one was home for and drying each other's dripping skin in the cold air.

Alan left the bathroom to turn into his bedroom. The pale stained wood of his bed reminded him of how it smelled when he first got it. Alan opened the headboard and inhaled deeply and relived the moment that he first got it. He had come home one evening from work after school, and it was there; a headboard, dresser, nightstand, desk. It was wonderful. The first piece of furniture he owned, and it was all his.

Inside the headboard were various magazines, books, and knick knacks he had no use for anymore. He opened the rest of his drawers in the dresser and the desk, and emptied them. In one there was stationary, in another pens, in another razors, in another baseball cards. He was so happy when he got these things, but living without them for such a long time, he didn't want them any longer. All he wanted was Mum; the Mum from before dad abandoned her. Arguably, she was the happiest woman alive.

He wasn't sure when she started to descend into madness, but it was certainly after she and dad had split. Maybe it was being a single mom. She had so many disappointments in her life, but Alan was one of the things she had that meant the most to her, and Alan knew it at this point. He was a symbol of everything that she was and everything she wanted to be. Alan's grandmother sent her to a private catholic school and she got awful grades. Alan went to public high school and graduated with honors. She went to college to get her teaching license, but left after getting her license but without graduating because she simply did not have the patience for it and would become anxious in her classes. Alan, for the time he was in college, did very well... He almost thought that he should go back to fulfill her wishes.

There was junk all spayed about the room. Useless things; useless material things that at one point meant so much to him to accumulate and meant absolutely nothing now. It was as if he had grown up in a terrible depression and people felt the need to keep everything from broken refrigerators and pens the bank gave away and junk just in the off chance that it would be needed. There were clothes in some of the drawers. They were great because he needed clothes quite badly, and the only bad thing is that they smelled damp and musty like a thrift store.

In one of the piles from the desk was a photo with frayed and yellowed edges. It was black and white, but Alan thought only because it was so old. It was a picture of his mum when she was only a teenager. When she gave it to Alan, she explained that it was taken with a Polaroid camera when they still used instant film instead of the instant digital printing that they did out of the back of the camera now. It was shiny, and if you had oily fingers, it would rub off on the matted black part on the back. That is also why, she said, there is the yellow and white on the edges and the uneven border. The picture would develop in your hand.

Alan remembered thinking that the device that took the picture would have to be really cool, but moreover how pretty his mother was when she was younger. He also remembered a picture of her in really high cut boots and a really short skirt and she had dyed her hair black that made her look like a fox. He wondered where she put the suitcase with all of the pictures in it. It would probably be very, very heavy.

Alan pocketed the picture and left his room a complete disaster, and turned the corner into his mother's room.

Whether it was a complete surprise, he wasn't sure… Alan had a romantic vision of how it happened ultimately; she went to bed, and never woke up. But opening the door, the first thing he noticed was that the windows were open, and the next thing, he breathed in and found out why the windows were open. The room smelled of bile, rot, and digestion. Vomit was caked in spatters in the bed and on the floor and leading to the bathroom that was part of the bedroom off to the left. There was still an impression of mum's body in the bed, a rubber glove on the floor, a tilted bottle of chardonnay, and dried vomit some more, and the choking feeling at the back of Alan's throat.

His stomach heaved and he turned and closed the door again, and his hands were shaking, and he dropped to his knees and on his hands, and he threw up. His vision blurred again, and he threw up again. And he felt dizzy, and sweat beaded out from his pores, and he threw up again, even though there was nothing left to expel but a string of drool coming from the back of his throat.

Alan could feel his heart beating, and he felt weak in his limbs. Why didn't he think he would see all of that? Alan stood for a moment, and ran down the hallway. What did he think happened in his imagination? He bounded down the stairs, almost falling down them, skipping two at a time, and gravity pulled a thousand times stronger. Did he think she would swoon and die perfectly in a bed of flowers like Romeo found Juliet? He darted through the living room, and straight for the door. Did he think it would be pretty? Romantic? There were two thick envelopes that were behind the door. It was violent and sickening. Suffered. He leaned his weight into the storm door, and swung it open. Sickening. Alan planted himself on the front steps in the cold end-of-December air, his stomach heaving on its own, his hand over his mouth, his body trembling.

This was how it happened, he thought. This was it. Was this how the life of a suffering and selfless being should have ended? Certainly not. She was beautiful, caring, and thoughtful. Why did this have to happen? Did she leave anything? Was there any signs pointing to this? Where were her friends? Was she that lonely? What the fuck. What the fuckity-fuck shit-ass fucking fuck. Alan turned his face over the side of the cement landing as his stomach continued to purge, but there was nothing left. His ribs hurt, it was trying so hard. As his stomach heaved, all that came from his mouth was a hanging line of drool, swinging back and forth.

Alan must have sat out in the cold, shivering on the pavement for at least a half hour, asking himself so many questions. Why? Why, why, why, why, why? So many authors and artists and people have taken their lives so often throughout history, and why did it need to be his mother? Why did she have to do it? Some did it because of notoriety and some to be romantic, but fuck, it was so cliché now, and why did she have to do it? It... She was nobody, and she took her own universe down around her like a curtain because of why?

Alan wasn't listening, he thought. He needed to listen, and gather his love for mum, and tell her every day, and tell her every five minutes, and... He wondered if it was because he ran away. He stepped to the edge of her patience and disappeared. Where were her dreams? Was Alan it? It couldn't be. He had never told mum anything but that he loved her with all of his heart. That was the world of mum that he knew, and he hoped that she didn't forget it up until her last moment. Her last sickening and horrible last moment.

Alan stood, and walked back inside. Tears were streaming down his face, and he was unsure if it was because he was upset or if it was the body's mechanism to tear up when you were throwing up so much. There was vomit on his shirt, and when he reentered the house, Sella looked up at him from the couch. The house certainly didn't feel the same at all, and all he was left with was a job to do.

Alan picked the envelopes up from behind the door, and he recognized the handwriting on the front of the packages. It was his own, and it was his name and his address written in his handwriting on the front. They were both the same weight and girth, and he opened one. It was one of his manuscripts with a rejection letter in the front. One of the *dear sir, we regret to inform you that this entry is not entirely suitable for our publication* letters. This one was from Atlantic Monthly. That was okay. Even though he was a Bostonian and he felt like he should have an in at the publication, these things happened. His 'Hungry' story sucked, anyway. The other package had the same contents from Playboy.

Alan shifted around and went into the kitchen. He retrieved a bucket from under the sink, a scrub brush for dishes above it, a bottle of soap, and a bottle of bleach. Alan went upstairs and into his bathroom and filled the bucket with the bleach, soap, and hot water from the tap in the tub, and as it filled, took a thick pile of towels from the cabinet. He wrapped one around his face, and tied it in the back. He ran back downstairs for some trash bags, and when he returned upstairs the bucket was full. It was time.

Alan opened the door to his mother's room again, this time with his eyes closed. It was just a room. It was just a room. It was just a room. He stepped over the threshold, and opened his eyes. His stomach immediately gave way again, and he dropped to his knees, heaving nothing up into the towel across his face. Where did he go... He wouldn't even have to do this... He shouldn't even-

Alan, from his knees, took the water and splashed it along the floor from the bed to the bathroom. The smell radiated from the floor and into his towel and into his nostrils. His stomach contracted at regular intervals, and he just closed his eyes, splashing water all over the carpet. Wasn't there someone that does this kind of thing? When he reached the tiny hall that went to the bathroom of the master bedroom with the counter and two sinks, he found the bottles. There were literally a hundred of them, all orange with white caps, and different names of the medications of the side. One said 'risperidone' and another 'olanzapine.' A bottle read 'lithium,' while one more read 'carbamazepine.' 'Gabapentin,' 'phenelzine,' 'fluoxetine,' 'tranylcypromine,' and 'isocarboxazid,' all shared the counterspace, too.

The bottles made Alan uneasy. Being in his mother's room, and digesting the names of all of these strange and unusual empty bottles made him think that he was smaller than the bottles, dancing among them on the counter, their bright orange luminescence lighting the way as he wore a funny hat, and shouted their names out. He was in a Dr. Seuss book, the meaning of his pseudonym being correctly adapted to this particular fairytale, singing aloud, being trailed by little creatures with fluffy horns and wide eyes. Devils and angels with pudgy faces and tall, skinny bicycles followed him as they all sang along;

> 'Come, come, everyone; even you venlafaxine,
> for we are traveling to the world of delight,
> of citaloprams, and paroxitines!
> Our adventures will bring us to nefazadone,
> Where we'll eat bupropoins fresh off the trees!
> But we must beware of mirtazepine,
> And her evil clomipramine diazepam buspirones!
> When we win the battle for lamotrigine,
> And defeat the king of gabapentin,
> We will celebrate like wild olanzapines,
> And clomipramine-escitalopram-sertralines!'

Alan put the bucket down after soaking the carpeting with water, all the way to the toilet. It was funny that she even bothered to run to the toilet considering the circumstances... He then took all of the bottles and swiftly shoveled them in one of the trash bags. Then he took the sheets and blankets and pillows off of the bed, and tossed those into the bag as well, stuffing it full.

He ran the bag outside, and placed it on the curb. He then ran inside, and upon seeing that there was a stain on the mattress, he decided to junk that as well. He pulled the mattress off of the bed as forcefully as possible, and slid it down the stairs, pulled it through the door, and brought it outside. While he was at it, he thought, he would do the same thing with the box spring mattress. He grabbed that, slid it through the hall, pushed it down the stairs where it slid down most of the way itself and put a small hole in the wall on the landing. He pulled it out of the hole, and got a splinter trying to maneuver it to the curb.

Upon returning to his mother's room, he turned her clock radio on full blast to the first station that came on, and listened to right wing talk radio for the next two hours, which took his mind off of scrubbing his mother's calcified vomit from the carpet leading form where her bed once was to the bathroom, where she probably died.

· · ·

Alan was late leaving for his mother's burial. He didn't mind considering the circumstances surrounding his first eight hours back in Massachusetts, one and a half of which was spent baptizing himself in the shower in his bathroom cleansing himself of his morbid occupation. He was soaked; soaked through. His skin wrinkled under the weight of all that water. He put on a fresh pressed suit that was probably sitting in his closet for at least the last five years without being worn, and enough Kayak cologne to mask what he had smelled for his next twenty years.

In his mother's room, in the closet that was next to her bathroom, were piles and piles of unopened envelopes stuffed with papers. There were manila envelopes, white envelopes, oak tag envelopes, brown envelopes, airmail envelopes, priority envelopes; and they were all filled with thousands of pages of manuscript. Alan's manuscripts. They contained letters that were addressed exactly the same; *Good Afternoon, Dear Mr. Levy, Greetings,* among others. They all had contents that were also the same; *We regret to inform you, Unfortunately, Thank you so much for your manuscript however, I am unsure whether you know that this is a feminist publication, and your submission… Signed, Sincerely, Regretfully, etc… P.S. Feel free to submit again at any time and we will review your work.* It was a depressing thesis… Alan wasn't entirely upset, aside from the amount of money he had spent on submitting his pieces and their return envelopes easily extended beyond several hundred dollars.

When he did leave, he and Sella were forced to tumble down interstate 95 at unsafe speeds. It wouldn't look good appearing at his mother's funeral ten minutes late. At this rate, he would be just on time. The speedometer read 130 kilometers per hour, but a taxicab passed Alan going at least 145. The time was displayed on the advertisement screen on top of the cab, and Alan wanted desperately to catch up to read it, but if he sped up, the cab sped up. Alan eventually pressed the accelerator as hard as he could, but the lanky and needlessly expensive rental car was no match for the tuned up taxicab.

Alan took the exit off of the highway that the funeral director told him to take. He followed the off ramp, crossed a small drawbridge that crossed the Neponset River, took a left a half kilometer down the road, and came upon the cemetery. He turned into the giant gates, and drove down the road. It was apparent where the service was taking place, as the hearse stood out as a black shadow at the far back of the cemetery covered in wilted grass and frost. Alan parked his car behind the hearse and took Sella out of the back seat. They walked the thousand paces or so to the grave site, and Alan originally walked directly past the desolate scene. He took Sella down to the low lying bushes that were twenty meters past the funeral site.

Sella sniffed around, and did her business, as Alan watched a Lincoln pull up behind his car, and a gentleman in a suit get out. He walked toward the grave, and was just about there when Sella finished her business. The two walked toward the gravesite as well. When they arrived, the man approached Alan with a hand outstretched.

"Alan? Alan." He addressed. Alan didn't know this man. "It is so good to see you," he continued softly, "it has been so long. Rabbi Morris?" Alan suddenly remembered this man, but vaguely as he was a figment of an important aspect of their family before dad left.

"Rabbi Morris... How are you?" His familiar smell of a musky and masculine cologne wafted over to Alan in the cold air. It smelled like home, authority, and elementary school.

"Fine, Alan, fine. I apologize that we must make our acquaintances again under such dire circumstances. Your mother was a great and strong woman. I am really sorry for your loss..." Alan had another vision of scraping the solidified matter from the carpet.

"Thank you, rabbi."

The rabbi reached into his suit pocket and produced a pile of black buttons with a piece of ribbon protruding from the rear and hanging down the length of it. He pinned one to Alan, one to himself, and after briefly looking at Alan with a wrinkled forehead, one on Sella's collar.

"I have so many of these... I guess that is a good thing." He then put his prayer book under his arm, and continued to sing a Hebrew prayer in a low and sad voice. He tore the ribbon on Alan's lapel, on his own jacket, and then on Sella's. When he was done singing, he began to casually speak to Alan again.

"I am sorry that your mum has to be buried here. I wish there was something I could have done..."

"That is okay,..." The rabbi continued to look at Alan with the wrinkled forehead, almost looking as if he wished that he could read Alan's mind. The way the rabbi looked at him, he almost felt better about the whole situation.

"Are you ready?" Alan nodded his head. They made their way over to the grave, and now there was another mourner standing by the grave. A woman with a blazer and a heavy dress on stood on the opposite side of the grave as Alan, the top half of her figure shadowed by a large black hat. It was comforting to see another human there, and Alan wondered why there weren't more people there to show their respects.

Alan looked down at the grave and inside was a box. It was plain, and with its stain and the star of David on the lid, it had a simple elegance. Sella patiently sat next to Alan.

"Alan, before I begin, would you like to recite the Kaddish?" It was the customary prayer for the deceased, and Alan did not remember it one bit. He was sure if the rabbi began, he could enter and contribute to it. He wasn't so much embarrassed as much as he felt bad. This was his mother's funeral.

"Could you help me?"

"That's fine, Alan."

...And they began. As they recited it in Hebrew, it came natural. Alan even remembered some of the translation. *May his great name grow exalted; In the world He created at His will; May He give reign to His kingship in your lives and your days; And in the lifetimes of the entire family of Israel; Swiftly, soon.*

Alan began feeling desperate. He was desperate for not having to be there. He was desperate for help. He was desperate for forgiveness if this was his fault. He was sad. He was sad for entirely different reasons now. He was just sad for his mother not being here with him at this moment. He was skyrocketed into a deep feeling, a deep feeling of desperation. He wanted so much to hold her, and smell her; this was his mum! Why? Why did she have to leave him?

Alan continued to pray, and his chin and voice began to quiver. The rabbi barreled through the prayer at what seemed to be a faster speed, but in reality it was Alan that was slowing down. His mind and his heart hurt. It was painful to be here with this and experiencing this, and his mother was in the ground right there and he felt like his knees were weak again, and again, he felt like he was going to throw up. He tasted saline on his lips.

Just then, a sound emerged from the trees and the bushes. A loud sound of an engine, or several engines, and Alan stopped praying and looked up just in time to see a train emerge beyond the trees and above the bushes farther off where Sella went to the bathroom, going ever so slowly. The engine was loud, the bass reverberating through his chest. He couldn't hear the rabbi over the roar. As the engine passed behind the trees, passenger cars that trailed behind it. The windows of the cars were open, and there was a man over a loudspeaker giving information out as if it were a tour. Passengers hung out of the windows watching something, all smiling. As the man on the loudspeaker instructed, so did the passengers hold themselves out the windows. And they were waving. And they were all happy.

"Hiiii!" some shouted... "Heyyyyy!!!!" shouted others. Some cheered and some clapped. They were all very, very happy, and they were all waving to Alan and the rabbi and the woman.

May his great name be blessed forever and ever.

A large decal on the side of the car said exactly what it was. It was the "United States Winter Olympics Team Countrywide Whistlestop Tour!" and they just happened to be on a train bound for the west coast. They just happened to be riding a train bound for the west coast at the exact same time as Alan attending his mother's funeral. His mother's funeral just happened to be at a cemetery that was next to some train tracks. The train tracks just happened to be next to the Neponset River.

Blessed, praised, glorified, exalted, extolled…

Yes… The words were nothing about sadness; they were nothing about sadness and nothing about being depressed, and nothing about death, but of happiness. They were words that explained how wonderful the creator is. How wonderful this all was. These words were nothing more than thanks for gracing us with this wonderful person on this earth.

Mighty, upraised, and lauded…

A helicopter passed overhead, and the train was still passing with cheering folks. They were all so happy. From the helicopter we must all look so small. We are so small. We are so small and fragile and there are almost nine and a half billion people on the Earth, and they were born everyday, and the died everyday, and here was one named Alan at his mum's funeral. There was a box, and there is some dirt, and there are some really happy people, and here are some really sad people. Alan began to laugh through his tears at how absolutely ridiculous this all was…

Beyond any blessing and song…

Mom was beautiful. Sella was beautiful. Jaime was beautiful. Alan was beautiful. Hobbeston was beautiful. Carson was beautiful. Everything was so beautiful and crisp and fresh and holy and wonderful and exalted… All thanks to Him? How could Alan have become so cynical? How could he have become so heartless? How could he have become so downright awful about this wonderful earth he lives on? How could he have treated the people he treated so badly the way he did? Why in the world was he so ignorant?

Never mind asking why mum killed herself; the world and the awful spiral of living is a test and it is difficult and it is horrible at times… But this is just an illusion. This life is just an illusion that leads to something so much better. The true ideals of living he has already found; compassion, virtue, making this world so much less of a struggle for as many people as he possibly could.

May there be abundant peace from heaven, and life…

As the last car of the train disappeared into the trees again, and a train's whistle was heard echoing through the vast hills and bouncing off of the river, Alan continued reciting the Kaddish, and he ultimately understood what it meant. The Kaddish is the praising of God, and it had been unbelievably misunderstood by Alan because of his connections with it, and it being recited exclusively about death. It wasn't a prayer about death, but of life, and happiness...

He who makes peace in His great heights, may He make peace...

It was about direction. It was about life! It was about purpose! It was about living! It was about destination! It was about life! It was about confidence! It was about life! It was about acceptance! It was about life! It was about everything that Alan was searching for!

Upon us all, and upon all of Israel!

Alan was not only reciting the Kaddish for his mum, but also for himself. He was burying his ungrateful and cynical and ignorant self. He was mourning for everything he had done wrong in his life and over the last year. It was the Kaddish for himself that was recited to cleanse himself of every broken heart and broken trust and broken embrace that he had made over the last few years.

Alan was laughing now... Or was he crying? Alan's breath was invigorating and his heart leapt knowing from this day forward, he would live by nothing less than truth. It took only a simple reciting of a prayer...

The service continued, albeit a short one. At the end, Rabbi Morris, Alan, and the woman in the black hat, all dropped a handful of dirt on top of the casket to bring final closure to his mother's life. Alan considered taking dirt and placing it on his head. This was the most enlightening funeral he had ever attended.

Alan said his goodbyes to the rabbi, as did the woman, and Alan just stared at the sky and the casket, wiping the remaining tears from his eyes. He wished it could have been different, but this was what it took. He sat down on the ground next to Sella, and stroked her mane. She was so wonderful. She was another thing Alan was grateful for. Alan was grateful for everything; he truly was.

A shadow approached the pair, as Alan daydreamed. Looking down, Alan saw the feet of the woman, and slowly looked up.

"Hello, stranger..." she said in a familiar voice. Beneath the big black hat, Alan recognized the face immediately. The only other mourner at the funeral stood before him, and she was beautiful, confident, and most importantly, there for Alan. She was the most there for him than anyone had ever been his entire life. "How are you feeling?"

Alan felt her heart in her voice, and the only thing that came out of his mouth was, "Jane?"

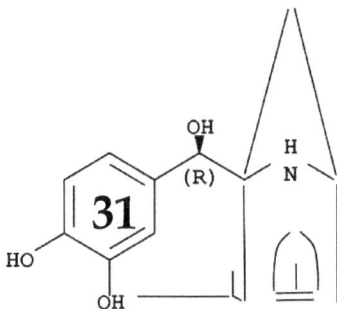

The welcome air in the house where Alan entered was uncanny. It was the same house whose backyard exploded. The same house with the depressing cat. The same house with the forlorn expression of guilt, broken hearts, and support when the odds were all against you. The house felt as though he were entering just after crying, the moist air teetering on the moment that you laugh while you wipe tears from your face.

This seemed as though it was more tragic than a woman dying in labor…

The kitchen was empty, as was the rest of the house. The moist saline in the air felt like a morning to Alan. It felt like he was awash in the river of Jordan. He was wet; soaking, sopping wet. The air was so thick with moisture it was almost unbearable; like breathing water. It was probably only because he had been in Massachusetts for a day and he was so used to the arid environment of the desert.

Sella darted into the house, and examined every possible square centimeter of the floor there was to smell. Jane walked him into the living room, and Alan followed her. They sat on the ratty threadbare couch in the wood paneled living room. She sat looking at Alan, and Alan looked back. How absolutely ridiculous it is that I end up here, he thought, right back where I started.

She looked at him, but she wasn't smiling. She was searching. Her forehead showed confused emotions, wrinkled like the tissue paper in an oversized gift bag. She looked as though she had been crying, and she looked confused, and she looked like she didn't even know why she was doing that with her forehead. They had taken separate cars for the hour or so drive it took to get back to Chapmansville.

She grabbed his hand, and led him up the steep stairs. It was musty. It smelled like cooking and vacuuming and dust and care. A familiar, sleepy smell that Alan had smelled back home in Southie. She led him upstairs, and she led him into her bedroom. Her hands rested on Alan's elbows as his arms sagged from his shoulders. She saw more. She looked at him and she looked thorough him. It was strange that she was looking at him in such a way, and Alan wasn't used to it. Was there something wrong with her? There was nothing wrong with Alan, at least not that he could think about at this exact moment because he was so busy studying Jane's face. She was looking at him like she would look at a bird that was laying in the yard after flying into the kitchen window. He was empty.

She pushed him so he was sitting on the bed. She stood over him, and looked down at him with the same face - what was that face for? She knelt down and took his shoes off, and then his socks. They were moist and sweaty, and burrs of lint clung to them helplessly. She took a tee shirt, and wiped his feet, and it felt wonderful to Alan. She then pushed Alan's torso down so that he was laying on the bed, and she pulled his feet around for him, so that he was laying down. He stared up at the tilted ceiling, and his comfort prompted him to think that there really couldn't be anything more wonderful than this right now. What he needed right now was a good long nap; he had been up all night and all day. This was the perfect opportunity.

But she didn't stop there. She unbuttoned his slacks, and pulled then down slightly.

"Jane-"

"Alan, don't think..."

"But you never; your folks-"

"Alan!" She whispered the loudest exclamation he had ever heard. "Don't. Think... Let me..." She trailed off like that, and took him into her mouth. She claimed her desire, and claimed Alan in the process. There was nothing more than he could possibly want at this exact moment. After stress, after stress, after stress he was comfortable and he didn't have to think or do anything less than let someone take care of him.

At this point he could have broken. What right had she to take him and tell him that he needed this or needed that? She had no right... But she was so warm. He trusted her so much... There was no way that she could have any feeling of how Alan felt at that exact moment... But she understood! She understood wholly. She understood where she went wrong, and she had her reasons for treating him that way, and Alan had his own reasons for treating her like he did.

He threw away everything to leave and shake and sway in the tides of passion and romance of getting up and leaving once and for all. No one could stop him. He was in control! The chains that moved as he left only provided further evidence of what he thought at this moment. The pain and the fear and everything he was experiencing one year later was only summed up in one statement. That statement existed only long enough to prove in his own head that he went on a journey, and on that journey he had a lot of growing up to do. While Alan was away, and in the harsh reality of how he left Jane, he thought that that gave her reason to grow up a little, too.

He wanted to ask her when it was that she came around; but that would be simply inappropriate. Simply inappropri-

Alan was sleepy; almost dreamy as she crawled up his body. Jane's face was centimeters from his face, and in the afternoon light, he felt like a furry little creature in her masterful, guardian, mothering touch. Her hair, draping like curtains over his face, smelled sweet and feminine. It ironically smelled like affluence; like the way his mother smelled before his dad left. He wanted to sob. He was happy, and comfortable, and didn't have to worry now.

"Is this okay," Jane had whispered. Alan just continued to look up at her, and he was crying. "Oh, god, I am sorry...."

"No, Jane," Alan whispered. "Don't stop..."

And in the afternoon of his mother's funeral Alan counted the stars that he saw as he transformed into a lemming and dove off the cliffs of passion and security. He knew that the lemmings never committed suicide, he thought as he drifted off to sleep next to Jane. The video of the tiny furry animals taking the terrible plunge into the icy depths was simply staged; the filmmakers shoved the tiny creatures off the side of the cliffs. It wasn't any documentary filmmakers, but amateur filmmakers of a proud children's corporation who did it. For the past year Alan had been those filmmakers, pushing himself over the edge. Now, Jane was Mother Nature telling him it was all a lie.

That was his last thought, looking into her white light of ecstasy, the stars encompassing him just before he fell asleep.

He didn't dream... Instead he woke with an empty bed hours later. He was still in Jane's house, and a spicy and tangy aroma wafted up into the bedroom. Something sizzled far away. His eyelids were heavy. There was nothing more; what time was it? Alan looked down at his water... His water? His watch. It was six thirty. He had been out for a few hours.

He got up, he felt a musky sex-sleep-sweat beneath his suit that was uncomfortable, but there was nothing to be done about it. His head spun like he had slept the whole day. It was dark out, and he felt off. He felt off like he had been on a plane the entire night before, stayed awake and cleaned up his mother's vomit at his childhood home, and gone to her fucking funeral. That was the only way to sum it up.

He slid down the stairs, and the mood in the kitchen was stunning. Jane's mother was dancing about in her apron. Her father was playing rough with Sella. Jane was laughing with it all. Who was this family? Certainly not the one he had met before... The one he had known; the one with broken dreams. But the only thing that was different, was... Was he the only difference?

"You're up!" Jane shouted.

"Alan," Her father walked over and shook Alan's hand. "Good to see you back." He said it in the most caring and unobtrusive voice he had ever heard. As if he never left.

"Hello, Alan" her mother said. "I am sure you'll stay for dinner, Alan...???"

"Yes," he replied with hesitation, but a deep confusion as if he was in a different family's home altogether.

And that night they feasted on meatloaf. And Alan felt under no obligation to be a host or tell any stories. And he took enjoyment of listening to the stories they had to tell. They all had lives as Alan was away... But of course, why wouldn't they? They all had their lives and their jobs and their struggles while Alan was gone, and it was wonderful just to eat his meatloaf and mashed potatoes and corn and take it all in. He felt in his own way, without the obligations, and he was in his own heaven. The chemistry of the moment was magical.

After dinner, Jane's father invited him out onto the front concrete steps. They sat in the cool air, just breathing. He produced two factory produced, plastic wrapped American cigars, and handed one to Alan. Alan took it in his mouth. Father lit a match, lit Alan's cigar, and then lit his own. The sting of the tobacco, and the sweet smoke entering his mouth was calming to Alan. What originally started as a macabre day, turned into one of the most relaxing Alan ever had.

"I remember when my mother died, Alan," father said, staring at the ground. "In many ways she died like your mother did... It wasn't immediately apparent, but she died of emptiness. Her heart dried up because she was so terribly sad. So terribly, terribly sad. My father died at the shipyard when I was very young. Then I ended up going to the war in Iraq all those years ago - you know, the one that no one knew why we were there... She was afraid every day. There was a reason they called it terrorism, of course. My friends were dying.

"I remember one time we were bringing food to this mosque in Baghdad, and we were talking to the head cleric there. He was very kind and very grateful. There was enough food there to feel people for a long time. So, as we were talking to him, I heard a little puff next to me - not even. It was like my buddy was snapping gum with his mouth closed... But then he was on the floor, and there was a pool of blood growing out from his head. Just like that. No sound. Nothing. And we were doing something nice,..." he shook his head. "I don't even know where this is coming from, but... Mother died when I got back. She smoked every day of her life until I went away. That is when she vowed to quit, and she did, but the lung cancer still came. This was back in the day, remember...

"Alan. I feel like I relate to you. I can say that you never saw the horrors of war, and I am grateful that you haven't. But it's weird. I like to think that we still have had the same struggles. We still have had the same struggles and you and I have had the power and the grace to overcome it all...

"I am happy you are here Alan. I am happy you are back."

Alan had no idea where this was coming from, but he understood. He hadn't exchanged a word with him for the years that he had been here before, and all of a sudden the compassionate 'son, you remind me of me' speech?

"Alan, I want to ask you a favor..." Alan just looked back at him, cigar embers dropping into the darkness. "I want to ask you if you would be willing to stay with us, just for a little while until you get yourself on your feet again. I don't want any money, and you can stay in Jane's room, no questions asked..."

"Well, I appreciate that Mr. Rarus, but frankly-"

"Frankly, what, Alan? All you can say is yes. I know you don't have anywhere to go; and I don't want you in that house after what happened..."

Alan looked at Father. He tasted coffee and cigarettes and cocoa and everything that was right in the world in his mouth at that moment. He did only what he thought of - to put his arms around Father. He held him for ten minutes, and an centimeter of ash collected on the stoop under where his cigar was. He felt like he was going to fall asleep again.

"You are probably still exhausted, eh?"

"Yeah..."

"Go to bed. You need it." He held his hand out, and Alan handed him the cigar. He rubbed it out on the stoop. "We'll save this for tomorrow night."

Alan got up, went inside, and began to walk up the stairs as Father's hand pat his back. He walked up the stairs, and lay down on Jane's bed. He could hear Sella bound up the stairs and plant herself at the foot of the bed. On the bed he drifted in and out of affliction with what her father had said. What in the world possessed Jane to get him to do that?

The women laughed downstairs. Their laughs echoed in the same intonation. The same pauses. The same decrescendo at the end.

Alan drifted off for a moment, and then came to again as Jane was changing for bed in the room and slid her body up the bed next to him. She was wearing cool silk, and her body felt like milk as it formed around Alan. She placed her head on his shoulder.

"Why did you ask your father to let me stay," Alan asked.

"I didn't..."

"Did you think I was like a dog or something that you found along the way? A pet? Why would you even do that?"

"I didn't, Alan, I told you. Dad told me when he came in from outside. He said you had a nice talk and that he had asked you to stay."

"Well,..."

"He said there was no pressure, but he and mom wanted you here... He said he wished he was in that place when he had to go through what you are going through."

Alan was unsure as to why he was so infatuated with being offended by someone wanting to take care of him. There was nothing he had to do right now... Nowhere for him to go, nor nowhere he had to be. This was the way it was supposed to work out and it was working out simply by virtue of the fact that there were people in this world that genuinely loved him without strings attached. Where was he going to go? Was he going to run away again?

More importantly, was asking these questions leading him down the path that he had originally run away from?

But then he thought about this: was this an inevitable decline from the beginning? Was he destined to be stuck in this rut? Was this even a rut? Alan had spent the last year analyzing other people's faith. Faith in god, in themselves, and in America. Faith in where they were going and faith in where they had been. Alan thought - it was time for him to have some faith in the idea that he could not rule the world even if he wanted to. He needed to have some faith in himself, and faith in the fact that his god would treat him well and put him in the places he needed to be. That god had done a pretty good job so far… Everything else was none of his business.

Holding Jane, he found the god he was looking for. That God was with him the whole time. He was here, watching over Alan as the people he needed to be there for him were there at that exact moment. He had a roof over his head. He had a creature at his feet and in his arms and in this roof that loved him very dearly. He had it in Overton, and he had it in Branson, and he had it in Virginia Beach, and he had it here. He had no right to ask questions; and he had no right for anyone to treat him this nicely.

"…You know - when I got to the house in Boston, all of my manuscripts were piled up in mum's room." Alan said. "Like she was hoarding them… It was just stacks and stacks and stacks of envelopes. It padded her room. I actually almost couldn't open the front door because there was a stack of them behind that, too."

"She was very proud of you, Alan. She was extremely proud of you and she kept them… They are like trophies to her."

"She never had even read any of them, I don't think…"

"But don't you think that she told everyone how great of a writer you are? That you are really going to make it?"

"I don't know." They sat in the silence, close together. Alan felt himself getting emotional again. The flutters in his chest and on his face were impossible to contain, and he really wanted to leave the place he had been over the last year. He wanted to concentrate on the important things. He missed mother already, and he wished he wasn't so neglectful.

"I'm sorry," he whispered. He was crying. Silently.

Jane also began to cry. Hers was audible, and she breathed heavy into Alan's chest.

"Don't be sorry," Jane said. She paused enough for her huffs to enter Alan's chest. "We're all sorry… I have been seeing someone, and-" and Alan began sobbing louder.

"What?" he mustered though his sobs.

"No, no, Alan, not seeing another lover… A rabbi…" and they continued to cry, silently, whispering. "I wanted to know what was going on with you. I wanted help, and that made sense, somehow. He said what you have been going through is very Jewish. The struggle. He said that it is very Jewish to struggle and to fight for truth; whether it be a sense of truth for God, or a sense of truth for justice. You, Alan, spent the last painful and struggling year on a search for the truthful self, and… I have so much admiration of you for that. You are amazing…"

"No, no…"

"You want to live with truth, live with honesty, live with freedom from our own mortal overbearing nature - and that is nothing less than beautiful. The further you got away, I realized the more I loved you, Alan."

"Me, too; me too…"

She kissed Alan, with the most powerful passion and energy that he had ever been kissed with. Their tears mixed upon their cheeks, and their noses dripped and mixed, and it was so natural and so very innate. Alan felt the chorus and the piano and the guitar in his heart, playing a strong and slow progression. The chorus sang and they sang 'everything we are now;' and the chorus sang 'we're everything we are now;' and the chorus sang ever so softly.

"Don't leave me, Alan. I love you." She sobbed.

"I love you too, Jane."

The chorus sang and the welling pangs of pins and needles at the back of his nose and in his throat sprang forth, and heat and pain and a waterfall of melt surged through his veins; and the chorus sang some more. 'Don't go away;' they sang; 'be with me;' they sang; 'hold me, oh, hold me;' they sang. 'this is heaven;' they sang. 'I love you.'

I love you.

Love. You.

Love is never wasted, oh God is it never wasted.

Thank you so much for this moment.

If I died this instant, it would be so terribly sweet.

I wouldn't want to remember anything else.

I would want this to be my last feeling of helplessness.

Because I love you.

I love you.

I love you.

I love you.

Thank you.

Thank you.

Thank you.

And they drifted off to sleep.

In his dreams, Alan was walking down the street in Overton, with the sweeping deserts on one side. It was nighttime. And then on his right were the shores of Virginia Beach. Straight ahead was the lush and towny street of Branson. It was warm out, and he had a tee shirt and shorts on. He was walking down the street, trees on both sides. It looked like Branson, anyway. It looked like Branson and it looked like Iowa and it looked like Michigan. It looked like the perfect tree-lined street. It was everywhere at once.

All of the houses lay dormant in the dark. There was one house he was walking to specifically; a one level with a huge yard, trees canopying everything. It was lush. He felt his hands, and his fingernails felt extremely long. They felt heavy, but he didn't look at them.

He walked toward the front door, and as he approached, the lights faded in inside, and in the yard. It smelled like pollen and spring. He looked in the window. There was something extremely familiar about this house. It was his house. He had bought it. He had bought it with Jane.

The window next to the door looked straight into the kitchen. Jane was sitting at the table, Sella at her feet. She was reading the newspaper with her back to him. Alan looked down at the door handle, and reached for it. Where his hand should have been, there was only a wrist. He used his left, and the same happened. There were two shiny perfect nubs where his hands should have been. There were just no hands. No hands. He was sad, but all he wanted to do was go inside. He just wanted to go inside and be with Jane.

He struggled with the door. He was pulling at it, rubbing it, stubbing it to get it open. He couldn't. He knocked with his stub on the window. Hollow pats resounded off of the glass. He could see Jane turn methodically from the chair, no longer holding the paper, and walk to the door. It wasn't even like she had opened the door, but suddenly Alan was inside. He was inside and Jane's arms were around him. He was sobbing again.

"I couldn't open the door... I couldn't open the door... I am sorry," he kept saying. He smelled banana bread through his choking crying. It was warm. Alan looked about and there was new furniture shrink wrapped and sitting about, not even opened. Jane just kept holding him tighter. They stood there in the dim light, just holding one another, swaying and rocking to nothing, for what seemed to be hours in the dream. And that was just fine.

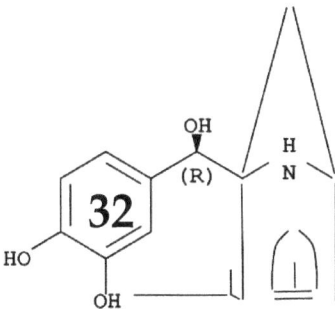

Alan woke up the next morning, and the house was silent. Everyone was gone. Alan was alone. They trusted him within their domain, and that was wonderful.

Sella's head arose, and her collar jangled. Alan made his way downstairs, and she followed. He walked outside, and she followed. She went into the backyard, and did her business. She completely avoided the dormant charred circle in the yard where the plane had crashed the year before. They entered the house, and Alan thought about what to do for the day. He should probably look for some kind of job... Or rest and recover from the day before... Or vegetate with the television. He deserved that much.

As they passed through the kitchen, there was a note taped to the handle of the microwave that was installed above the oven. *Alan, we went to a short Christmas get-together. FYI, there is food in the fridge. If you need anything you can call us on the cell phones. Also, we set up a makeshift thing in the office next to the dining room for you... Check it out. Relax! Have a good day! ~The Raruses*

Alan took the note off of the fridge, and Sella clopped around and doing her own thing. Alan went into the living room, took a right into the adjacent dining room, and then walked straight back into the small three by four meter room. The desk had a typewriter on it, and a fresh, unopened ream of paper. Another note in the roller of the typewriter said *I'm sure you have a lot to say now. Good luck!* They had set up a little writing station for him. Alan removed the note from the typewriter.

He turned out of the room, and actually thought about writing. That would be therapeutic for him. He would walk upstairs, get his notebook, and just let it fly. He went upstairs, grabbed his jacket, and reached into the lapel pocket for his little black notebook. He probably wouldn't even need it considering that there was so much he had been thinking about in even the last twenty four hours. Yes, this would probably be very good for him. He placed the jacket back on the chair it was sitting on, and turned to leave. He would write about life, the universe, space, faith, the world, mortality. He had so much material now. This would be very good indee-

Alan noticed a stack of black videotapes on a shelf. He probably wouldn't have even paid any attention to them except for his name scrawled on black marker on the side of the tapes. *Alan* they all said. There were about four or five total. He was always unsure of why Jane's family still used video tapes, as they were very difficult to get, but their ease of use and vast recycleability seemed to outweigh the durability of the extremely fragile nature of the magnetic tape. This magnetic tape that had something to do with Alan.

Alan grabbed the stack and brought it down to the living room where the very inexpensive and retro entertainment center sat. He fed one of the tapes to the player, and turned the television on.

Static. Then a commercial for a telephone company. He was unsure of where this was headed. Until the screen cut in... It was a newsroom. They were covering the afternoon's news. There was a kidnapping in Ohio. Something about foreign delegation. Then the search for Hobbeston's wife briefly. And then...

"And a bizarre story we are following out of Cortez, Colorado. A protester has been holing himself up nightly in the ValuMart here in Cortez until he is kicked out. Local authorities say that he is currently under investigation, and may be charged with trespassing, although there is no speculation as to why he is doing it..."

Alan fast forwarded the tape...

"...it seems as though there is another man with him, and they are gaining a following. People are coming from neighboring towns to become part of the protest or just to see what is going on. Frankly, this is the...."

He watched more...

"...ink that a man would hole himself up in a ValuMart?" the newscaster asked.

"Well, I think that some people are diss-a-POIN-ted with the e-caw-nomy, and diss-a-POIN-ted with themselves and diss-a-POIN-ted with the warld... All they hay-uve to to with themselves is make a ruckus at the local staw-re and make us shaw-ppers miserable. Thay-ut's what AH thaynk." the overweight interviewee with a southern drawl responded.

And he watched more.

He watched more and more and more. An hour passed. Two. He couldn't take his eyes off of the screen, and he was wondering why he was so obsessively watching it. There was even a small melee outside of the store one of the days that he hadn't even been aware of. When the first tape was finished, he switched to the second. When the second was finished, he switched to the third.

One particular part of the third video was familiar...

"... without hesitation that we do something about the oppression and poor treatment of the staff with poor hours, pay, and benefits!" a crunchy girl said.

The reporter returned the microphone to her own face. "So your means are merely political in nature?"

"In a sense, yes. We are unofficially following the lead of Michael Carson who has been coming here every night for the past few years. He is a multimillionaire, and yet he sleeps here every night as a protest to his own selling-out as a corporate trading success story. Carson curls up as if he was the fetus in the womb of corporate America. He protests by posing as the bastard *(beep)*-child of materialism and excessive capitalism!" and a group of people screamed in triumph behind her.

Alan watched more. He watched more and more and the time passed. It was as if the time wasn't even passing, but was more of a fluid entity that whispered in his ear. He was in a trance by mass media. He hated the news because it did this to him. Every exciting thing; every exciting next thing on was the more important and more troubling and scarier news than before... And what was funny about this all was that it all already happened. It happened months ago! And Alan was there! He knew how it ended!

Later on in the fifth tape, you could still rewind and faintly see Alan jump up in the air as the authorities and the angry mob swooped in to take him away. The apex of the whole five film series. The dénouement! It was beautiful. He played it in slow motion, and he looked like an angel floating up to the sky, the thick clouds of tear gas slowly creating a triumphant ethereal arc over the crowd!

And if he rewound it! Oh, if he rewound it! If he rewound it, he landed and the smoke gracefully sucked itself back into the canisters, and as his feet would have touched the floor, the crowd scattered backward and into uniform rows. It was lovely and artistic...

Alan peeled himself from the floor and collected the tapes. He ran upstairs and placed the tapes back as uniformly as he could in relation to where they were before. He ran downstairs, let Sella into the backyard, and then walked down the street. It was time for a drink, and there just so happened to be a bar three blocks away.

He walked down the hill in the cold air, without a jacket, contemplating his course. He has had so much. Some on Earth could ever experience what he did in a single year. Among the awful things that happened while he was away, some great things did, too. All of it was great, frankly. The good and the bad set him up for a lesson in living. People come and people go, and Alan was lucky enough that he made it back alive and into the arms of Jane and her family.

But what was next for Alan? He didn't know. He had to go back to school. He had to get a place. He had to get a job... But being received so well last night, it seemed that he had the opportunity to take all of that in. He wondered if there was an estate left to him by mum – there was the house, after all. He wondered where he would end up with Jane. He wondered what was next.

At the base of the hill was the main route. The drag he took out of the town. Further up the street a half a kilometer was the bowling alley. Straight ahead was the bar next to the thrift store. To his right was a convenience store.

He walked over to it, and entered. There was something he wanted to get.
There was something comforting in the cigar he had the night before. He
walked up to the counter.

"Could I have a pack of cigarettes?"

"Sure, what kind?"

"I don't know... what ones are good?"

The teller looked at him with a strange look. He reached up and
retrieved a yellow box of cigarettes with Native American designs on them.
He handed him the box, and charged him twelve dollars. Alan took a book of
matches, and walked out of the store. He removed the cellophane, removed a
cigarette, and placed it in his mouth. He lit a match, lit the cigarette, and
inhaled. The smoke entered his lungs, and nicotine entered his blood.

He examined the simple packaging. There was a large picture of some
rotten teeth on one side, on the other a giant black warning from the surgeon
general. The few spots that were covered in words that had to do with the
cigarettes said words like *100% natural*, *ultra light*, and *Spirit*. Alan had
remembered reading a short story by one of his favorite authors when he was
in college. It was called something about a Woodpecker, but it was about a
girl and in it she had a pack of cigarettes back in the day that had no writing
on them but the packaging designs.

The little girl fantasized about being in the packaging, and romancing
the beautiful ideals and symbols that the packaging emanated. She would
stare at the package, and feel like she was in the Middle Eastern Turkish world
of intrigue and beautiful architecture, and mysterious women in veils, and
gritty men on camel-back. It was certainly a small adventure. She had
crawled into the packaging, and at the end, you realized that her romance was
simply surrounding the ideals of what the package actually advertised and not
what was inside... She never opened the pack.

But Alan was happy with his cigarette. It was in his mouth, and he
felt like a free man; like he would never die. Like Jane was the young secretary
he just left his family for. Like this day was his first. It was a supernova of
epic adventure, ready to hit the world and explode with a wit about him and
his writing and he was gonna make it, dammit!

But he probably looked like an idiot with a cigarette on the stoop of
the convenience store. He held it like people held them... But in all actuality,
he probably looked like a boob. He would need a couple of martinis first.
Alan walked through the parking lot, off the curb, across the street, through
the parking lot, put his half-smoked cigarette in the receptacle next to the door,
and went in.

Alan ordered a vodka martini, extra dry, no olives. He received it in a
small tumbler with no ice (which he didn't want anyway) and he wasn't even
sure if there was any vermouth in it, but it didn't matter. It tasted delicious. It
took him a half hour to drink it down, studying the television that was playing
an afternoon court show and then looking over at the television playing lottery
numbers you could play every two or three minutes.

He ordered another, and drank it down the same way. As he was sipping on it, he wondered if things didn't work out this way. He wondered what would have happened if he had felt he had something to prove like Clark did, and felt the need to stay with her without having the chance to grow. Without her having the chance to grow. He took out his notebook and scribbled some notes; *What if the last year never happened? If love is never wasted, how did one feel as though it were? Regret? Never growing? Waiting too long to?* He wrote on the page opposite read *'the loneliest of days'* and *'wife'*. What had that been in reference to?

Alan finished the martini, and sauntered out of the bar with a small buzz, enough to get him home, in front of the typewriter, and a few paragraphs out while still keeping him laid back enough to produce something that wasn't entirely crap.

When he got back to the house, he retrieved Sella from the back yard, and retrieved the small bag of food he had in the rental car parked out on the street in front of the house. He poured Sella a small dish of food and water in the kitchen, and then retired to his cozy little office. It smelled like a library in there; the musty and moist air had a lovely aged papery smell.

He fed the fist page into the typewriter, and opened his notebook to what he had written in the bar. He stared at the blank paper, and then the notebook, and then the screen. He had thought to himself that he wanted to put the pain and the energy of what he had felt in the last two days, and the last week, and the last month, and the last year into words. He wanted to make readers feel it. He wanted readers to feel as sorry as he did. He wanted readers to be grateful. He wanted to make an impact on the overall being of a reader. He wanted to prove that there is a greater and more pure trance that someone could enter besides the banal waste of consciousness that the television provided.

Mostly, he just wanted to get published; he finally had the opportunity, it seemed, to start his career somewhere.

He pressed the first key, and faded away into his own head… This time, he thought, it would be so much simpler.

• • •

Emilene was dead long before the paper arrived that day. Long before it was printed, long before Harold picked it up with jittery hands and shuffled it into the kitchen, and long before he even considered the thought. It only crossed his mind as he steadied his sixty-four year old hand over the crossword puzzle convulsing out the word pestilence; a ten letter word for "Venomous, fatal affliction."

He looked up from the inky mess, reflecting on the last time he heard her voice. It was months ago, and yet he wasn't inspired to call… He only leafed to the obituaries and the odor of the cold, wintry, fresh ink washed over his nose from her name. Emilene Holmes. She kept Harold's name despite her new marriage, and his heart burned molten over the rest of the sentence, "loving mother and wife left behind her husband Rock and daughter Margaret."

He read the sentence fruitlessly several times over. It was as if she were leaving behind only a man whose namesake bore no resemblance to dead Hollywood actors of demure quality, and a daughter who would love her more than anything this cruel world could provide. Yet, this same cruel world provided no mention of Harold, a man that would discover he loved her more than the spans of heaven and the beauty of Eden. Harold could only speculate that he would make it to the gates of paradise to even see Emilene again.

"How is the portfolio business treating you, Harold?" Rock asked after mass. Regardless of the divorce, they still attended the same church.

"Well, very fine indeed..." although certain politicians were causing the market to dramatically digest one's nest egg as a serpent. "Your practice?"

"Couldn't be better! I am actually helping Margaret with her college bills... I really wish you would too. A custom investment portfolio would assist her quite nicely." Harold envisioned reaching his jaw as if he were to surprise him with a kiss and then tearing at his neck flesh with his teeth like a reptile. Emilene politely stared at him, her pale blue eyes mercurially elevating Harold's spirits enough for a pleasant transaction.

"How are you, Harold?" ever so softly.

"Okay, I suppose..." Harold responded, his bobbing, shaking head nullifying his masculinity, "very well, thank you." She just stared at him. A quick, pert, meaningless smile crossed her face, right before she and Rock turned to leave. Yes, it was a pleasant transaction; a pleasant transaction at the bank.

Harold last spoke with her on the phone the last day he was allowed to call. Rock had instructed her that she wasn't to talk to Harold without him present, as the pair of them were too prone to "emotionally unstable outbursts," as he put it. She had told him how she was doing, how the house was, the inane activities of her new cat, and the last time she had spoken with their daughter.

Harold began his side of the conversation with an embarrassing venture into why he missed Emilene, when would he see her, and how very much he loved her, although he wished he never did. They would weep at each other, making it impossible to solve anything. After every conversation, they were reminded of Emilene's great mortal tragedy; the rotten cancerous onion munching at her side. He pleaded to Emilene as he could to stay with him, return and forget his misgivings, but she wouldn't.

After a lengthy discussion on the eve of their thirty-second wedding anniversary, Harold decided that he had a simple decision to make. As nothing more than a compulsive introvert, it was time for him to move out. He liked being alone, and with a new apartment downtown he would be afforded the luxury of solitude for the first time in decades.

Through a muffle of tears, Emilene mustered, "when can I visit, then?"

"No."

"When will I see you, husband? My love?"

"No."

They didn't speak, but after his liquor store excursions, Harold would often find aromatic pink envelopes on the doorstep addressed to him in cursive. But he wouldn't open them, rather, he lined them up on the kitchen counter to serve as decorative coasters for the ever-growing chorus line of empty square whiskey bottles chronicling his historic months of sloth and depravity.   But he was perfectly happy being utterly depressed and heartbroken.

It wasn't until years after the undemanding divorce that he had found out about his wife's marriage to a prominent doctor of otolaryngology practicing in Boston. It was that day that he remembered she was missing, and that he loved her. He was then willing to give her anything, and in one cold late-October evening was almost struck down by a car as he shouted, "You are so pretty, here is my blood! You are so lovely! Here are my bones! I miss your heart and flesh!" He realized after dodging the rusty clunker that neither the doctor nor his new wife were at home at all.

As the weeks and months passed, Harold missed Emilene exponentially, and after talking to her a week after she hung up on him sobbing incoherently, he found out about her cancer. No, it seemed there was no time to waste after her diagnosis. Harold called her twice as often, but also called the best hospitals for hours on end, and was unofficially diagnosed as a sociopath by everyone he interacted with.

Recalling his life as he hovered over the early morning paper, he drained his heart and his soul. While a fire in his ribs grew and glassy oil ran from his eyes, he didn't realize that he was sucking on the bitter pulp Emilene's obituary was printed on; he was only aware that October relished in allowing the loneliest days for man, and the expansive drift of Autumn and abandonment existed immortally in life's chaotic spiral.

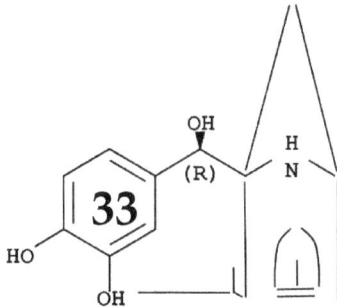

It was two weeks later when he had edited the work to its final product. It was lovely, and at such a short length Alan thought of it as one of the greatest things he had written. The ultimate question remained, 'what would have happened if I had not taken a journey and been by myself, but instead, felt as though I was settling?' It seems as though this similar question echoed off of every bad relationship and marriage. Every year, it seemed like more people were marrying the wrong people. Alan felt he had written about it the best possible way in a piece that was the best he had ever composed.

Alan and Jane were driving to the post office to drop off Alan's manuscripts to send them to the big magazines. Alan felt that this, 'October Allows the Loneliest Days,' was everything they were looking for. Short, meaningful, contemporary, and timeless. This work would span time; that much was certain to Alan. But would their relationship? Alan was sure that he could want nothing further from this life than the way it was going right now...

"Jane?"

"Yeah?"

"Do you... Do you want to get married?" Her face reflected that she was taken aback by this question.

"Don't be ridiculous. You aren't ready for that, I know that much. I am also certain that I am not either. So I hope that is a good explanation for you..."

"Well I suppose it is. I just figure that if we end up moving in together and then totally hating each other..."

"I worry about that too, Alan, but I am not worried in the least. You know why?"

"Why?"

"Because we could live in a cardboard box and I would be completely infatuated with being with you. We could have nowhere to go to the bathroom, or shower, and be cold and wet every night. But you know, I would like nothing more than that.

"That is all I could think about while you were gone," she continued. "I would rather be with you in complete squalor and degradation, and know that you are okay - that we're okay - than ever go through not having you like last year. Do we need to be married to make that happen?"

Alan realized that he was the crazy one. He thought that because he didn't necessarily feel that marriage was a viable institution anymore, it would almost mean more for a couple not to get married and stay strong and happy and... and he reminded himself of someone he once knew.

"I love you, Jane..."

She smiled as she drove. They pulled into the post office and Alan shipped them, giving a customary kiss to each as it left his hands. He felt nervous handing his money to the cashier, and he wanted a cigarette. He had smoked one each time he sat down to edit the piece; he would cut, and respell, and the cigarette just seemed to work in keeping him from feeling awful about what he was doing. Alan wanted to be one of those romantic writers that told everyone that they survived on a diet of coffee, cigarettes, and fingernails... Hell, he looked like he did. Regardless, now was not the time for a cigarette... Jane was in the car.

He returned to the car, and Jane smiled at him.

"How did you do?"

"Fine..." he sighed. "Fine. I would rather they just keep them and shred them than send them back. Then I could keep wondering and guessing. I'm sure it's my poor-ass fault for sending the return envelopes inside because resending the same ones was cheaper than printing it out every time."

"You know, Alan, a lot of people have respect for you for doing this – I don't think many people do that anymore. People who like to paint go to work at the factory or the accounting office just to make a buck, and they tell everyone that they are accountants and manufacturers... You actually tell people you are a writer, and you prove it. That is commendable, and I am proud of you."

Jane was precisely what he thought was great and good. In the time she was stuck in Chapmansville while Alan was away, she grew out of the worst part of her. That part of her that made anyone not from Chapmansville know that she was from Chapmansville. She shed her brutal and selfish self. More importantly, so had Alan.

As they drove, Sella was in the back seat. It had begun to snow, and Alan began to think about his father. He was exactly what Alan was. They were the same... But rather than adjust and wring his own heart out, rather than becoming numb and leading himself around until he couldn't take it anymore; rather than leave a life that he had built and a universe and family structure that he was a cornerstone of, Alan disappeared until he was strong enough to return.

Alan evaporated into thin air as he found out for himself that there was nothing in the world that was much better than the world he had. There were snags and burrs in the fabric of his world, and the very act of exploration and rocket science of disappearing and then materializing again seemed to fill in the missing strands of fate that were missing. Now he was tuned in... He was plugged in with golden fibers to what he needed... To what was generated by the destruction of that old world. Today it was all new.

While he wished he could have rewound his mother's and Jaime's deaths just as he could the news footage of the ValuMart disaster, he couldn't. It seemed as though they were martyrs for the absolute glory he felt. It was time to meet dad; for no other reason than because of the fact that he could. They were both alive, and it was time to meet the man. Alan wondered if they were at all similar. What kind of person was he? Did he even know about what happened to mum?

Alan watched the windshield as snow softly fluttered to the glass, landed for a moment, and was sent careening off to the side. He looked at Jane as she drove. She was so graceful... Flesh and electrical impulses that fired for only him. Alan could never have understood in a million years how wonderful this was before. He was grateful, oh so grateful. When he arrived back at the house, he would write everyone a letter. It would be a ten page letter, outlining what it was like being in such comfortable bliss. This was what happiness and life was all about.

"Do you want to move to Cambridge, Alan?" Jane asked. Alan thought about it... He did. He wanted to be in the middle of it all again, but he also recognized that he already was.

"I don't know."

"That's okay. You don't need to know... We can save up some money and figure it out..."

"I suppose we could always go stay in the house in Southie..." Alan looked up at her driving. There was a definite dreadful look on her face. "...Or I could sell it. We can save up some money. You're right."

They turned a corner, and they were driving up in the center of a great big bowl of strip malls. It was easily a square kilometer of pavement. There were strip malls on all sides, and Jane drove them to the very edge of the bowl, and parked in front of a coffee store that Alan had always meant to go in. They opened the windows a crack so Sella could breathe, and they opened the car doors.

Alan began to walk into the coffee shop. Jane grabbed him by the arm, and he spun around. She was looking at him from the top of her eyes, and she looked magnificent.

"I. Am. So. Glad. You. Are. Here." Alan smiled, and she moved in and kissed him.

They walked into the small café, which had a sort of rugged mountain theme with wooden tables, and mini lanterns, and a wood plank floor. There was moose regalia everywhere, and a soft stereo filled the air with adult contemporary jazz. Not like the prepackaged stuff, but actually enjoyable.

Alan got a large cup of black coffee, and Jane got a cappuccino. They sat at a table. Jane stood up, walked away, and returned with a Scrabble board. They opened it, and played. The coffee was delicious and warm, and tasted even better as Alan looked outside at the snow, which had started coming down rather hard.

Mask.

As they sat, Alan thought that it was about time that he sent a letter to Clark. See if he ever made out with that girl. He should send a letter to the Stillers and give them an update on how he was doing. Send a letter to Carson. He should send a letter to Hank most of all. Alan owed Hank so much. He was truly a glorious man.

Trees.

Jane smiled as she drank her cappuccino. The froth form the oversized mug caught on her lip, and she would wipe her face after every sip. She felt like summer, and felt like the coffee Alan was drinking. She felt like a blanket, a blanket of butter being spread on toast. She looked at Alan as if the entire future rested in his eyes. Everything that was to come in the world rested just so, right there. How could she be so warm?

Sway.

Alan wanted to know what she saw. Alan wanted to know what the future was, for himself, and for the both of them. Alan was happy that he had the opportunity to throw away everything he lived for create an entire new world. Would he become bloodthirsty again? Probably. We all did. Will he fall in love again? Probably. We all did. What was important was what he had to do with all of these feelings now. He couldn't throw this away, not now. He was invested in this life. He would be happy, and if he wasn't, he would have to find an answer. Running off on Jane again would not prove to be suitable, no matter what the reward. The cost would be too great to risk his heart for another dead end in any aspect of his existence.

Coyote.

The snow faded outside, and it was just Alan and Jane. The lights faded inside, and it was just Alan and Jane. The world faded, and it was just Alan and Jane and their scrabble board and their delicious coffee. This was what it was all about. There was nothing more. Virtue, Alan learned, was Compassion and Connection. They had it between each other at this exact moment. There was nothing more to comprehend about life and the universe. All that was left was God.

Specter.

And it was God that was in this moment, as every moment that Alan experienced when he had come home. Cleaning up his mother's vomit. Burying her. Dropping a clod of dirt on her casket. Ending up in Chapmansville again. Staying with the Raruses. Writing another great story. The magic of the moments at the coffee shop. Alan would not have made it through them without a higher power, and he almost had to experience them in order to clean out his previous cynicism about everything. The memory eroded of who he was and the world he was in.

Warmth.

The time Alan coexisted with Jane was slowed to a spark in the ultimate cycle of everything. Their lives left behind the simple shadow of their former selves, and they reminded themselves of the price they paid to get to where they were. Alan and Jane felt so alive; so alive. Their worlds were only each other. They tuned out work and the rest of the world. They were invincible. There were no problems that they couldn't overcome. There was nothing but them, in their own bodies and souls flowing like smoke between them, walking in heaven.

Gourmet.

They would go back to this coffee shop every week and play scrabble. It was homage to themselves, and homage to their company. It was pure, and comfortable, understanding, and served as a chronicle to their existence. It gave them a reason to exist. They were there the first month Alan returned, the week of Jane's first promotion, the week of Alan's first publication, the week of Hobbeston's guilty verdict, the week Sella died, the week they moved from Chapmansville, and the week they got married.

Bandage.

This special place was among others that they shared. They shared physical spaces, and the spaces that were in between were not spaces at all, but a dense matter that was an emotional bonding epoxy between them. The universe was built in seven days just for them, and they reacted to it as if they were all seeing it and tasting it for the first time. Tragedy was a word no longer in either of their vocabularies.

Light.

Their world was their kingdom; their kingdom their universe. Created from a single cell between them, an undeteriorating mass evolved into a great castle reaching great heights and spanning decades and planes of physical matter and song and thought and presence. As King and Queen on their great thrones, they looked at each other and they looked at the vast plains of existence. Day turned into night, and sobbing at one another for how absolutely beautiful the earth and the heavens and the creatures were, they looked to the sky and saw only that they were dust and atoms and particles created from a much grander scale; fission; ashes tossed into a vacant vacuum and exploding into what was reflecting off of their tears at that exact moment…

Stars.

About the Author

Solomon Deep was born in 1969 in Memphis, and currently spends his time between New York and Northampton.

He is best known as the creator, producer, and head writer for the weekly live radio program FortNight. Elements was his first published novel, followed by several novels and collections produced and released by independent publishers.

Deep is a dedicated writer, poet, beekeeper, gardener, actor, and traveler.

www.ingramcontent.com/pod-product-compliance
Lightning Source LLC
Chambersburg PA
CBHW051227260626
47162CB00002B/313